The Northeast Quarter

S. M. Harris

The Northeast Quarter

Published by Wheatmark®
2030 East Speedway Blvd., Suite 106
Tucson, Arizona 85719 USA
www.wheatmark.com

ISBN: 978-1-62787-376-5 (paperback)
ISBN: 978-1-62787-377-2 (ebook)
LCCN: 2015959469

rev201602

For Annis and Henry Harris

Part One

CHILDHOOD

1

ANN LOOKED UP FROM HER PLACE at the long table. The man was still outside by the entrance gate near the row of carriages. He had been staring at the house for about fifteen minutes, but Ann couldn't see who it was because a branch of the maple in the driveway drooped just low enough to cover his face. The rest of him was clear enough, though: a dark silhouette against the green of the cornstalks beyond. Ann couldn't imagine what he wanted.

She turned back to the other guests at the table, wondering if someone else had noticed him. They were all adults and were having grown-up conversation. Ann was ten years old, and subjects like bushels of corn, the spring planting, and the price of grain had been part of her world as long as she could remember, but she was too young to pay much attention.

Twenty-four guests sat on each side of the long table. Under the pointed ceiling and crossbeams of the dining hall of Carson Manor, everything felt large and magnificent. The gentlemen were in their Sunday best, and the ladies wore bright dresses in the latest fashions—at least for a country in the middle of a war. It was July 4, 1918. Before each guest was the finest china and crystal. Decanters of wine and platters of corn, potatoes, fried chicken, and roast beef had been arranged in a perfectly ordered sequence all the way down the table. Most of these platters were empty now in preparation for the large vanilla and chocolate layer cake on the rolling cart by the fireplace. Most families kept the dessert out of sight until the right moment. But on the Fourth of July at Carson Manor, the cake was something special.

Ann was the only child in this multitude. To her, they were all old folks— quite old, for not a one was under thirty-five and none had a favorite dolly on her pillow. That was all right with her since they were family and friends. Ann liked most of them and loved some of them. She felt protected among them. Everyone present was happy, and everything was going right. Yet something did not feel right. It had nothing to do with the man out in the road. To Ann's knowledge, no one else had seen him. But his presence seemed to accentuate her feelings of uncertainty.

She gazed down the table at Zachary to see how he was doing. Zachary was the only one who could feel and appreciate this aura of love and protection from the adults in the room. Technically he was Ann's uncle, but at forty years old, he had the mind of someone three decades younger. Zachary was in fine spirits. He saw Ann and waved timidly. His mouth formed the words "Happy birthday." Ann waved back. For a few seconds, she felt the warmth she had felt when she was younger. She would be having her own tiny cake with some school friends later in the afternoon. Slowly, she looked back out the window. The man had not moved.

To Ann's left at the end of the table was her father, Jack Hardy, involved in a discussion with two gentlemen. Since Jack had come home from the war, he'd had a number of ideas about agricultural improvement, such as ways to enrich the soil and increase the harvest. Ann enjoyed it when her father got on a subject that inspired him. Then he seemed more alive, and it was like the troubles in Europe had never happened.

Ann's mother, Lucille, seated beside her husband, appeared worried. While the conversation and laughter of the celebration buzzed around them, Lucille focused on her father, Colonel Wallace Carson, the man at the head of the table.

Wallace Carson seemed two feet taller than the average man when people first met him. With his white beard, Ann thought he looked like one of the Titans Homer had written about. She'd had a dream once that years ago Grandpa had grown bored with the inactivity on Mount Olympus and decided to settle somewhere else. He had wandered the world for decades, and when he found the place that pleased him, he called it Franklin County, Iowa. He was an older man now, but the force of his personality was as vital as ever. His eyes flashed, and his voice was a benevolent rumble.

Grandpa had built Carson Manor. Twenty years after the Civil War he and his wife, Lady Ann, had settled on a farm in the middle of Franklin County. He began to grow corn, and one farm had led to another over the decades. Lady Ann's people were from England, and so, as a gift to her, Wallace Carson had bought a Cotswold manor in Surrey and had it dismantled and brought stone by stone to Franklin County where it had then been rebuilt to watch over the thousands of acres of the Carson empire. Lady Ann was not of royal birth, but in every respect, she and Colonel Carson were the reigning monarchs of Winfield.

Stationed on the highest hill for miles around, the Carson home dominated the scene. It was the center of Franklin County and the center of the town of Winfield. Everyone at the table had something to do with the Carson empire in one way or another—except the man outside.

Ann glanced over to her father. "I see him," Jack said. "It's Warren Hyatt."

"What does he want, Papa?" she asked.

"Who knows with that man?"

"But what's he doing out there? He's been staring at the house for fifteen minutes."

"Well," Jack said, "sometimes a fella has to feel bad about something just to get through the day."

They looked back out the window. The man had vanished. Jack smiled at his daughter. "See? He's gone. Forget about him. It's your birthday. Let's enjoy the party."

Ann knew her mother had been watching her. Although she had a loving smile on her face, Lucille's eyes were red around the rims, as if she had been weeping sometime earlier in the day. Ann's parents generally seemed optimistic about the challenges and fortunes of life. But concern over Grandpa's health had become an issue. Her parents had told her that Grandpa would be all right if he took it easy, but Ann could see the difference between what they said and how they were behaving. Suddenly Ann had that feeling again.

"Mama, Grandpa's all right, isn't he?"

"Of course he is."

The answer didn't reassure Ann. Still, the colonel was having a roaring good time at the end of the table. As Ann watched him, she remembered all the other Fourth of July celebrations at the manor. Everything led up to what was going to happen at any moment.

"Mama, when's the speech?" she asked.

"What?"

"When's the speech? I like it when Grandpa gives his speech. It's like a magic moment. Everything stops and we all feel safe. He goes around the table and gives everyone a big hug."

"That's your grandpa, all right," Lucille said.

"It sure is," Jack added. "Everybody gets a hug."

Lucille's eyes went down the row of guests to the colonel. He was enthrall-ing a small group with a story. His large hands were moving in firm, deliberate movements to emphasize a point. Lady Ann was seated beside him, listening. The perfect wife and hostess, she was an elegant and fashionable woman of sixty with gray hair and delicate features. But today she also appeared con-cerned.

"I'm worried about Papa," Lucille said.

Jack reached over and gently touched Lucille's arm. "He'll be all right."

"This is the first time that Mama hasn't sat opposite him at the head of the table."

Lucille stared at the row of guests. "Doc Powell doesn't look too festive. He wanted Papa to skip the party entirely."

"He'll be fine, Lucille."

Doc Powell, a gray-haired man, was seated next to Lady Ann and was smiling along with the other listeners.

On the other side of the table, Van Burin, the banker, was finishing a story of his own. Van Burin always seemed to be operating at one level of energy higher than he actually needed.

"They're both telling stories, Papa."

"Van Burin always seems to be making a sale," Jack said. "He's our bank president, but if anyone was born to be a door-to-door salesman, it's Patrick Van Burin."

A chorus of chuckles erupted around Van Burin. A man of fifty, he had a flashing mane of red hair that complemented his gray suit. In his lapel there was his white carnation—part of his daily order from Sidford's Florist.

Colonel Carson tapped his crystal glass. This was the signal.

Van Burin's face lit up. "We were waiting, Colonel. I was just saying that July fourth wouldn't be July fourth without you." Appreciative laughter rippled up and down the table.

"Now, why does he have to do that?" Ann thought. "Grandpa'd be just fine without old Van Burin backslapping his way into the center of things."

"It's that time of year," the colonel said. His voice was low, but it could be heard all over the room.

When Carson stood up, his six-foot-five frame seemed to tower over the assembled guests. At seventy, he was not a shell of his former self—merely an older edition. He was about to speak when he caught his breath and stopped to inhale.

"Wallace?" said Lady Ann.

Carson looked down at his wife. "I'm fine. It's getting so a man can't get up and stretch without someone worrying about his health."

Lady Ann nodded.

"See?" Carson said. "On my own two feet. I could still climb onto this table and shoot the eye out of the weather vane."

Van Burin leaned forward to the other guests. "That's the colonel, all right. Come wind or rain, he stands right up there."

"So does our bank president," Jack whispered.

Sometimes Van Burin seemed to hover around conversations like an eager puppy.

"We have given our blessing for the meal," Carson continued. "But it is always a tradition in this family to give thanks to our country for what it has given us during the year."

Everyone at the table clapped accordingly. There were cries of "hear, hear," the loudest of which came from Van Burin.

Ann knew the procedure. The door to the kitchen opened, and Olga Christensen appeared in the doorway. A massive Danish woman in her fifties, Olga was the household cook and practically a member of the family. Her appearance at this time was part of the tradition. She gave Ann a little wave. Ann blew her a kiss and waved back.

"I have a lot of gratitude," Carson said. "The first thing I am grateful for is to look down this table and see three generations before me. All together. All safe from harm's way, which brings me to our second birthday. The birthday of my granddaughter, Ann."

Ann felt a warm glow inside. This was what she meant about the feeling of being hugged during Grandpa's speech.

"Olga," the colonel continued, "every year on this occasion, you prepare the best meal any family could ask for, and every year I say you've outdone yourself. And you know what? I'm going to say it again. Thank you."

Another round of applause.

"Thank you, sir," Olga said. "Thank you, everyone."

"Thank you, Olga," Ann echoed from her seat.

"This is your day, child," Olga replied with a wide smile. "You enjoy it now." She stepped back into the kitchen, and the door closed.

Carson surveyed the room. "July fourth, 1918," he said. "We are a country at war. The Germans are still holding positions in France, but they are weakening. God willing, the war will be over soon, and America can return to peaceful times. Farmers can get back to the land." A number of nods from the guests and words here and there of "Amen" and "Speedy victory."

Carson resumed. "First, I give thanks to Lady Ann, my devoted wife, who organized clothing drives and sewing circles to send supplies to the troops. You managed to have every quilting group in the state working at one time or another. From the letter we received from the War Department, you made a difference for the boys overseas. My dear, you were—no, you *are*—magnificent." A round of applause and cries of "Lady Ann, Lady Ann."

"Second, I give thanks to my daughter Lucille for all the fund-raising you did for the Red Cross. The troops needed medical supplies. You helped ensure that they received them."

Carson stopped. His thoughts carried him in another direction.

"You know, I have always favored the vote for women. Since women share so much of our lives in good times and in bad, I hope we see the day when they will share in the decision making of our country as well."

The colonel froze. "Ah, I seem to have run out of breath here."

"Wallace?" Lady Ann asked.

"Maybe a rest, Colonel," Doc Powell said.

"Almost finished," the colonel answered. He gathered himself for a couple of seconds.

"My son-in-law, Jack," he continued. "Speaking of doctors, we've both had our share of them recently." Ann patted her father on the arm. "Jack, you had the courage and foresight to recognize the troubles across the sea. You went over there and enlisted with the British. Fought alongside some of your mother's people. You faced the enemy, and you incurred some injuries. But instead of sitting around in the hospital while your lungs healed, you figured out new ways to improve our agricultural endeavors. We will try some of them in the next planting season. I am proud and grateful for what you have done."

More voices of approval from the company. Zachary got up from his seat and moved around Lady Ann to the colonel.

Lady Ann noticed it. "Oh, Zachary," she murmured. It was too late, for Zachary was already beside his father, holding out a small object.

"Papa...Papa," he said eagerly.

The colonel gave him his full attention. "What is it, son?"

"I made a gift for you."

"Let's see it."

Zachary held out a small wooden box, crudely painted red, white, and blue. Carson took the box. It was a gift from his son, and knowing that, the colonel gave it his undivided attention.

"Thank you, son," he said. "It's a beautiful box."

"Are you proud of me, too?"

"Yes, Zachary, I am proud of you."

The colonel took his son's face in his large hands in a movement that was both powerful and gentle.

"I am always proud of you. God gave you a good heart and a noble spirit. Not many men have that. You are special, son. Don't forget it."

Zachary seemed overjoyed, almost tearful in his happiness. The colonel held him, patting him on the back.

"Good boy," the colonel whispered. "Good boy."

Carson released Zachary and watched him go back to his seat. His gaze returned to the other guests at the table. He focused on Little Ann.

"And now," he said, "we get to my granddaughter, who will one day inherit all this. Of course, there are others between me and you in the line of succession—your grandma, your parents—but sometimes a man wants to look down the line to the one at the very end, who someday will be standing where I am now, giving this speech on our country's birthday."

Ann sat up in her chair.

"You're young. And where I stand in life must look like a hundred years away. Look at the people along this table. Listen to what they say. Watch what they do. Follow their counsel. Learn from them. Remember our traditions. Do well for the land. Do well for the people. And give thanks for the harvest."

Ann listened intently. This was more than a passing acknowledgment. She had heard these words bandied about all her life, but they had never been addressed directly to her.

"Ann," the colonel said, "the world is a place of limitless possibilities. There are all kinds of people in it—good people, like the ones seated around us, but bad ones as well."

The colonel stopped to catch his breath.

"Watch out for the bad ones. They come in all shapes and sizes. Some are easy to spot...crooked as a rail and plain to the eye, but the others...the really bad ones...the demons...the monsters...they're the dangerous ones. They're tougher to see. They move through the world, corrupting everything. They hide in the shadows of our day-to-day existence, just waiting for a moment to pounce."

Ann thought she understood. On the other hand, she'd never seen a demon before.

"I do believe that God put these miserable creatures among us to keep us on our toes...keep us alive. They stir up the pot down here so He won't be bored with His creation. That may well be. The point is that you can outsmart them. They come to you with the voice of a friend. So you listen to what they say. And you watch for what they don't say. If you keep your guard up, you can spot them before they have a chance to strike."

"We'll help her, Colonel," said Van Burin. "We can spot that kind like a skunk in a dog show."

There was a chorus of "Yes...Yes...We'll be there...We can help. Count on us."

"Thank you, my friends. All of you," said the colonel. His attention returned to his granddaughter.

"And finally...and this is most important. Remember...Remember the Northeast Quarter. Everything around you began...years ago with the Northeast Quarter—the finest, most fertile land in the state of Iowa. Out of that jewel grew a kingdom of ten thousand acres. All that and everything you see from one piece of fertile land."

"The Northeast Quarter," whispered Lucille.

"Yes, Mama," replied Ann. She was getting a little tired. It was nice being included, but she was thinking of the ice cream and presents that were yet to come.

"The Northeast Quarter," repeated Colonel Carson. "I want you to make a promise to me."

"What, Grandpa?" Ann sighed.

"This is important, young lady," the colonel thundered. "Never give up the Northeast Quarter."

"I won't," Ann said.

"You understand?"

"Yes, Grandpa."

"Promise me. Say it…say it as if your soul depends on it."

Ann was still looking at her grandfather. She understood the importance of his request, although she didn't comprehend the consequences.

"I promise, Grandpa," she said.

"As if your soul depends on it."

"As if my soul depends on it. I promise, Grandpa."

"Good," answered the colonel. He took a breath. "I'm going to have to stop now."

Colonel Carson looked somewhat bewildered—as if suddenly he had forgotten what he was going to say or he had felt a chill in the air but was unable to see its origin.

"It's been an excellent party, dear," Lady Ann said.

"I'm worried about Grandpa," Ann whispered to her mother.

"He'll be all right," Lucille answered.

Then Ann saw him—Warren Hyatt, the man from the road. He had entered through the kitchen. A pampered-looking man around thirty, with pudgy cheeks and brown hair, he was poised in the kitchen doorway, with a smug and arrogant smile. Olga stood next to him, looking worried.

"One more thing," the colonel said, not noticing the intruder. "Hell, the most important thing."

Slowly Colonel Carson took his glass in his hand and raised it in a toast. As he did, everyone at the table took a glass and did the same.

"To the United States of America," the colonel said. "Our thanks and happy birthday."

The guests followed with "Happy birthday. God bless America."

Everyone drank the toast. As they were lowering their glasses, Colonel Carson spotted the intruder.

"Hello…" Carson said.

"I'm sorry, sir," Olga said. "I told him it was a private party."

"Good afternoon, Colonel," Hyatt said. "I thought I would drop by and pay my respects."

"This is a family gathering," Carson said.

"It's my daughter's birthday," Jack added.

"Yes...a birthday party for young Ann Hardy." Hyatt was crossing the room to Ann. "You're lucky to grow up in a house of privilege and good fortune: everything given to you; everything done for you."

"Is there something we can do for you?" the colonel asked.

Lady Ann was watching everything with a cool façade that covered her embarrassment.

"Olga, fix him a place," she said quietly.

Ann looked to Lucille. "Why is she doing that, Mama?"

"Sometimes we have to be sociable," Lucille said.

"Yes, it's nice to see how the other half lives," Hyatt announced. "However, young lady, all these preparations in your honor are quite troubling to me."

Ann was staring directly at him. "If you'd stayed outside, maybe you wouldn't be so troubled," she said.

"Shh," Lucille said.

"I heard that, young lady," he retorted. "Actually I'm here because I'm writing an article about your birthday...for the *Sentinel*."

"I didn't know you worked for the *Sentinel*," Jack said.

"I didn't either," Van Burin chimed in.

"Yes, I work for them."

"No, you don't work for the *Sentinel*," Carson said.

"I beg your pardon!"

"You don't work for them. You just sit around the office and bother the typesetters. What do you really want here?"

"All right, I'll tell you. You challenge me. I'll tell you," said Hyatt, his voice rising. "I grew up in this town, and ever since I can remember, everything in the community pointed up to Carson Manor. The Carsons of Winfield. The Carsons of Franklin County."

"So?"

"The point is, you're living on borrowed time," he said with mounting glee. "That's right—borrowed time. A new and glorious revolution has started over in Europe, and when it comes here, your traditions...your ways...where everyone salutes and bows to the high and mighty Carsons...will be over...All over."

"What the hell are you talking about?" roared the colonel.

The pudgy cheeks were flushed with happiness: the joy of the recent convert. "I'm talking about Russia. Glorious Mother Russia. Over there the rich don't own the land. The workers own it. The workers."

"Russia's in chaos," muttered Doc Powell.

"Comrades and commissars all over the place," offered another voice.

"Oh no, it's a boiling and beautiful beginning. The workers pulled all the big landowners off their mountaintops and took over. Made a community of equals where no one has more than the other. No one wants more than the other. A man like me can look down on a man like you because we're equal."

"How can one man look down on another if they're equal?" Ann said to Lucille.

Hyatt began to stride proudly around the room.

"I've been waiting to tell you people all about this for weeks. Waiting for the right moment to come and share this with you. Then today I saw my chance. I was walking by the bakery. I saw the cake. The *big* cake. This reckless display of opulence for one little girl."

"The big cake, eh?" said the colonel. "Did you read the inscription on it?"

"I didn't have to," Hyatt replied. "It was obvious."

"Better read it, Warren," said Van Burin.

"I'll say," muttered another guest.

"Read us the inscription, Mr. Hyatt," said the colonel.

Hyatt sauntered slowly over to the cake, obviously relishing every step.

"Happy Birthday…"

"Now finish it."

"To the United States of America."

"Big country," the colonel declared. "Big cake."

Warren Hyatt was facing the guests with a distressed expression. This wasn't fair. As a budding social revolutionary in Iowa, he had hoped for a more dramatic announcement.

"I didn't know that. Nobody told *me* that," Hyatt whined. "But that doesn't matter. Yesterday you outbid my father for that Kentucky mare at Stegelsen's auction in Exira. You knew he wanted that horse. So you went there and outbid him."

"Wait a minute," the colonel interjected. "Who's talking about horses? What's this all about?"

"Another thing you Carsons get away with. You knew my father wanted that mare. So you showed up with full knowledge and outbid him."

There were murmurs from the other guests.

"Who told you that?" Lady Ann asked.

"Where'd you get your facts, Warren?" echoed Van Burin, adding his voice to the controversy.

"I know. I just know."

"Charlie McMahon bought that horse," the colonel said.

"My father wanted that mare," continued Hyatt, his tone rising again. "But when he heard you were coming, he stayed home."

Colonel Carson stared at him in disbelief. "What the hell did he do that for?"

"You know very well, sir. You know very well."

"No, I don't," the colonel answered. "I wasn't there. I never went to the auction."

"I don't believe you."

"It's true," Powell interjected. "The colonel wasn't even there."

"That's right," Van Burin added. "I saw him at the bank yesterday."

"He was in town. Yes. Yes," everyone agreed.

"Oh no, he was at the auction," Hyatt said. "My father was certain he'd be there."

"I was helping my wife and daughter buy food for this party," said the colonel.

"I don't accept that," Hyatt said. "It doesn't matter anyway. You'd have tried to outbid him if you did come. That's the trouble with rich people like you. It doesn't matter what the truth is. You cover for each other. You lie for each other. Just so you can look down on the rest of us."

With a resurgence of energy, Hyatt took a single step forward.

"Tell me, Colonel," Hyatt said in triumph. "When you're in town and say good morning to people in the street, do you *really* know their names?"

"Of course I do."

"I hardly believe that." Hyatt sniffed.

"That's because I'm where I am and you're where you are," the colonel thundered. "If you do business with someone, you better know his name. You better know the name of his wife and all his children. And you better know how old each child is and the dates of everyone's birthdays."

The colonel's eyes twinkled, as he drove home his final point. "And if you're really good, you won't have to work at it."

"That's the truth, gentlemen," Van Burin bubbled. "The colonel here knows 'em all, forward and backward."

Ann was enjoying this. Her grandfather was handling Warren Hyatt very well. This self-righteous heckler must have rehearsed the scene in his mind many times, yet he was not at all prepared for the outcome.

Colonel Carson studied Hyatt.

"What have you done in life, boy?" he asked. "Your father has tried to buy you into more jobs than you could shake a stick at. You don't work. You didn't enlist—"

"I have a bad back," Hyatt said. "And on philosophical grounds, I have an aversion to conflict."

Chuckles came from those at the table.

Olga appeared in the kitchen doorway with a napkin, some silverware, and a plate.

"He won't be staying," the colonel said. His breathing had become heavier, his expression uncertain. Lady Ann and Doc Powell caught it immediately.

"He's just leaving," the colonel said. Hyatt was seething. He had come too far to stop, so he decided to stand his ground.

"Go ahead," Hyatt jeered. "Throw me out. When the revolution comes, people like you will have nothing."

"We've heard enough, Warren," Powell stated. "You'd better go."

Ann watched the faces of the other guests. There was a growing anger toward the intruder.

Ignoring them, Hyatt forged ahead. "You've had everything for so long. You deserve to see what it's like to have nothing. Tell me. Have you ever had nothing?"

"Of course I have," replied the colonel. "I started out with nothing, and I built this place. I built everything you see around you."

Doc Powell was concerned. "Colonel, forget about him. Take a rest."

"Papa, please," Lucille added.

Powell turned to Hyatt. "Warren, I'm telling you. Get out of here. This isn't good for anybody."

"You too, Doctor?" Hyatt asked innocently. "Hostility from the good doctor?"

"And before you go, you little pup," the colonel roared, "if what you glowingly describe ever happened around here, I'd find another plot of land and build the empire all over again. I'd build it from scratch!"

"I didn't mean to touch a nerve," Hyatt replied with a smile.

"Get out!" the colonel bellowed. He was attempting to stay on his feet when suddenly, as if his legs gave out, he collapsed into his chair.

"Colonel!" Powell cried.

"You get out of here!" Carson shouted from his seat. He was lunging forward and backward in an effort to stand. "Get me a buggy whip! Somebody get me a buggy whip!"

"You're just upset," suggested Hyatt. "I didn't mean for everyone to be upset."

Suddenly, Carson struggled to get to his feet another time, but with his strength weakening, he fell back.

"Wallace!" Lady Ann cried. Powell had already grabbed his medical bag and was rushing over to the colonel.

"Get him to the sofa," Powell said.

"I'll be all right," the colonel muttered. "I feel faint, that's all...It's getting so a man can't raise his voice in his own house."

With Lady Ann following, Van Burin, Powell, and two other men helped the colonel over to the sofa. Jack and Lucille were up from their seats.

"Jack," Powell whispered, "get the buggy hitched. We're taking him to the hospital."

Jack headed out the side door to the stables.

"Stand back," said Powell. "Give him some air." Already he had opened his bag and was starting to examine the colonel.

"Easy, Colonel," he said.

"Hospital," the colonel murmured. "Don't like the sound of that word."

"Lie still, dear," Lady Ann said.

Powell took out his stethoscope. Warren Hyatt was still standing in place—looking less defiant and more foolish by the minute.

Finally, Powell looked up. But then, as if not believing his verdict, he put the stethoscope down on Carson's chest and listened a second time. When he raised his eyes this time, his expression was heartbroken.

Lady Ann began to weep. Lucille took her in her arms. They hugged for a moment and knelt down beside the colonel. Already he seemed to be leaving them.

"What's this?" the colonel whispered. "I'm all right. It's the Fourth of July."

The two women were sobbing quietly.

"Now, now. None of this. Tomorrow we'll all go riding."

Then he saw Warren Hyatt.

"Get him out of here," Carson rasped.

All eyes turned to Warren Hyatt. Facing a wall of disgusted and disapproving expressions, Hyatt withered.

"I didn't expect the discourse to become so heated," he offered. "I don't want people thinking I had anything to do with this."

Ann had been watching Hyatt with a growing contempt. Inside, she knew that a person accepts responsibility for his actions. Hyatt's denial and self-justification were too much for her to take. She left her mother and crossed over to Hyatt. She stared up at him.

"I didn't cause this," he said, squirming in her glare. "I don't want anyone to think... Why are you looking at me that way?"

"You came here and now my grandpa is sick," she said. "We saw it. You know it. Now you get out."

"Very well, young lady," he said, attempting a last ditch effort of sanctimony. He moved to the front door. Ann followed. He opened the door and then turned back to Ann.

"Don't you look at me that way," he protested. "Don't you look at me like that. I'm not to blame for what happened here. I came in a friendly manner."

He stepped outside. Ann began to close the door behind him.

"I'm not to blame... I'm not to blame at all."

Ann shut the door and returned to her grandfather. Lady Ann was weeping. Lucille was comforting her. The colonel's eyes were closed, as if he were sleeping peacefully. His breathing was slower.

Doc Powell was taking his pulse. Time seemed to stand still.

The breathing stopped. Powell listened for a heartbeat again. After a moment, he looked to Lady Ann.

"He's gone," he said.

Little Ann reached out and took her mother's hand.

2

THE FUNERAL WAS FOUR DAYS LATER. Riverside Cemetery was located on a sprawling hillside that overlooked the town of Winfield. It offered such a spectacular panorama of the town and its surroundings that local folks often walked up there just to enjoy the slope and roll of the farmland that extended for miles in every direction.

It also afforded a view from one end of town to the other: from Pomphrey Park and the courthouse at one end, all the way down Market Street to the lumberyard, corral, and warehouses at the other. Market Street was the one major thoroughfare, running parallel to the railroad tracks. Along it were the major businesses—Van Burin's Iowa Trust Bank, the hardware store, the dress shop, the pharmacy, and the local café. All of them were closed for the funeral.

Ann had ridden to the cemetery in the buggy with Jack and Lucille. She missed her grandpa. She had spent a good part of the last three days listening to neighbors who came by to offer condolences to Lady Ann and her parents. She had also spent a lot of time consoling Zachary. The problem that faced Ann was how to offer sympathy and advice for something she was just learning to experience herself. She wanted to say the right thing to Zachary, but all she could come up with was "He's all right," or "He's in heaven with the angels." But what seemed to work best was taking Zachary's hand and saying, "I know. I miss him, too."

The road up the hill was lined with horses and buggies and the occasional car. The area around the coffin was a blanket of red, white, and blue flowers. Covering the hillside beyond appeared to be a mosaic of mourners. In 1918 a thousand people lived in Winfield, and the vast majority had shown up to pay their respects to the man who had founded their community.

Ann sat between Jack and Lucille in the row of chairs beside the flag-draped coffin, and Zachary and Lady Ann sat beside Lucille as Reverend Clarence

Bidwell conducted the service. Ann felt loved and protected, surrounded by her family. They were still a strong unit and always looked out for one another. Ann knew many of the mourners by name, but many she did not. The colonel's presence held everything together—family and town. But now the colonel was gone. With no one to look up to, would his traditions continue, or would they begin to change?

As Reverend Bidwell began the eulogy, Ann found herself tuning in and out of his words. Bidwell was a good man, but there was nothing in the eulogy that he had not spoken about in various Sunday services about the travails of life and the heavenly reward at the end. Ann found herself thinking of her promise to her grandpa. He had asked her to do something, and she had promised she would. This was serious.

Of course, Lucille and Jack had assured her, "Don't worry about the promise, Ann. We'll all be here to help." Ann felt more confident knowing it would be a group effort.

Then, as she was listening to the eulogy, a strange feeling came over her. Everything and everyone looked the same, but with Grandpa gone, she felt something more than a sense of loss. She felt alone. It was as if everyone around her was on the other side of a large cold room. She could see them, even hear them, yet they seemed strangely distant. She tried to put it out of her mind since her mother was right beside her, but Ann still felt alone.

3

FIVE DAYS LATER, LADY ANN AND her granddaughter took the horse and buggy and headed into town. Lady Ann was clad in black. Ann could see that her grandmother was still in a state of shock. It wasn't just losing the colonel that seemed to affect her, but how she would cope without him. Lucille had offered to come along, but Lady Ann assured her that everything would be fine.

Ann would always remember the silence of that day the most. The dome of blue above them and the surrounding cornfields seemed to swallow up any sound. Indeed, the lack of noise became a sound of its own. The roll and thud of the wagon wheels crossing the ruts and grooves on the dirt road and the clop-clopping of the horses' hooves seemed to be the only signs of movement. Whenever Ann and her grandmother spoke, their voices seemed muffled in the roll of the landscape around them.

Her grandmother was going to a meeting at the bank, something she did not look forward to, but something she had to do. "It's part of life," she told Ann. "Your mama will have to do it one day, and sometime after that, you'll have to do it, too." Ann knew Lady Ann was telling her the truth, but all that seemed so far away.

They were approaching town. It would be about ten minutes before they passed the corral and warehouses and started up Market Street to the bank at the other end. The 10:40 a.m. train would be at the depot. Except for when the train departed, Ann knew the town would be quiet, with only a couple of wagons and horses in front of one of the stores and maybe a motor car here or there. Most of the citizens were out working on their farms.

What they didn't know was that there were already preparations going on at the bank for their arrival.

Ann had always likened the Iowa Trust Bank to a small cave, with its walls of shadowy, knotted pine. Upon entering the main lobby, visitors were immediately struck by how dark it was. Patrick Van Burin had wanted to brighten the customer areas of the bank in order to demonstrate to clients how important they were, but doing that entailed darkening the employee work space. Across the lobby from the street entrance was the enclosure containing the teller's window. Ann always thought it looked like a cage. To the right were three doors. The first was a door to the alley; the second, in the corner, led to Van Burin's office, which, when the curtains were open, offered a view of Pomphrey Park and the courthouse; and the third opened to a spare office that was used as a sort of storeroom. Van Burin always saw to it that the bank was decorated with plenty of bouquets from Sidford's.

At this moment he was fussily double-checking the propriety of his office. Warren Hyatt stood by the counter, looking concerned. Behind the bars in the teller's cage stood Royce Chamberlin. Poised in the dark, only his tall and gaunt outline with long arms and a pair of dark eye sockets was visible to those in the room.

Chamberlin was watching Van Burin as he finished a trip around the room and then began a triple-check.

"I'll say it again," Hyatt said. "Everyone looks at me differently now. Why this morning I passed Mrs. Leland in the street, and she ignored me. Just walked by. Right by me."

Van Burin checked the clock on the wall behind the teller's cage. It was nine forty-five. "Time to go, Warren."

"Even here," Hyatt whined, "I feel like a persona non grata. Even here."

Van Burin examined a bouquet beside the sofa. Were the flowers wilted? Or did they only seem that way in the dim light?

"Every petal is fresh, Mr. Van Burin," Chamberlin said from the cage.

Surprised, Van Burin turned around. "Oh, I didn't see you there, Royce."

"I've been listening."

"I wish someone would listen to *me*," Hyatt said.

"Warren, this is important," Van Burin declared. "We've got the richest woman in five counties coming in here. We want her to feel comforted in her grief."

"Did you hear that, Warren?" Chamberlin asked. The tone was low and insinuating. Chamberlin always made Hyatt uncomfortable.

"Yes, yes, I heard it," Hyatt replied. "I just wish that people would stop associating me with what happened to the colonel."

"And why is that?"

"I...I already explained. The colonel had a bad heart. The conversation got out of hand."

"You induced the man to have a heart attack in a roomful of family and friends."

"You-You can't blame me for that," Hyatt sputtered. "I didn't mean for that to happen."

"Then why were you out at the manor?" Chamberlin asked. He leaned closer to the bars. "Do you want me to tell you it wasn't your fault?"

"It wasn't..."

"OK, it wasn't your fault," Chamberlin said in an almost soothing voice. "Feel better now?"

"Now that that's settled...," Van Burin said.

"I'll go... I'll go," Hyatt said, edging toward the door.

Suddenly, he rushed back to the teller's cage.

"Royce... please... would you put in some kind of good word for me?" he implored. "I know the Carsons have hardened their hearts against me. I know they're unforgiving, but I have to live here. Will you please...?"

"I'll be glad to."

"You will? Thank you, Royce."

"You can go home now and feel perfectly fine."

Lady Ann and Ann pulled up in front of the bank. With a panicked expression, Van Burin grabbed Hyatt and propelled him across the room like a bouncer removing a drunk.

"Oh Lord, she's here. Quick. Out the back."

"Yes, I'm leaving, Patrick," said Hyatt. He stepped out into the alley and was gone.

Van Burin sighed in relief. "That was close. I don't know why we put up with him. Calls himself a reporter. Spends most of his time at the barbershop."

"He's our court jester, Mr. Van Burin," Chamberlin said.

Ann and her grandmother entered the bank. Van Burin greeted them, a small folder under his arm.

"Lady Ann... and Little Ann. Good to see you. Come in. Come in." He looked down at Ann. "It's wonderful you could be along, too."

"I wanted to be with Grandma." Ann could never tell whether Van Burin was sincere or not. All she ever saw was the effort.

"It was a beautiful service," Van Burin said. "The colonel was very much a part of our lives. Let me tell you again how very sorry we all are for your loss."

"Yes, thank you," Lady Ann said.

"Why, I remember my first day at work here. I was working as a teller behind that window right there. The colonel came in, looked at me, and said, 'Van Burin, you have an honest face. I think we can do business.'"

"I remember," Lady Ann said.

"And we've done business for all these years."

He became more direct. "By the way, I took the liberty of contacting Fred Brubaker. He should be joining us at any minute."

Lady Ann stiffened. "Oh, Patrick, I hadn't intended this to be a full business meeting."

"It won't be. We'll just have a few words in my office. We can schedule a more formal gathering in a few weeks." He looked at her. "How has everything been?"

"It is what it is."

"I'm sorry," he said. He handed her the folder. "This is the planting record for this year. The colonel asked for it before the..."

"I understand," Lady Ann said. She took the folder, opened it, and began to go over the contents. To Ann, her grandmother seemed lost, although she was trying so hard not to show it.

While Lady Ann read, Ann wandered over to the teller's cage. She had been to the bank before—in more agreeable times. Like everything else, the place seemed both familiar and strange. As she stood in the area beneath the cage, Chamberlin's form seemed to loom up behind her like a dark cloud on the other side of the bars. He seemed at home in the shadows. His gray eyes focused on the little girl below him for a long time—like a beast in a cave contemplating a smaller and defenseless creature a few inches away. Ann continued to watch her grandmother read the folder.

Finally, Chamberlin spoke. "Hello, little girl."

Ann looked up. "Hello." All she could see was the outline of a head and the flicker of two eyes.

"It looks awfully dark in there," Ann said.

"Mr. Van Burin likes it that way. From our side it's not dark at all."

Ann studied him for a moment. "Are you people friends with Warren Hyatt?"

"Why do you ask?"

"When we arrived, I saw him running up the alley."

"You're very observant," Chamberlin said. "No, we're not friends with Warren Hyatt. We have to do business with him. The man lacks social graces, don't you think?"

"I don't like him."

"I don't either. I hate to see him coming, and I can't wait for him to leave. Word has it he had a hog trough for a crib." Ann had to smile at this. "It was a terrible thing he did on your birthday."

"Warren Hyatt hurt my grandpa."

"I know," Chamberlin said with great empathy. "I can't think of one good word to say about him."

Fred Brubaker entered, carrying some folders under his arm. He was dressed like the prosperous country lawyer he was. At fifty with a ruddy complexion and pressed, well-fitting suit, he matched up with Van Burin's meticulous appearance.

"I'm late," Brubaker said. "I apologize."

"No need, Fred," Van Burin said. "This meeting is impromptu. Shall we go inside?"

Van Burin ushered Lady Ann toward his office. She glanced back to check on Little Ann.

"She'll be all right," Van Burin said. He pulled the curtain wide open. The office held four bouquets of flowers: two on the bookcase behind his desk, one on the desk, and another on the writing table across the room. The one on the writing table had already started to droop because of the darkness.

"Flowers," remarked Brubaker. "You always have your flowers."

"Yes," Van Burin said. He settled behind his desk and motioned for Brubaker and Lady Ann to sit in the two chairs in front of him. "I couldn't do a thing without a bouquet somewhere. They're my Achilles' heel."

Ann watched through the open door as Lady Ann and Brubaker sat down in Van Burin's office. They had rolled out the carpet for something. And her grandma had already been through a lot.

"First," Brubaker said, "I want to say that we are at your service, Lady Ann. We'll assist you in any way possible."

"Thank you, gentlemen," Lady Ann said.

Still behind the bars of the teller's window, Royce Chamberlin stared down at the little girl below him. He studied her slightly upturned nose, her small red lips, and her soft complexion. She had her mother's auburn hair. The longer he looked at her, the more he felt that, although she was small, here was a girl of some courage. And she was the granddaughter of the richest man in five counties.

"I have two daughters," Chamberlin said softly. "A little older. But good girls. Like you."

"Carol and Cassie," Ann replied. "I don't know them very well."

"Yes . . . Carol and Cassie . . . Carol and Cassandra. They're the twinkle in their father's eye. I'm very proud of them. How's everything out at Carson Manor?"

"Why do you want to know?"

"We watch over you," Chamberlin said. "You and your family, that is. We guard your money, and we protect your livelihood."

"We're doing . . ." Suddenly, Ann stopped. This man was a stranger, and he seemed friendly, but she was thinking of her family. "We miss Grandpa," she said. "And my grandma is so sad."

"She loved the colonel. She depended on him. It's a big loss for us, too," Royce whispered. "We just want to know if everything is all right."

"It is," Ann replied. "But if something comes up, we can handle it."

"Of course you can. You're a fine little girl."

"Excuse me," Ann said. She started across the room to Van Burin's office. As Ann arrived, Brubaker was speaking to Lady Ann.

"In a nutshell, you have twenty farms. Ten thousand acres. The total value of the estate, not counting the expenses for upkeep and the coming harvest, is nine hundred and fifty thousand dollars."

"An empire of properties all over Franklin County," Van Burin said.

"The colonel left the whole empire to you," Brubaker said. "He was quite clear in his wishes. You're a very wealthy lady."

Lady Ann sat still in her chair. She appeared tired. "I know how I am financially, gentlemen, but right now I feel like my world has fallen out from under me."

"Yes," Van Burin said. "And once again our sympathies."

"Anything you need, we're there for you," Brubaker added.

"That's right, Lady Ann," Van Burin gushed. "We're here to be there for you."

"Ah, and here's Little Ann," Brubaker said.

Ann saw her grandmother had been carefully watching them. She must have had the feeling she was being prepared for something. Ann couldn't tell what it was, but then she saw Brubaker put his folder on the desk and take out a few sheets of paper.

"Lady Ann," Brubaker began gently, "we won't take up much of your time. Did the colonel ever mention the security codicil to you?"

"No," Lady Ann replied.

"It's another word for custodial addendum. It's set up so we can assist you in the management of the estate."

"It makes it easier for you," Van Burin said. "We know your wishes, and we carry them out."

"You do that already," Lady Ann said.

"Yes...in a manner of speaking."

"But this takes a tremendous load off your shoulders," Brubaker explained, "and lets us do the work."

"You're describing a power of attorney," Lady Ann said.

"Well, yes, that's one word for it." Brubaker leaned back in his chair as if to compose his words carefully. "We know your wishes. We carry them out. You're just giving us the power to do it."

Lady Ann knew these men had been friendly and obedient to the colonel, but now the situation had plainly changed. Her only recourse was what she called The Dying Swan Act. She had learned it years ago from a cousin in the Deep South. She began to fan herself lightly.

"Gentlemen, my apologies," she said. "This is all a little much for me. Could we talk this over in more detail in a few weeks?"

"Of course," said Van Burin.

"In truth, there's nothing to change or decide," Brubaker said. "We can continue the way we did when the colonel was alive."

"And we'll be right there for you," said Van Burin.

"Thank you, gentlemen." Lady Ann looked down at her granddaughter. "We have to go."

"Yes, Grandma."

"I apologize, gentlemen," Lady Ann said as she rose from her chair. "I'll be more receptive a little later on. This has all been so much."

"Of course," said Van Burin.

"We understand," Brubaker added.

Lady Ann and Ann stepped out of the office.

"Give my best to your wives," Lady Ann said. "Their condolences were much appreciated."

"We will," said Van Burin.

"Thank you, gentlemen."

"Thank you, Lady Ann," Van Burin said with a smile. "Good-bye, Little Ann. You're a brave little girl."

"Thank you, Mr. Van Burin." They walked out the door and onto the sidewalk.

Van Burin and Brubaker watched the door in silence. They heard the hoofbeats and the wheels as the carriage pulled out into the street.

"I think that went well enough," Brubaker said, without much enthusiasm.

Van Burin remembered there were three of them in the room. He looked over to the teller's cage.

"Royce, you've been awfully quiet. You usually have something to say."

"I've been listening."

"There's something on your mind. What is it?"

"Do you want to know?"

"I'm asking."

"I'm thinking that if a man played his cards right, he could end up with a million dollars and never leave the county."

Van Burin stared at the cage. He could never understand Royce Chamberlin. The man could count money, but he just didn't think like other people.

"Uh, what brought this on, Royce?"

"As I said, I've been thinking," the voice in the cage resumed. "You spend all your time back here. You begin to watch your customers. You size them up. You take account of their strengths and weaknesses. Pretty soon you know them better than they know themselves. They're out there. You're right here. And you handle their money. After a time, it's not difficult to imagine that their money belongs to you."

"Well, yes." Brubaker replied. "The responsibility...You're almost a member of the family."

"I don't understand this," Van Burin said. "What are you saying?"

"I'll explain it another way," Chamberlin said. He moved out of the shadows of the teller's window and into the waiting area. "My father used to tell me a story when I was a little boy," he said. "It was about a tiger in a zoo. This tiger spent all his days in his cage, staring out between the bars and wondering what life was like on the other side. Some days he concentrated with such ferocity that he tasted blood in his mouth. There was a world to feast upon if he could just get free of his cage. The monkey in the cage next door used to laugh at him and say, 'You can't get out of there. You're a tiger. It's your lot in life to stay behind those bars in your cage.' But the tiger wanted more. So much more."

Chamberlin's voice was sardonic and knowing. He had transformed this narrative into something more than a childhood reminiscence.

"Well, the tiger began to watch the zookeeper come to the door of the cage every day with his ration of meat. He watched the way the zookeeper flicked open the latch on the gate. He saw this was the way to get in, and he knew this was the way to get out. He studied the flicking motion until he learned it. Finally, he realized the only thing keeping him in was the latch. 'Don't you do it,' said the monkey. 'Don't you think it. You belong in here in the cage. It's your lot in life.' At last the time came. One day after the zookeeper left, the tiger walked up to the door and opened the latch. With nothing stopping him, he stepped outside and was free of the bars and the expectations that were holding him in. In short order, he tore apart and devoured the monkey who had laughed at him. Then he killed the zookeeper who had kept him locked in all these years. The tiger was free of his cage, but he was still hungry. He had a ravenous appetite now, and the whole world awaited him."

Royce Chamberlin, a middle-aged man with gray hair, high cheekbones, and a handlebar moustache, was standing before them with a fixed and unnerving smile. He studied the two men in front of him like a cobra watching a couple of sparrows in a birdbath.

"Royce," Van Burin asked nervously, "are you unhappy with your job in some way?"

"Unhappy? Oh no."

"Then what are you trying to tell us?"

"Gentlemen," Chamberlin announced, "I am going to marry the rich widow Carson."

"You *what?*" Brubaker gasped.

Van Burin and Brubaker burst out laughing. Chamberlin stood his ground. The laughter continued for a while, and then it stopped.

"My God . . . you're serious," Van Burin said.

4

NEITHER ANN NOR HER GRANDMOTHER MENTIONED the conversation at the bank right away.

Ann saw that Lady Ann had become quiet and subdued. Once they got home, she retreated to the big bedroom upstairs that she had shared with Colonel Carson.

A few days later, Ann was sitting in the dining room area with Lady Ann, Lucille, and Olga. The banquet table had been removed. In its place was the regular dining room table, which seated six. Zachary was nearby, watching everyone.

Sunlight streamed through the big window, illuminating the living room from the wood floor to the pointed ceiling and crossbeams. It was still summer, and soon they would have to open the windows, but right now the sunlight served to emphasize the vastness of the downstairs area. Without guests, the present gathering appeared forlorn.

Silver polishing was a tradition in the family. It served both a practical and therapeutic functions. If a decision needed to be reached or a problem reduced to manageable size, the act of polishing kept one's focus off the worry and allowed the family members time to resolve the dilemma in their heads.

Ann counted the assorted silver pitchers, knives, forks, and spoons on the table. They were about halfway done. She had been polishing a soup spoon.

"I can help, Mama," Zachary said.

Ann took a cleaning rag and spoon off the table and handed them to Zachary.

She rubbed the spoon with the cloth. "Like this, Zachary."

Zachary took his spoon and began to polish it. They all continued in silence.

"I'm glad you told Brubaker to wait," Lucille said. "You did the right thing."

"I did. He and Van Burin were trying some fancy footwork. I could see it.

Wallace told me that bankers and lawyers are like good hunting dogs. Keep them on a short leash and point them in the right direction, and you'll get along fine."

"Papa knew that, all right," Lucille said.

Lady Ann polished a ladle. "So what do I do now?" she asked.

"We're doing it, Mama," Lucille said. "We're running the estate. We're hanging on."

"We're polishing silver," Ann said. "That's what we're doing."

"Are we polishing silver because we're worried, Mama?" Zachary asked.

"No, son. We're polishing it because it needs to be polished."

"You don't have to polish it, ma'am," Olga said. "I've done this for years on my own."

"I know," Lady Ann said. "I've got to do something—something to keep busy."

"It's going to be fine, Mama."

"Is it?"

"We're all right here," Lucille said.

"And God bless you for that."

Lady Ann tossed her silver and rag onto the table. "No, it's not going to be fine. I thought it would be better after I refused Brubaker and Van Burin, but all I did was bluff them. I did it so they'd believe we could manage things. Now I feel more alone than ever. I wasn't prepared for this."

Ann could see the British reserve of her grandmother's ancestors slowly crumbling away. It made her sad. Lady Ann had been through so much grief in such a short time.

"Wallace could do anything he set his mind to—anything. I walk around this house. It's so big and so empty now. I try to find some tasks to occupy my thoughts. To calm my nerves. But all it does is help me avoid my feelings."

"You're doing work."

"Not the real work. I have to run things here. I don't know how."

"I think you do," Lucille said. "You went with Papa on his rounds many times. You saw what he did and how he did it. Sometimes when he was out of town, you took instructions to the managers and field hands on your own."

"Yes, I did," Lady Ann said. "But they were his instructions, not mine."

"But, Mama, the responsibility for running it and the action of running it are the same thing."

"But he was running it. Not me. We're talking about twenty farms, each one with its own foreman and crew."

"I know that, but I don't see the difference."

There was a knock on the front door. Lady Ann turned toward it with a worried expression. "Now, who could that be?"

"I'll get it, ma'am," Olga said.

"No, I'll do it," Lady Ann said.

Ann watched Lady Ann cross to the door and open it. Standing on the step were Cyrus and Doss, two of the hired hands. Cyrus was scrawny, serious, and concerned, while Doss was plump with a smirk on his face. Ann had always thought Doss looked like a woodchuck.

"Morning, Lady Ann," Cyrus began. "Sorry to bother you, but we need you to settle something."

"Now, that's not really the case," Doss drawled. "We really got nothin' to settle at all."

Lucille glanced at the others at the table. "It's Doss Claypool."

"We do, ma'am," Cyrus said. "I need the wagon to go into town and pick up the wire for the boys out on Section Eight. They're waiting for it now."

"Now, you just wait a minute," Doss said. "I need the same wagon to go out to Five and bring in those bales of hay."

Lady Ann knew the ways of the Woodchuck pretty well by now. "Doss, weren't you supposed to do that yesterday?"

"Well, I did half, ma'am," Doss said.

"You were supposed to finish it," Cyrus said

"I'd get the rest done today if I had the wagon."

"We need the wagon on Eight."

"I think I see the problem, gentlemen," Lady Ann said, in an effort to control the conversation.

"I'm just sayin'," Doss said with a smirk, "that since I had the wagon first, maybe I could go out and finish the job."

"That's no guarantee you *will* finish it, Doss," Cyrus snapped.

"Hey, let's not go talkin' that way to Old Dawz here," the Woodchuck replied with a laugh.

"Lady Ann. Everyone's waiting on Eight," Cyrus said.

"Well, life's full of waiting," Doss said. "So, Mrs. Carson, if you could just make a decision here, then Old Dawz can get…"

"That's enough. Please, gentlemen," Lady Ann said.

"It's not tough to make a decision, ma'am," Doss drawled. "If the colonel were here, he'd tell Cyrus to wait his turn…"

"Gentlemen, stop."

Lucille put down her silverware and started for the door.

"I didn't mean to get you upset, ma'am," Doss said. "I can see you're upset."

"I am not upset," Lady Ann declared.

Ann saw Lucille arrive at the door. With her daughter beside her, Lady Ann appeared to regroup herself.

"Cyrus," she said, "you take the wagon. Doss, you finish the bales when he's done with it."

"And when I give it to you, Doss, try to finish the job," Cyrus said.

The Woodchuck stepped back to address the others. The sly grin had an edge now. "So it's decided then? Everybody sure what everybody wants?"

"My mother said we've decided," Lucille said.

"Then it looks like he's got the wire and I sit with the hay."

Cyrus ignored the remark. "We'll get back to work now. Thank you, ma'am."

The two men started out the driveway.

"I don't like Doss Claypool," Lucille said. "Papa almost fired him a couple of times."

"He calls himself Old Dawz when he wants to get out of trouble," Ann scoffed. "Which means half the time he opens his mouth."

Lady Ann's attention was still on the two men in the driveway.

"Now they'll know," she finally whispered. "Now everybody will know. People talk. They saw I couldn't decide. Here I am hemming and hawing when I should have been decisive. They saw it."

"But you did decide, Mama," Lucille said. "You did fine."

They took their places at the dining room table.

"No. It was a show of weakness," Lady Ann said. "It was a simple decision. What if it had been something where our lives depended on it?" The woebegone expression returned. "Can't you see? I don't know how to do this. I wasn't prepared for it. Wallace always said if you reveal your insecurity, people will take advantage. How am I going to cope with that?"

It was only morning, but already Lady Ann looked tired.

"I don't consider myself weak," she continued. "But right now, whenever I open my mouth to make a request to any of the hands, there's a little voice inside me that says, 'Can't do it. Not prepared. You're a woman in a man's world.' I become paralyzed."

"We can fight through this," Lucille said.

"We can, Grandma," Ann said.

Lady Ann smiled at them. "You all know the consequences when you're a woman. If we fail and we lose everything, we're out on the street."

"We're not on the street," Lucille said.

"We could be if we aren't careful. We have to be so careful." She sighed. "If I was prepared, I could do this."

"Mama, Jack's here. He can help."

"Jack's a good man, but since he came back from the war, he's changed."

"He can do it."

"He's got the will, but not the temperament. And then when his lungs flare up, he's away at the hospital for weeks on end. If he hadn't gone and enlisted . . . if the Germans hadn't used gas in the trenches . . . he would have been our answer."

"He still could be," Lucille said.

"Jack's an idea man. He's an innovator—not a leader. "And now . . ."—Lady Ann paused as if trying to reach some kind of solution—"I feel dazed just thinking about it. And then I get very angry at myself for feeling this way."

"I can help, Grandma," Ann said.

"God bless you, child. You're too young."

5

FOR THE NEXT FEW MONTHS, LADY Ann and the family were able to make do with running Carson Manor in spite of their concern that the townspeople would fathom their insecurity. The problem was their lack of confidence and fear of consequences, which made every day seem more arduous than the one before.

Finally, on November 13, 1918, came the news that the war in Europe was over. The men would be coming home. For many in Winfield, life would return to the way it was before the war. Fall had come, the crops were harvested, and the temperature had dropped. However, for Lady Ann, the seasons were only a change of scenery, and today was just another day. She was sitting at the dining room table with a cup of tea and the newspaper. Ann and the other schoolchildren had been sent home early, and she was upstairs in her room. Olga was dusting the fireplace and furniture.

"Ma'am, that place where they signed the treaty..."

"Rethondes," Lady Ann said.

"That any place near where Mr. Jack served?"

"No, he was near the coast. That was when everybody just dug in and held on." Lady Ann put the newspaper on the table. "They held on. Just like we're doing."

Ann went to the top of the stairs to listen. She could not understand why her grandmother was unable to see how well they were actually doing.

"We've done better than that, ma'am," Olga said. "We got through the harvest. Some of the corn we shipped. Some is in storage. We're doing just fine."

There was a knock on the front door.

"I wonder who that could be," Olga said. "It's near eleven o'clock. Everyone's at work by now."

Lady Ann started to rise.

"I'll get it, ma'am," Olga said, crossing to the entrance with her feather duster. She opened the door. Royce Chamberlin was standing outside, dressed in a winter jacket and boots. He had a folder under his arm, and he was moving back and forth in the chilly air.

"Good morning," Chamberlin said simply.

"It's Mr. Chamberlin from the bank," Olga called back into the room.

"May I come in?" he asked. "Just for a moment."

"Let him in, Olga," Lady Ann said.

Ann crouched along the railing upstairs. She knew who the visitor was, but she had never seen him out of the shadows, and here he was in broad daylight.

"Thank you," Chamberlin said. He started into the room. Olga closed the door behind him. "I hope you don't mind that I took the liberty of dropping by, but I have something I thought you should see."

Lady Ann was crossing the room to meet him.

"Oh, is it something from the bank?"

"Please," Chamberlin said, "I believe this is important." He was already reaching for a paper inside the folder.

"What is it?"

Chamberlin handed her the paper and watched intently as she read it.

"It's a savings account," Lady Ann said. "Number 23622. Called the Grain Funding Account." She looked up at Chamberlin. "I don't understand. Whose account is this?"

"Do you recognize the signature?"

Lady Ann looked at the paper again.

"I do," she said. "Bradford Brenner. That's Buddy Brenner. One of our hands."

"And the balance is one thousand and eighty dollars. It was opened in August. Deposits in August, September, and October. Three deposits of three hundred, four hundred eighty, and three hundred."

"Is there a problem? We pay him good wages. He's saving his money."

"Do you pay him that much in so short a time?'

"No."

"Do you mind if we ask him where he got it?"

"I don't mind," Lady Ann said. "But why?"

"In August didn't you have some pilferage at a grain storage facility?"

"We did. Three weeks after Wallace passed away. On Section Ten. So much has happened since then . . . so much."

"Weren't Brenner and another man—Bob Ishie, I think it was—weren't they in charge of that facility?"

"That's true. They said there was an accident up the road, so they left the property to help. When they came back, Section Ten had been robbed."

"I think we're looking at your missing grain."

Upstairs, Ann leaned forward to hear. Chamberlin and her grandmother were speaking in low voices. Chamberlin seemed quite calm, taking in everything.

"This?" Lady Ann said, pointing to the bank statement. She was trembling. "They couldn't have. They're trusted hands. Both of them."

"Possibly."

"Are you sure, Mr. Chamberlin? I know these men."

"How well?"

Lady Ann was silent, uncertain of how to answer.

"There's one way to find out," Chamberlin said. "This is why I came to see you privately."

"I understand."

"No sense word getting around about this."

From her position upstairs, Ann was able to get a better view of their visitor. At first glance he seemed undistinguished and average—the sort of person one might pass on the street and barely acknowledge. However, when focused on a goal and obsessed with achieving it, he could be startling. His cold eyes and eerily calm smile made him seem inhuman, even monstrous.

"Does Patrick know about this?" Lady Ann inquired.

"No, I thought this should be handled with a minimum of fuss."

"I appreciate that, Mr. Chamberlin."

There was another knock. "Excuse me," Lady Ann said.

"By all means."

She crossed to the front door. The Woodchuck was slouching in the doorway.

"Lady Ann, you wanted to see me?" he drawled.

"Yes, Doss. We need to get some rolls of wire out to Section Fourteen."

"Oh yeah, I'll get to it."

"You were supposed to do it last week."

Chamberlin slipped over to the entrance. Ann was surprised at the suddenness of the move.

"Somethin' got in the way, ma'am," Doss said. "The cold weather and all."

"The job needs to be done."

"We'll get it done, ma'am," Doss answered, seeming mildly annoyed. "Don't you worry now, Lady Ann."

Chamberlin stepped around the door to confront the Woodchuck.

"Excuse me, did you mean that?" he said sharply.

"What? What are you doin' here?"

"If you meant it, you should have already done the job." An expression of surprise and shock appeared on the Woodchuck's face.

"Four weeks ago there was a wagonload of wire ordered for Sections Twelve and Seventeen," Chamberlin said. "On my way here, I went by Section Sixteen. Joshua Barnes's place."

"I know it's Piccolo Barnes's place. So?"

"There are two rolls in front of his house. He's already used *his* wire. If you want to do something, you'll pick up those rolls and do Fourteen today."

"What are you talkin' to me like that for? You ain't supposed to be out here."

"Claypool, I'm saying if you're serious, you'll retrieve that wire and do the job you were told to do last week."

"I don't like the way you're talkin' to me. You just work at the bank."

"Get the wire and take care of it, Doss," Lady Ann said.

"Another thing," Chamberlin interjected. "Have you seen Brenner and Ishie this morning?"

"Well, now, I don't know."

"They should still be at the bunkhouse. Tell them we'd like to see them," Lady Ann said.

"OK, OK, I'll do it, Lady Ann," Doss grumbled. His glare moved to Chamberlin. "As for *you*, enough said. All right? Enough said."

The Woodchuck stalked out the driveway.

From her perch Ann had observed the entire scene. It was entertaining to see her grandma and the visitor cut the Woodchuck down to size. Lady Ann seemed more relaxed. It was as if the pressures and anxieties of the present had been lifted from her shoulders.

"Thank you, Mr. Chamberlin."

"I'm glad I could help."

"It was much appreciated."

"You handled Claypool well enough. The man was just feeling his oats—testing his limits. Sometimes people just like to see how much they can get away with."

Lady Ann was regarding Chamberlin with some interest. He seemed to instinctively understand her predicament.

"It's not an easy time right now," he said. "Things seem to pile up right and left."

"They do. They most certainly do," Lady Ann said.

"You'll get through it. It may not seem so right now, but you will."

They watched the approach of Buddy Brenner and Bob Ishie. Upstairs, Ann could see them, too. She always felt the best word to describe this pair was *vague*. Brenner's eyes seemed to endlessly search the air in front of him for an answer that never materialized. Ishie was more concerned with his immediate surroundings—so much so that his gaze never focused on anything for very long.

Lady Ann and Chamberlin stood in the doorway to greet them.

"Morning, Lady Ann," Brenner said.

"Doss said you wanted to see us," Ishie offered.

"Good morning, gentlemen," Chamberlin said.

"Mr. Chamberlin wanted to ask you a few questions," Lady Ann said.

Chamberlin held out the paper to them. "Do you recognize this?"

"Yeah, sure," Brenner said. "Uh, why?"

"These three deposits. They were made in cash, were they not?"

"Yeah, yeah," Ishie said uncertainly. "They were made in cash, all right."

"You know it was cash, Mr. Chamberlin," Brenner stated. "You're the teller. I gave it to you."

"May I ask where you got the money?"

"What?"

"The money you deposited."

"You never asked before," Brenner declared.

"I'm asking now. After the third deposit, I became curious."

"OK. I earned it."

"That's right. We earned it," Ishie said. "Are we in some kinda trouble?"

"Where did you earn it?" Chamberlin repeated.

"I know this is an intrusion, gentlemen," Lady Ann said, "but it's important."

"It's no intrusion," Brenner replied. "But what I'm sayin' is…"

"What we're sayin' is," Ishie continued, "we did some odds and ends on Section Seven."

"That's right. Odds and ends. Seven, it was."

"How can that be?" Lady Ann asked. "You two have never worked on Seven."

"Maybe it was Six," Ishie offered.

"Yeah. Six maybe. What I'm sayin' is…"

"The money didn't come from Carson Manor," Chamberlin stated.

"No. No, it didn't," Ishie replied. "I mean, it did and it didn't."

"And what we're sayin' is…"

Chamberlin looked at them calmly. "Come again? You better get your facts straight."

From where Ann was seated, the man from the bank seemed to be regarding them and staring through them at the same time. He had made up his mind, and there was no reasoning with him.

"Last August," Chamberlin resumed, "you two were working Section Ten. You said you were lured away, and the place was robbed."

"Yeah. Shorty Allen's buckboard went off the road," Brenner answered. "That's what happened."

"It's what we told Sheriff Dierkes."

Chamberlin held out the paper. "Two weeks after the theft of some grain, you start making deposits in a grain funding account."

"So?"

"And two days before every deposit, one of you managed to take a trip to Cedar Glen."

"That's the grain elevator," Lady Ann said in surprise. "What about this?"

"You think it was us?" Ishie said with some alarm.

"This is your account."

Ishie appeared discouraged—as if two thoughts began to merge in his head. "Oh, Nellie," he murmured. "Oh, Nellie…"

"Now, let's just wait a second," Brenner interjected. "What I'm sayin' is…"

"We need to clear this up," Lady Ann said.

"Maybe we should speak to Dierkes again," Chamberlin said.

"Don't do that," Brenner said quickly.

"So what happened?" Chamberlin demanded. "I have a very good idea. Why don't you save us a lot of trouble?"

Bob Ishie took a step backward, shaking his head, as if trying to clear his mind.

"No…no…I don't want this hangin' over us," he said.

"It's hanging over both of you right now," Chamberlin said.

Brenner was staring helplessly at the floor,

"Sheez," Ishie said. "Sheez Louise, Buddy. Are you gonna tell 'em, or am I?"

"Looks like you're tellin' them right now, Bob. Talkin' that way sorta lays it out on the table."

"Gentlemen?" Chamberlin said firmly.

"We took it," Ishie finally said. "We took it. And I'm man enough to admit it."

"We didn't mean you no harm," Brenner added. "You got enough corn as it is."

"That's hardly the point," Chamberlin said.

Lady Ann was still stunned. "Why did you do it?" she asked. "You could have come to me."

Ishie shook his head again. "I know. I know."

"Instead, you stole," Chamberlin said sternly. "You stole from your employer. And you made the bank an accessory to your low-level chicanery."

"Yeah, yeah, we were wrong," Ishie announced. "And I'm man enough to admit it."

"We trusted you," Lady Ann said. "We were fair to you."

"You got other sections," Brenner replied. "Nineteen other sections. We figured no one would notice."

"Not an ounce of remorse," Chamberlin said in dismay. "Not a flicker of regret."

"I know it looks bad," Brenner said, "but what I'm sayin' is..."

"I don't care what you're saying," Chamberlin snapped. "You stole from Carson Manor. You stole from an employer who treated you fairly—a woman who was mourning the loss of her husband. A great man. An honorable man. Is this how you repay her?"

With an earnest expression, he turned to Lady Ann. "Do you want to bring charges against them? You have every right."

"They'll have to be dismissed," she said.

"And the charges?"

"The charges?"

"The criminal charges. It's up to you."

Lady Ann pondered a moment. "No," she said slowly. "We caught them. We've got the money. I don't see much purpose in taking it further."

"You two be out of Franklin County by nightfall," Chamberlin said. "If you ever come back, I'll bring charges against you myself."

With downcast eyes, the two men started for the driveway.

From her seat above, Ann noticed that as Brenner was leaving, he glanced back to Royce Chamberlin and Lady Ann. Chamberlin nodded curtly. Was it a nod of approval, or was Chamberlin acknowledging to himself that an unpleasant episode had been concluded? Ann couldn't tell. It was there and then it was gone—a flash and over.

"Thank you again, Mr. Chamberlin," Lady Ann said.

"Royce. Please call me Royce."

They remained in the doorway, watching Brenner and Ishie as they returned to the bunkhouse.

"You know," Chamberlin said, "the world would be a lot better place if people looked out for one another. Neighbors looking out for neighbors, like it says in the Bible. They preach it in church every Sunday, but somehow, out here in the real world, it's another set of rules."

"It certainly is."

Chamberlin was facing Lady Ann. "I took a chance when I first arrived. Now I'm going to take another. May I call again?"

Lady Ann did not reply immediately. "Yes," she finally said. "Yes, of course, Royce."

Ann did not leave her spot at the top of the stairs. She was not sure what to make of Chamberlin. The man had come to help, and he had delivered. Lady Ann was free of the fears and anxieties that had plagued her. Her confidence seemed to have returned.

Ann decided to give Chamberlin the benefit of the doubt—at least for now.

6

ROYCE CHAMBERLIN MANAGED TO CALL ON Lady Ann at least once a week for the next four weeks. Usually, he would arrive with some problem or decision from the bank that he would present to Lady Ann and then proceed to solve for her before his departure. Ann began to liken his visits to the routine of a door-to-door broom salesman—the sort of man who would give his pitch about the broom's quality, sprinkle a few wood chips on the floor, and then sweep them up.

By the fifth visit, their conversations had begun to touch on more personal topics. Chamberlin had lost his wife several years before.

They were seated in the living room, waiting for Olga to bring the tea.

"Royce, after your Sara died, how did you manage?"

"It was difficult for me. At first, everyday things suddenly seemed unfamiliar, even confusing."

Lady Ann's eyes widened. He had touched on something she understood.

"I was concerned—not just for myself, but for my family."

"Family."

"My inspiration," he said. "The strength of family. It was never an obligation. My two girls, Carol and Cassandra, were my foundation. I relied on them, and they sustained me."

Chamberlin continued carefully. "I admired the colonel very much, and I think of you often. We're both in the same position. I went through it sometime before you, but I have the experience to tell you that it will work out."

"Oh, easier said. Easier said."

"It was a lesson that took me time to learn," he continued. "The obstacles seemed terribly large, so I learned to focus on the steps that solved the particular task at hand rather than the obstacle, and certainly not the bigger picture, which at the time seemed perilous."

"Were you afraid?"

"I was. So I forced myself to behave as if I weren't. I did everything one step at a time, putting all thoughts of conditions and consequences out of my mind. You have to put fear and doubt out of your mind and concentrate on the individual steps."

"You make it sound so simple."

"No problem is simple. Life isn't simple. Breaking our actions into steps makes the resolutions much easier."

He saw something in her eyes. That flicker he was waiting for.

"I'm saying you can do it, Lady Ann," he declared. "You've done very well already. You're not saying to yourself, 'I'm a woman. I'm not prepared for this. I fear the consequences of my inexperience.'"

Lady Ann was about to speak—to reveal the fears and anxieties she had been feeling for all these months. Just admitting it would remove some of what she had allowed herself to bottle up inside. At that moment Olga entered with a tray holding a pot and two teacups. She placed it on the table and served them.

"You're not saying those words, Lady Ann. You're not even thinking them," Chamberlin said when Olga left. "You're a strong woman."

"You only see the outside."

"It's the outside that counts. It's the outside of each and every one of us that deals with the world at large. We keep the inside to ourselves . . . and to our loved ones. And that's as it should be." He changed tack. "I've seen you coping with duties and obligations—seen you taking charge and never relying on someone to do it for you. You're a strong woman. I appreciate strong women. I learned that from bringing up my girls. I respect women. I admire them."

"I believe you," Lady Ann said. "I believe you do."

"You could run this place with no fears or anxiety," he said tentatively. "Providing you had the proper help."

"Help?"

"Advice. Counsel. Someone to master the more difficult situations. But always there."

"It's been a daunting task."

"Perhaps it isn't for you to do alone," he said slowly. "I don't mean to force myself upon you, but at the bank I am familiar with all things financial concerning the Carson empire. I know what was proposed, how it was accomplished, what the bank paid, what we got in return, and what it cost in taxes and financial expenses."

He pointed to his right temple. "I've got it all up here. I was almost like a second pair of hands for the colonel." He lowered his eyes bashfully. "Of course, I'm not the man the colonel was, but I am a man."

Lady Ann was trying to decipher what he said. Here was a person who understood her predicament.

"Everything I'm trying to share with you, I had to learn by trial and error," he said. "But I did learn, and I learned there are some things one can't do alone." He watched her out of the corner of his eye. "I was thinking that perhaps we might overcome some of these difficulties for our children."

Lady Ann stared straight ahead. Her mind was on all she had been enduring for the past months. "There are difficulties."

"But don't you see? We both lost loved ones. We both have children. You have a daughter and granddaughter. I have two daughters with no mother." Then with great sensitivity he continued. "Perhaps I'm pressing my case too hard, but if we pooled our resources, we might make an unfortunate situation work for us and for our children."

She had heard him, but did not respond. Neither did she recoil at the suggestion—a fact that surprised her all the more. "Do I shock you?" he asked.

"No, no...it's just that so much has happened recently."

"I know the workings of the estate. I can help," he said. "At least think it over."

The kitchen door opened. Ann and Zachary entered, chuckling at some joke. When Zachary saw Lady Ann, he went to her immediately. Chamberlin maintained his fixed smile.

"I helped today, Mama," Zachary said happily. "I helped...I..." He looked to Ann. "What did we do?"

"We took some feed out to the barn."

"That's right. We took feed to the barn. That's right...and...oh yes...the bags were heavy, so Chester and Billy stopped baling the hay and helped us."

The more Ann looked at Chamberlin, the more uneasy she felt. The smile and the expression in his eyes didn't add up. There was something about his eyes that seemed both animated and dead.

"I helped, too," Zachary said to Chamberlin

"Very good," Chamberlin answered. "Helping the family is an admirable quality."

"Yes," said Zachary. "I don't want Mama to be unhappy. Mama's been unhappy."

Everyone heard the remark and interpreted it in a different way. For Chamberlain, it was a validation for his visits. But for Lady Ann, it was an admission—an open declaration of the state of the household that she had been trying to conceal for so long.

"Ann," she said abruptly, "perhaps you and Zachary could help Olga in the kitchen."

"Come on, Zachary," Ann said. "Let's get some milk."

When the door closed behind them, Lady Ann spoke. "That was very nice what you said to Zachary," she said.

"Uh...about Zachary...forgive my curiosity..."

"When he was little, he slipped and fell down those stairs. He hit his head, and..."

"I'm sorry. He's a good boy."

As the conversation continued, Ann crept back to the kitchen door. She crouched down on the floor and pushed it ajar. From her place, she was able to keep her eye on Zachary at the kitchen table and listen to her grandmother and her visitor.

"Royce...a moment ago...were you proposing marriage?" Lady Ann asked.

Chamberlin smiled. "I wouldn't dare to be so forward."

Ann listened intently. She was surprised that the visits had been so frequent, and she began to see that all these offers of help and advice concealed a hidden agenda. This man was up to no good.

"It would strengthen our families," he continued. "But no...it's too soon. Too soon."

"No...no," Lady Ann said. "I understand."

"It all seems so vast...almost regal out here," he said. "It seems like a tremendous task. Still, I'd like to help."

"No, no," thought Ann, "this kind of help we don't need."

"But, Royce...there could be no love."

"Oh?" Chamberlin asked mildly.

"In what you're proposing."

"I'm thinking more of the strength of family," he said. "Family union. Family values."

Ann was amazed that his man seemed to be getting away with his strategy.

"I don't know, Royce," Lady Ann said. "This is all so overwhelming."

"Please think about it. I am always at your disposal."

Ann shifted her weight, tired from being in a crouched position. The floorboards creaked. Before she could get away, Lady Ann stepped over and opened the door.

"Ann, what are you doing back there?"

"Hello, little girl," Chamberlin said gently. "Were you playing?"

Ann glared at him. He was trying so hard to be innocent and proper, but his eyes gave him away.

"I'm speaking to you, little girl."

"You're not the colonel," she said pointedly.

"Ann! What a thing to say," Lady Ann said.

"It's already forgotten," Chamberlin said. He looked down at Ann. "I never claimed to be the colonel. And you should be careful where you play."

"Go back in the kitchen," Lady Ann said.

"Sometimes I forget I have two growing daughters. I should be going."

"I'll walk you to the door," she said.

Olga appeared with Chamberlin's coat. He put it on.

Olga opened the front door. Chamberlin glanced back to Lady Ann.

"Next Tuesday?"

Ann watched. Her grandma didn't answer immediately. "Please say no, Grandma," she thought. "Please say no."

"Yes," Lady Ann replied. "Yes, of course. Next Tuesday."

7

MANY OF THE MEN WHO FOUGHT in the war were returning home. There were celebrations, but since they were returning to working farms, most of the festivities were held in the privacy of homes. Besides, it was winter and most of the countryside was barren—empty rows slashed across the sloping hillsides where cornstalks had stood a few months ago and would stand next year.

It was late December at Carson Manor. Outside, the snowflakes were fluttering past the window, but tension brewed within the household. Every other day since Royce Chamberlin's proposal, a dozen white roses had been delivered to Lady Ann from Sidford's Florist.

Lady Ann, Jack, and Lucille were gathered in the main hall. Ann was along the wall nearby. The adults were sitting at the dining-room table for a grown-up conversation. There had been a fair number of these since Grandpa died and a lot more since Royce Chamberlin showed up. For Ann, this was part of the adult world—a place she would enter soon enough. She liked the look of it, but there were many things she didn't understand.

Ann had always wondered why adult conversations took such a long time to resolve anything. If a child's growth went from crawling to walking to running, then by that logic, an adult should be able to make a snap decision and move on. Instead, they would hash it over for hours.

Today they were discussing Royce Chamberlin. Ann wondered why they didn't simply say yes or no—preferably no—and be done with it.

The adults were contemplating the latest bouquet on the hall table. Jack's face was slightly red. He claimed it was the cold outside, but his cough had returned, and he had been trying to hide it from Lady Ann.

"What are you going to tell Mr. Chamberlin, Mama?" Lucille asked.

"You want to think it over more. Much more," Jack added. "I think this is all too sudden."

"I just don't like opening up our family to someone so soon after Papa died," Lucille said. "It hasn't even been a year."

Lady Ann took Lucille's hands. "Lucille . . . I loved your father. I'll always love him, but this situation is too big for me, and it isn't going to change. I thought I would get used to it through habit, but every day—every morning—begins with uncertainty, and every evening ends with doubts. Some days I just want to walk out that front door and never come back."

"Don't do that, Grandma," Ann said.

"I won't, child," Lady Ann said. "I'm just speaking figuratively."

"Go play with your dolly, little one," Jack said.

Ann moved away and sat in a hall chair to listen. She didn't want to get her doll. She knew that holding a doll would lessen her credibility in an adult conversation.

Jack felt a tickling sensation welling up in his throat. It was like a powerful itch. He couldn't clear his throat to make it stop, and it seemed to dig in. He put his hand over his mouth and turned away. He had stifled the attack, but Lady Ann had seen it.

"Jack?"

"Winter cough."

"That's right," Lucille said.

Lady Ann was not convinced.

"Winter," Jack said. "That's what it is." He hoped everyone would chalk it up to the weather. This one burned worse than before.

Ann felt sad for her father when these attacks came. If he were in the middle of something important, their manifestation seemed to reduce his stature.

Lucille had seen it, too. She wanted to divert the attention from her husband and back to the subject at hand.

"Letting another person in to help run things. That's a big change," Lucille said.

"I know that," Lady Ann answered. "That's why I haven't said yes or no."

"Say no, Grandma," Ann said from her seat. She wanted to give her father some support.

Lucille looked over at her daughter. "Ann, we're having a serious discussion here."

"A family discussion," said Jack.

"I'm part of the family."

"Bless you, child, you are," Lady Ann said patiently. "But this is something we have to decide ourselves."

"You play with your dolly, or you go to your room," Lucille said. The doll or the room. Neither one was a good choice.

Ann went over to the steps where she would be out of sight but close enough to listen.

"Mother Carson, *we* can help," Jack said.

"I know you can." Lady Ann's tone became more entreating. "But don't you see? I'm not considering this because I'm lazy and want someone to take care of me. Not at all."

"We know that," Lucille said.

"During the war, our quilting bees didn't pop up like ragweed. We went out, knocked on doors, and organized. We're not lazy people who are waiting for someone to fan us. We're practical, and when we have to, we act on our principles. Now, Royce does know the business. He knows all the farms: the profits and debts of each one, and the specific needs of each property."

Ann was puzzled. She wasn't sure if Lady Ann wanted to be talked out of it or into it.

Jack knew the situation called for a man to step forward and declare himself. The problem was that nobody in the room seemed to acknowledge him.

"What about hiring a manager?" Lucille asked.

Lady Ann recoiled. "No...no. Never. That would be an admission of defeat to the whole county. It would show we're weak. What would people say? What would they think?"

"I don't think they'd care, Mama."

"They'd care, and they'd know. When Wallace Carson founded this town, he set a standard for everyone who settled here afterward. We have to preserve and protect that standard. We'll do whatever it takes."

"But what has Chamberlin done?" Jack asked, more as a challenge.

"Let's examine that for a moment," Lady Ann said. "We're having a discussion. Let's give him his due."

"Are you taking his side?"

"Jack, I'm trying to make a decision," Lady Ann said impatiently.

"He caught Brenner and Ishie," Lucille said.

"They were out in the open," Jack declared. "Someone would have caught them sooner or later."

"All right, I'll concede that."

"Barlow Fence in Des Moines," Lady Ann said.

"That was Fred Brubaker."

"It was Chamberlin first," Lucille added. "Right after Papa died, Barlow sent a bill to the bank for new fence. He claims we had ordered it, but Chamberlin checked, and it turns out there was no order."

"Exactly," Lady Ann added. "We didn't know, and Royce stepped in to protect us."

"To his credit, he has been a help," Lucille said.

"Yeah, but how did he discover these things?" Jack asked.

"In files and book work at the bank."

"Don't you think it's a little strange how they've popped up at regular intervals?"

"They didn't pop up. They were there, and he discovered them," Lady Ann said.

"I don't think it matters, Jack," Lucille said.

"I think it does. These things are important."

"We can haggle over this forever," Lady Ann said. "Right now, we have our own issues. The point is, he's declared himself, and he's demonstrated it by his actions."

"But is he family?" Jack asked, exasperated.

"No."

"Then please…let me take it on."

Ann began to feel sad again. Jack had declared himself. He had done it several times, and no one seemed to hear him. In fact, on some occasions, they seemed to be addressing him as a child.

"Let me try," he said. "I've been in this family fifteen years. If it's a matter of issuing instructions, tell me what to say. Tell me what to do.

Jack started to cough but then caught it. His face became red again as he struggled to control the attack. "All right, it's the inflamed lung, but it goes away after a stay in the hospital."

"That's the point," Lady Ann said. "You're away a lot of the time."

"Mama's right, Jack," Lucille said.

"I thought you were on my side," Jack said to Lucille. "I'm as competent as the next man."

Ann couldn't stand it any longer. She had to speak up for her papa.

"Papa can do it," Ann said from the stairs. "I know he can."

The emotions and tension of the discourse seemed to affect Jack's cough. He sat there, breathing heavily.

"Sometimes you're away six weeks at a time," Lady Ann said.

"What does that have to do with running a farm?" Jack cried. "We could put in one of those new telephones. They have them in the city. We can get one here."

"No," Lady Ann said. "Every call goes through Sallilee at the switchboard in town. Two phone calls and the whole town would know our business."

"But that's not important, Mother Carson."

"This is twenty farms. That makes it important. We need somebody here all the time."

"Listen, please," he said urgently. "If it's experience, I can learn. If it's…"

Another attack swept through his lungs. When it subsided, his voice became more pleading. "What you're hearing…the cough…that's not me, not my capabilities. Tell me. If it weren't for the lungs…if it weren't for the…"

Lady Ann was regarding him with a sad expression. This would be one of the most difficult things she ever had to say. "Jack," she began, "if good intentions and good will were all it required, you could do it, but we need more."

Jack was out of his chair and crossing to the liquor cart beside the kitchen door. He took a bottle of scotch and poured himself a glass.

"Jack, it's ten thirty in the morning," Lucille cautioned.

"It stops the cough," he said. He downed the glass in a gulp. "Alcohol…cough medicine. Who knows? But it works."

He returned to the table to renew his argument.

"Mother Carson, when I was courting Lucille, it took me a year to prove myself to the colonel. I didn't mind. I loved Lucille. It took time to become a family member."

"I know that."

"What do we know about Royce Chamberlin? Very little or nothing at all." His tone became almost imploring. "Please don't do this. I have a feeling that if you do, it will be a terrible mistake."

Lady Ann's voice became softer, more reasonable. "I've spent the last month questioning myself. Am I being an opportunist? Am I afraid and just using him, knowing that he might be using me in return? I've been as honest and scrupulous as I can. I'm not caving in here…I'm fighting for the estate in the only way I know how. I'm doing this for us."

As she spoke, she saw how sorrowful Jack had become.

"I know you're disappointed," she said. "I'm sorry."

Jack's demeanor was resigned. He had tried, but the family came first.

"Well then, I suppose I'd better get packed for a stay in Rochester Clinic," he said. "This cough's been with me for a day and half. I tried to hide it. Everything's out in the open now."

Ann watched Jack start up the stairs to the bedroom. She felt sad for him, but in a way she felt proud. He had stated his case, and he had done his best. At that moment he looked as if he had been pulled in all directions until there was nothing left. It was then that Ann realized how much she loved her father.

Lucille waited till he was upstairs. "He has been trying to hide it," she said. "It comes. He goes to the clinic. He returns home. It's back. Same pattern all over again."

"But Papa can help. I know he can," Ann said.

"I know you love your papa," Lady Ann said.

"What about the promise to Grandpa?" Ann asked.

"We have to consider what we need the most. There's no getting around it."

Even though the discussion had covered all possible arguments, it appeared that the decision was already made.

"What are you going to do?" Lucille asked.

"I'm telling him yes," Lady Ann said.

8

BY SPRING OF THE FOLLOWING YEAR, the crops were already in full growth. Ann had spent much of her time in the company of her friends Judy and Ellen. She didn't like the upcoming marriage of her grandmother and Royce Chamberlin. She tried to discuss it with her friends, but her grandmother's sudden remarriage was something they had never considered.

Ann imagined that the remarriage was causing gossip around the town, but not the supportive kind that her family had hoped for. She never heard any, but it didn't stop her from imagining. Then there was the promise to Grandpa. She had given him her word, and now everything seemed to be heading in a direction nobody had foreseen.

On April 5, 1919, Carson Manor was decked out for the wedding celebration of Lady Ann and Royce Chamberlin. With the line of carriages along the road beside the cornfields, it looked very much like the Fourth of July celebration only nine months before. The temperature was cooler, and the roads were still muddy from rain a few days earlier. The slippery areas in the dirt made the arrival of the guests seem precarious. As they navigated around the treacherous parts, everyone appeared to be tiptoeing apprehensively, rather than arriving enthusiastically, to partake in the celebration.

The long table was set once again with the finest china and crystal. The guests were arranged up and down the sides with groupings of white roses down the middle of the table from one end to the other. The painting on the wall of Lady Ann and the colonel had been removed. However, even though no expense had been spared, there was something off-kilter about this celebration—perhaps because Lady Ann had paid for it. There was also the underlying reality that everyone concerned was trying too hard.

A small orchestra was playing softly while the assembled feasted on roast beef, baked potatoes, and assorted vegetables. The musicians performed well

enough, but they would have looked more at home in a country club in Phila-
delphia than in Winfield. Ann thought that one moo from a cow and this bunch
would scamper for the nearest buckboard.

Royce Chamberlin was at one end of the table. Dressed in a fine blue suit, he
was beaming triumphantly, as if he could hardly believe his good fortune. Lady
Ann was at the other end—almost like a miniature of herself in a photograph.
She wore a happy expression, but anyone who knew her could see that it never
approached the radiance she had shown when she was in the company of the
colonel. She and Chamberlin were married, but they still seemed disconnected.

To Lady Ann's right was her family. Lucille, Jack, Ann, and Zachary were
seated in a row. They were putting on a good show for the company—smiling
and saying, "We hope Mama will be happy," but never elaborating. Beyond
them and extending all the way up to Chamberlin were the legal and business
interests of the town. This included Van Burin, Brubaker, Judge Farnell Post,
and assorted merchants. The one wild card in the company was Sheriff Dierkes.

Ann had always liked Tom Dierkes. A tall, middle-aged man with a weather-
beaten face, he was a loner, yet he had a voice of moral authority that everyone
respected. Dierkes had been the town lawman for ten years. Ann admired him
because he seemed mysterious. She had guessed he had been a gunfighter out
west who had tired of shooting snake-oil salesmen and cattle rustlers and decided to settle in Winfield. All anyone knew was that he'd arrived in town thirty
years ago—rode in on a flatcar of the eastbound freight. Sheriff Baxter had given
him a job sweeping cells at the jailhouse. Then he'd made him deputy. When
Sheriff Baxter had retired, Dierkes ran for the top office and won. Wherever he
came from, he had found his home in Winfield, Iowa.

With the exception of Dierkes, it seemed that Chamberlin had crowded his
end of the table with the local chamber of commerce. Family had been relegated
to the other end—with Lady Ann. This included his two daughters, Cassie and
Carol.

The girls were seated directly across the table from Ann, Lucille, and Jack.
Chamberlin had managed to avoid presenting them to his new family until now.
This had been a red flag to Lucille, Jack, and Ann, but Lady Ann felt certain that
everyone would work together once they realized the importance of their task.

Cassie was eighteen. In looks and behavior, she came across as a fluttery
southern belle, minus the accent. Life seemed to be one gay party—her oohs and
ahs and giddy laughter seemed to greet every situation. But then one noticed her
blank eyes; it was as if something inside her had shut off years before and what
remained was a vivacious shell. Carol was a year older. She wore severe clothing
that hid every bit of her sexuality. With long sleeves and a high, buttoned collar,
Carol seemed a decade older than her sister. She never smiled. Her gaze moved

all around the room, missing nothing and evaluating everyone. This was her father's wedding, but she regarded her surroundings with the cold authority of a guard monitoring a prison ward.

The orchestra finished. Chamberlin tapped his crystal goblet and stood up to address the company.

"What a glorious day this is," he said grandly. "Not only for my new bride and myself, but for the town." There was a chorus of agreement up and down the table. "I look around the table, and I see several representatives of the powers that be."

"Judge Post," he said, leading a round of applause from the guests. "Van Burin, my banker and my friend." Another round of applause as Van Burin smiled to the assembled, forever working the crowd. "At a party that tried too hard, he was the perfect guest," Ann thought.

"Lawyer Brubaker, my legal representative." More applause as Brubaker nodded politely.

"And finally Sheriff Tom Dierkes, my representative of the law." A final round of applause. Ann noticed that Dierkes was smiling back, but he did not appear taken in by the flattery—at least Ann hoped that was the case.

"You might say that I have all the powers that be eating off the plates at my table," Chamberlin said graciously. "It has been a long road to this moment."

He tapped his glass. "To all of us...a toast."

Everyone at the table raised a glass. Dierkes did, too, but without as much enthusiasm as the others. More and more, Ann felt that Dierkes didn't want to be there and that he was putting in an appearance.

"Why the long face, Tom?" Chamberlin boomed out.

"Best wishes on your day," Dierkes returned and drank his toast. The others at the table followed him.

"There's something behind this," Ann thought. "It was like Dierkes was saying, 'I know you're a skunk,' and the skunk answering, 'I know that you know.' There's something here."

"You've had enough, Jack," she heard her mother say.

Ann noticed that her father had drunk the toast with the others. No more than that. Jack seemed embarrassed that Lucille had spoken out in front of the others. However, from his end of the table, Chamberlin had not missed a thing.

"Let him have one more, Lucille," he said generously. "It's a celebration, isn't it?"

"Biggest one in years," echoed Van Burin.

"One more never hurt anyone," Chamberlin said, holding out his glass. "Here, Jack, drink with me."

Jack reached for his glass and slowly raised it. With his eyes fixed on Jack, Chamberlin slowly downed the remainder of his glass. Jack did the same.

"If any of you hearing me this afternoon," Chamberlin continued, "if any of you believes that there will be radical changes to the Carson farms, I promise you there will not."

His gaze moved among the faces of the invited. "We all watched while Colonel Wallace Carson created this magnificent monument to Iowa and its citizens. We witnessed a miracle. One man's dream became a beautiful reality. Today, I pledge to you that Lady Ann and I—along with our families and you, my friends—we will all become caretakers of that dream."

The room burst into applause.

"Do well for the people. Do well for the land. To that I must add, do well for the family. For what are we all, but part of the bigger family? The human family. That was the colonel's dream...that is Lady Ann's dream...and that is my dream."

Everyone applauded again. Van Burin appeared to be shaking his head in wonderment at the beauty of the words. With a sly smile, Brubaker seemed to be acknowledging the shrewd tactics of a fellow attorney. Ann saw Lucille and Jack clapping, but without much heart. And at the end of the table, Lady Ann was applauding, even though she was all but forgotten in the uproar. To Ann, her grandmother seemed more like a bewildered guest who had wandered into another person's party.

As the clapping died down, Chamberlin nodded to the orchestra. They began to play a waltz.

"Ah," Chamberlin said. "A cue for a dance." He looked down the long table to Lady Ann. "My dear?"

Chamberlin moved along the row of chairs toward his new bride. He had married the rich widow Carson, and now they were going to dance in front of the entire town. He was smiling proudly and extending his arm to Lady Ann when Cassie scrambled out of her seat and darted around the table. It was so quick that nobody had time to react.

"Dance with me, Papa," Cassie said eagerly. "Dance with me."

"It's my wedding day, Cassandra."

She grabbed her father's arm. "Dance with me, Papa."

"No, I'll dance with you next."

Cassie was looking at Lady Ann with a hurt expression. Chamberlin took Lady Ann by the arm and escorted her to the area between the orchestra and the long table. They began to dance. Cassie stood along the row of chairs, fuming.

"Careful you don't have them fighting over you, Royce," Van Burin said loudly. There was a smattering of laughter. Others sat in polite embarrassment as the waltz continued.

"Well, Royce finally has his day," Brubaker said.

"Good old Royce," Van Burin burbled. "Man of ambition, man of his word."

"Royce has become a pillar of the community overnight," Judge Post said.

"He sure has. A real pillar."

"How's his deal going in Omaha?" Post inquired.

"He's signed an agreement between the bank and Rose Grain and Feed. Royce thinks there's money in it."

"He's come a long way from the teller's cage," Brubaker mused.

As Chamberlin and her grandma danced, Ann noticed the scowl on Cassie's face. She had not seen one like it since Tommy Taylor offered his little sister an ice cream and then threw it in the horse trough.

"Why is she so unhappy?" Ann asked.

"I don't know, little one," Lucille answered. "We never got a chance to know them."

Carol's voice slashed through the summer air like a cold blade. "Our family has special ways of doing things. You'll learn that after we move in."

"Yes, I suppose we will," Lucille replied.

"If Cassie is unhappy, Papa will make it right. It's family."

"But we're going to be family, too, Carol."

Ann studied Carol. With no makeup, restricting clothing, and her hair pulled into a tight bun, this nineteen-year-old girl already seemed like a bitter old woman.

Carol's tone shifted to cool condescension. She turned to Lucille. "Tell me, are we to call you mother?" And then pointing to her father and Lady Ann. "Or are we to call her mother?"

"I don't know," Lucille answered. "Call her mother. Call me Lucille."

The music stopped. There was mild applause. Chamberlin escorted Lady Ann back to her seat. Cassie raced eagerly to her father.

"Me, Papa. Me, Papa."

Chamberlin gave the orchestra a signal, and they began to play another waltz. He and his daughter began to dance. Cassie was radiant. She seemed to bask in the attention. From her seat at the table, Carol watched them with a grimly approving expression.

Ann had never seen people like this before. And they were moving into the family house!

Lady Ann stepped down the long table to her family. She had a happy face, but she seemed concerned.

"Ann," she said, "aren't you having a good time?"

"It's a good party, Grandma."

"Please. Try to get along with everyone, for your grandpa's sake."

"I will."

Lucille leaned over to Ann. "All right?" she whispered.

"I don't know, Mama. I don't think I like them."

From his seat Dierkes watched Chamberlin and Cassie. His mind was not on the current festivities—it was back on a hot night in August, a few weeks after the death of Colonel Carson.

Dierkes lived alone, and often, when he couldn't sleep, he would saddle his horse and patrol the areas around Winfield and the surrounding farms. He never encountered any trouble, nor did he expect to. But he found that a solitary night ride was restful.

This particular night was extremely hot—as summer nights in Iowa can be—and so around 3:30 a.m., he went out for a ride. On most of these rides, the only sounds he encountered were the crickets, an occasional hoot of a horned owl, and the constant clop-clopping of his horse along the dirt road.

He had ridden alone for a while, and, perhaps out of a sense of protectiveness, he decided to take more time to patrol the Carson farms. There was a full moon that gave a blue cast to the rows of cornstalks.

As he approached Section Fifteen, he realized he wasn't alone. This sixth sense came from his years as a cattle drover; it was an awareness that something as insignificant as a leaf falling to the ground or the cessation of cricket sounds might indicate the presence of another human being.

The corner of Section Fifteen rose slightly into a hill that afforded a view of several of the Carson properties, extending outward to the horizon. As Dierkes's eyes searched the terrain ahead, he saw a figure standing on top of the hill. "Who the hell is that? What's he doing out here in the middle of the night?" Dierkes wondered. The man was alone—standing motionless with the white circle of the moon behind him. He appeared to be in deep thought as he surveyed the Carson property that lay before him. Dierkes recognized the man to be Royce Chamberlin.

Dierkes rode over to the road that passed Section Fifteen and started along the road that led uphill. When he arrived at the top, the man had disappeared.

9

THE NEXT FEW WEEKS WERE DIFFICULT for Ann and her family. Chamberlin and his daughters moved into the manor. The activities focused mainly on the physical act of moving—purchasing new furniture or bringing in old items from Chamberlin's former home. There were dealings with visiting workmen. Other than giving voice to Lady Ann's instructions in running the farms, Royce Chamberlin was careful not to make any major changes. After all, he had made a promise to Lady Ann and the town—and in May of 1919, it was not even the first anniversary of Wallace Carson's death.

Young Ann spent much of her time with Judy and Ellen—either at their farms or in town. She preferred to be with them than at the manor. Even though everyone claimed to be making an effort to be a family, Ann rarely saw it. Chamberlin and his daughters were demanding; Lady Ann's people were accommodating. It was a difficult place to live, yet whenever she tried to escape, she felt she was letting the family down. And so, she always ended up returning home sooner than she had planned.

On May 12 Royce and Lady Ann had hitched up the carriage for a trip into town. Lady Ann had some shopping to do at Caldecott's Linen and Dry Goods. She had asked Ann to come along, and wanting to spend time with her grandmother, Ann readily accepted. Royce objected to Ann's coming, but Lady Ann persuaded him to change his mind. For Ann, this was the first major warning. What could Royce have against her accompanying them to the dry goods store?

The three made the trip into Winfield with little or no conversation. When they reached Market Street, they let Ann off at Caldecott's and continued on to the bank. Ann started toward the store, but her curiosity was piqued. She remained on the sidewalk, watching the carriage approach the bank on the far side of the street.

Ann did not know it, but inside the bank they were already making preparations for Lady Ann's visit. There were a few more bouquets around the interior. Van Burin had hired a new teller, but she was not due to start until the following week. Until then, Van Burin was doing the job himself. He was at the teller's window, counting out some bills for Warren Hyatt, and quite eager to see him off the premises.

"Thank you, Warren," Van Burin said. "It's always good to see you."

"Are you trying to get me out of here? I'm a customer, too."

"I know you're a customer, but Lady Ann and Royce are due any moment." Hyatt had begun to recount the bills. "Can't you do that somewhere else?"

"This sure wouldn't be happening in Mother Russia," Hyatt grumbled.

"Now, don't start with that."

"Over there, the money belongs to the people," Hyatt declared.

"Then you wouldn't be coming in every month to cash your father's allowance check."

"That's not fair. You know I can't get a job in Winfield. No one will hire me."

"No one will hire you because you haven't been looking."

"I've been looking…I have…or I would. Don't you see, Patrick? No one would hire me anyway."

"Have you applied for a job at all?"

"It wouldn't matter if I did. I know that. Everyone seems to think I caused the colonel's death. There's no point in applying for anything. We know how it is here…what people think. Even you think it. You don't say so, but you do."

"I don't want to hear anymore," Van Burin said.

"I don't deserve that," Hyatt whined. "All right…I'm leaving. See? Right out the door."

He collided with Brubaker, who was coming in from his office next door.

"Sorry, Fred."

Brubaker entered the bank with several folders under his arm. He looked back to Hyatt. "Where's he off to in such a huff?"

"Probably the barbershop until Cecil boots him out," Van Burin said.

"Lady Ann and Royce just pulled up outside."

"That means they saw Hyatt."

"So what?" Brubaker smiled slyly. "How does it feel having your teller as your best customer?"

"Times have changed."

"Better get used to it."

Chamberlin and Lady Ann entered. Chamberlin was polished and authoritative—the perfect model of a wealthy landowner. Beneath her fashionable manner, Lady Ann appeared tense.

"Lady Ann…Royce. So good to see you," Van Burin gushed.

"Thank you, Patrick," Lady Ann answered.

"Good morning, Lady Ann," Brubaker said.

"Good morning, Fred."

"Royce," Van Burin said, "you haven't been in lately, but it's always good to see you."

Before Lady Ann could say a word, Chamberlin took over the discourse. "That's why we're here. Lady Ann and I have been discussing family finances, and we want to make some changes in her accounts."

"Shall we step into my office?"

Chamberlin, Lady Ann, and Van Burin walked into the bank's corner office. Brubaker quietly crossed to the front door, put the Closed sign against the glass, and quickly rejoined the others, who had found seats around Van Burin's desk. Van Burin pulled the curtains to let in more light.

"Now. What may we do for you?"

"I want to have signing privileges on all accounts. And I want to have power of attorney over the entire estate," Chamberlin announced.

Van Burin was stunned. Lady Ann clutched her hands together in her lap. Only Brubaker regarded the proceedings with the same affable expression.

"I'd like to talk it over first," Lady Ann said, her voice quiet but firm.

"You mean talk it over more," Chamberlin replied.

"This is a big step," she said.

"And an important one."

"You would be sharing the administrative duties," Brubaker suggested.

"We discussed that," Chamberlin added. "We agreed it would be better for you."

Van Burin listened in astonishment. Chamberlin and Brubaker were moving together in perfect stride.

"It's still a big step," Lady Ann said. Despite her genteel manner, she seemed to be standing her ground.

"Let's examine it again," Chamberlin said, adopting a patient tone. "First, nothing would occur without your knowledge. Nothing would occur without your permission. We want to maintain the values and traditions of the colonel."

"Traditions and values. Very important," Brubaker chimed in.

Up the street, Ann was outside Caldecott's. She had seen her grandmother enter the bank with Royce. She had also seen Brubaker go in shortly afterward with his armload of papers. This wasn't unusual. But she had also seen him place the Closed sign in the front door window. If Lady Ann was making a quick stop, why were they closing the bank? This didn't seem right. Ann left Caldecott's and started down the street.

Inside the office, Chamberlin was watching his new bride. "You were so agreeable at the house, Lady Ann," he said.

"I'm still not sure if it's the right thing."

"When you were running the estate by yourself, it was a heavy responsibility. You were alone, and you were right to consider the lot of a woman alone in the world as well as the consequences of attempting to go it alone."

"Hazardous for a woman alone," Brubaker echoed.

"I'm taking some of that responsibility off your shoulders," Chamberlin said.

"Working together as a team," Brubaker added. "That's what it is."

"I'll phrase it another way. In a sense, I will be shielding you. If, God forbid, we had a loss, I would take responsibility."

"But with every success, you'll share the benefits," Brubaker said.

Lady Ann became more uneasy. The three sets of eyes were fastened upon her. She felt pinned to her seat, and it was too late to try The Dying Swan Act.

Ann had arrived at the door to the bank. What was going on in there? She was about to knock, but she decided to try the handle first and found that the door was unlocked. Cautiously, she slipped inside. It was quiet and empty—except for the activity in the office.

Nobody inside had heard her. Everyone's attention was riveted on Lady Ann. It looked like a business meeting. Ann tiptoed closer to listen.

"I know you were worried," Chamberlin was saying. "If you let me help, you won't have to worry anymore."

"That's what we discussed," Lady Ann said.

"In the long run, this is so much better," Brubaker added.

"Think about it, Lady Ann," Van Burin said, finally joining in.

"I am," Lady Ann said. "I want what's best for my family."

"Best for the land. Best for the people," Brubaker added.

"Best for the family," Chamberlin said. "You want what's best for the family, don't you?"

Lady Ann was staring at the desk, appearing to be in deep thought. Inside she felt trapped, unable to act.

"Don't you?" Chamberlin prodded.

"Of course I do."

"Have you thought it over?" Van Burin asked.

"I have," Lady Ann said, finally caving. "I've thought it over."

"And?"

"I'll sign."

"A wise decision," Brubaker said.

"Yes…yes," Lady Ann said, "It'll make everything smoother. The last year has been quite difficult."

"A difficult year," Van Burin said. "We can draw up the papers and..."

Brubaker opened one of his folders. "No problem, Patrick. I have them right here."

He placed them on the desk before Royce and Lady Ann. Lady Ann glanced at the three men around her. She looked more uncomfortable than resolute.

"Wait. Isn't this all a bit sudden?" she said.

"It might seem that way," Brubaker replied. "We wanted to consider this while everyone was present."

Chamberlin began to sign. "For the record," he said, "I am doing this in a managerial capacity only."

"In a managerial capacity. Exactly," Brubaker affirmed.

Chamberlin handed the pen to Lady Ann. "Now you, dear."

Lady Ann looked at the paper for several long seconds. Then she took the pen and began to sign it. When she finished, she slid the paper across the desk to Van Burin.

"Is that all?" she asked.

"It's done, Lady Ann," Van Burin said.

Ann knew something important had happened. The three men looming around Lady Ann and her decidedly unenthusiastic reaction made her even more suspicious.

"What are you doing out there?"

Chamberlin had spotted her. Ann walked over to the doorway.

"How did you get in?" he demanded.

"I opened the door," Ann said. "What happened?"

"Setting up some paperwork to help Lady Ann," Brubaker answered.

"Family business," Van Burin added.

"Why was the Closed sign on the door?"

"I must have forgotten to take it off," Van Burin said. "I'm doing double-duty right now."

"It's all right," Lady Ann said quietly.

The three men were still hovering. It was as if they expected her to say something more.

"I was waiting for you at Caldecott's, Grandma. I got worried when you didn't come."

"We'll go now," Lady Ann said.

She seemed more tired than eager to do any shopping.

"We're finished here," Lady Ann said. "Let's go."

Lady Ann knew that she had to get out of that office. She had made her decision, and she felt stung with hurt and disappointment. She had to get outside to breathe.

"Royce, we'll be at Caldecott's or the dressmaker. Excuse us."

"I'll join you in a while," Chamberlin said

"Good day, gentlemen," Lady Ann said hurriedly.

With Ann beside her, Lady Ann was out of the bank and onto the street. She never saw the Closed sign on the door. A carriage and horse went clopping by. Sal Sims, a farmer from one of the sections, waved at her—but she did not see him either.

"Well, that took care of that," Van Burin finally said. "You think Little Ann heard anything?"

"Wouldn't matter if she did," Brubaker said. "Lady Ann signed willingly. Nobody can say otherwise."

"It's certainly a change," Van Burin said.

"The whole world is changing out there," Chamberlin said. "We want to grab it while we can."

Van Burin was still nervous. "Speaking of that, I have a slight question, Royce. How will you be able to control the finances at Carson Manor?"

"I'll do it here in town."

"Come again?"

"Lady Ann will watch the property. I'll watch the finances."

"You've got to adapt, Patrick," Brubaker said.

"Adapt? I've adapted. Royce was an employee. Now he's an important customer."

"I'm more than that," Chamberlin said. "Right now, I control most of the money from the farms. That's about seventy-five percent of all the funds in the bank—one way or another."

"One way or another," Brubaker echoed.

"It so happens that we had an offer from Parkins Savings and Loan to move all our accounts to their office in Omaha where our new business interests are located."

Van Burin became pale. Seeing the reaction, Chamberlin smiled.

"I turned them down, of course," he said. "I told them we were perfectly happy here."

"Thank you," Van Burin blurted out. "We have a happy relationship. I know we do. We're all working together. We're all happy."

"That's right," said Chamberlin. "We like it right here."

"I'm glad. I'm grateful."

"We'll all work together, Patrick," Brubaker said.

"The war's over," Chamberlin said. "There's going to be a boom in the stock market as America goes back to work."

"A rich bank...a rich bank president," Brubaker said. "Would you like that, Patrick?"

"Of course I would. Any man would, but this is confidential. This is just among the three of us."

"Of course," Chamberlin said.

"You can count on me," Van Burin said.

"I'll be setting up my office right here at the bank," Chamberlin said.

"Here? Excellent," Van Burin said. "That's a wise move."

"I think so."

"Of course, you'll need an office here. Access to the files and paperwork."

"Yes."

"We can make room for you," Van Burin said, indicating the spare office.

"I'll be needing something larger."

Brubaker became serious. "Patrick, he needs a view. Some light. Room to move about."

"Where would that be? The only other room is my office."

"With responsibility comes space," Brubaker intoned.

Van Burin was aghast. "You want my office?"

"I'm asking," Chamberlin said.

"You're very astute and very generous to offer it, Patrick," Brubaker said.

"I am? It's just a surprise. That's all."

"You're part of the deal," Brubaker said. "Small sacrifices. Big rewards."

"Money for all of us," Chamberlin said.

"Money for all of us," Van Burin said, still in shock. "But where do I go?" His eyes fell back on the wall of the adjoining office. "In there? That's the spare room."

"Not any longer," Chamberlin announced. "That's your office."

10

History recognizes October 1929 as the official start of the Great Depression, but the first signs of its coming occurred years earlier in the rural areas of the country. Nobody paid much attention, except the people directly involved. The country had gone through a great war, and the Roaring Twenties were near at hand. People in towns like Winfield believed that everyone in the big cities was enjoying an economic boom, dressing up, and going to one party after another. Prohibition existed, but people in the cities got around that. Their lives were different.

In Winfield, the first sign of the imminent depression came in the fall of 1919, when Olie Marchussen's farm went under. For days, nobody in town even knew it had happened. Olie's son was killed in the war, and Olie, a veteran himself, had depended on the boy for help. When the war came, Olie borrowed from the Iowa Trust Bank in Winfield. Van Burin encouraged him to extend himself. Food prices were high and interest rates low, so Marchussen fell into step with the supply and demand. When his son was killed, Olie couldn't keep up. All at once, prices dropped, the interest rates went back up, and Olie found he had corn he couldn't sell. He was stranded. The bank was ready. When they foreclosed, Olie left his keys on the front step on the way out. It was a day or two before anyone realized he had left for good.

When Chamberlin learned of this, he decided to move ahead. Many of the farms and businesses in Winfield had installed their first telephones. So for his maiden phone call from Carson Manor, Chamberlin telephoned Brubaker and Van Burin. They were to meet in Van Burin's former office.

"Gentlemen," Chamberlin began, "we've had our first foreclosure."

"Marchussen," Brubaker said.

"There will be others, I'm sure. The future for us is not farms; it's investment. To do that, we want collateral. The farms will provide it."

"Are we going to put Marchussen's place up for sale?" Van Burin asked.

"We are. There's a land boom right now. The farms will become our currency."

Chamberlin tapped his new mahogany desk. "We follow a pattern. We put the farm up for sale at a lower price with the current interest rate. Never sell for the full amount—always a partial payment with a mortgage attached. Someone goes for the offer, and we invest a portion of his payment. He pays interest; we invest a portion of the interest. Sooner or later with current prices, he'll find he can't keep up with the higher interest rate. He'll default. We'll foreclose and put the property up for sale all over again. The farm is a self-generating investment machine."

"Like a teat on a cow," Brubaker said.

"Right now, there are at least sixteen farms in Winfield that are in trouble."

"It's a harvest," Brubaker said to Van Burin.

"Some of these people are old customers," Van Burin said. "We've known them…"

"These are difficult times," Brubaker interjected. "It boils down to a man thinking of his family. You don't want to see your family slinking out of town in a wagon, do you?"

"No."

"Then we have to protect our families."

"And it's waiting for us, gentlemen," Chamberlin said. "We have the capital and wherewithal to create a financial institution of our own, and we'll use the Carson empire and Franklin County to fund it."

"What do you propose, Royce?" Brubaker asked.

"Power and electricity. Right now, they're building a dam to the north of us."

"Kanaha River Dam…Everybody knows that."

"Four hundred thousand horsepower coming out of that dam…a lot of electric power," Van Burin said.

"Daniel Rose alerted me to the formation of Pheasant Valley Power and Electric Company. Small company…new, but they're behind the dam. When their market officially opens, their stocks will be a pittance. I propose we buy up a majority of Pheasant Valley stock. In a few years, we'll have a fortune."

"What about Daniel Rose?" Brubaker asked.

"I promised I would join his consortium to purchase a fourth of Pheasant Valley. I'll do that."

"And what do we do?"

"We'll buy up another third for ourselves."

"Does Rose know about this?" Van Burin asked.

A slow and knowing smile appeared on Brubaker's face. He understood perfectly.

"He doesn't know?" Van Burin said.

"We have to insure our investment, Patrick," Brubaker said. "Royce here is going to make us rich."

11

FOR THE NEXT YEAR, LIFE FELL into a routine at Carson Manor. Chamberlin made sure every action or decision concerning life on the farms was carried out in an open and forthright manner. Before giving any orders to the hired hands, he always conferred first with Lady Ann. The Carsons and the Chamberlins were polite to one another, but if quizzed privately, each family wouldn't have minded if the other family moved out.

Ann continued to spend much of her time with her friends. With a telephone in many homes, they could frequently talk, but it was still more fun to meet in person. They would go to Minnie's Ice Cream Parlor, and being girls of twelve and thirteen, they could indulge themselves with a new flavor.

One afternoon, Ann, Judy, and Ellen were at what they called their usual table by the window that looked out on the street and the Iowa Trust Bank. They were not concerned with banks. They had just been served a new concoction that Minnie was introducing to her clientele. It was not a scoop but rather a small slab of chocolate-covered vanilla ice cream on a plate. Invented in the town of Onawa—on the other side of the state—it was rapidly becoming popular. The slab had begun life with the name I Scream Bar, but more people were calling it the Eskimo Pie.

Ellen was half-finished. Ann was taking another bite, and Judy was observing their reactions. Her I Scream Bar was languishing on its plate.

"What do you think?" Judy asked.

"I like it," Ann replied.

"Mmm," Ellen added, her mouth full.

Judy became meditative. "There's one thing I don't understand."

"What?"

"Why is it called the I Scream Bar?"

"I don't know," Ellen said. "Who's thinking about that?"

68

"I just wonder why they don't call it what it is. Ice cream. That's what it is. This is Minnie's Ice Cream Parlor."

"It was when we came in," Ann said.

"Ice cream. Nobody's yelling. Nobody's afraid."

Ann had to smile. They were going to get into one of their discussions. And for Ann there was a comfort in this. Usually one of the trio—either Judy or Ellen—would seize on a word or an idea. They would analyze and discuss a point down to where whatever pithy idea it contained was chewed to a pulp. All that remained was a tiny speck. Ann never partook in the discussions. Someone had to be the audience—or the referee.

"Then what's all this screaming going on?" Judy inquired. "I Scream sounds like Halloween or murder at the ice house."

"Not murder," Ellen said. "Nobody said anything about that."

"They're screaming, sure enough."

Ellen put down her spoon. "No, no. You're missing it. They're talking about happiness—people yelling for joy. They're happy to have their ice cream."

"Then why don't they call it the Happy Bar?"

"Judy," Ann said, "you'd better eat your bar before it melts."

"Yeah," Ellen added. "You keep wondering anymore, and you'll have to sip it from the plate."

Judy took her spoon and scooped off a chunk. She looked up, as if remembering an important thought. "You know, my grandma says that eating ice cream is a sure sign of laziness."

"How so?" Ann asked.

"I don't know, but that's what she says. Grandma says corn bread is good. Apple pie is good. Stewed prunes are good. You prepare it. You cook it. You do the work, and you get the reward."

"You eat the reward," Ellen said.

"But people who eat ice cream are always sitting around on a hot day doing nothing."

"Like what we're doing?" Ann asked.

"No. We're different."

Ellen thought a moment. "You know, Judy...your grandma's a Bible thumper."

"Oh no."

"She sure is. She told me that people who drink and smoke are going to hell in a handbasket."

"She doesn't always say that, Ellen."

Ann remembered one of the traits of her grandfather. If a family discussion was heading into touchy territory, he would change the subject. In Ann's case, there was one specific way to do it.

"How's your doll, Judy?" Ann asked. She could hear the colonel's voice thundering across the room. "How's the doll, Ann?" It sounded odd coming from the head of a farming empire.

"I don't know," Judy said. "I guess she's OK. I put her on my pillow when I left."

Ellen was studying Judy's plate. "It's going to melt."

Judy glanced at the spoon on the plate. "Sheez, it sort of sank on the plate."

"Maybe it's lazy," Ann quipped.

Judy took a bite. "That's good. That is very good." Her eyes returned to the plate. "They should have given me a bigger serving."

"They did," Ellen said. "But it got lost in the discourse."

"What?"

"It melted while we were talking."

Judy became serious again. "Now about my grandma…"

"She's pious," Ann said.

"That's right."

"Deeply religious."

"Absolutely. That's my grandma. Deeply religious."

"Let's talk about ice cream," Ann said. "Why don't we have another one?"

Ann felt good. These were her friends. And they had been having these discussions ever since the first grade. They never resolved a thing, but they were fun while they lasted.

"Who's that?" Ellen said.

Outside a wagon had pulled up and parked in front of the bank. It was packed to the hilt with furniture. Brooms and a shovel stuck out of the load like a cluster of quills. Brubaker and Van Burin stepped outside to speak to the owner of the wagon. The man appeared distraught.

"Old Man Rudubaugh and his family," Ann replied. "My grandpa knew him when he started the farms."

"Looks like he's leaving town," Judy said.

"Looks like the bank foreclosed on him," Ellen said.

"I'm surprised Royce isn't out there supervising," Judy commented.

"Royce is still in Kansas City, thank God," Ann said. "Let him stay there."

"Your mama and papa are away, too. When are they coming back?"

"In a few days. It's just Grandma, Zachary, and me at home."

The farmer was making what appeared to be one last appeal. Van Burin tried to seem cool and collected as he refused the request. Brubaker attempted a serious and understanding demeanor as though he wanted to show that this hurt him as much as it hurt the Rudubaughs.

Finally, Rudubaugh turned away, his shoulders slumped in defeat. Brubaker and Van Burin watched him climb into his wagon. He began to comfort his sobbing wife.

Ann stood up.

"Where you going?" Judy asked.

"I know these people," Ann said.

Ann left Minnie's and crossed the street to where the Rudubaughs were sitting in the wagon.

"Hi, Mr. Rudubaugh," she said.

He looked down to see who it was. "Ann, I didn't see you."

"We better go," Mrs. Rudubaugh whispered.

"You can see...we're leaving," Rudubaugh said.

"Do you have to?" Ann asked.

"They got us," he replied. "Can't pay my mortgage...crops, payments. They got us good."

Ann looked over at Brubaker and Van Burin.

"They can't do anything," Rudubaugh said. "Or they won't. They talked about bein' on my side when they made the damn loan. Moment I slip up, they're waitin' to take it all away from me."

"I'm sorry." Ann felt empty. Their misfortune didn't affect her directly, but the whole scene drew her in.

Ann walked over to the two in front of the bank. "Mr. Van Burin, this man was a friend of my grandpa."

"Now, now, we understand that, Ann," Brubaker said.

"We don't like doing it," Van Burin added. "But times are tough on all of us."

Rudubaugh shook his head. "Tough times. Yeah...with their pressed suits and diamond stickpins. Really tough times."

"Now, we don't want to go talking that way," Brubaker chided. "We've been square with you right down the line."

By now, Ellen and Judy were standing beside Ann.

"What are you going to do?" Ann asked.

"Got a cousin in Kansas...we can work on his farm," Rudubaugh answered. "We'll get by."

Ann was unsure how to answer. This was more serious than merely getting by.

"I want to thank you for comin' over," Rudubaugh said. "Not many would do that. They see a family leavin' town, and they suddenly don't want to speak to their old neighbors anymore. Your grandpa was always proud of you. He'd be proud of you now."

"Thank you, Mr. Rudubaugh."

"This sure ain't the way I thought it would turn out. The colonel and me...we helped settle this whole area. We put our lives into it...every planting...every season."

Rudubaugh took the reins in his hand. "You take care now, Ann Hardy." He gave a sharp command, and the horses and wagon moved away from the curb. Mrs. Rudubaugh looked back at Ann for a few seconds and then turned to the road in front of them.

Ann, Judy, and Ellen watched the wagon move up the street and start around the park.

"I better get home," Ann said.

"But you just got here," Judy said.

"I had my ice cream. I promised my grandma."

Ann was twelve now, and she had permission to go into town by herself. She had become a good rider. She rode one of the gentler horses from the manor's stables.

It took her about half an hour to get home. Every now and then she waved to a farmer working in the fields like her grandpa had done. When he said he knew everyone's name, he was telling the truth.

The wonder of this man who had been her grandpa! To build an empire from scratch and know the names of everyone who lived in it. To encourage them in good times and look after them when things got tough. It was incidents and encounters such as the one with Rudubaugh that made Ann appreciate Colonel Carson. To her, he was becoming more than just the titan who gave the speeches she'd loved on the Fourth of July. She could see the manor house up ahead. Its stone walls and pointed roof made it look like an imposing citadel among the smaller farm houses. It had been home for her whole life, but now it was occupied territory.

Ann arrived at Carson Manor, passing the small, one-room house at the front of the driveway that everyone referred to as the gatehouse. She returned the horse to the stable.

Lady Ann was standing at the front window. Ann noticed she did that now and then. She would be reading, and after a while, she would put down her book and cross to the front window to look out. Ann couldn't tell if she was trying to remember the outside as it was during happier times or merely wishing she and her family were somewhere else.

"Hi, Grandma," Ann said.

"Have a good time in town?"

"Yes," Ann answered. "Well...No. I saw Old Man Rudubaugh. He was leaving town."

"Willie Rudubaugh?"

"In front of the bank with Mrs. Rudubaugh and all their belongings. Bank had foreclosed, and they were on the way out."

Lady Ann turned to Ann. "This is not good…Wallace would never have permitted it."

"No, he wouldn't."

"Willie Rudubaugh helped your grandpa build Winfield. His fortunes were never as good as Wallace's, but that didn't stop them from being friends."

"They were good friends."

"Everything's changing," Lady Ann said. "I can feel it. Outside, it looks the same, but it's not."

Ann paused to look out the window with her grandmother.

"Who were you looking for, Grandma?"

"Oh, I was just looking."

"Papa and Mama have been away for two days. I miss them. I want Papa to get better. And Royce? I don't care if he falls into a ditch."

"He's my husband," Lady Ann said. "Ann, I know it's been difficult for you…just don't let Carol or Cassie hear you."

"All right. I'm sorry."

"Try to get along with them."

As if on cue, there was the sound of footsteps coming down the stairs. Two pairs of footsteps.

"Here they come," Lady Ann cautioned.

Carol and Cassie entered the room. Cassie was flouncing about in a colorful dress with her hair in baby doll curls. Carol, as usual, was clad in black with a tight, high collar and her hair twisted into a severe bun.

"We enter a room, and suddenly everyone is quiet," Cassie observed with forced gaiety.

"Were you talking about us?" Carol said.

"Have you heard from your father?" Lady Ann asked. "I've been getting a little concerned."

"Must I keep telling you?" Carol replied formally. "If there's a change in plans, Papa will send word."

"I understand," Lady Ann countered. "But he did say he'd be back two days ago."

"Papa will come home when he is ready."

Zachary entered, carrying a small box. "I found the jam, Mama," he said. His voice trailed off when he saw Cassie and Carol.

"What have you got there, Zachary?" Carol demanded.

"Nothing."

"Why don't you two go outside?" Lady Ann said to the daughters.

"We'll go if we want to," Cassie said.

"Why don't you put Zachary outside?" Carol blared. "If you want to put people outside, why don't you start with him?"

"You leave Zachary alone," Lady Ann said firmly. "You girls find something to do now."

Carol's lips curled into a smirk. It was the closest she ever came to a smile.

"I'll be in the kitchen," she said. Everyone watched as Carol disappeared.

"It's all right, Mama," Zachary murmured.

"No, it's not all right."

"Wouldn't matter if it was or it wasn't," said Cassie brightly. "He's not *our* family."

"Mama didn't mean anything," Zachary said.

All of a sudden, a commotion erupted behind the closed door of the kitchen. There were shouts, drawers slamming, and the sound of the refrigerator door closing. First Carol, then Olga, and then Carol.

Lady Ann turned. "What in the world . . . ?"

"Something has upset Carol," Cassie said. "It doesn't sound very good."

The kitchen door swung open, and Carol stormed back into the room.

"What happened to my gelatin?" she bellowed.

"Your what?" Lady Ann inquired.

"Who was it? I prepare gelatin in a very special way. And someone has eaten half of it."

Ann stifled a grin. Seeing Carol throwing a tantrum was always a perverse kind of treat. Usually Carol lost control over some triviality, but when Ann noticed Zachary looking uneasily at his mother, she realized this episode might have more serious repercussions.

"We don't eat your gelatin, Carol," Lady Ann said. "We know to leave it alone."

"None of us have bowel trouble," Ann quipped.

Carol glared at Ann. "What do you know about this?"

"Carol, calm down," Lady Ann said. "We know your special place in the fridge. We respect it, and we leave it alone."

"Somebody didn't. I have a very delicate constitution, you know."

Carol froze when she saw Zachary's expression. She stomped over to him until they were almost face-to-face.

"Was it you?"

"No, Carol."

"I don't believe you."

"Leave him alone, Carol," Lady Ann said. "He said no."

"It was you. It had to be. Nobody else would make a mess and leave the spoon in it."

Zachary lowered his eyes.

"Don't you know any manners, Zachary?" Cassie trilled. "Don't you have any social graces?"

Zachary looked imploringly at Lady Ann.

"Was it, son?" she asked.

"Yes, Mama."

"It was my food. My gelatin…"

"Calm down, Carol."

"I live here. I have my special place in the kitchen."

Ann watched as Lady Ann took Zachary's hands. "Why did you do it, Zachary? It was hers. Were you hungry?"

"No."

"I bet he was," Cassie said.

"What then?"

Zachary had his eyes on Lady Ann. He had to be sure it was safe to reply. "I was in the kitchen. Olga and Cyrus said the back door was making those squeaks. When you opened it, it made noise. I wanted to help. They were looking for some oil, and I wanted to help. So I went to the fridge."

"And so you got some gelatin."

"Yes, Mama."

"You used my gelatin to fix a squeaky hinge?" Carol bawled.

"I'm sorry, Carol."

"I have a delicate constitution. A very delicate constitution."

Carol paced around the room, muttering and cursing.

"Did it fix the door?" Ann asked impishly.

"Oh yes," Zachary answered. "Right away, Ann. No squeak. No nothing."

"I'm going to tell you something," Carol snapped. "This is the last time you're using my gelatin on a screen door. I want my things left alone."

"He said he was sorry," Lady Ann said.

"And so he should be. Creeping around. Going through our things. Making a mess. Somebody should put him on a leash."

"Carol, that's enough!" Lady Ann cried.

Ann was surprised at the outburst. Usually Lady Ann was quite soft-spoken, but being under the same roof with the Chamberlins was bringing out the worst in everyone.

"You heard him say he was sorry. There's no harm was done. We've all had our say. I think we should all apologize and be done with this."

"You want us to apologize to him?" Carol said indignantly.

"Why should we?" Cassie added. "He's not our family."

Carol noticed the contempt in Ann's gaze. "What are you looking at?"

"Nothing at all," Ann replied.

"Stop it now," Lady Ann said. "Please."

"I'm trying to figure out what makes you two the way you are," Ann said. "Is it because you have no gentlemen callers?"

Cassie gasped. "Carol, did you hear that?"

Carol was already crossing toward Ann with her hand raised. Lady Ann stepped between them to protect her granddaughter.

"No you don't, Carol! You stop right there."

The women were glaring at each other in a sort of deadlock when there was the sound of an automobile in the driveway. Carol's eyes went to the front window. Her anger evaporated in a second.

"It's Papa," she said happily. "Papa's home."

Cassie was radiant, a child thinking of Santa Claus. "Papa? Is it Papa? Is it Papa?"

Cassie skipped to the front window. Carol followed her like a patient governess. They both looked out expectantly.

"Whew," Ann whistled to her grandmother. "I stopped skipping seven years ago."

Olga appeared from the kitchen. She had heard the car's approach and opened the front door. Chamberlin entered wearing a long coat and carrying a briefcase.

"Mr. Royce," Olga said.

"My bags are in the car," Chamberlin said without looking at her. He took off the coat and held it out. Olga hung it in the closet and went out the door.

Cassie and Carol dashed across the room. "Papa! Papa! Papa!"

Chamberlin opened his arms. The two young women rushed into his embrace as if they were little children.

"Now, now," Chamberlin said. "How's a father's pride and joy?"

"Did you bring me anything, Papa?" Cassie gushed.

"Did you, Papa?" Carol echoed.

Chamberlin became aware of Lady Ann standing nearby. He released them and gave Lady Ann a peck on the cheek. "You didn't think I had forgotten you."

"No, Royce," Lady Ann said.

"It's all set. Grain shipments go from here to Omaha to Kansas City to all points east and west. Starting in a month."

"If you think it's a good system," Lady Ann said warily.

Olga entered, followed by Billy, one of the hired hands. Each was carrying one of Chamberlin's suitcases. They started up the stairs with the bags.

"We talked about it before I left," Chamberlin said.

"But it seems to cost so much, Royce."

"Successful business can be expensive."

"But if these businesses were already in existence…"

"They existed separately. Now we've connected them."

Ann knew he was not answering her. And Lady Ann was not going to give up.

"Why does it cost so much?" Lady Ann asked.

"I just told you why."

"But if all it meant was getting them together to sign a paper…"

Chamberlin's expression became frozen like a statue. Ann noticed a similarity between him and Carol.

"Are you doubting me?" he demanded.

"I was just asking," Lady Ann said.

His eyes probed her. "Sometimes asking is a form of doubt."

"No, I don't doubt you, Royce."

Olga and Billy came down the stairs. Billy left, while Olga returned to the kitchen.

"Now, Papa! Us, Papa! Yes, Papa!" Cassie and Carol cried.

"What did you get me?" Cassie said.

Chamberlin reached into his suit pocket and took out two tiny matching boxes.

"My two princesses," he said, handing them out. "One for you… and one for you."

Giggling, Carol and Cassie opened their boxes. Each took out a small necklace.

"Oh, Papa! Thank you, Papa! Thank you! Thank you!" Cassie bubbled.

"Thank you, Papa," Carol said, watching Cassie put on her necklace.

"I'll do yours, Carol," Cassie said. Chamberlin smiled at them approvingly.

"See what he brought us?" Cassie said to Ann. "We're his special girls."

Lady Ann was regarding this scene with an expression of shock. It didn't seem to bother Ann as much as it did her grandmother.

"Royce," Lady Ann said, "did you bring anything to Ann?"

"Lucille can bring her something."

"But she's with Jack at the hospital." Lady Ann said. "Don't worry, child. I'll buy you something."

"I don't need anything," Ann said.

"Don't you want something, too?" Carol said.

"Don't you want something, so you can be like us?" Cassie added.

"No."

"And why not?" Carol challenged.

"Why would I want to be like you two?"

With a pouty expression, Cassie looked to her father. "Papa, you heard her. You heard what she said."

He stared reproachfully at Ann. "I certainly did."

Before the conversation could escalate, a pounding began on the front door: first several sharp blows of a fist, then a pause, then another series of blows.

Olga entered rapidly from the kitchen, wiping flour off her hands with a towel.

"See who that is," Chamberlin said.

"Yes, Mr. Royce," she muttered. "First the gelatin and now this."

Olga went to the front and peered out. "Some young man, Mr. Royce," she said. Chamberlin nodded and Olga opened the door. Standing on the doorstep was a man in his twenties. Obviously overwrought, he pushed his way past Olga and into the main hall.

"Wait! Stop!" she cried. "No!"

The young man halted when he saw Royce and the others.

"I want to see Royce Chamberlin. Are you Royce Chamberlin?"

"What if I am?" Chamberlin asked. If he was surprised at the intrusion, he didn't show it.

The young man stood his ground. He was sizing up Chamberlin.

"So you're Royce Chamberlin," he said.

"And you're in my house."

Olga moved for the front door. Leaving it open, she continued outside, heading for the stables.

"You don't have to run for help," the young man said. "What I have to say is very simple."

"Who are you?" Lady Ann asked.

"My name is Delmond Rose, ma'am," he said. "I doubt if that will mean anything to you." He resumed his attack on Chamberlin.

"You know my parents…Daniel and Beth Rose."

"In business dealings, yes."

"A lot more than that," Rose stated. "You stay away from my mother."

"I'm not sure what you're implying, young man."

"I'm not implying anything. You come into my father's life. You make friends with him. Then you start lying to him and playing up to my mother."

"They're business friends," Chamberlin said.

"You used them. You use my father. You betray him. My parents are having troubles, and you're the cause of it. So I'm telling you to stay away from my mother."

"What's he talking about, Royce?" Lady Ann asked.

"I don't know. I really don't."

Ann was watching all of this with interest. She was starting to believe his story.

"You people watch out," Delmond said to Lady Ann. "You don't know what you married here. He comes into your lives. He lies. He deceives. He destroys everything he touches."

"Now, you hold it!" Chamberlin snarled.

"Who is he?" Ann whispered to her grandmother.

"You be quiet, Ann," Carol said.

"See what you've done? You've upset my family," Chamberlin said to Rose. "How dare you come into my home with these wild accusations?"

"I have letters. I have proof," Rose retorted.

"I never wrote anyone any letters."

"No, these are letters she wrote to you and never mailed."

"It's not my fault that she writes letters and doesn't mail them."

"It's your fault that she's writing them at all. Now, you stay away from her."

The front door opened and Olga returned, followed by Doss, Billy, and another hand. The Woodchuck had his usual knowing leer. The thought of a possible altercation with three-to-one odds seemed to enliven him.

"Are you threatening me?" Chamberlin asked.

"I'm warning you. You stay away from her."

"Sounds like a threat to me," Doss drawled.

With witnesses present, Chamberlin adopted a sanctimonious tone. "You come into my house...where the welcome mat is always out...you insult my bride, my family, and my hospitality."

"Your hospitality can go to hell. This is between you and me."

"You've had your say, and now it's over," Chamberlin said. "Throw him out."

The three hands grabbed Rose around his arms and waist.

"You people don't know what he is!"

"Time to go," the Woodchuck drawled.

"I'm not afraid of you! I'm not afraid of you!" he screamed.

"Enough said," Doss muttered. "Enough said."

They reached the front door. Doss opened it while the others followed closely with the irate intruder.

"You stay away!" Delmond shouted. "You stay away from our family!"

The door slammed shut.

"Oh Lord, what a calamity," Olga said. "I couldn't stop him, Mr. Royce."

Ann watched as they brought Rose's horse over to him. Rose glared at the manor house for a few seconds. Then he rode out the driveway.

"No trouble...he's leaving," Chamberlin said.

"The business world is complex and demanding," Carol said. "Papa says some people are just not meant for it."

"What was that about, Royce?" Lady Ann repeated. "That young man seemed to know what he was talking about."

Ann hated to admit that her grandma sounded afraid. She could stand up to Royce, but she had to do it within limits. Ann wanted to help her.

"I said it was nothing. Merely the ravings of an adolescent."

"It seemed more than that."

"What are you saying, Lady Ann?" Chamberlin asked simply. "Are we going to have our discussion again?"

"He said he had letters. I just want to know what's going on."

"And I'm telling you there's nothing."

As Ann listened, she began to realize that Lady Ann may have had some doubts before Delmond Rose had ever arrived.

"Over the past two years you've made more trips to Kansas City than Wallace made in a decade. He only went in summer and harvest time."

"The colonel was here, building the empire," Chamberlin said. "I am merely extending his work. If you were more appreciative, you'd see I'm trying to make things run smoothly for our families."

"It doesn't look so smooth to me," Ann said.

Across the room, Cassie was already beside her father. Carol remained where she stood, her eyes riveted on Ann.

"She's a very willful girl, Papa," Carol said.

Chamberlin glanced down at his girls. "We'll discuss it at another time," he said as a gentle reproach. "Go enjoy your presents. Go on now."

As the sisters started for the stairs, Carol veered off and sauntered up to Zachary. Slowly, she leaned forward. "Boo!" she whispered in an exaggerated manner. With a cackling laugh, she rejoined Cassie as they went upstairs.

Lady Ann was shocked—not only at the cruelty, but at the suddenness of Carol's act. Both daughters were past adolescence—one was near twenty. But they remained capricious and sadistic children. Ann went over to Zachary, who looked mystified and hurt.

"Royce," Lady Ann declared, "we have to stop this immediately."

"I think we should," he agreed.

"I'm glad you feel that way. This treatment of Zachary has to stop."

"This conversation has been a long time coming," he said. "You don't trust me...That's what it is."

"I'm talking about the conduct in this house."

"So am I . . . Trust and doubt and conduct. Right here in our household. It's disappointing that you doubt me."

"I'm talking about my son, Royce."

Chamberlin opened his briefcase and poured the contents onto the dining room table.

"Contracts. Contracts signed in Kansas City," he said with a pained expression. "For you. For the family. For our children . . . and particularly for Ann over there, who shows no appreciation at all."

"No, Royce. No," Zachary was murmuring. "Ann's a good girl."

"Zachary," Lady Ann cautioned.

"Ann's a good girl, Royce," Zachary said. "Ann's a good . . ."

"Will you keep his mouth shut?" Chamberlin ordered.

Ann took Zachary's hand. "It's OK, Zachary."

The anger in the room was making Zachary more and more unsettled.

"But you're good, Ann. You're . . ."

"It's OK. We're all right," Ann said softly. "Let's be quiet now. We're OK."

Chamberlin's tirade continued. "Lady Ann, this is more than just trust and doubt. I've sensed this for some time. It's because I'm not the colonel. I've borne up under it because I'm your husband, but I'm crushed that you don't recognize that everything I do is for you."

"I was talking about our families, Royce."

"Do you remember how it was before? You didn't know how to run things until I came along. I offered to take the load of your shoulders."

"I know, and I appreciate that."

Ann could see her grandmother was beginning to cave. She had stood up as long as she could, but Chamberlin knew her weak spot and how to play on it.

"Aren't my efforts good enough? You were concerned about the consequences of going it alone—more than just concerned. You were afraid and rightfully so. You knew what would happen if you made a wrong decision."

"Yes, I know that . . ."

"And you know what life's like for a woman who's destitute. Alone. No financial remuneration. I saved you from that."

Lady Ann was silent. He had worn her down. There were sounds on the stairs as Cassie and Carol returned to the living room. But he was not finished.

"It is only thanks to me that you're still living in comfort at Carson Manor."

"I know . . . I know," she sighed. "You don't have to repeat it. I know."

His expression became solemn.

"I'm going to move into the guest room for a while . . . so you may have time to think. You're going to have to show me."

The sisters' faces brightened.

"If you're moving, may we move, too, Papa?" Cassie inquired.

"Yes," Chamberlin said. His eyes found Ann, who was standing with Zachary. "Ann, it's time to bring you down a notch. Your room is way too big for you. You'll be moving down here to the spare room."

"That little room?" Ann asked incredulously.

"The girls will take your room."

"Next to the guest room," Carol agreed.

"Next to Papa's new room," Cassie echoed.

"Royce...please," Lady Ann interjected. "Don't take it out on Ann."

"It's better for all of us," Chamberlin answered.

"Is it, Grandma?" Ann asked.

Lady Ann had a sad, defeated expression. "Better let him have his way," she finally said.

Ann knew she couldn't let this happen. Her grandpa always said if something's wrong, you say so.

"Who says this is right?" she asked. "Who says any of this is right?"

"We say it's right," Carol said.

"Papa is always right," Cassie added with her usual dimple-cheeked gaiety. Zachary noticed it. He didn't understand it. But he was a Carson, too.

"Why is he doing this, Mama? Why is he doing this?"

Lady Ann was immediately beside her son. "Come along, Zachary. Let's go outside."

"Why?"

"Come along. Your mama's taking you for a walk." Lady Ann and Zachary went out the front door and closed it behind them.

Ann was facing them alone. She had never liked the Chamberlins. Now her dislike was growing.

"You wish to say something?" he challenged.

"Just because there are more of you, that doesn't make it right."

Chamberlin felt a stirring inside, which was something he did not expect. Ann's stubborn nature enraged him, but at the same time, she was the only person who stood up to him without fear. This little girl touched him in some way.

"So it boils down to you and me," he said.

At that moment Ann realized that his man was regarding her as an opponent and not just a child to be pushed out of the way. It seemed like some kind of turning point, although she wasn't sure what it was.

"Come along, girls," Chamberlin said to his daughters. "We have to make some changes around here."

Chamberlin and the girls started for the stairs. Cassie was wide-eyed and expectant. Carol was approving until she caught sight of Ann. She left her father and sister and walked over to Ann. Ann looked at her with a steady gaze. Carol stared back, her face like a totem. Suddenly, she slapped Ann hard across the face. Ann fell to the floor. She lay still for a moment. Her face hurt, but there was no taste of blood. Ann looked up at her attacker, ready for another blow. Carol was staring down at her with a total lack of emotion—she might as well have been looking at a spot on the floorboards. Slowly, Carol turned away and followed Royce and Cassie up the stairs.

12

ANN COULDN'T UNDERSTAND WHY THE ADULTS had not fought back against Chamberlin. Her grandpa would have done something long before now. She wondered how one man could develop so much power over other people. He must be one of the monsters her grandpa had described. But who was he really? Before he showed up at the front door, he was always in the background—the man in the last row that no one could quite remember, the man whose face was blurred in the corner of the photo. Now, though, Chamberlin was out in the open. Everything had changed, and everyone around him seemed afraid.

A month later, Lady Ann and Lucille were in the living room of the manor house. Lucille was working on a needlepoint, and Ann was sitting beside her. Now and then Lucille would glance over at the day's edition of the *Winfield Gazette* resting nearby on the coffee table. The *Gazette* was the local paper; each edition was no longer than ten pages. Today the headlines were trumpeting something special: CONSTITUTIONAL AMENDMENT RATIFICATION NEAR. VOTES FOR WOMEN.

Ann noticed her grandmother glance over at the paper as well. It had been there for several hours.

"So far away," Lady Ann mused. "All around us and so far away."

Lucille looked up from her needlepoint. "What, Mama? You think it's going to go through, don't you?"

"The Senate and House passed it last year," Lady Ann replied. "It was signed into law last month. All it needs is ratification."

"It's a great thing for women."

"It is. It is," Lady Ann said. "Sometimes I have to step away from our situation to appreciate what's going on in the rest of the world."

"Would Grandpa approve of it?" Ann asked.

Lady Ann smiled. "Your grandpa was all for the amendment when the movement started two years ago. He'd have been pleased."

"Votes for women? That means one day I can vote."

"That means we can all vote," Lucille added.

"I wish we could vote Royce out of here."

"Ann," Lucille cautioned.

"Him and that gelatin-eating daughter of his. Delicate constitution, my foot," Ann said.

Lady Ann moved away from the paper. Whatever cheer and optimism she had gotten from the headline had departed.

Ann was still looking at the words "Votes for Women." She had not meant to put a damper on the discussion, but she felt they should face facts.

"What does this do for us?" she asked.

"It means women can vote," Lady Ann said.

"But it doesn't change a thing right here."

"Maybe it will one day," Lucille said.

They were all silent. Ann realized her words had dried up the conversation. The only thing left was for somebody to change the subject.

"You know," Lady Ann began, "an Iowa lady played a big part in the creation of this amendment."

"A lady from Burlington," Lucille added.

Ann could see the attempted spontaneity from the two adults. Usually, she withdrew from the conversation, but this time the subject intrigued her.

"Who?" she asked.

"Her name was Arabella Mansfield," Lady Ann answered. "A great lady. First female lawyer in America."

A female lawyer. Ann had never heard of such a thing. It was unexpected, but it sounded right to her.

"She's gone now. Passed away before the war."

The idea of a woman lawyer was appealing to Ann. The image of a woman taking charge was such a contrast to their current predicament.

"How did she do it?"

"Back in sixty-nine, there was a rule that only men over twenty-one could become lawyers," Lucille replied. "Arabella Mansfield studied, took the exam, and passed."

"First female lawyer in America, and she was from Iowa," Lady Ann said.

"Did you ever meet her, Grandma?"

"No, but your Grandpa and I heard her speak once in Des Moines."

"She never practiced law," Lucille added. "Afterward, she dedicated her time to helping the suffragettes."

"They were the ones behind the amendment," Lady Ann said. "And if Tennessee ratifies it, it'll become law."

Ann could see her grandmother's enthusiasm returning from talking about a political event several states away.

"I'm sure they will," Lucille said. "It's so close now."

Outside they heard a carriage pull up. It was Owen the mailman. Lady Ann went to the door and came back with a few letters.

She began to sort through the mail. Lucille stopped to watch her mother.

"Anything important?" Lucille asked.

"No, it's just bills, ads, church," Lady Ann said.

She stopped. Her eyes were on the unopened letter in her hand.

"What is it?" Lucille asked.

"A letter to Royce . . . from the county farm."

"What?"

"What is it, Grandma?" Ann said.

"It's addressed to Royce. From H. Hester . . . Harvest Horizons . . . Nighthawk Flat. That's Horace Hester."

"That's the old place outside of town," Ann said.

"Yes," Lucille said. "Why would they be writing to us?"

"I don't like that place," Ann said. "It smells like a big outhouse. Everybody living there wears nightshirts . . . sitting around or wandering in the halls. It's like the people in charge stuck a Welcome sign in the front yard to hide what's going on inside."

"That's the county farm," Lady Ann said. "They're writing to us because somebody here wrote to them."

Lady Ann started to open the envelope.

"It's addressed to Royce," Lucille said. Lady Ann stopped to look at envelope.

"It may be addressed to Royce," she said. "But I want to know what's in it."

She took the letter out of the envelope and began to read. Her sad expression returned.

"What's it say, Grandma?"

"Royce wants to have Zachary committed."

"He what?" Lucille gasped.

"He can't do that," Ann said.

"He has the power of attorney, little one," her grandmother said. "I'm afraid he can."

She began to read. "'Dear Mr. Chamberlin: In response to your inquiry, we can have a place for Zachary. We pride ourselves on providing residence for those among us who, unable to fend for themselves, require management in day-to-day living. As a father myself, I can understand your caution regarding

Zachary's attentions toward your girls, but being head of the household, you are responsible for everyone. You are to be commended for your concern for Zachary's welfare. As you have already furnished the proper paperwork from the county seat, all that remains is for us to arrange the date of Zachary's arrival. Sincerely, Horace Hester.'"

The three sat in shock.

"But Zachary wouldn't hurt anyone," Lucille said.

"I know it. We all do, but if a family member contacts the county about another family member with mental problems..."

"He hasn't hurt anyone, Mama."

"He's been living here at our discretion. According to this, Zachary has upset Cassie and Carol. Royce will say he's doing what's best for the family."

"Why is he doing it behind our backs?" Ann asked.

"I don't know," Lady Ann said. But inside she did know. Everyone knew.

"If it's best for everyone, why can't he be open about it?"

"Whatever the reasons," Lady Ann said, "Zachary was safe with us and now..."

"Do we have to?" Lucille asked. "He'll be so hurt."

"This is a request for state committal, Lucille."

"Grandma," Ann said, "I've seen that Harvest Horizons. I went out with Ellen when her Grammie Lynn was sick. It's not good. The people who work there make fun of the residents."

"Maybe we could send him somewhere else," Lucille said.

"It's not fair," Ann said.

"Yes, it's unfair," Lady Ann replied.

"Maybe Jack can help," Lucille suggested.

"Yes, Grandma. Papa'll fix it. He'll sit down with Royce. Papa's not afraid. He'll fix it so Zachary can stay."

As soon as Ann said it, the words felt hollow. She wondered if her papa could handle Royce Chamberlin.

Lady Ann had become ashen. It was as if some long-standing emotion had risen to the surface.

"I'm afraid I owe you both an apology," she began. "A big apology..."

Lucille reached out to comfort her.

"No, no, hear me out," she said in a soft voice. "I made a horrible mistake—a horrible error in judgment—when I married Royce Chamberlin."

"You didn't know," Lucille said.

"Please listen. He wasn't what he said he was. We know that now. He controls everything. He's set up that bank as his own private office. I never saw it coming. I would never believe that he could have the banker, the lawyer, and the judge running errands for him. But he has. And he's turned this house into...I'm sorry...I'm so sorry."

"Don't cry, Mama," Lucille said.

"Don't cry, Grandma," Ann said, wanting so much to be a part of the situation and resolution.

Lucille, however, wasn't about to give up. "We can still do something," she said. "We're Zachary's family. We'll figure something out."

"We can think about it. We can talk about it," Lady Ann said. "But what else can we do? With the law on his side, he can have us out of here anytime he wants."

"I wish we could get rid of him," Ann said. "If we can't vote him out, then kick him out."

"If only life were that simple," Lady Ann stated. "But he's got the power and we don't."

"There must be something," Lucille said.

"There is...and God forgive me for suggesting it," Lady Ann answered. She waited a few seconds, as though enunciating her solution was something morally repellant. "We live with it."

"Live with it?" Lucille exclaimed.

"We bite the bullet, and we weather the storm. We're strong. We've survived blizzards and droughts...We'll survive this."

"But I promised Grandpa I'd protect the Northeast Quarter," Ann said.

"I know. And this will protect it. We're not surrendering. We're rising to the occasion. Don't you see? The only thing to do is to live the best way we can under the circumstances. It's the only way to keep what's ours."

Ann didn't understand this way of thinking. In her mind at her age, to defeat a bully, a person should fight back. She didn't lie down, let the bully walk over her, and then call it a victory.

"You're saying if we leave him alone, maybe he'll leave us alone," Lucille said.

"Don't you think I want to take back what I was forced into? I'd give anything to undo it. But sometimes you have to compromise in order to keep what you have. I made a mistake, so we'll have to live with that, but this isn't the end of the world."

Lucille and Ann did not reply. Once again, Ann felt her grandmother was trying to convince herself instead of them.

"He's already sold one farm, and he's using another as collateral for this business scheme he won't talk about. He doesn't consult me anymore. He just does what he wants."

Lady Ann walked over to the front window. She looked out at the field across the road. The stalks were already full. They would make a fine harvest in the fall. Seeing them gave her a momentary respite from her despair.

"I long to see the day when women can stand up for themselves, a day when they don't have to fear men like Royce Chamberlin. Maybe this vote's a beginning. But it's a long way from this room."

She turned back from the window to face Lucille and Ann.

"I got us into this because I was weak. I was afraid. I never had the confidence to trust my own abilities."

There was a loud knock on the front door. The three seemed to jump at the sound.

"Look at us," Lucille said, attempting to laugh. "Getting scared of a knock at the door."

"Is it Royce?" Lady Ann asked.

"Royce doesn't knock," Ann said.

Lucille went to the door. Doss Claypool was lounging on the front step.

"It's me—Old Dawz," Claypool drawled. "Just want to tell you that Cal Olsen got back from Kansas City, and him and me got all the seed put away."

"That's good, Doss."

"That's just in case somebody around here starts sayin' I don't get things done on time."

"Just so we get the job done," Lucille said.

"Yeah, yeah, but that ain't why I'm here. Olsen came back with some interesting news. That Delmond Rose kid is dead. I thought you might want to know."

Delmond Rose. Ann didn't know him except for the one time he came to Carson Manor to warn Royce away from his family. Still, the news made her anxious.

The Woodchuck had the pleased expression of a purveyor of choice gossip. "You know, that loudmouthed kid who came here to the manor."

"I know who you're talking about."

"He fell down a stairwell at the warehouse in Kansas City. Went upstairs to fetch a box for his father. Next thing you know, the kid comes down instead of the box."

"That's terrible," Lucille said.

"Guess he shouldn't have come here and sassed Mr. Royce."

"Excuse me?"

"Well, Mr. Royce didn't take too kindly to him comin' here. Guess that goes to show…Now, I'm not sayin' there's any connection. I'm just reportin' what I heard."

Claypool started to leave but leaned back with one more statement. "Funny thing...I'd heard that Delmond kid was a real athlete back in school and all. Just seems funny that he'd take a dive down a stairwell, don't you think?"

"Thank you, Doss," Lady Ann said, closing the door behind him.

Ann had been watching Lady Ann conduct this conversation. Her grandmother remained by the door.

"What's wrong, Grandma?"

"I think we should be careful what we say and do around here," Lady Ann said.

"You don't think there's a connection, do you?" Lucille asked.

"I don't know. But when you're living on the defensive, you can start making connections that may not exist, but then again, your instincts may be correct."

"So which is it, Grandma?" Ann asked.

"I don't know. I'm not sure. All I can say is that when I heard the news, I felt a chill."

"Me, too," Ann said.

"Maybe it comes from living in this house under these circumstances."

"We'll be careful," Lucille said.

Lady Ann put her arms around her daughter and granddaughter.

"I was afraid then. I'm afraid now," she announced. "But that will not prevent us from helping Zachary. I'm going to help him. One way or another, I'm going to help my son."

13

AFTER DISCUSSING ZACHARY'S PREDICAMENT WITH THE family, Jack decided to go into town for a meeting with Fred Brubaker. Ann had her doubts.

Chamberlin and his growing entourage were only half the problem. Ann's family and their idiosyncrasies were the other. They were good people, but they weren't prepared for the forces that had gathered around them.

On this particular morning, they rose earlier than usual. Jack was set to leave for town while Royce was upstairs getting dressed. Royce usually took his time and left the door closed.

"Be careful, Papa."

Ann had followed her father over to the hallway mirror where he was adjusting his tie. He wanted to be sure he was wearing the proper attire for a business meeting.

"I'll be all right," he said. "I'm going to see Fred Brubaker. It's just Fred. He's been our lawyer for years."

"You didn't see him working on Grandma."

Jack could hear the concern in Ann's voice.

"Ann, Fred was our lawyer before Royce ever showed up. He was hired by your grandpa. That has to count for something."

"Maybe."

"I know I can talk to him. If I can get to him when Royce isn't around, I think I can work something out. We want to help Zachary, right?"

"Yes."

"Then that's what we have to think about."

Ann didn't answer. She knew the current situation, but she could also see the battle lines being formed for the larger conflict. This meeting would only be a skirmish or a postponement.

"I just want you to be careful," she said.

"I'll be fine. Just fine," Jack said with a grin. "I'm just going to see if Fred will help. If he can't, then nobody's the worse, OK? Nobody's going to force your papa into something he doesn't want to do."

Jack patted her lightly on the cheek. "I know you worry about me. I haven't been doing as much as I could around here."

"You're doing your share."

"No, I'm not. Not with this cough and these trips to Rochester." He placed a handkerchief in his coat pocket. "When the war started, I made a choice. I'm still convinced I did the right thing. A lot of men stayed home, but I enlisted, and if I had to do it all over again, I would."

"I know you would. We're all proud of you."

Suddenly, Jack became serious. "I want you to be proud of me now. I'm going to town, we'll have a talk, and I'll be home with an answer."

"Good luck, Papa," Ann said.

"Don't you worry now."

Jack Hardy took the carriage and headed for Winfield. On summer mornings it was a pleasant ride. On nearly every farm, a neighbor stood out against the rows of green that seemed to spread out in all directions. Red-winged blackbirds would swoop and fly across the dirt roads, and every now and then, a pheasant would dart across the road and disappear at the base of the cornstalks.

The new telephone poles intrigued him. These poles with the wires strung between them didn't exactly interfere with the look of the landscape, but they would take getting used to.

In town, the bank and attorney's office looked quite fashionable. The walls were painted a brighter color, which gave the entire waiting room a more welcoming air. There was a lamp in the teller's cage that provided Sonya Fornerod, the new teller, with a modicum of light. Chamberlin had moved all of Patrick Van Burin's possessions into the former spare room. In addition to the new mahogany desk in Chamberlin's office, the entire space had been done over in polished wood. From his desk, Chamberlin could look out the window at Pomphrey Park and the courthouse on the other side. Everyone looked prosperous, and everyone seemed to be enjoying it—everyone except Patrick Van Burin, that is.

Van Burin and Brubaker were in the lobby as Sonya counted out some bills and change for a customer.

"What's the matter, Patrick?" Brubaker said after the customer left.

"This takes getting used to," Van Burin said. "Encouraging our neighbors to buy, all the while knowing we plan to foreclose."

"This is business," Brubaker said.

"No, this is different."

"Tell me how."

Van Burin couldn't tell him how. All he knew was that the current plan didn't set well with him. He was a banker. He lent the money. He gave the clients their chances. If it didn't work out for them, then he began foreclosure proceedings. He wasn't always popular, but the process followed a set of rules and ethics. But this was a different game.

"You've done this many times, or you wouldn't be bank president," Brubaker said. "Remember last year? You foreclosed on three farms at once."

"They defaulted on their mortgage payments."

"Couldn't let them stay rent-free and interest-free, could you?"

Van Burin had always admired Brubaker's unperturbed demeanor during business transactions. He wished he had the same coolness, or, to put it bluntly, the same cold-bloodedness in selling out a neighbor or family friend.

"How do you do it, Fred?" Van Burin said. "When a customer comes in here, suspecting something questionable. And we've known this customer for years..."

"What you're asking me is 'How do we handle them?'"

"Yes."

"You think of your family. I've told you that. These are tough times. We have to make hard choices and do things we wouldn't normally do just to put bread on the table. We're all in this together, Patrick."

"What if the client accuses us of wrongdoing?"

"If it's an accusation, deny it."

Jack's carriage pulled up in front of the bank.

"It's Jack Hardy," Van Burin said. "What could he want?"

"Coming to see me for reasons I strongly suspect. Stay with me, Patrick. I'll answer your question."

The two slipped into Van Burin's office. It was more than a little cramped.

"Why are we in here?" Van Burin asked.

"Starting point. Jack will be looking for us, and we're not where he expects us to be. That puts him off guard."

Outside, Jack looked into Brubaker's office. Seeing it was empty, he went over to the bank teller. Sonya glanced up with a bored expression.

"May I help you, sir?"

"I'm Jack Hardy. I'd like to see Fred Brubaker."

Van Burin stepped out of his office. "Oh, Jack, it's so good to see you. We've missed you here at the bank. What's the matter? Too busy to see your friends?"

"I came to see Fred."

"Can't Royce help you?"

"No. I need to see Fred."

Brubaker appeared in the doorway of Van Burin's office. Jack wondered how two people could fit in there at the same time.

"Jack," he said jovially, "how are you?"

"Fine."

"The hospital does wonders. You go there, stay awhile, and come back good as new."

"I'd like to see you for a minute."

"Of course," Brubaker replied.

Brubaker and Jack returned to the lawyer's office. Van Burin followed.

"You don't mind if Patrick joins us, do you?"

"No," Jack said, although he did mind.

Jack and Brubaker sat on opposite sides of the desk. Jack's eyes moved around the office, taking in the new maple desk and matching bookcase.

"Things have changed," he said

"Haven't they? Royce was telling me the other day about all the plans he has for the manor house and the town. Do you want to hear about them?"

"I have another matter to discuss."

"Are you worried about something?" Brubaker asked.

"No."

"You look worried."

"I'm not."

"Before we start," Brubaker said warmly, "I was just telling Patrick the other day that I wish I'd gone off to the war and done my part. I see you and some of the other boys who served and came home. Duty. Country. I wish I had that sense of patriotism and pride that you boys had. I wish I could be able to stand on my plot of land and say, 'Yes, yes, I did my share.'"

"I'd like to talk about Zachary," Jack said.

"Yes, yes, Zachary. Special boy."

"Royce wants to put him away."

"He must have a good reason."

"I was hoping we might figure out something else."

"I don't know what that could be, Jack," Brubaker said in a matter-of-fact tone.

"What troubles me is you seem to agree with him."

Jack was becoming more and more frustrated. He thought of Ann. She had warned him.

Saying nothing, Brubaker slowly leaned back in his desk chair. Van Burin hovered nearby. Here was a clear demonstration of what he and Brubaker had been talking about.

"You seem to be taking his side, Fred," Jack said.

Again, Brubaker simply sat attentively with his eyes on Jack. This was a different Brubaker.

"Is there anything we can do to help Zachary?"

"I thought that's what we were doing."

"It's not. Zachary's been living quietly out at the manor house. He's not hurting anybody."

"Royce and his daughters live out there, too, Jack. Zachary's a full-grown man, and Royce's girls are vibrant young women."

"But what can we do for Zachary?" Jack said. "I'm trying to help him."

Anger was building in Jack. The sight made Van Burin uncomfortable. He wanted to speak up. He just didn't know what to say.

"You know," Van Burin blurted out, "I was just thinking. They just signed this law giving women the vote. What's that going to do to us?"

"I'm not here about the vote, Patrick."

"I was just telling my wife that women better learn which side of the bread the butter's on. Voting's important. A lot of people vote like they just fell off the peanut wagon."

"I'm sure we can talk about voting later," Brubaker said. "Right now, Jack has other things on his mind."

"I'm . . . I'm trying to find out whose side you're on."

More silence.

"What about Zachary?" Jack said impatiently. "We've been talking about Zachary."

"There's not much we can do, Jack," Brubaker said. "The papers are already prepared."

"You didn't tell us."

"I thought you knew."

Jack's frustration and anger seemed to curdle. This was no discussion.

"You prepared the papers, and you didn't consult us," he said. "You're supposed to be helping us."

The ticking of the clock was the only sound in the office. Brubaker watched Jack as if studying a specimen.

Finally, Brubaker spoke. "You've got to face the bigger picture. Any time there's a remarriage and each party has children, there has to be some give and take on each side."

"Give and take," Jack said bitterly. "With Royce there seems to be more taking than giving."

Jack was trying to do his best, but he knew he was losing ground with every effort.

"You're not going behind Royce's back, are you?" Brubaker asked cautiously.

"I'm trying to do what's best…"

"Because if you are, as your family attorney, I would strongly advise against it."

"Who are you working for, Fred?" Jack cried. "Royce or the family?"

"The family, of course," Brubaker replied calmly. "I signed a contract to be legal representative for the entire Carson estate."

"He did, Jack," Van Burin added. "You know that."

Van Burin had spoken up. He was relieved to have jumped in. As usual, though, he hadn't changed a thing.

"When Royce gets here, you ought to go in his office and talk it over with him," Brubaker said helpfully. "Sit down with him and really hash it out."

"Hash it out?" Jack exclaimed.

There were footsteps and the bustling of long skirts as Chamberlin and his daughters entered Brubaker's office. Each girl was carrying a package under her arm.

"Royce, we were just talking about you," Brubaker said.

"I was up at Caldecott's with my daughters."

"The dress shop," Van Burin beamed. "You girls are lucky to have a generous papa like Royce."

"Oh yes," Cassie gushed. "We're Papa's special girls."

"You're both special to your father," Chamberlin purred. His gaze became cold and reproachful as it settled on Jack. "Something I can help you with?"

"That's just what I was telling him," Brubaker said. "Now that Royce is here, you two can sit down and hash it out."

"Come into my office," Chamberlin said.

"All right," Jack said bitterly. "We'll go in and hash it out."

Jack followed Chamberlin into the bank and on to his office. The girls trailed along quietly, with Brubaker and Van Burin bringing up the rear. Jack paused once they were inside.

"Uh, couldn't we make this more private?"

"My daughters are family," Chamberlin responded.

Chamberlin sat down at his desk, facing Jack. Brubaker and Van Burin remained outside in the lobby. As Jack sat down across from Chamberlin, Cassie and Carol brushed around him to position themselves on either side of their father like matching exclamation points.

"Now, what may I do for you?"

"I want to talk about Zachary," Jack said. "I don't think we should send him away."

Chamberlin reached into the right-hand drawer of his desk, took out a bottle of whiskey and two glasses, and placed them on the desk.

"Drink?" he offered innocently.

"No. Lucille says I have to be careful."

"I'm having one."

While Cassie and Carol watched admiringly, Chamberlin poured a drink into one of the glasses just slowly enough that every gurgle was audible in the room.

"I think your concern for Zachary is noble," Chamberlin said. He emptied his glass and set it back on the desk. "Real Kentucky sipping whiskey. With the Prohibition going on, you don't find much of it in this county. Sure you won't join me?"

"No."

"It's quite a thing to help shoulder the responsibility for Zachary when you married into the family. He's not even related to you."

"We're not talking about me."

Chamberlin poured himself another drink. Jack felt its taste and texture in his mouth. He fought the sensation. He was going to do right for the family. He was going to make Ann proud.

"I don't think Zachary should be sent away," Jack said.

"But, Papa, he frightened me," Cassie said.

"He crept up behind Cassie when she wasn't looking," Carol said.

"And what did he do?" Jack asked impatiently.

"He scared her. He scared my sister, and he offended her. And he makes a mess of my nutrition in the kitchen. I have a delicate constitution."

"So you tell us."

"It doesn't matter what he did or didn't do," Chamberlin said. "It's what he might do."

"I think it does matter," Jack said. "If we look at what really happened…"

"He scared me," Cassie wailed.

"But what did he do? What happened?" Jack repeated.

Chamberlin slowly downed the glass. "Zachary isn't a little boy," he said. "My daughters are young women. You have to consider their feelings."

Chamberlin held out the bottle. "Sure you won't? You said it was good for the cough."

"I thought it was, but I'm back from the hospital now."

Chamberlin eased the bottle a few inches closer. Jack tried to ignore it.

"And how was the hospital this time? I haven't had time to ask."

"It was good," Jack said. "The air in Rochester helps."

"You know, Jack, a convalescent residence is a safe place for people who are incapacitated."

"I'm *not* incapacitated," Jack said suddenly. He realized he had gotten so nervous that he was jumping at anything.

Chamberlin smiled. "I was talking about Zachary."

Chamberlin poured whiskey into the other glass. Then he poured himself another drink.

"That's why I'm here," Jack said. "Zachary's not incapacitated. I'm not incapacitated."

"Of course, you're not. We're very much alike, you and I. We both married into the family. We both care for our families. We both have to do what's best for them. But we also have to face the way things are."

"The way things are?"

Jack took the glass and downed the contents "We still have to decide something, Royce. I promised we'd decide something."

Chamberlin poured another drink in Jack's glass. "Haven't we already decided?"

"No. No, we haven't. We haven't decided a damn thing."

"But, Jack, for you the only decision is to keep Zachary at home."

"I know what you're doing," Jack said suddenly. "I know what you're trying to do to me."

Chamberlin took a tiny sip from his drink.

"Royce," Jack said urgently, "if you could just give me a chance here. Sending him away is wrong. All wrong."

Jack took the bottle and poured himself another glass. Chamberlin and his daughters watched him. Chamberlin placed his half-empty glass back on the desk. It had served its purpose.

"How do you think we should remedy that, Jack?"

Jack downed his glass. "By talking. By communicating. By presenting sides and listening. Listening—not trying to take advantage."

Chamberlin and the girls continued to observe him. Brubaker and Van Burin hovered in the lobby. Jack felt their eyes on him. He knew he had slipped, but he had to try one more time.

His tone became pleading. "Listen to me, please. Listen. You sit there like it's all been decided, like there's no point in talking, like nothing I say matters at all."

Chamberlin slowly reached for the bottle. "I'll pour my own," Jack said. "I'm just saying that we're not a family anymore. You've got everything tied up here. You sold one farm, and you're planning to sell two more."

"We need collateral."

"You didn't tell us. We had to find out on our own. And Zachary, too. This isn't right. The women are dealing with this the best they can, but suddenly you've got all the power."

Jack downed the glass and put it on the desk. The alcohol was beginning to take effect.

"So you're suggesting that we change everything back to how it was when the colonel was alive and I go back to the teller's cage."

"Yes!" Jack cried. "No, no. What I'm saying…I'm not sure what I was saying…I'm trying to say that…"

"You're saying I should be more lenient."

"Yes."

"You're saying I should be more open about what I do here."

"Yes, yes. Exactly. That's what you should do."

Jack's eyes fell on the empty glass.

"Kind of burns, doesn't it?" Chamberlin purred. "Real Kentucky sipping whiskey. I ordered two crates for the manor house and another for right here."

"I shouldn't have had any. I shouldn't have had one drop."

"Nature's cough medicine or gentleman's beverage. Take your pick. We've had a good talk, Jack."

"But we haven't decided anything," Jack said.

"I'm open to suggestions. Right now I have a business meeting out on Section Two."

"What'll I tell them at Carson Manor?"

"Tell them the truth, Jack. Tell them we had a good talk."

Jack was still looking at the half-empty bottle on Chamberlin's desk. He had let his family down. He had let himself down. He had to face everyone at Carson Manor, and he was not sure what he would say to them. He rushed out of the office, passing Van Burin and Brubaker in the lobby.

When he reached his carriage, he climbed into the front seat and sat. The taste of alcohol was still fresh in his mouth. He felt mocked, used, and defeated. He wondered what he would do next.

14

WHEN JACK RETURNED HOME, ALCOHOL ON his breath, he told everyone he had had a good talk with Fred Brubaker. About an hour later, Ann discovered her mother crying alone in an upstairs bedroom.

At her age, Ann could not fight Chamberlin and his clan. She would have to bide her time. Her mind kept returning to her promise to her grandpa: hold on to the Northeast Quarter. More and more, that promise changed into a resolution. It would become her personal objective—even though the family resolve was crumbling.

Chamberlin informed them that Zachary was moving to Harvest Horizon on September 13. Lady Ann counseled everyone that they would visit Zachary every day. That was small consolation.

Nobody slept well the night of the twelfth. Ann woke up around dawn. She had discovered that her move to the downstairs room carried a hidden benefit: it was close to the kitchen. On this particular morning, she decided to get a glass of juice before the others awakened. The early light was beginning to seep through the windows and give a clearer outline to the furniture in the main hall. Outside, a mockingbird was beginning to sing in a field far across the road. Listening to the birdsong, Ann realized how alone she was in her own house.

When it was time to go, Lady Ann, Lucille, and Ann walked with Zachary to the front door. Jack, feeling ashamed of how he had let everyone down, found an excuse to run an errand in town. Zachary was dressed in his only suit, but he had grown since he got it. It was seven years later, and everything about his wardrobe seemed one size too small.

Lady Ann was speaking to Zachary, trying to conceal her sadness. "I promise we'll come to visit you. Every day one of us will. I know I've said this to you at least fifteen times this morning, but I want you to understand."

Zachary was close to tears. "Why do I have to go?"

"I don't like it either, Zachary."

"We'll come and visit," Lucille said.

"I don't want to leave, Mama."

"Don't be afraid now. We're not far away."

"I don't want to leave, Mama. Why do I have to go?"

Lady Ann felt drained. She had been through this discussion so many times with her son.

"You're a big boy now," she said. "When big boys grow up, they have to leave the nest."

"I don't want to leave the nest," Zachary said.

"And we're not far away," Lucille said. "We'll come see you every day."

"You've got to go there and show them you're a big boy," Lady Ann said. "Can you do that?"

"You are a big boy," Lucille said. "Papa said so many times."

Zachary frowned for a few seconds. "Papa said it. He did, didn't he?"

"We're all very proud of you," Lucille said.

"And that's why we're asking you to do your share," Lady Ann said. "These are difficult times. We all have to do our share in our own way. Lucille, Jack, Ann, me, and you, Zachary."

Zachary studied them for a long time. He was trying to work something out.

"Will it help the family?" he asked.

"Yes," Lady Ann replied. With tears in her eyes, she gave her son a hug. "It's a big thing we're asking. You'll be doing your share."

"OK, I'll go," Zachary said.

"I love you, son."

"I love you, too, Mama."

"I'll get the car," Lucille said.

"Yes," Lady Ann said to Zachary. "We'll get our car and drive you. We'll take you right to your new room."

Lucille pulled up in front of the manor house. Ann ran over to Zachary and gave him a final hug. Olga appeared from the kitchen to say her farewell.

Ann watched them until the last sound of the engine had been swallowed up by the breeze over the fields. When Grandpa was alive, family members always went to the door to wave someone off. It was a tradition. Now it was different. Now they were no longer a family. They were simply occupants of the same house.

Ann stayed out by the gate for about twenty minutes, her eyes on the spot in the road where the car had vanished. She noticed Olga standing beside her.

"It's a sad day, Miss Ann." Olga gave Ann a big hug. "You poor child...you poor child," she said softly. "You're being forced to grow up real fast."

"Don't cry, Olga."

"Life goes by so fast as it is. You should be able to remember what it was like to be young. But you're being robbed of your childhood. Of all the good times. It's not fair for you. It's just happening."

Olga leaned down to look Ann in the face.

"Miss Ann, it's not often I speak to you like family," she said quietly. "But I've got to say this, and I want you to remember this conversation—this moment here by the gate. Remember what you feel right now…as a child. And when you get to be a big girl, a young woman, I want you to promise me that when you have children of your own, that they'll never have to feel the way you feel right now."

"I promise."

"You keep that promise."

"I will…I won't let it happen. And I'm going to keep my promise to Grandpa, too."

"Good for you."

Ann and Olga went back inside. Upstairs, the door to the girls' room was opening, and Cassie and Carol stepped out, dressed for a day of shopping.

"Did Idiot Boy get off?" Cassie asked.

"Don't you call him that," Ann said.

"You better be careful, Ann," Carol warned. "They say his affliction runs in the family."

Ann wanted to hand it back to them, but she remembered some of her grandpa's teachings. Never let an enemy know what you know. And never tell an enemy what you've got planned for them. So she said nothing.

"Come on, you girls," Olga said. "Leave Ann alone."

Outside two motorcars pulled into the driveway. One was sputtering and popping. It wasn't Lucille and Lady Ann.

"It's Papa," Carol said.

"Yes," Cassie echoed brightly. All at once, her gaiety unraveled. "Oh Lord. He's brought Jago and Kurt."

"It's business, Carol."

"But they're common field hands. Why does Papa have to bring them to our house?"

"You listen, Cassie. You go out there and be sociable. You do it for Papa."

Ann and Olga were at the window. They saw Royce's car and another beat-up gray vehicle with two men in it. Behind them, seated in a row were three large hound dogs, a trio of snobbish canines being chauffeured around the county.

"Who are those men?" Ann asked.

"I don't know. I've never seen them before."

Carol opened the front door. With forced smiles, she and Cassie walked outside to greet Chamberlin and the visitors.

Climbing out of the mud-splattered open car were Kurt Hudsen and his son Jago. Kurt was a large bear-like man in his fifties with a deep, rumbling voice and a wide, mischievous smile. Jago was thin as a cornstalk. His features were sharp and angular—like they'd been carved out with an axe. His eyes were squinty, his movements sudden and bird-like, a contrast to the rolling and swaying of his father. Jago opened the door and out of the backseat poured the three dogs, Achilles, Hector, and Ulysses. The dogs immediately started circling and sniffing around the front yard.

"Those are hound dogs," Olga said.

"Papa said they use them as guard dogs around prisons."

"Worse than that, child. They use 'em to hunt down the convicts if they escape."

Chamberlin was looking at the house. "Ann!" he called. "Ann! Come out here!"

"Maybe he wants to feed me to the hounds," Ann said.

"Miss Ann, don't say those things."

"Ann!"

"I better go," Ann said.

She went outside. Chamberlin was standing with the girls a few feet away from the Hudsens and their car. She noticed Jago staring dreamily at Cassie.

"Come here, Ann." Chamberlin commanded. "I want you to meet somebody."

A wide grin creased across Kurt's shaggy face. Ann slowed to a stop.

"What's the matter?" Chamberlin said.

"Looks like she's afraid of us," Kurt said.

"My papa told me to keep my distance with strangers," Ann said.

Kurt burst out laughing. Jago snickered at Ann until his eyes found their way back to Cassie.

"Ann, this is your Uncle Kurt and your Cousin Jago."

"Hello, girlie," Kurt drawled.

"They're going to move into Section Two and keep an eye on the Northeast Quarter."

Ann froze. This was the first time Chamberlin had ever spoken of the Northeast Quarter. Before she could think further, she was surrounded by a swirl of sniffing noses, brown hair, and bobbing tails. She stood her ground as the dogs moved all about, sniffing and jostling her.

"Don't mind them. Say hello to your Uncle Kurt."

"He's not my uncle," Ann said.

Kurt smirked. "Now, girlie," he cautioned, "I wouldn't go talkin' like that."

"You're not my uncle. I've never seen you before in my life."

"Well, maybe up here at the manor you're all high and mighty. People out there who work the land call each other aunt and uncle all the time."

"She's a tough one, ain't she?" Jago said.

"Your Uncle Kurt used to work at the grain warehouse in Kansas City," Chamberlin said. "Now he's decided to take up farming."

"The life of a gentleman farmer…That's for me."

Jago's eyes darted around the yard. "Hey, Papa!" he shouted. "Where's Goliath?"

"Ain't he with us?"

"No."

"Damn dog. Train him so he'll be big and ferocious, you end up with Goliath."

"Maybe he's tearin' up a chicken coop, Papa."

"More likely the chickens are tearin' him up."

By now Ann could tell that this pair of miscreants had not come to till the soil. They weren't there to manage any property, either. Who were they?

"Any news from Jick?" Chamberlin asked Kurt.

"He don't write much, Mr. Royce. His time isn't his own, if you know what I mean."

Jago was gazing wistfully at Cassie. Slowly, he approached and stood beside her, smiling. Pretending to ignore him, Cassie instinctively clutched at her collar. Cassie was the only highborn lady he had ever met and was by far the most enchanting woman he had ever seen.

"Hi, Miss Cassie. Remember me?"

"I'm afraid so," Cassie answered.

"Don't back away. It's me, Miss Cassie…It's Jago. You know, the tall guy from the warehouse. Remember me?"

"Yes, I do remember. Uh, please, stand downwind of me."

"Be a lady, Cassie," Carol whispered.

Jago stepped around Cassie to stand on the other side. "Isn't it amazin'? Of all the farms in the state of Iowa, you and me just happen to be together in the front yard of this one."

"I…I can't imagine why," Cassie gasped.

"Bet you're wonderin' what happened to my brother Jick."

"No. No, I really wasn't."

"I can tell you."

"You don't have to."

"After my mama run out, Jick left for the city. First night there he tried to rob a store. On his way out, he shot a cop."

"Oh, please..."

"Terrible thing. For Jick, I mean."

"Oh Lord...you don't need to tell me."

"Old Brother Jick's in prison now. Fifty years to life."

"I feel faint."

"I was just thinkin'. Now that I've moved here and all, do you mind if I come callin'?"

"I wish you wouldn't." Cassie was inching her way backward, but Jago dogged her every step.

"You think our youngsters are courtin', Mr. Royce?" Kurt asked affably.

"One of them is," Chamberlin replied.

"Papa, make him stop," Cassie wailed.

"I don't mean nothin', Mr. Royce. I didn't bring flowers, but I can next time. I'm 4-H, proud and true. I'm askin' permission to call on Miss Cassie."

"Tell him no, Papa. Tell him no."

"I think you've got your answer, Jago," Chamberlin said.

"All right, Mr. Royce. Sorry, Mr. Royce," Jago said obsequiously. "I mean well. I really do."

"I know that."

"Would you tell me what I'm doin' wrong? What I can do better?"

"Another day, Jago," Chamberlin said.

"Thank you, thank you, Mr. Royce," Jago said. Then he noticed Ann. "You got somethin' to say to me?"

"No."

"Sure you do. I can see it in your eyes. Go on. Less'n you're afraid. Say it."

"You're mighty slow on the uptake," Ann said.

Suddenly the hawk face became ferocious. "You sayin' I'm slow?"

"Maybe Miss Cassie is already spoken for. Maybe Cassie and Carol have gentlemen callers parading through here like a string of mules."

Ann realized she had violated her own rule for keeping quiet. All three Chamberlins were frowning at her. She wished she had not spoken.

Inside the house, Olga saw the exchange. She began running for the front door.

"Now, little girl, you don't mean that," Jago snarled. "You better not mean that."

Olga was out the door and racing to Ann.

"She didn't mean anything, Mister," Olga cried. "Nothin' at all. She's just a child."

Jago wasn't satisfied. He didn't like the idea of Cassie being courted by some- one else, and he certainly didn't like Ann's remark. He would have to teach her a lesson—scare the daylights out of her, so she'd never make a crack like that again.

"I heard a story the other day," Jago began. "There was a wagon full of little girls, all from the Sunday school in Keokuk. They were passin' about five miles from here. Wagon fell in a crick, and all the little girls drowned. They drowned screamin' for their mamas 'cause they didn't know their manners."

Ann didn't know whether to laugh or not. The image was grotesque, but his anger was real.

"Of course, I would never try to frighten you with any big stories," Jago leered. "I'm not that kind of guy."

"I know that," Ann said.

"Come on, Jago. This is Mr. Royce's home," Kurt said.

"You watch that trash talk. Miss Cassie's a lady," Jago said to Ann.

"She didn't mean anything, Jago," Chamberlin said. "You're worth ten of our best field hands at harvest time."

"You're a good hand in the field," Carol added, nudging her sister.

"On the other side of the field," Cassie said.

"Kurt, why don't you and Jago get out to the property and get settled in? We'll talk in a few days."

"All right, Mr. Royce," Kurt replied. "Come on, boy."

Kurt cupped his hands around his mouth and emitted a deep cry that sound- ed like "Maaw!" The hounds stopped milling around in the yard and headed for the car.

"Look, Papa. It's Goliath!" Jago had caught some movement out in the driveway.

The Hudsens and their pets were such a bizarre collection that Ann won- dered if this missing dog wouldn't be some sort of leviathan—an oversized ca- nine carnivore who trampled the corn and sent everyone running for the house. The announcement and name certainly suggested such a creature. The problem was she couldn't see him.

Her eyes searched the road and the fields beyond for the monster. Then she saw the creature. Scurrying timidly up the driveway was a bull terrier. He scampered along and stopped, then resumed and restarted in spurts all the way to the car.

"Look at the little bastard." Jago snickered.

"That dog is a major disappointment," Kurt agreed.

This four-legged anticlimax stayed away from human contact, as if afraid he would be struck or kicked. When he saw Ann, he stopped in his tracks and looked at her.

"Goliath?" Chamberlin asked.

"I name all my dogs after the big heroes," Kurt explained. "Achilles. Hector. Ulysses. Figured if I gave this one a big heroic name, it might rub off on him...make him grow. Make him tough and mean. But look at the little son of a bitch."

Ann was intrigued. Underneath the coating of dust and mud, she guessed Goliath was pure white—but one couldn't tell it now. He peered up at Ann, the only person who wasn't laughing at him. He took a step toward her, then stopped, unsure of what to do next.

"We got to go," Kurt said. He opened the door and the hounds piled into the backseat.

"Doesn't he go with you?" Chamberlin said, indicating the terrier.

"You ride with us, you gotta earn it," Kurt said. He climbed into the front seat.

"That's right...You gotta earn it," Jago added. "Thank you, Mr. Royce. Bye, Miss Cassie."

Jago shut the door. With Goliath scampering along behind in the dust, the car turned and headed down the road.

Carol strode angrily over to Ann. Her footsteps made a dull, clumping sound on the earth.

"What's the matter now?" Ann said.

"You're a mighty willful girl," Carol snapped.

Carol raised her hand and slapped Ann across the face.

"No, Miss Carol!' Olga screamed.

"What happened, Carol?" Ann said. "Somebody spike your gelatin?"

Carol raised her hand again and struck another blow to Ann's face.

"Mr. Royce! Stop them!"

Chamberlin was observing the proceedings with a peculiar smile, more fascinated than concerned. This little girl was a tough one.

"Please, Mr. Royce!"

At the entrance to the driveway, another car appeared. It was Lucille returning to the manor. She had left Lady Ann and Zachary at the farm and come back to pick up Ann so they could help Zachary settle into his new quarters. She saw Ann facing a very angry Carol and swerved toward them. In seconds she was out of the car and beside her daughter.

"What's going on here?" She gently wiped the blood off Ann's mouth. "What happened to you? Who did this to you?"

"She's a very willful girl," Carol said.

"This is the last time either of you lays a hand on her."

"I'm all right, Mama," Ann said.

Chamberlin was annoyed at the interruption. "Are you telling me how to bring up my daughters in my house?"

"Your house?"

"That's right," Carol said. "You're not our mother. You're not our stepmother. You just live here."

"What?" Lucille exclaimed.

Royce was beside her now. "Lucille, there's a balance here," he said. "For Zachary. For you. Your mother. Everyone. Do you want to upset that balance?"

"What are you talking about?"

"You're going to have to realize the way things are, Lucille," Chamberlin said. "You're going to have to accept it."

Ann saw her mother take a deep breath. Something in that exchange had gotten through to her—on a deeper level than the words themselves.

"The way things are," he repeated.

"All right," Lucille said with some emotion. "I'll make a deal with you. You've been pushing for this the whole time. I won't stand in your way. You can do what you want. But you leave my daughter alone."

Ann could see what was happening. "No, Mama."

"That's the deal. I don't cause trouble. You leave Ann alone."

Cassie was grinning. "You think she means it, Papa?"

"You're damn right I mean it," Lucille declared. "I'm not one to give in without a fight. But this is different. You don't touch my little girl again."

The Chamberlin girls smiled—two cherubs waiting for Papa to issue the edict.

"We have a deal," Chamberlin said.

Lucille gently touched Ann's face. "Let's get you fixed up."

They started inside the house. "Why did you come back, Mama?" Ann asked.

"Out at the county farm I got to thinking…I said to myself, 'Ann's back there, and I'd feel a whole lot better if she was with me right now.' Call it mother's intuition."

"How did it go?"

"He misses us already. And Tracy Stabb, that nurse out there, she started pestering him, and he wanted to leave. Let's get your face washed, and we'll go back out so you can see him."

Ann glanced back at the Chamberlins. Royce and his daughters were watching her. This was not the arrogant and derisive expression she usually saw from the trio. It was direct and emotionless.

The three of them were contemplating an adversary.

15

Two days later Lady Ann arranged a secret meeting for her side of the family. She had been carrying a triple load of woe for a long time: guilt for having given in to her insecurities to marry Royce, shame for having had the insecurities at all, and finally, anger at herself for having signed the power of attorney.

She had waited for a morning when Chamberlin had left for town and the girls were still asleep. Since it was harvest time, all the hands would be out working, and for a few hours, the barn would be deserted, making it a perfect place for a meeting. She didn't tell Lucille, Jack, or Ann why she wanted to see them.

Lady Ann was the first to arrive. She stood inside the door, listening to the breeze blowing through the cracks in the wood in the hayloft. The wagons and horses were out in the fields, so the interior of the building seemed larger than usual. It was like she was alone on her own farm.

Lucille, Jack, and Ann showed up a few minutes later. Lady Ann glanced back at the manor house to verify that no one was around to see them.

"Did you check when you left the house? Are we alone?"

"We are," Lucille said.

Lady Ann moved to the middle of the barn, looking up at the hayloft. "Nobody up there?"

"Doesn't look it," Jack said. He started up the ladder to check.

"Wait," Lady Ann said. Jack stopped. They all paused, looking up at the loft. There was no sound except the breeze. A couple of swallows darted around the rafters and out the big doorway.

"No one, Mama," Lucille said. "We're alone."

"What did you want to see us about?" Ann asked.

She had been observing her grandma. In the past months, Lady Ann had seemed to age. She'd stopped putting on makeup, or if she put on any, she was using a nearly empty jar.

"I've been doing a lot of thinking lately."

"What is it, Mama?" Lucille said.

"I've made some mistakes here. God knows, I've made so many since Wallace died."

"No one's blaming you," Jack said.

"I knew, Jack. Somewhere deep down I'm convinced that I knew...I knew and I gave in to a softer way. It was unforgivable. I said we should try to get along with Royce and his family. To some degree, I still hold to that principle. That is the safest path. But sitting back and enduring their cruelties isn't the best way either. We are not born victims."

"You're saying we should fight?" Lucille asked.

"I'm saying we should investigate the possibilities. I know it's a tremendous risk. That is why I suggested we meet in secret."

"What do you propose?" Jack said.

"I'd like to investigate the prospects of taking Royce to court. See if we can't break this power of attorney."

Jack sighed.

"You're saying I shouldn't?"

Lucille's eyes seemed to flash at his reaction. She was starting to fear that Jack would become the weak link in their defense.

"I'm just saying it's sudden."

"Of course it's sudden," Lady Ann said. "I realize we're taking a chance. But living in that house under their conditions is no longer acceptable. We have to do something."

Jack knew she was right. In the old days, he used to visualize the successful outcome of every venture. Now he only saw the dangers.

"The power of attorney. That's a difficult point to attack," he said.

"It's worth a try."

"I agree, Mother Carson, but..."

"But what?"

"You signed it in front of three witnesses, four counting Ann. They'll all say you were given plenty of opportunity for reflection and you signed it willingly."

"Yes, I did it willingly," Lady Ann declared. "And God forgive me for that. I was in full command of my faculties and signed it in complete accord with them."

"Then what can we do?" Lucille asked.

"Maybe we can argue I signed it under duress. I was bereaved. Pressured into it. We'll probably have to pay a fortune to buy our way out, but we won't have to live in fear anymore. We'll be a family again."

As Ann listened, she began to feel some renewed pride in her family. They were talking about standing up for themselves, not lying down and taking it. She also realized the importance of lawyers and their role in helping people in tough situations. Royce had bought his lawyer long ago. What about their side?

"I say we go ahead," Lucille said.

"Good. We're together on this," Lady Ann said.

Ann was thinking. What would Arabella Mansfield have done in their place? How would she have handled it? Too bad they couldn't have gone to her. She would have known what to do.

"We look for a lawyer," Lady Ann said. "See if we have a case. If we don't have one, nobody will know the difference, but at least we tried."

"We have to be careful," Jack said. Again, he hadn't meant to say it. It just came out.

Lady Ann raised her voice. "Jack, are you with me on this or not?"

"Of course I am."

"It seems like you're not. When I come up with a plan, you rush in to point out all the hazards and defects. I need to know if you're with me."

"He's with us," Lucille said. "You know that."

"What can I do, Mother Carson?"

"I want you to start looking for an attorney. I'll do the same."

"A good strategy," Lucille said.

"We'll start in Exira," Lady Ann said. "If no one's available, we'll keep looking till we find one."

Jack seemed to gather some determination. "We'll do it. We'll find our lawyer," he said. "We've sat on our haunches long enough."

Lady Ann smiled. This was the young Jack from years ago—the one who had charmed her and the colonel and married Lucille.

"All right. It's settled," she said.

"Good," Lucille said. "Lord willing, we might have an answer by the end of the month."

"Lord willing," Lady Ann added.

Lady Ann peered outside the door. A wagon full of corn was passing on the road outside.

"We'd better get back to the house now."

Lucille took her mother by the arm. "Mama, I'm proud of you."

The four of them started across the yard to the manor house. They had been gone for about twenty seconds when some hay began to flutter down from the loft above.

Doss Claypool sat up and yawned. He had stopped off in the barn for a brief morning repose, and he had overheard the entire conversation. He had been working on Section Eight when he was sent back to retrieve some husking knives. He could always say it took longer than he expected to find them—just as long as he had them when he returned.

Doss climbed down the ladder, opened a drawer in the storage cabinet, and took out five knives. He slipped over to the door to watch Lady Ann and her family as they entered the main house.

What Doss did not realize was that he was also being observed. Carol had been awakened by the sound of Lady Ann and the others as they entered the house. When she went to the window to investigate, she saw Claypool furtively leaving the barn—fully rested and feeling quite important.

16

Royce Chamberlin had no love for Doss Claypool. In fact, he had been intending to give him the sack for some time. And being aware of this, Claypool had managed to stay out of Chamberlin's way, or he made sure Royce could see him working enthusiastically with the other hands. When Carol told her father she'd seen Claypool sneaking out of the barn, he decided that Claypool's time was over at Carson Manor.

The following day, when Lady Ann and Lucille had gone into town to pick up Ann at school, Chamberlin took the carriage and went out to Section Eight. As he approached, he could see the three horse-drawn wagons inching their way along the rows of corn. Several of the hands moved down each row, pulling the ears of corn off the stalks and tossing them into the back of the wagon. Chamberlin could hear the whack each time an ear landed against the inside wall, the part of the wagon that had come to be known as the bang board. That was not the place to find Doss Claypool, Royce decided. Sure enough, Claypool was leaning against one of the wagons, while the other hands were twisting the corn off the stalk and tossing the pieces into the back.

Chamberlin stopped the carriage to observe. Doss noticed him watching, but it was too late for him to resume work with the others. Chamberlin motioned him over.

"I want a word with you, Claypool," Chamberlin said.

"Yeah, I could see this one comin'," Doss muttered.

"I don't think you're happy here."

"That a lead-in to tellin' Old Dawz he's through? 'Cause if it is, there's someone around here been spreadin' this rumor. Says if you want a job done by nightfall and you put Old Dawz on it, you won't see it done till the end of the week."

"You think there's any truth in that?" Chamberlin asked.

"Pure spite, if you ask me."

"You were in the barn yesterday instead of out here working. They sent you back to dig up some more husking knives. It took you two hours."

"Uh-huh. If they were all out here workin', what dumb son of a bitch told you I was in the barn?"

"My daughter Carol."

"Oh, well, I guess I was in the barn then."

"Carol's a very observant girl. But that's not what we're here to talk about."

"So what happens now? You gonna fire me?"

"What do you think?"

"After all the years I put in...summers and winters...and the damn frosts."

"You knew this was bound to happen. You aren't earning your salary."

Doss saw that Chamberlin was implacable. He grinned slyly. "Maybe you better think again about givin' me the heave-ho."

"Why?"

"Yesterday in the barn I heard somethin'. No, I *saw* somethin'. I got a real bargainin' tool here."

"And what is that?"

"What's in it for me, Mr. Royce?"

"Nothing if you keep wasting my time."

"What would you say if I told you that Lady Ann, Lucille, and Jack are plannin' to find a lawyer? They want to break that agreement you signed when you came here."

This was a surprise. The story was too incredible to have been made up on the spot, yet it answered some of the suspicions he had been having about Lady Ann and the others. Claypool had to be telling the truth.

"Tell me more."

"I knew that'd interest you. See? Old Dawz is good for somethin' after all. Well, anyway, I was up in the hayloft. Yesterday morning. They come in for this private meeting, thinkin' nobody in the house would see them leave."

"A lawyer. Who are they going to hire?"

"Don't know yet. They're going to start in Exira and work from there."

"Exira."

"I thought you should know," Claypool drawled.

Chamberlin took in the cunning look on Claypool's face. The Woodchuck was an easy man to read and an easier man to stay ahead of. Still, his guile and insolence were not to be put aside.

"And when were you planning to tell me this?" Chamberlin inquired.

"Soon...when I got to it...I mean, right away. Knowledge is a heavy responsibility."

"I can see that."

"Don't write me off," Claypool added. "I seen other things too. Stuff when you're not around. Little Ann, for instance. I've heard her askin' her father these... business questions. Managerial questions."

"At her age?"

"I know. It isn't natural, Mr. Royce."

"What exactly was she asking?"

"Little things... like why we're shippin' grain to this place and not to that one."

"So?"

"It's like she's tryin' to get a handle on how to run the place."

"Maybe she's just curious."

"That's what I'm telling you. It isn't natural if you ask me."

Chamberlin listened with interest. This little girl was definitely the colonel's granddaughter.

"I tell you, Mr. Royce. Women get the vote, and everything goes straight to hell."

Claypool noticed that Chamberlin had a strange smile on his face.

"I don't see you givin' this much reaction," he said.

"I react in my own way," Chamberlin answered.

"Aren't you going to do anything?"

"In time, I will. It's like chess. They make their move. You make yours."

"You'll figure a good one, Mr. Royce. You always have everyone in the right place. Never get your hands dirty."

"What do you mean?"

"Like with Jack, for instance. He drinks now. Everybody knows it. Anytime there's a decision, you always find time for a little refreshment with Jack, or you leave a bottle lyin' around."

"I think you're misinformed."

Claypool heard the warning, but he had to show what he knew.

"Sure you do. The other day I saw you slip him a flask out on the front porch. You told him it was for his cough."

By now Chamberlin was staring at Claypool. His temper had risen, but at the same time he reluctantly recognized that this man could be useful.

"You're just full of information."

"I know who to come to, Mr. Royce. Hired man's got to show his loyalty."

At that moment Chamberlin thought of the ideal place for the Woodchuck.

"Now that you've told me all this, you probably expect to keep your job."

"It's the decent thing to do."

"Well, you're not going to keep it."

"I knew it. I knew it all along. You're givin' Old Dawz the sack."

"You're going to be transferred."

"What?"

Chamberlin's expression was blank—except for a twinkle in his eye. "Claypool, I'm looking for a bona fide loafer who'll do anything for a dollar."

"What are you askin' me for?"

"I'm only going to say it once. In town at the depot, Stationmaster Dobbs needs an assistant baggage handler. You're going to work there. I'll have a word with Dobbs."

Claypool became apprehensive. "Baggage? That means heavy liftin', don't it?"

"Maybe two or three times a day. I need a pair of eyes and ears in town. I need to know who's arriving. Who's leaving. Who's shipping and receiving. All you do is sit on a crate outside the baggage room and watch."

"Sounds like a responsible job, Mr. Royce."

"With your wages here and the railroad salary thrown in, you'll be paid double."

"Two times the wages."

"Double pay for doing nothing. That's right up your alley."

Doss knew he had to put up with Chamberlin's occasional sarcasm. He was a local success story. Doss liked being a part of it.

"When do I start?" Claypool asked.

On his way back to Carson Manor, Chamberlin reviewed all that he had been told. His first decision was that he would not confront Lady Ann. There would be time later. The other consideration was Little Ann. Within the scheme of things, she might become useful.

⁓

That afternoon Chamberlin had tea with his daughters. They met at Minnie's across the street from the bank. They were seated beside the window at the table normally occupied by Ann and her friends.

Minnie's had the usual scattering of afternoon customers, but none of them were seated near the Chamberlins. Every table around Royce and his daughters was empty. Many people feared Chamberlin. The girls, especially Carol, figured this avoidance was a form of respect for their position: people didn't approach royalty unless they were invited. Chamberlin knew better, and it didn't matter to him as long as people stayed out of his way.

He had a reason for inviting the girls to tea. He was sipping from his cup while Cassie and Carol were poking their Eskimo Pies with their spoons.

"So what are you going to do, Papa?" Cassie asked.

"About what?"

"About Lady Ann."

"Nothing," Chamberlin said.

"They're trying to put us out of our house," Carol declared.

"Fred and I made sure to do business with attorneys in all the surrounding counties to shield ourselves against this sort of thing."

"You'll win, Papa," Cassie trilled. "You always do."

Chamberlin smiled. "It's going to take them a long time to find a lawyer."

Carol prodded her ice cream around the plate.

"In the meantime, I want you to stop hitting Little Ann."

Carol looked up in surprise. "I hate her, Papa."

"She's rude and ill-mannered," Cassie said.

Chamberlin took another sip. The tea was still warm. "In her way she's special."

"I thought we were special," Cassie said.

"You are. But Ann can be useful for us. She's the only one in that family with the courage to stand up for herself. Times are changing out there. With proper handling, we might turn her to our advantage."

"That's an awful lot of turning, Papa," Carol said forcefully. "What could she do?"

"Don't raise your voice, Carol," Cassie whispered.

"She's right," Chamberlin added. "In public places everyone's a potential eavesdropper."

"Sorry, Papa. She just gets me angry."

Chamberlin placed his cup on the table. "If we train her in the right way, we might have her working for us."

Both girls were puzzled. They never thought of Ann as being useful. She was more of an annoyance.

"But you're running things," Cassie said.

"You're not thinking of leaving her anything, are you?" Carol exclaimed.

"You know me better than that."

"Sorry, Papa."

"She's young," Chamberlin continued. "She's got spirit. She's got the Carson name. And she seems to be developing an interest in business."

"I haven't seen it," Carol said.

"I didn't either till Claypool mentioned it. If we mold her the right way, I see her working for us as a paid manager."

"Her? Working in business?"

"It's a changing world," Chamberlin said. "If we're wise, we'll change with it.

With women getting the vote, the social landscape is evolving. If we put her in as a figurehead—a symbol with the proper bloodline—and if we control her the right way, we can move right along with the times."

Cassie regarded her father with a curious expression. "I thought you didn't want women to vote, Papa."

"They shouldn't," Carol scoffed. "It's a man's world anyway."

"In truth, I never gave it much thought," Chamberlin said. "I do think the running of the world is better left to those who can, but that's not what we're here to discuss."

"You put a lot of faith in the little brat," Carol said. "You don't even like her."

"Like has nothing to do with it," Chamberlin replied. "This is business." The eyes in the stone face twinkled. "You want someone to take care of you in your old age, don't you?"

"Of course I do. It's expected."

"One's business; the other's family," Chamberlin said. "A figurehead only. All decisions and purse strings would be managed by the bankers and lawyers. She would answer to them."

"I should hope so."

Cassie's face brightened. "I think I know what Papa is telling us. When we're old ladies, we'll be sitting on top of everything. All we do is cash the checks, and the brat does all the work."

Chamberlin smiled. He tried his tea. It was cold.

"If you've got a plan for her, we better start soon," Cassie said.

"I'm going to send her away to school," Chamberlin said. "I want a place where she'll learn discipline. Knock some of that willfulness out of her."

"Teach her proper femininity," Carol said. "They'll have to pound it into her."

"Teach her a little respect," Cassie agreed.

"Teach her to respect us," Carol declared.

"Imagine this. A private school away from here," Chamberlin continued. "Break her down and build her back up. See what's left standing. Any ideas?"

Cassie looked up from the pool on her plate. "I do. Send her out of the county."

"Send her out of state," Carol said.

"Someplace chilly. Someplace cold," Chamberlin suggested. The twinkle was back.

Carol grinned. "I know where you're sending her, Papa."

"All I say is make it far away. Send her to the edge of the world," Cassie said.

"Not that far," Chamberlin said.

"Where then, Papa?" Cassie asked.

"Minnesota."

17

THE FOLLOWING MORNING ROYCE CHAMBERLIN WENT into town early. When he arrived at the bank, he went immediately to his office. His purpose was to conduct an enrollment interview for Ann at the Clearwater School for Young Women in Coon Falls, Minnesota.

He knew the number, and he knew whom to call. Miss Nadia Fairchild, the headmistress, would be in her office at this hour of the morning. He dialed the local operator and placed the long-distance call. He knew that Tessa, the new Winfield operator, might be listening in, but this was a family matter and not a business transaction, so an eavesdropper would not matter.

Chamberlin waited while the number rang. Finally he recognized a familiar voice on the other end. Miss Nadia's intonation might be described as a muted foghorn. She was a heavy woman in her fifties, and the combination of poundage plus personal authority created a distinct tone.

"Good morning, Miss Fairchild. This is Royce Chamberlin."

"Hello, Mr. Royce. How good to hear from you. And how are the girls? How are Carol and Cassandra?"

"Very well. They're remarkable young women."

"Yes, yes, they were fine maidens at my school. I knew they would turn out well. You know, I've always been fond of those girls."

"And they have fond memories of you and Clearwater."

"I am glad to hear that. So many young women today do not know their place in the world. It takes a devoted parent and a patient educator to mold a young woman properly for the demands of today's society."

"Women have the vote now."

"Ah, but it's still a man's world, Mr. Royce. It always has been."

Van Burin arrived. He nodded to Royce and went into his cubbyhole.

"There's a special reason I called you, Miss Fairchild," Chamberlin said. "It's my step-granddaughter. Her name is Ann Hardy. She's twelve, and she's a very willful girl."

"They are at that age."

"Frankly, Miss Fairchild, I need your help."

"Clearwater School is always ready, Mr. Royce. We develop feminine integrity, and we discourage unmaidenly patterns of behavior."

"I've always regarded your school as a tumbling barrel for life. We send you the pebbles, and you give back the polished gems."

"Integrity, Mr. Royce. Feminine integrity."

"About Ann. I've never had a problem like this. You see, after my Sara died…"

"And my condolences once again."

"And I remarried—for the sake of the girls, of course."

"Of course."

"Well, when you remarry, you can't always be sure what you're in for."

"I see your problem."

"I'd hoped you would."

"Tell me. Does she cry?"

"Excuse me?"

"This Ann Hardy. Does she cry? Does she weep?"

"I've never seen it," Chamberlin said.

"Never?"

"No."

There was a long silence at Fairchild's end of the line. Chamberlin could hear slow and measured breathing. It was Nadia Fairchild pondering a circumstance with all her pistons at work.

"That is…very disturbing to hear."

"I was hoping to enroll her at Clearwater to see if there is any hope for her."

"There is always hope."

"She's very hostile to everyone around, especially Carol and Cassandra."

"Terrible. Terrible."

"I want to submit her to the salutary process at Clearwater. See who she is. If there is any way to reclaim her, it's in your hands."

"You realize it is late in the year. Our fall enrollment is almost complete."

"I could make that worth your while. Perhaps a donation to the Clearwater Building Fund. I know you're planning to build a new residence for the upper classes."

"We are, as a matter of fact."

"Let us say regular tuition with one thousand dollars added to ameliorate Ann's stay."

"That is very acceptable."

"The full six years. I put her in your hands."

"I will do whatever it takes, Mr. Royce."

"Thank you."

"It takes a very special kind of man to appreciate our methods."

"Miss Fairchild, I've never questioned your methods, and I've always appreciated your results."

"We open officially in two weeks. Can you have her with us by then?"

"I can. And thank you."

"Thank *you*, Mr. Royce. I look forward to working with her. I shall gladly meet the challenge."

Chamberlin once again said good-bye and thank you. He placed the receiver back on the telephone and sat back with a grin of satisfaction.

18

WHEN CHAMBERLIN ANNOUNCED THAT ANN WAS going away to school, Lady Ann and her family naturally objected. To bolster his argument, Chamberlin presented Clearwater as the exclusive private school where he had sent his own daughters. Anything good enough for Carol and Cassandra was good enough for Ann Hardy.

Emotionally Ann found herself stranded between feeling defeated and wanting to fight. She didn't want to leave, and everyone around her was allowing it to happen.

"Do I have to go?" she asked.

Ann was in the living room with Lady Ann and her parents. It was the morning of the day after Royce had issued his edict. They were all speaking in low voices, as Royce was still in the house.

"We'd like you to," Lady Ann said.

"He said Clearwater's a good school," Lucille added in a helpful tone.

"That's what he told us, all right," Ann said wryly.

"He said he's doing it to bridge the differences between our families," Lady Ann said.

"Do you honestly believe that, Grandma?"

"Ann, shhh," Lucille cautioned.

Jack glanced across the main hall to the closed door of the den and study.

"Door's closed. He won't hear us."

"What happened?" Ann asked. "Did Carol complain? They moved me downstairs, and I've handled it pretty well. In some ways, I've grown to like it. That must really stick it to them."

"I don't think that's the reason," Lady Ann said. "If Carol were behind this, she would have let us know right away."

"Trumpet and bellow," Lucille said. "That's our Carol."

"Carol would make a mighty poor poker player," Jack added. "Whine with a weak hand, gloat with a good one, and throw a fit when she lost."

"Then what's the reason?"

"I don't know," Lady Ann said. "But I know Royce." There was a bitterness in her voice. "He never does anything unless there's something in it for him. For the moment we should play along with him."

Ann's anger was beginning to rise. She knew the decision for her departure must have been made some time ago. She knew she should appreciate that they were going through the motions of having a family discussion about it, but right now she didn't feel very appreciative.

"That's right," Ann replied. "He never does anything unless something's in it for him. And we always do what he says no matter what's in it for us."

"Ann, that's not fair," Lucille said.

"Why, last Sunday after church, when they were christening Sudie Strommen's baby, I heard Old Man Strommen talking. He turned to the man next to him and said, 'You know, that Chamberlin's a devious bastard.' That's what he said. Reverend Bidwell had just blessed the baby, and the first thing that popped out of Old Man Strommen's mouth was 'that Chamberlin's a devious bastard.'"

"All right, but a lot of people don't like Royce," Jack said.

"He controls everything. Our money. Our lives. Now he's sending me away. I have a life here, Papa. Doesn't that mean anything?"

"Of course it does."

"And?"

"We do know how you feel."

Jack's words had a finality about them. He was acknowledging her words without offering a direct response to anything she said—almost like a wall. Ann felt they had been walking her along, agreeing and cajoling her right up to the wall.

Ann was silent. Her eyes were moving around the main hall, taking in the walls, the furniture, even the draperies. She had not left, but already she was beginning to miss it. That she could miss it before she had even left was bringing tears to her eyes.

"I'm not going to cry," she thought. "I will not cry. I will not show them how I feel."

Lady Ann could see the struggle going on within her granddaughter. "Ann, I know this is your first time away from home."

"It's not far," Lucille added. "Two . . . maybe three hours by train."

Even though she felt a knot in her chest from holding onto her emotions, Ann had to stifle the urge to smile. Their words sounded like a repetition of their farewells to Zachary. And Zachary had been quite brave about it.

"I know we're asking a big thing," Lady Ann said.

"Right now our hands are tied," Jack added.

Ann's eyes were on the area where the long table was always set up. She remembered her grandpa holding court in the big seat at the very end. She remembered their last Fourth of July celebration. Then she realized she was staring at an empty chair.

"Please understand," Lady Ann said.

Ann walked away from them to the front window. She was looking outside, almost desperately. Her gaze settled on a rake near the gatehouse wall that was tilted alongside the back window. Focusing on the details took her attention off the pain inside. The rake looked abandoned and forgotten. Looking at the rake didn't help. Its solitude reminded Ann of her current circumstance.

"I've got to make this work," she thought. "Grandpa always said, 'When the going gets bad, then turn it to your advantage.' I've got to find something in this. Anything. Even if it's not there, I've got to find something."

Ann turned back to face them. "I'm going to sound like Zachary," she said. "If I go along with this, will it help the family?"

"Yes, it will," Lady Ann answered. "We'll make it up to you some way. And you'll get a good education."

And there they were. Back at the wall. Ann knew she couldn't change what was about to happen. Her family had their own plan to take on Royce at a later time, and her refusal might jeopardize it. The colonel had also said, 'If you can't turn it to your advantage, then settle for something that works best for everyone.'

"All right," Ann said, unsure whether she was betraying herself or not. "I'll go. Knowing it's for the family makes it easier and makes me feel like we're all together on this."

"We are together," Jack said. "Don't ever forget that."

Lady Ann frowned. "It won't be forever, Ann. Right now we mustn't cause any ripples. We play along with Royce while we look for our attorney. It's a strategy, that's all. When we find one, things will be different around here. Then you'll come home. You have my word."

"If Zachary can go to the county farm, then I'll go to Coon Falls," Ann said.

"That's the spirit!" Jack exclaimed. For a moment Ann thought he sounded like Van Burin. "It's a little like the Trojan horse. Stealth and strategy won the day. Same thing here. We pretend everything is fine while we quietly make our move."

Ann was puzzled by the remark. "The Trojan horse? Oh no, Papa."

"What's the matter with that?"

"Mrs. Long taught us about the Trojan horse at school. That kind of stealth and strategy didn't do anybody any good. The Trojans were tricked and destroyed, but the Greeks had a terrible time getting home. It took some of them twenty years."

"I'm talking about the idea. The theory," Jack answered. "Not the outcome. None of that other stuff's going to happen to us. We're going to be just fine."

Lady Ann glanced over to the closed study door. "Royce is in the study," she said. "I think that awful Mr. Hudsen has left. Ann, go to the study and tell Royce you're willing to go to Minnesota. And thank him for sending you."

Ann was stunned. "Thank him? Oh no."

"Why not?" Lucille asked.

"I thought she understood," Jack said.

"Why should I let him kick me out and then go grovel to him?"

"Please, Ann," Lady Ann said.

"Grandma, he'll know we're up to something."

"Please."

Ann could not understand her family. Even with their strategy, they hadn't learned a thing about the opposition.

"He'll know," Ann continued. "We're working so hard to avoid ripples, but we're making a big one right here."

"Royce is trying to be civil," Lady Ann replied impatiently. "And we're answering in kind. That's all we're doing."

"Who says he's trying to be civil?"

"For appearances," Lucille said. "Please, Ann, two or three minutes. That's all."

"It'll be fine," Jack said.

Ann felt a sour taste in her mouth. She started across the main hall to the study door. As she arrived, she heard the rumble of Kurt Hudsen's voice. He had not left after all. She thought about turning back, but she was going to have to do this sometime. Better to get it over with.

"What about Charlie Nelson's place?" Hudsen was asking. "It looks like he's going to have a good harvest."

"Next week pay him a visit," Royce answered. "Let me know how he's doing."

"Jago and me'll take care of it."

Ann knocked on the door and entered. "Get it over with and get out," she told herself. She had rarely visited the study since Colonel Carson had died. It was another room she associated with her grandpa, so it only reminded her that he was gone.

The first thing she noticed was the haze of cigar smoke. All the books were in the same place, but any tokens of the colonel had been removed. Even reminders of Lady Ann were absent. In their place was a pair of photos and two etchings of Royce and his daughters.

"Hello, girlie."

Kurt Hudsen was sprawled in the big leather armchair facing the desk. Royce was seated on the other side. Their cigars were in separate ashtrays on the desk.

"Ann, this is a surprise," Chamberlin said. "I'm busy."

"I can see that."

Ann took a step into the room.

"I came to tell you that I'm willing to go to Clearwater School. And to thank you for sending me there."

Chamberlin was mystified. This was not like Ann at all.

"Did somebody put you up to this?" he asked.

"I knew this would happen," Ann thought. "Nobody," she said to Royce. "I'll let you get back to work."

"It's good you're so agreeable about it."

"I'm agreeable."

Hudsen snickered. "I don't think you have any choice in the matter."

"I said I was agreeable," Ann said evenly.

"That's what you said, girlie, but that sure ain't what you mean."

Ann turned to go.

"Don't you want to know why I'm sending you?" Chamberlin said.

Ann stopped.

"I'm thinking of the future. One day you and my girls will be the voices of authority around here. I want you prepared for the responsibility. We noticed you've taken an interest in how the place is run."

"Yes, I live here," Ann replied.

"And he's doin' this all for your benefit," Kurt rumbled. "Take it from your Uncle Kurt here."

Ann shot a glance at Hudsen. He always had a way of insinuating himself into the conversation. "I'll remember that," she said.

"I'm sure you will." Kurt had that knowing leer that he used to cover rising emotion. "I can see that look in your eyes a mile off. See those eyes, Mr. Royce? And that ever-so-polite smile? She's sayin' thank you, but she's sure not thinkin' it. Ever wonder what she's really thinkin'?"

"I know what she's thinking," Chamberlin said. "I'm hoping in time that will change."

"What are you thinkin', girlie?"

"I'm thinking I better go," Ann replied, turning to leave. "Excuse me."

"Oh no," Kurt bellowed. "We're not done yet."

Ann instinctively stopped again. She wished she hadn't.

"Maybe we got off on the wrong track here," Kurt said in a jovial tone. "Maybe I jumped the gun. Mr. Royce is sendin' you off to school. Gesture of good will on his part. And speakin' of good will, maybe you and me shouldn't be fightin' either."

"Funny," Ann thought. "We're fighting right now."

"Why don't we smoke a peace pipe?" Kurt asked innocently.

"A what?"

"Peace pipe." Kurt scooped the cigar out of the ash tray. "Peace offering. Ever smoke one of these?"

"Nope."

"It's big stuff. What big people do. Why, some women in the cities smoke these things."

Kurt held the cigar out to Ann.

Ann glanced over to Royce. He was enjoying the scene. If he had meant what he said about good will between the families, he had dropped his guard. Ann remembered talking with Judy and Ellen about smoking cigars. When Judy's younger cousin had tried to smoke a cigar, it made him sick to his stomach.

Kurt and Chamberlin were smiling at her like a couple of sharpsters setting up a rube.

"She isn't takin' it, Mr. Royce. Maybe she's afraid."

Ann knew she should never have gone to the study. Whatever good intentions Lady Ann may have had were lost in the cigar smoke. The only thing left was to get out with some dignity.

"He's offering you a peace pipe, Ann," Royce purred.

Ann thought she should excuse herself. But the idea of them making her sick in exchange for a few laughs made her angry.

"What do you think I should do?" she asked Royce.

"Smoke it."

"You want me to smoke it?" Ann said. "OK."

Ann reached out and took the cigar. Kurt was grinning avidly. Suddenly, she bit off the end and spat it out on the floor. Before the two men could react, she tossed the other part onto Kurt's ashtray.

"Thanks for the puff," she said and walked out of the study.

"Trojan horse, hell," she thought. "Let's keep this fight in the open."

19

A WEEK LATER ANN WAS READY to leave. Two suitcases and a trunk were set by the front door. Lucille would be taking her daughter to the school, which was located on the outskirts of Minneapolis.

Ann was dressed for travel and standing with Lady Ann, who was at her usual place by the front window. As always, she was staring out at the landscape. It was harvest time again, but Lady Ann did not seem to notice. Ann could see that her grandmother was upset, and for the first time, this grand old lady looked old.

"Remember, little one," she was saying to Ann, "you'll be coming home. I promise."

Olga entered the room. She was red-eyed and carrying some warm biscuits wrapped in a handkerchief.

"I made you and your mama some biscuits for the train." She handed them to Ann.

"Thank you, Olga," Ann said without much feeling.

"I know you don't like going, Miss Ann. I wish you could stay here."

"It is what it is," Ann replied.

"Does she really have to go, ma'am? I know Mr. Royce says his daughters went there, but when you see how they turned out..."

"Olga, we've been through this," Lady Ann said.

Olga saw she had not helped the situation. "I'm sorry, ma'am."

Lady Ann took Ann in her arms. Her whole demeanor was one of despair. She attempted to rally herself.

"Ann, I know you're angry."

"I said I would go, and I'm going," Ann said.

"I know it's unfair, but at least you're away from here for a while. Think of it: you'll be at a new school. You'll meet other girls your age. You'll...you'll..." She stopped, realizing her effort to sugarcoat the situation was leading nowhere.

Lady Ann hugged her granddaughter. Ann stood motionless, surprised at how long it took her to return the hug. In the past she would have reacted immediately—as an instinctive show of affection. Here the delay was only a few seconds, but it was long enough for Ann to realize that the impending separation among family members was far deeper than a geographic difference.

"Promise me you won't cry," Lady Ann said. "Promise me you'll leave like a young lady."

"I won't cry, Grandma."

Looking into her granddaughter's eyes, Lady Ann saw the hurt that Ann was trying to conceal. "Ann, when you're older, I hope you'll forgive me for what I've done."

There it was again. That same nagging guilt. Ann hated it. To her it was a sign of defeat.

"We all have to live with our mistakes. I'll live with mine for the rest of my life."

Ann felt she should make some kind of response. Every time Lady Ann brought up her marriage, she was asking for some kind of absolution, and every time the family member listening to her would say that there was nothing to forgive. But for Lady Ann those words were never enough.

"I traded insecurity for . . . for this. I should have lived with the insecurity. At least then we had hope."

As Lady Ann stepped back, she appeared to lose her balance. She reached for the windowsill and kept talking.

"Promise me that for as long as you're there, you'll do your studies and take your vitamins."

"Grandma, are you feeling all right?"

"Old age. It's nothing." She gave Ann a faintly mischievous smile. "I've been to Doc Powell. Just old age, that's all."

"I'm worried about you."

"No need for that . . . We're down, but we're not out. We're family. We'll always be family. We're as strong and united as when Wallace was alive. No matter what happens, we're still a family."

Ann wanted to tell Lady Ann that she loved her. To reach out to her some way. But the clenched-up emotions and the desire not to cry prevented her from opening her mouth. All she could do was look back at her grandmother.

They heard the puttering of the car's motor as it grew louder and then shut off. Lucille and Jack came in, followed by Erik, one of the hands. Erik took the bags and began to load them into the car.

"Ready to go," Jack said.

When she heard those words, Olga began to sob. She rushed over to Ann.

"Oh, child…oh, child…My baby's going to purgatory."

"Olga, I'm going to Minnesota."

Olga gave Ann a hug. Ann saw her father smiling and went over to him. Jack opened his arms for a hug as well. Ann returned it, almost dutifully.

"You're doing a brave thing. Your papa's proud of you."

There was an awkward silence.

"I love you, Ann."

"I love you, too, Papa," Ann said. "And please don't drink. It makes Mama so unhappy." Ann hadn't intended to be so blunt, but there was no time to rearrange her words.

"I'll be careful," Jack said.

No one had noticed Chamberlin and the girls as they quietly entered the room.

"How interesting," Carol said. "She's comforting them."

"Why isn't she crying?" Cassie trilled. "She's the one who should be crying. She's going to be all alone now."

"Time to go," Lucille said from the doorway. Not wanting to start in with Carol and Cassie, Ann was on her way outside.

"Do you think we'll miss you?" Carol jeered as Ann passed her.

Ann had wanted an uneventful exit, even hoped for one. But this required a response.

"Carol," she said sweetly, "in San Francisco if they want to get rid of someone, they knock him on the head and toss him on a slow boat to China. And the best you could come up with is Coon Falls?"

"Let's go, dear," Lucille said from outside.

Carol turned angrily to her father.

"Let her go," Chamberlin said.

"You heard her, Papa."

"Let. Her. Go."

Chamberlin advanced a few steps away from his girls. He extended his hand to Ann.

"Aren't you going to say good-bye to your grandfather?" he asked.

The hand remained extended.

"This isn't good-bye," Ann said to the Chamberlins. "I'll be back."

Without a word, Ann followed her mother out to the car. Erik was behind the wheel. Lucille was getting into the car.

Chamberlin lowered his hand as Ann got into the car beside her mother.

Everyone watched as the car headed out the driveway and turned up the road.

"And I'll be waiting, Ann," Chamberlin said. "I'll be right here."

Part Two

EDUCATION

20

LUCILLE, ANN, AND ERIK DROVE INTO town without much conversation. The Carson family made it a point of never airing their problems in public. It was part of Lady Ann's practice of maintaining the proper image. Everything that needed to be said had been said back at the manor.

Doss Claypool had been working at the Winfield depot for several weeks, and they had not looked forward to seeing his smirking visage. As it turned out, they didn't have to. The Woodchuck saw them approaching. The contrasting auburn hair of the passengers told him it was Ann and her mother. But when he spotted the trunk and suitcases, he ducked into the luggage room, remaining hidden until Erik and Stationmaster Dobbs had loaded the bags onto the train.

Ann and her mother were waiting on the platform when the train arrived in Winfield at ten twenty. They found a seat in one of the two coaches.

At ten twenty-five, Ann heard the puff and slow chug-chug from the engine and then a rapid series of creaks and squeaks as the cars shuddered and moved forward. Outside, the platform and station of Winfield began to creep past the window.

Before long, they were moving through a verdant sweep of land, speckled here and there with wagons. Ann was watching a pheasant as it flapped away from the brush along the tracks when she realized this was the first harvest she was going to miss.

In twenty minutes they crossed the last parcels of land on the edge of Franklin County. Here were smaller farms—established long after Colonel Wallace had founded the town of Winfield. They were the farthest away from town, but the colonel had made sure their owners felt as much a part of the community as one of the founders. As these plots were being settled, the colonel had ridden out to each farm to welcome them. "This is Winfield," he had said. "The winters can be cold and the summers can be hot—but it's nothing a person can't handle.

If you need something, ask me or a neighbor. In this town nobody's more important than the next man. There's us and there's the land. God gave us a glorious
gift, and we're going to make it bloom."

The train was passing one of these farms—a smaller parcel of land with a
red water tower that sat next to the barn. Ann did not know the owners, but she
liked the red water tower. Before she could point it out to Lucille, the train had
already passed, and the farm was vanishing in the distance behind them.

An incident was about to occur at this farm that would have a direct bearing
on Ann's life. It would also affect the lives of everyone involved in the present
conflict over Carson Manor. The reverberations would not be felt for nearly
another ten years, but the seeds were planted that morning in the fall of 1920.
Though Ann did not see it, the beat-up old motor car containing Kurt and Jago
Hudsen was bouncing and jostling along the dirt road toward the farm.

The farm belonged to Charlie Nelson. Royce and Kurt had been discussing
his mortgage and probable good harvest before Ann interrupted them in the
study. Nelson, like many of his neighbors, had done well during the war years.
As long as interest rates were low and prices were high for the crops, he had followed the financial advice of the local bank and financial institutions and he was
making money. Then, when the war ended, when prices dropped and the interest rates went back up, he found himself in debt and struggling to stay afloat.
He and his wife, Susannah, and son, Peter, were among the landowners who'd
found themselves in a newly adversarial position with Patrick Van Burin and the
Iowa Trust Bank.

Charlie and Peter were out in the field with their wagon. They had been up
since daybreak, walking behind the wagon, twisting off the corn and tossing it
into the back. It was tiring work, but it went with the life they had chosen. Since
there were only two of them, they had to put in long hours. However, with this
harvest, it looked as if they might make the payment to Van Burin and stay on
the farm another year. They had been working hard for the past week; it was too
early to officially rejoice but far enough along to relish the victory in the effort.

Then they heard the car. Kurt turned into their driveway and headed directly for them in the field. The car pulled to a stop about twenty feet from the
Nelsons.

Kurt and Jago got out, smiling affably. The three hounds followed them,
sniffing and circling over the Nelson property. The hounds did not understand
what their masters were up to, but they certainly enjoyed the travel benefits.
Whenever they paid a business call to a farm, there was a whole yard of scents
to follow and terrain to explore. Only the little bull terrier seemed to sense what
was about to transpire. Goliath followed the other hounds out of the car, but he
hid under the car and peered around the left rear tire to watch.

"What do they want?" Charlie asked his son.

"I don't know, Pa."

"Morning," Kurt said, flashing his grin. There was no reply from the Nelsons. The Hudsens kept walking until they were face-to-face with Charlie and his son.

"What can we do for you?" Charlie asked.

"We just happened to be in the area," Kurt said. "Thought we'd pay you a neighborly visit."

"We're busy right now," Charlie replied.

Jago's squinty gaze fastened on Peter, who pretended not to be aware of it.

"You know why we're here," Jago said pointedly.

"Yeah, yeah," Peter said. "Listen, I'll get it for you. I promise."

"That's what you said you'd do," Jago replied. "So far you ain't done it."

"What's he talking about?" Charlie asked.

"Financial matter," Kurt answered. "A matter between gentlemen."

"A man's supposed to fess up to his responsibility," Jago said. "So far you ain't done it."

"Peter, what's going on here?" Charlie said.

"Tell him, son." Kurt said. "You'll feel better."

"What is it?"

"I owe them some money, Pa."

"How much?"

Peter stared at the ground with a hangdog expression.

"How much?" his father repeated.

"Eight hundred dollars."

"Eight...hundred...dollars?"

Peter flushed. Charlie stared at his son in shock. The Hudsens regarded the scene with a mock seriousness.

"I'm sorry, Pa," Peter said. "I am."

"What did you get into?"

"I can pay it. I promise."

"What did you do?"

"Dice game. Over at Billings barn. I thought I could win something to help us around here."

"You know how I feel about gambling."

"I was only gonna do one game."

"One game? It's never one game. Why did you do it, boy?"

"I thought I could help, but then one thing led to another. I won a few times. Really, Pa, and then I started losing..."

Charlie couldn't stay angry at his son for long. He knew that Peter had been trying to help their situation. It was the way he had chosen to do it that exasperated him.

"Eight hundred dollars."

"We're tryin' to be neighborly about this," Kurt said. "We're just wondering when you can settle up."

"I will. Just give me some time," Peter said.

"We didn't expect this," Charlie said. "Mister, we'll pay you when we can. Right now we need the money. Times are hard."

"We need the money, too," Kurt said.

"We come here as gentlemen," Jago added.

"We can't do it," Charlie said. "Not right now. Give us two months. We got a good crop this year. We'll have some money by then."

"But a gentleman always fesses up to his responsibility . . . Or ain't you a gentleman?"

Charlie shot a look at Jago. The knowing insinuation in that remark bothered him.

"Billings place is on the other side of the county. How'd my son get out there anyway?"

"Ask your son," Jago replied.

"I'm asking you."

"Maybe we saw him outside the barn and invited him in," Kurt said.

"What was he doing outside the barn in the first place?"

"Forget it, Pa. I was wrong," Peter said.

"They tell you about the game and invite you to tag along?'

"We were just bein' neighborly," Kurt said.

Charlie was apprehensive. This pair knew more about the situation than they were revealing.

"I'm not trying to squirm out of this," he said. "Look around you. We're farmers. Our money comes with the crops and the seasons. Peter shouldn't have gotten into your dice game, but we'll pay you. If you'll just be understanding . . ."

"We're understanding," Kurt said. "We can see right here it's only two of you workin' the place."

"That's right."

"And if, God forbid, you had an emergency, you got some family over in Creston. They might come and help out around here."

Charlie was growing fearful. He began to suspect the entire situation was a set-up. It wasn't about a gambling debt. It was something else.

"How do you know about my family?"

"I know a lot of things about you," Kurt said. "I know your cousin Joe's just barely hangin' on with his spread over there. He's got his wife, Melanie, and son, Joe Junior, and daughter, Eliza, helpin', and even that isn't enough."

"Just a coincidence you know that?" Charlie asked bitterly.

"No such thing as coincidence in a small town," Kurt said. "A few people livin' close together. Can't help gettin' into each other's business."

"We're just bein' neighborly," Jago said.

"Neighborly, hell. I know what you're trying to do. You come out here for the money. We tell you we can't pay, so you start making threats."

"Maybe you could have a little talk with your family," Kurt said.

"They can't pay, and I won't ask 'em," Charlie said.

"That's mighty unfortunate. That sorta leaves you all by your lonesome."

"You'll be paid. Right now we got to work. Why don't you get out of here? Take your damn dogs and go."

The big man's mouth twisted into a snarl. "Now there's no count in takin' it out on my dogs. You don't talk about my dogs."

"What?"

"You don't ever talk about those dogs."

"All right, all right," Charlie said.

"You don't ever talk about them."

"You'll get your money, Hudsen. I promise."

"Hell, I know that," Kurt said, jovial once again. "We just got off on the wrong track here."

"Long as we understand each other."

Kurt winked at his son. "You know," he said to Charlie. "We're all neighbors. Why don't we give you and the boy a hand for a few hours?"

"No, none of that," Charlie said with suspicion.

"Why not?" Kurt drawled. "Quicker the harvest, quicker we get paid. Our way of makin' amends."

"Amends means we're offerin' to help," Jago added.

"How about it?" Kurt said. "Just to show there's no hard feelin's."

"I don't think so," Charlie answered. "Maybe you fellas better go."

"Come on." The grin widened. "Just bein' neighborly."

Charlie climbed up on his wagon. He gave the reins a jerk and the wagon started to move. Kurt and Jago fell into step behind Peter. Jago's attention remained riveted on the boy.

"Ain't this better?" Kurt said with a hearty chuckle. "Out here by yourselves...one of you moves the wagon six feet or so, then he gets off. You two work till you catch up to it. Then he gets back on top and moves it again."

"Works for us," Charlie answered from the seat.

"I'm sure it does," Kurt said.

"Hey," Peter said, "you two don't have any gloves. How are you going to work without any gloves?"

"We'll manage," Kurt said. "We're used to this."

Charlie had turned to the horse in front. Kurt eased his way up almost next to him. All at once Jago kicked Peter in the knee, tripping him. As Peter staggered to regain his balance, Jago shoved him under the wagon. Peter scrambled to get away, but Kurt slapped the horse, and the wagon lurched forward. Peter screamed as the wheel rolled over his arm.

21

"THAT'S ONE HARVEST THEY AIN'T GONNA finish," Kurt said.

It was an hour later. The car was puttering along the dirt road past the half-finished cornfields. The hounds were seated in the back with their eyes straight ahead, oblivious to the natural surroundings.

"They said they was goin' to Dierkes," Jago said.

"They won't go."

"They said they would, Papa."

"Dierkes can't do anything. It was an accident. Tripped and fell. He can't say it wasn't."

"Dierkes," Jago snickered. "I could take him."

"What did you say?"

"Dierkes...Used-up old lawman. I could take him easy."

Kurt jammed his foot on the brake. They were all alone on the road in the middle of nowhere.

"You don't listen to a damn thing I tell you," Kurt said. "I've told you so many times I've got calluses. You don't go against the law. That's why your brother's in prison. If he'd just stuck to what he was after and left the lawman alone, he wouldn't be in the pen."

"Lawman got in his way."

"I don't know how many times I've got to go over this. We do what we're paid to do. No more than that. In the world of ethics and commandments, we walk the riverbank—between the wet and the dry. It's a fine line. You step in the water now and then if you have to, but no more than that. A man with a badge comes along, he's got the laws of God almighty, the state, and every courtroom in the country behind him. Take him on and you're finished...Just ask Brother Jick on visitor's day."

"Still, it's a waste if you can take him, Papa."

"And then what? You got ten more, a hundred more, just like him on your tail. Don't even think it."

"Yeah, I see your point. Shouldn't be that way, but I see it."

"You get real respectful of that badge and everything it represents. Stay on the riverbank. Swallow your pride and live longer. Jick, he never understood that."

"They got Jick, all right."

"Am I gettin' through to you? It's a sucker move, boy."

Kurt started the car moving again. "You and me, we got a good deal. We settle differences for Mr. Royce. We live rent-free like gentleman farmers."

"I said I'd be careful, Papa."

The car bounced along the road. The two men were in front and the three hounds seated in a row in the backseat. Goliath had what spot remained—on the floor.

"Papa, why you think Miss Cassie tries to avoid me?"

"You forget about Miss Cassie."

"Why? She's a great lady, and I mean well. I don't understand why she don't give me the time of day."

"Maybe she don't like you."

"That's not it, Papa. She just ain't took the time to know me. She'd see I was a real catch if she got her head on straight."

"You keep your attention on what Mr. Royce tells us to do. We're here because he needs us in Winfield. We stay put on the riverbank. That's all."

"But what about Miss Cassie?"

"Jago, sometimes I think you're dumb as a post. I'm sayin' that the Chamberlins are one family you don't want to get close with. We work for 'em. That's fine. But get any closer? There's somethin' about them even I have second thoughts about. If you ask me to tell you what it is, I can't. It's just a gut feelin'."

"He's a hard man, ain't he?"

"More than that. Him and them two girls, they live by their own set of rules. Like it was just them and nobody else is welcome. Anybody gets too close or crosses them in some way…"

"What, Papa?"

"I remember one time…years ago back in Cedar Rapids when his wife was sick…He had an opportunity to move his family into a bigger apartment. Wife couldn't be moved, but it was a prime rental. One day he left the wife alone and took the girls to see this new apartment. They stayed out all day. Said they'd left the wife home with a nurse. Turned out he sent the nurse home in the morning and hid all the medicines. Wife wasn't dead when they got home, but almost."

"You think he was tryin' to kill her?"

"I don't know...I don't want to know...I heard it from Barney Sills, the manager of the place. Mr. Royce had asked him to drop in on his wife about an hour before he got back with the girls...She was alive, but just barely. She died the next day."

"Whew."

"So you remember this. You work for Mr. Royce. But you don't get too close to him. I lost one boy. I don't want to lose another."

22

WHEN ANN AND LUCILLE ARRIVED IN Minneapolis that afternoon, they transferred the bags and trunk to a taxi and started out of town. The city was alive with motor cars and carriages. Ann noticed a barrage of city noises that she'd never heard at home. In Winfield there would be an occasional car in the main street, but always on an individual basis. Mr. Smith's motor car would be going one way, Mr. Brown's carriage going the other. Here the noise was on all sides: the honk of a horn, the chorus of engine noises, wagon wheels, horses here and there. It was not overpowering—just new. It all seemed so disorganized.

They left the city and followed the path of the river. When they came in on the train, much of the terrain was flat and green. Here it was rockier—full of thick fir trees with cliffs jutting through.

It took them about thirty minutes to reach Coon Falls. The town itself looked like a Winfield that had never gotten started. There was a general store, a post office, a city hall, a fire station, and a couple of cafes. All of them shared a faded, gray-brown clapboard exterior. The tiny city park had grass whose shaggy appearance had been determined by the limestone deposits in the soil that surrounded the town. Although the businesses were open, Ann did not see a single person anywhere.

After twenty more minutes on a narrow two-way road, they turned off onto a smaller one. Ahead of them was the school.

Clearwater was on a hillside to the left of the road. At first glance it looked like a huge abandoned bunker with windows. Below the building was an empty corral and a sport field whose grassy areas needed mowing.

The school sat on the shore of the river whose ash-gray current was dotted with whitecaps. The road they had left continued on to cross a bridge and then vanish into the woods on the other side.

"Here we are," Lucille said.

Ann glanced out the window as they passed the sport field. "It looks like they raise weeds out there."

"Give it a chance. You won't be here long."

As they were moving past the sport field, they caught a glimpse of a group of students under a tree on the perimeter. There were twenty girls in their teens—all clad in olive-khaki uniforms. They were listening to a lecture by an immensely large middle-aged woman who was holding a parasol to protect herself from the afternoon sun. Ann did not know it yet, but this was Nadia Fairchild, the headmistress. When the taxi drew nearer, the large woman stopped talking and turned to see the car and its occupants. The students were curious as well. They stared silently, their eyes following the taxi as it passed.

At the entrance, Ann and Lucille had a better look at the building. Formerly, it had been a hospital. Each room had its own balcony and a folded up awning that had long since rusted and frozen shut. Except for the occupants and some of the furniture, nothing much had changed since the hospital days.

Ann and Lucille entered, taking the suitcases. The lobby area contained several well-worn sofas and couches. Except for a crouched and squinty gray-haired woman at a desk in one corner, the place was deserted.

Ann and Lucille put down the bags and walked over to her.

"Yes?" the woman asked.

"My name is Lucille Hardy, and this is my daughter Ann. Ann is going to be attending your school."

The woman peered suspiciously at Lucille and Ann. Ann thought she was decidedly unusual—her hair, her dress, even her skin appeared gray. "She looks like she's never seen sunlight," Ann thought.

"We were wondering what we should do now," Lucille finally said.

"Well...I suppose we'll have to wait," the woman said. "All of the staff are either in class or on a nature walk. Your daughter..."

"Ann."

"Yes. Ann will be shown to her quarters in due time."

"In due time?"

"You're free to take a seat in the waiting area."

"I hadn't expected this," Lucille said. "Do you have any idea where her room is? I'd hoped to be able to see her room before I left."

"We can't allow people to roam freely in the living quarters."

"But I'm her mother."

"Yes. But your daughter hasn't taken acquisition of her quarters."

"Meaning I could see it after she moves in."

"Of course."

Ann looked forlornly around the lobby. It was like a well-aired cavern. She couldn't imagine anyone gathering here for any length of time.

"You're free to take a seat while you wait," the squinter offered.

"How long will that be?" Lucille asked.

"An hour. Maybe longer. They just left."

"An hour?" Lucille exclaimed. "I can't do it. I won't make the train home."

"You better go, Mama."

"I don't want to."

"Go on. You'll see it next time."

"Miss Fairchild changed the schedule at the last minute," the squinter explained. "When the beauty of the day inspires her, she decides that maidens should engage in a promenade."

"Maidens?" Lucille inquired.

"Your daughter is in good hands now. She will be well taken care of."

Ann felt her anger building. She had been brought to a place no one in her family knew much about. And now that she was here, nobody was sure what to do next. She saw the driver placing her trunk inside the door beside the suitcases. This, more than anything, told Ann she was here to stay.

She'd promised herself she'd try to control her temper. It was a losing battle. "Mama, did you ask Royce anything about this place?"

"Don't be like that, Ann. Please."

"Like what?"

"You were so good about coming. Try to be understanding."

"I'm understanding. It's like Grandpa died, and it all went wrong."

"You'll be all right," the squinter said. "You're just homesick."

Ann wandered among the sagging couches. "Don't let it get you," she said to herself. "You agreed to this. Get through it. Make it work."

"She's just homesick, Mrs. Hardy."

With a melancholy expression, Lucille crossed over to Ann and gave her a hug. "I love you, Ann. I'm very proud of you."

Lucille turned and started for the waiting taxi. Ann stood alone in the lobby, watching her.

"Let her go. Let them all go," Ann thought. "She doesn't like it any more than I do."

It was then that she realized that Lucille was on the verge of tears herself. It was the first time she had not consoled her mother when she was unhappy. At that moment, it didn't matter where they were. Her mother was crying, and she had done nothing.

Ann saw Lucille getting into the taxi. The car door was closing. She couldn't let her leave without telling her she loved her. In a flash, she was racing across the lobby.

"Hey!" the receptionist cried.

Ann was out the front door. The taxi was moving somewhat slowly down the driveway. Ann began to run after it. The car was picking up speed.

"Mama!" Ann called. Inside the car, Lucille did not hear. She was looking out at the sport field and remembering Ann's comments.

Ann raced along, running faster and faster, but the car turned out the driveway and was gone.

Ann stopped. She was staring at the spot in the trees where she last saw the taxi. Now she was truly alone.

She felt her eyes filling up with tears. "I won't cry. I won't. Someday I'll cry. But not today."

Ann started back to the lobby. She glanced over to the group under the tree, wondering if they had noticed. She was surprised to see they were all watching her intently. The huge woman. The girls in olive khaki. Every eye was on Ann. Every face was pale and colorless. Every expression full of puffy indignation. It was as if Ann's dash out the front door was a violation of some code of etiquette, known only to them.

"What's the matter with them?" Ann thought. "They all look dead...What in the world have I gotten into?"

She returned to the lobby and sat down on one of the sofas. This one seemed to have no springs left—just a big sinkhole in the cushion where countless students had plopped themselves over the years. As Ann looked around at the indentations on all the sofas, she wondered how many rear ends it had taken to create this collection of craters.

"I'm angry. That's why I'm not afraid," she thought. Ann pondered a moment. "Grandpa said that sometimes when you're in a tough situation, if you think of the future, you'll find the strength to get through it. I'll hold to my promise. The Northeast Quarter. It's my responsibility. That's it. Getting through this place will help me keep my promise. And thinking of the promise will give me the strength to get through it."

A woman in her fifties entered from the hallway. She looked tired, as if life at the school had weighed so heavily on her shoulders that she could hardly lift her feet. When she walked, the soles of her shoes made a sliding sound along the surface of the floor—more of a shuffle than a step. When she spoke, it was in an urgent whisper.

"Oh, there you are," she said. "I hope you haven't been waiting long."

"She just arrived, Miss Bruner," the receptionist said. "I thought everybody was either in class or out with Miss Fairchild."

"Ah yes, Nadia likes to take them out on a nice day."

"This is Miss Hardy."

"I'm Miss Bruner," the woman murmured, barely audible.

"There isn't much choice of rooms since you came to us so precipitately. But we have you at the far end of the building in the last hall."

Ann glanced over to her bags and the trunk, wondering which one to take first.

"We'll have your things brought to your room in short order," Bruner said. "Shall we start?"

They began to walk down the hallway, passing a series of classroom doors. Ann saw that every door was wide enough to accommodate a bed or a hospital cart.

"You notice the doors," Miss Bruner said. The scuffing of Bruner's steps accompanied them. "They're from the days when this was a hospital. This was a place where sick people were cured. Now it's a place where young minds are nurtured."

They reached the end of the hallway, went down some stairs, entered another hallway, and began to pass the doors of students' rooms. There was less light here.

Bruner's shoes continued scuffing.

"Is this your first time away from home?" Bruner whispered.

"Yes, ma'am, I guess it is."

"You seem remarkably poised for a young lady away for the first time."

"It's my first time away, but someday I'm going back."

Ann's view of the passing doors was blurred.

"Of course. You'll be home on vacations."

"No. I mean for keeps."

They reached the end of the hall. Miss Bruner began to fidget.

"What is it, ma'am?" Ann asked.

"One more hallway." She was pointing to a stairway at the end. They went down these stairs and found themselves in a darker hallway than the one above.

"Was this part of the hospital?" Ann asked.

"This used to be the morgue. But that shouldn't affect your studies."

"The morgue?"

"We're a school now, Miss Hardy. A citadel of life. Miss Fairchild is an inspired educator. All that other stuff is in the past. If I hadn't told you, you would never have known it."

As before, they were facing two rows of wide doors in a passageway that was lit only by lamps along the side. As far as Ann could figure, they were underground. When they began walking, Ann could hear a muffled yet steady rumbling sound in the background.

"What's that noise?" Ann asked.

"The river. The Mississippi starts up the way at Otaska. It's far enough away, but when it's quiet, you can hear the water flowing past."

"I do hear it."

"Up the river are the falls, and downriver are the rapids."

They stopped again.

"Now some rules," Bruner whispered. "No unexcused absence from school grounds at any time."

"That's understandable," Ann said.

"What?"

"Where could we go?"

"No smoking in rooms or anywhere on school grounds," Bruner resumed. "Young ladies do not indulge in the vice of the tobacco leaf. Every student will be up and ready for morning exercise at five thirty, and every student will be in her bed and ready for sleep at eighty thirty. A well-rested maiden is the bodily dwelling of a well-rested mind."

"Yes."

"On the school grounds every student should speak in a dulcet voce."

"A what?"

"A dulcet voce. That's a feminine vocal whisper as I am doing. Young ladies do not caterwaul or bellow. Every student should treat every other student with the utmost respect and every staff member with even more respect."

They resumed walking. Ann felt like Red Riding Hood lost in the woods at sundown.

"Class times are from eight until eleven forty-five and one until four. Meal times are breakfast at six thirty, lunch at eleven forty-five, and dinner at six. We'll have a uniform for you before the evening meal."

They had reached the end of the hall. Ahead of them, the passage split in two. The one on the left ended abruptly. On the right a small offshoot accommodated one more room.

"Are we here, ma'am?" she asked.

"Yes. The last room on the right. It seems like a long way down, but you'll learn the way. Just follow the hall and when you see a stairway, go up. Just go up."

Ann was still feeling abandoned. But she put her insecurities aside to deal with the current situation. "I'll react later," she thought. "Right now, I've got to learn my way around."

"I'll leave you to get settled in."

She watched Miss Bruner scuttle up the hall, scuffing all the way, until there was only silence.

Ann opened the door and found herself standing in an empty room with a single spring bed along the right wall. A dresser and a table with a lamp on it were against the left wall. The walls were the same faded green color as everywhere else in the school. The only window was six feet above, almost along the ceiling. A rectangle of thick glass, eight inches tall and eighteen inches wide, it opened inwardly and had not been cleaned for decades.

"Six feet under sure enough," Ann thought.

Ann glanced around the room.

"I'm not afraid," Ann thought. "I ought to be. But I'm too busy getting used to this place."

She had found a way to deal with her new surroundings. Think of the promise. Take the rest as it comes.

⤳

A dour handyman brought Ann's trunk and bags to the room. Without a word, he dropped the luggage by the doorway and then left. Ann shoved the trunk into the room and started to unpack.

A sullen upper-class student appeared at the doorway a short time later with Ann's uniform. Instead of greeting Ann, she simply placed the olive denim on the nearest bed and left.

Ann changed into her uniform. Dinner was called—a ripple effect that began with the tinkle of a faraway bell. followed by muffled voices in the upstairs hall, and ending with a mélange of half-hearted murmurs from the top of the stairs to their hallway

They made the journey through the main building. Ann noticed the other girls in their rooms, preparing to leave or stepping out into the hall. Nobody paid much attention to anyone else, and as before, no one spoke above a whisper.

The dining hall was a large auditorium with long tables running up and down the center of the room. Along the far wall was the faculty dining area. This was another long table, situated on a three-foot-high platform stage that gave those seated there a view of the entire room. Situated directly in front of this table were three steps and a speaker's podium.

To the left of the entrance were the doors to the kitchen. Between them was a long table set apart from the wall, holding two stacks of plates, metal containers for silverware, and three trays containing cups of warm tea.

Ann was the last to arrive. With the drab green of the walls and the multitude of olive khaki bobbing about, Ann's first impression was that she had walked into a large bowl of bean soup. Most of the other students, aged twelve to eighteen, were gathered along the wall in pockets according to their age and class. And even in this crowd, no one spoke above a whisper.

She fell into line with the others. The staff had arrived and were being served their meals by a kitchen helper, pale skinned and blond.

The kitchen doors swung open and two more helpers pushed in the evening meal of meat loaf, mashed potatoes, and peas. One of the helpers gave a signal to the front of the line. These students picked up their plates and moved forward to have their meals doled out to them.

When Ann arrived at the front of the line, she could see that the first helper shoved a portion of meat loaf onto each plate, the second slopped a ladle of mashed potatoes beside it, and the third added peas. Each of the girls took a cup of tea from one of the trays and then returned to her place. Ann found an empty spot at one of the tables.

A red-headed girl looked up at her.

"Is there a...?"

"Shh," came the response.

Ann sat down at the table. It was then she noticed that nobody had begun to eat. This time there was not even a whisper. After a minute, a door opened on one side of the room.

Standing in the doorway was a large woman in a formal gray dress. With her hair pulled into a tight bun and her coarse complexion, Ann was not sure if she was male or female. Nadia Fairchild was a tall woman—perhaps an athlete in her youth. Her head was the size of a watermelon, and her upper arms had the bulk of a Christmas turkey. Her large-boned form assumed the shape of a pear. Despite her bulk, she gave the impression of possessing tremendous physical strength.

Miss Fairchild strode to the steps of the faculty dining area. She remained standing in front of her seat, surveying the room and the students gathered below her. Then she nodded to some inner thought—satisfied that everything and everyone was in the proper place.

"Good evening," she said aloud. Her voice seemed to blend high-pitched male and low-pitched female vocal tones.

"Good evening, Miss Fairchild" came the reply from the students.

"And now the blessing." Her eyes searched the eighty upraised faces assembled below her. "Tillie Thompson, let you say the blessing."

"Let you?" Ann thought. "Sounds biblical..."

A young girl about Ann's age left her seat, solemnly mounted the stairs, and crossed the stage to the podium.

"Oh Lord, Jesus, Mary, and Joseph," she began.

"Just the blessing, child," Miss Fairchild bellowed. "Not the weather report."

"For what we are about to receive, may the Lord make us truly thankful. Amen."

"Thank you, Tillie," Miss Fairchild said. She made a small twirling motion to the students with her hand to signal that they could begin.

For the next thirty minutes, everyone ate in almost total silence. The only communication was an occasional whisper requesting salt or pepper. The only sounds were silverware touching the plates, the occasional creak of a chair, or a cough here and there. Ann noticed some of the students watching her. They were scrutinizing her, trying to figure her out. They seemed to pick up on the fact that she looked uncomfortable in new surroundings, but that she seemed more questioning than accepting in her outlook, which made her stand out from the rest.

At the conclusion of the meal, Miss Fairchild tapped her glass and strode to the podium.

"Young ladies," she began, "I have waited to make my traditional introductory speech until we were all here. We had three late arrivals, the last of whom joined us today. We are now assembled and ready to begin."

She paused for dramatic effect.

"We are a special school. We are special because we endeavor to teach you not only the basics of education, but the key to using that education in your daily lives. There is a world outside, and every one of you will venture into it. How you get on when you get there is what we are about."

Another pause as her eyes moved around from face to face below her.

"The key to feminine success and survival is self-knowledge: knowing who you are, knowing your limitations, and finally, knowing your place in the world. This is very important. You are all maidens—young women. And the tragedy that befalls so many young women today is that they confuse their strengths with their limitations. They destroy themselves because they do not have self-knowledge. They do not know their place."

Another pause. Her eyes became riveted on Ann. She had found the new face.

"Just so we do not misunderstand each other, a woman is a capable, intelligent creature. We share many of the strengths which our creator gave men, but within limits, of course—within limits. Men are reckless, adventurous, and it is a woman's place to stay out of that world. Away from that brouhaha. Do not attempt what you were not meant to achieve. Venture into forbidden territory, and you hurl yourself upon the rocks of incautious fortune. Know your place. Accept yourself for who you are. Then and only then will you blossom threefold and become the perfect creature our creator meant you to be."

She stepped back with a proud smile.

"You are dismissed," Miss Fairchild said. "May I see Ann Hardy?"

Ann got up from her chair and walked over to the stage. Up close, this headmistress looked more enormous than ever. She was at least six feet tall, like a circus tent with a face on top. Already the other girls were filing out of the dining area with occasional whispers and a giggle here and there.

"Miss Hardy?"

"Yes, ma'am," Ann said.

"Let us go to my office. We can talk there."

Ann followed Miss Fairchild out of the dining room and across the lobby. They entered another hallway, and after passing a door marked Bureau, they stopped at the next one, which had Miss Fairchild's name on it.

The inside of the principal's office was lit by a pair of lamps. There was a large window looking out at the sport field and the driveway, a large desk and leather chair, and a pair of less comfortable seats for students or guests. Ann noticed a small wind-up phonograph on a fragile table to one side of the leather chair.

"Let you sit, Miss Hardy," Miss Fairchild said.

Ann went to one of the chairs across from the desk.

"So you're Ann Hardy. Your grandfather speaks very highly of you."

"He does?"

"He thinks we might be able to help you."

"How, ma'am?"

"He says you have emotional problems."

"Oh?"

"Miss Hardy, your grandfather is concerned for your welfare. He wants to fathom your aptitudes and, if at all possible, to redeem them. You should appreciate his efforts."

"Yes, ma'am."

"Somehow I am not convinced that you do. Why, the moment you arrived, he was on the telephone with me. He had called to see if you arrived safely."

"I didn't know that," Ann said. She wondered how Miss Fairchild managed to talk on the telephone in her office at the same she was outdoors, lecturing students under a tree.

Ann was about to address this lie, when she remembered some advice from Colonel Carson. If you keep quiet, you might learn something. And she was already learning about Miss Nadia Fairchild.

"Didn't Carol and Cassie go here?"

Miss Fairchild leaned back in her chair, closing her eyes as if she were relishing a fine wine.

"Ah, Carol and Cassandra...Cassandra and Carol...The crème de la crème. Whip-smart and properly feminine. They are a standard to which you should aspire, Miss Hardy."

Ann felt a knot form in her stomach. It could have been the meat loaf, but then again, maybe not.

"Aspire to be like them…that's a tall order, ma'am."

"Frankly, Miss Hardy, I am distressed that you are having problems relating to their father. Royce Chamberlin is a credit to humanity."

Miss Fairchild was scrutinizing Ann, looking for any quirks or reactions. This little girl was clearly not like the other students.

"Let us step back a moment, Miss Hardy. We have talked of your family. Let us talk of you. You are twelve years old."

"Yes, ma'am."

"We're a six-year program. That means you are with us until you are eighteen. That is a long time. Did Miss Bruner explain the rules and regulations of the school?"

"Yes, ma'am, she did."

"And you come to us from Iowa."

"Yes."

"I don't like Iowa," Miss Fairchild announced. "All those cornstalks growing and nothing to do. You walk around in the fields all day, and when you go into town, there's no theater, no culture, no art. Nothing, just nothing."

Ann stifled a grin. Miss Fairchild could have been describing Coon Falls.

"What do you say to that?" Fairchild challenged.

"What do I say to what, ma'am?"

"About Iowa."

"Nothing."

"Nothing? I offered an opinion of your state."

"A person is free to believe what she wants. That's what my real grandpa used to say."

"Don't you agree with me?"

"No, ma'am."

Fairchild's temper was rising. Obviously, Ann was not taking the bait.

"You seem quite reserved for a maiden your age. Why is that?"

"I don't know, ma'am."

"I intend to find out, Miss Hardy. Reserve means repression. Repression means holding in, concealing all those angry voices in your head that rage deep inside. When I look into a maiden's eyes, I want to know where she is at all times. My school is here to nurture you from childhood through adolescence to young womanhood. I intend to know who you are and what makes you tick."

Ann was puzzled that anyone could arrive at such a conclusion after five minutes of conversation. "I don't think I'm that far gone, ma'am," she said.

Miss Fairchild's expression changed into a sneer. "Are you angry, Miss Hardy?"

"No, ma'am."

"I think you are. I hear your anger, Miss Hardy. Together, we will understand your rage."

Again, Ann wanted to respond to Fairchild's words, but she caught herself.

"I'm not angry, ma'am."

"Yes, you are. You are angry. Already our conversation has assumed an antagonistic edge. You are. I'm not. Yes, you are. No, I'm not."

"I can't say I'm angry when I'm not."

Miss Fairchild was out of her chair and lumbering toward Ann. She stuck out a carrot-sized forefinger and roughly tapped Ann on the head.

"I know you're *in* there," Miss Fairchild said. "I shall find you out whoever you are. I shall find you out." She stepped back. "And I have plenty of time."

The large woman was staring intimately at Ann, still waiting for some kind of antagonistic response. Ann just wanted to get out of the office.

"Miss Fairchild, may I ask something?"

"Very well. What is it?"

"If I have any news from home, will you tell me?"

"Of course, any news from home, you will be the first to know."

"And letters?"

"The same thing, Miss Hardy. We're not the Barbary Coast here."

"No, ma'am."

"Miss Hardy, this school is a positive antidote to your rural upbringing. We are a pulse of feminine enlightenment. Why, sometimes I feel Clearwater is the only thing that stands between my girls and the pitchforks."

Even from Fairchild this sounded bizarre. Ann had never thought of a school in this way before.

"You may go, Miss Hardy. We shall talk again."

"Yes, ma'am."

Miss Fairchild returned to her place behind the desk.

23

ANN SETTLED INTO HER FIRST YEAR. Initially, she told herself that her attendance at Clearwater would be temporary. That was what her parents had said. But the weeks began to pass. Weeks that seemed like months. On the occasion when Jack or Lucille did call or write, they told her, "Have patience. Jack has been to Crawford Glen." Or, "In ten days Jack is going to Cedar Rapids." She soon realized her stay was going to be longer than anyone anticipated, but she held in her heart that one day she would return to Winfield.

Beneath her hope, there was always the bitterness, but she would counter it by reminding herself what Colonel Carson had always said: no matter how legitimate, anger is a load that gets in the way of day-to-day living.

She was in a class called Hearth and Home, an activity for first-year students. Essentially, it was a group letter-writing session in Sunday study hall—intended more for the parents and guardians than the girls themselves. The students would copy a short letter dictated by a staff member. At the conclusion, the girls would sign their letters and turn them in. On the following day, the letters went out with the morning mail.

This particular session was held in late afternoon. Miss Kramer, the school science teacher, dictated the letter. The choice of words gave Ann the opportunity to consider her own feelings.

Kramer strolled along the rows of tables, composing the text as she walked.

"Dear Father and Mother," she began. "I hope you are in good spirits, and everything is well among the family."

"Ridiculous," Ann thought. "Since when have I ever said that to Mama and Papa?"

"I am doing very well here at Clearwater School. I love my studies, and I say my prayers every night."

"Who are they kidding?" Ann said to herself. "That's not my story. My whole life was spent in a place I loved. A special place. Carson Manor in Winfield. Then suddenly I was moved out just to make it easier for them. I was sent here because they're afraid of Royce Chamberlin."

Kramer stopped. She walked over to the window. The afternoon sun was streaming down on the forest around the school. It looked like the entire landscape was covered with Christmas trees. In the distance the Coon Falls church bell was ringing.

"It is autumn right now," Kramer dictated slowly. "And we are all enjoying one of nature's true wonders…the glorious fall foliage."

"The what?" It was Tillie Thompson, the girl who gave the weather report at the start of Ann's first Clearwater meal.

"What is it, Miss Thompson?"

"Forgive me for speaking. What are we enjoying?"

"The foliage. The changing colors of the leaves."

"But they're pine trees, Miss Kramer. They don't change colors unless they're sick."

"Write the sentence, Miss Thompson."

"Yes, Miss Kramer. Sorry, Miss Kramer."

A flurry of indignant whispers among the girls.

"Grandpa's right," Ann thought. "Being angry doesn't help me here. It gets in my way. I have to think of myself right now. Put it aside while I deal with this place."

Kramer stopped to look down at Ann's letter. She nodded approvingly and continued her stroll.

"I am making friends with many other girls," Kramer intoned. "School days are a wholesome and special time for me. I look forward every week to writing my letter home, for family is very important to me. Until next week, Your Loving Daughter."

～

Christmas recess was two months later. Lucille came to school to bring Ann home. As Ann waited for her in the lobby, her emotions were mixed. She had gotten used to the school and its ways, and she had made some nodding acquaintances, which was as close as she would ever get to a friend at Clearwater.

When the taxi arrived and Ann saw her mother, she raced over to give her a hug. It was as if the resentment had evaporated.

Ann did not talk much on the trip back. Most of the time, Lucille told her the latest news from Winfield, including their difficulties in finding an attorney. Ann noticed how detached she felt from what her mother was saying. Lucille was describing people and places Ann had known all her life, but somehow they did not mean as much.

"This time I've only been away three months," she thought. "It seems longer."

Jack met them at the depot with the car. It had snowed a few days earlier, and the ground was covered with splotches of icy mud. They bundled up and began the drive home. Ann was glad to see Winfield again, but somehow she didn't feel a part of it. Had the school and its ways ingrained themselves so deeply that it made her feel like a visitor in her hometown? "I hope not," Ann thought.

"We hope you understand about the lawyer," Jack began tentatively. "It would hurt us more than anything if you didn't understand."

"I understand," Ann said, beginning to feel irritated.

"Do you?"

Ann hated it when her father started agonizing. When her grandpa was alive, Jack never moped and complained. She hoped her father wasn't drinking again.

"How's Grandma?" Ann asked.

"You'll see a change," Lucille answered. "She spends a lot of time at the front window, just looking out."

"I'm sorry to hear that," Ann said. This was one image she couldn't brush aside—Lady Ann at the window. She kept thinking of it during the drive.

Up ahead a wagon was inching its way in the opposite direction. Ann could see that it was packed to the hilt with furniture and possessions. Three people were huddled together on the driver's seat. Another family leaving. Jack slowed down and moved the car as far as possible to the right side of the road.

"It's Bill Roundtree," Lucille said.

"Yeah," Jack added. "Another one."

"That makes five in East County, and it's Christmas to boot."

"Foreclosures don't keep banker's hours," Jack replied. "They got you when they got you."

Jack stopped to let the wagon pass.

The driver, a grim-faced man in a heavy topcoat, nodded curtly at Jack and Lucille. The woman and the young girl beside him stared straight ahead. Jack waited as the wagon passed.

"Some people don't talk to us anymore," Lucille said.

"Why? You're not to blame," Ann said.

"Particulars don't matter when you've lost everything," Jack said. "We're Royce's family now."

Ann looked back at the wagon. The chill in the air and the barren landscape around them created a feeling of desolation.

"What's going to happen to them?"

"They'll manage," Jack said. "People here are tough. Flood or drought, they manage. Sometimes it's better not to think of it."

Nobody spoke for the next few minutes. The encounter had left an impression.

"We've talked to six different attorneys," Lucille said finally. "Every one turned us down. They gave various reasons—from full caseload to conflict of interest. We think the real reason is that they're afraid of Royce."

"We haven't given up," Jack said.

"We did learn something interesting," Lucille said. "Remember Brenner and Ishie?"

"Sure," Ann said. "Grandma fired them."

"It seems that Royce gave each of them money to buy his own spread."

"Really?"

"They both own farms over in Albert Mill," Jack added.

"How did you find out?" Ann asked.

"Morgenstern's Law Office in Keokuk. They told me."

"I thought Royce caught them cheating Grandma," Ann said.

"Looks like Royce had it all staged to win us over," Lucille said. "The two farms were a payoff."

"Royce has his hands in everything. That's why we have to be careful," Jack said.

In a few minutes, they were approaching Carson Manor. The sight of it filled Ann with joy. Here was home, the place where everything had been safe and loving. For a few seconds, it was as if nothing had happened. But the nearer they drew, the less like home it seemed. Everything seemed different. Returning home was not supposed to be this way.

"Royce isn't here," Jack said. "He and Cassie are in Kansas City."

"What are they doing there?" Ann asked.

"Shopping trip. They'll be back tomorrow."

"What about Carol?"

"She's still here."

"That's strange—just Royce and Cassie going and leaving Carol behind. No wonder she's so mean."

"The Chamberlins are a strange family," Jack said. "The three of them live like they're the only people on earth."

Lady Ann and Olga greeted Ann at the front door. There were hugs and salutations. The interior of the house had been decorated for Christmas with mistletoe and wreaths. Carol hovered sternly to one side. She said nothing to Ann.

Early that evening, while the others were preparing for dinner, Ann had time to speak with her grandmother. Lady Ann looked tired. She was standing in her usual spot beside the front window, watching the snow falling outside. It was dusk, and the flakes were fluttering through the light cast from the house.

"Look," Lady Ann said.

"Yeah."

"I still like to watch it."

They stood side by side for a long time, watching the flakes landing in the driveway.

"I was remembering how I met your grandfather," Lady Ann said. "I do that now and then." Lady Ann smiled. "Back then, he didn't have that majestic beard. There was a handsome man under that white mane."

Ann could see her grandmother reliving this moment: a retreat to earlier and safer times.

"I was a young woman. I had just arrived from England. That's where my people were from. Oxfordshire. Have I told you that?"

"Yes, Grandma. Cotswold country."

"That's right. Where so many of the big houses look like this one. The Cotswolds. Look at that flake, Ann."

They watched a particularly large flake quavering its way past the window.

"Wallace was visiting his army friend, Roland Moss. Rolie had an idea of bringing Hereford cattle out to Kansas and Nebraska. Others had been doing it. Rolie wanted to buy a pair of bulls from my papa, and he talked Wallace into coming along."

Ann had heard the story many times. She wanted to reach out and hug Lady Ann and tell her everything would be all right.

"When I saw your grandpa, I thought he was the most handsome man I had ever seen. He stood there like a big statue. Full of life. Loving life. I'd met other young men, but this was different. Have you ever felt that way?"

"No," Ann said.

"You will. And when it's the right one, you'll know, Ann. You'll know."

"Not many boys around Clearwater."

"That's all right. You're young. You're still a child."

Olga appeared in the kitchen doorway.

"Dinner call, Miss Ann. I've fixed you chicken and corn bread."

"Thank you, Olga," Ann said.

Lucille and Jack were coming down the stairs. Carol hovered in the entrance to the study. Lady Ann and Ann started for the table.

～ convolution ～

The following day Royce and Cassie returned with two bags full of Christmas presents. Four of them were for Lady Ann and her family. The other fifteen were to be exchanged among the Chamberlins. This did not surprise Ann, but the shopping trip did. Why was Carol left behind? Was there a division in the Chamberlin family?

That afternoon, Royce summoned Ann to the study. As she was crossing the main hall to the study door, she remembered the previous time when she had made this trip—the cigar episode with Kurt Hudsen. When she arrived at the door, she heard the voices of Royce and Carol on the other side.

"You love her more, Papa. That's what it is," Carol was saying. "It's true."

"Carol, we've been through this..."

"It's true, Papa. You love Cassie more."

Ann could hear sobs on the other side of the door. She had never thought Carol was capable of any kind of emotion. She wanted to feel good that Carol was suffering given that Carol had earned every tear, but somehow Ann couldn't rejoice. Celebrating another's misfortune wasn't in her.

The sobs continued.

"We're special people," Chamberlin said. "You know that. We were meant for great things. We live our own way. By our own rules. We do more, and consequently, we feel more. It's what makes us who we are."

Ann leaned closer to hear better, pressing against the door.

"Papa, someone's out there."

"Special people, my foot," Ann said to herself. She knocked on the door and entered the study. Royce was at the desk. Carol was positioned across the room. Her cheeks were red, her eyes bleary.

"You were listening," Carol snapped.

"I just got here," Ann said.

"What may I do for you, Ann?" Royce said.

"Papa said you wanted to see me."

Royce smiled approvingly. He obviously still expected immediate obedience. Ann bristled.

"I was wondering how you were doing at Clearwater."

"Didn't Miss Fairchild tell you?"

The smile continued, but they both knew that nothing had changed. The enmity was right back on the surface.

"I was hoping to hear it from you," Chamberlin said.

"The place takes getting used to," Ann replied.

"Don't tell me you're homesick already," Carol jeered.

"I don't know what to tell you," Ann said to Royce. "The last time I was here, you stuck a cigar in my face."

Chamberlin's eyes twinkled. "Ann, I was hoping we could be civil about this."

"We're being civil," Ann said.

"I had hoped you might show some appreciation. I have plans for you. For your future."

"I'd sure like to know what they are."

"Suppose you leave that to me."

"I don't like being part of a plan unless I know what it is," Ann declared.

"You little ingrate..." Carol snarled.

"Anything else you wanted to talk about?" Ann said to Royce.

"We won't give up on this, Ann," Chamberlin said. "We'll talk again."

As Ann left the study and started into the main hall, she heard Chamberlin's voice behind her. "It's a contest of wills. Ann and me. It won't last forever."

The next five days everyone went through the motions of celebrating the holidays. Ann was home, but the atmosphere was anything but home-like.

Ann decided to keep her emotions in check. "I won't feel anything on these visits because it's all temporary. I'm here and then I'm gone again. I won't feel joy. I won't feel sadness. I'll keep it in. I'll wait till I'm home for good."

⁓

Before she knew it, the holiday was over and she was back at school. The classes resumed, and Ann began to think of the next time she would visit Winfield. She had visited Zachary at the county farm. He wanted to come home. Everything seemed to be waiting for something else to happen.

Three weeks after her return, Ann received two letters. One was from Lucille and was full of Winfield news. One item, however, stuck out. "Some disturbing news. When Lapp and Dode Swaybill were on their way back from visiting their grandchildren in Cardinal Springs, they were attacked on the road. Lapp is in hospital. No one says what happened or who did it. The Swaybills had a note at the bank and lost their farm. A lot of this is starting to happen. We think it is the Hudsens. Everyone's afraid to talk."

The second letter touched closer to home. The page was almost blank, except for a few sentences, written by Jack. "We are so proud of you. We love you and keep you in our hearts. Love, Mama and Papa." And beneath their signature was written in a shaky scrawl "Love Always, Your Grandma." It was almost a caricature of her usual graceful penmanship. This, more than anything, told her how Lady Ann had been dealing with the conditions at Carson Manor.

Ann remembered her conversation with Lady Ann at the window. She had wanted to reach out to her grandmother and reassure her.

"I missed a lot of opportunities back there," Ann thought. "I won't do it this time." In study hall she wrote a short note to Lady Ann. "Grandma, if you are feeling sad, think of me. I am always here for you. Love, Ann."

Ann mailed it herself from the letter box in Coon Falls.

24

The years passed. Ann was fourteen and in the ninth grade.

The morning of November 15 was unusually cold. With the coming of winter, breakfast now included hot cross buns along with the usual servings of oranges, oatmeal, and biscuits and gravy.

At 11:00 a.m. Ann was sitting in Feminine Ethics with nine other students. Each one had a notebook and a dark-brown hardback book in front of her. The class was taught by an elderly woman named Miss Webber in a dusty classroom. Everyone sat in wooden desk chairs facing the teacher's desk and a blackboard. On the blackboard were printed the words "Proper Ethics. Proper Femininity." Hovering over the blackboard was a poster of a saintly woman in a shawl with eyes raised heavenward in supplication. To the staff, she was Saint Gertrude De Greves—Patron Saint of Feminine Humility. Ann called her Gravel Gertie—the Patron Saint of Getting the Hell Out.

"Be not dismayed," Miss Webber was saying. "You are all young maidens in a world full of hidden dangers and public wickedness. We are preparing you in the socially and morally proper manner. You must learn to recognize sin and embrace virtue."

"Yes, Miss Webber," recited the class.

Ann had little time for this lesson. She doubted if anyone in the room had faced the kinds of morally testing situations Miss Webber described.

Webber was looking out at the cluster of faces. "Who can tell me how to recognize sin?"

Two or three hands went up.

"Miss Tuttle."

A blond girl began. "You recognize it when you see it as it is. When it is a revulsion to your personal values as a maiden."

"Excellent. Simply excellent," Miss Webber said. "A maiden's personal values should be sheltered and protected—hidden away from all the savage brou-haha."

Another hand.

"Miss Ryan."

"A woman's role is to protect the hearth and home. In addition to her role as homemaker for her husband and children, she must act as guardian of decency within the family."

"Exactly . . . All of that and nothing more."

Suddenly, she was focusing on Ann.

"Ann Hardy, you have been with us for two years now, yet you always seem hesitant to join the discussion. Why is that?"

"What a stupid question," Ann thought. She took a breath. "I'm sorry, Miss Webber. I didn't mean to give that impression."

"You always seem to have something else on your mind."

"I don't, ma'am. My mind is always on the lesson at hand."

"I think not, Miss Hardy. I think you have your own thoughts, and you keep them to yourself."

Miss Webber was using the standard Clearwater technique of repeating the charge until the student finally agreed.

"If I have my own thoughts," Ann began slowly, "then it's proper that I keep them to myself."

"Caution, Miss Hardy. Caution."

Ann knew she shouldn't get into a discussion. Something about this class ir-ritated her. It reminded her of everything at home. Define evil and then sit back, hoping it leaves you alone.

"May I speak frankly?"

"Within reason."

"I wonder what we would do if Sin walked into this class and introduced himself."

A collective gasp around the room.

"That is not an appropriate question," Miss Webber exclaimed. "Such a thing would never happen."

"But what would we do if it did happen? What if the most evil man in the world walked into this room and said hello."

"It would never happen. Our ethical considerations prepare us to avoid such an occurrence." Her eyes narrowed into an accusatory stare. "You're a trouble-maker, Ann Hardy."

"I don't mean to be." Ann sighed.

"But you are. Don't you see? Your questions are . . . upsetting."

"I'd sure like to know what everyone's afraid of," Ann said.

"Afraid?" Miss Webber exclaimed. "Afraid?"

"Yes, ma'am. Nothing will ever get solved if everyone's afraid."

"That's enough from you, Miss Hardy!" Webber cried. "Report to the office and tell them you have ten demerits!"

"Yes, ma'am."

"You need to reflect on word and deed."

Ann started for the door. "That's the mop and bucket," she said.

"Of course it is. You know the punishment. You mop the floor to cleanse soul and spirit."

"Yes, ma'am."

Ann was out of the classroom and on her way to the office. She arrived to find Miss Bruner alone at one of the desks. Before Ann could speak, Bruner was on her way over with a plain white envelope.

"Special correspondence for Miss Hardy," she said.

"Thank you."

Ann opened the envelope. There were two letters inside. She opened the first and began to read. All at once, she stopped. It was as if all the air had gone out of her.

"Oh no, my grandma died."

"Oh Lord," Bruner murmured.

Ann felt tears crowding into her eyes. She wanted to have control over her emotions, but she couldn't. She spun around and paced over to the office wall.

For a few seconds she stood in silence with her eyes closed. Although the hurt inside was tremendous, she would deal with it later.

She returned to the letter. It was from Royce Chamberlin. It read: "It is my sad duty to inform you of the passing of your grandmother on November 8. The funeral was on November 10."

Ann's eyes flashed as she looked up. "It was five days ago."

"What?"

"She died a week ago."

"You mean, they didn't tell you?"

"No. The funeral was on the tenth. I never got to go to my grandma's funeral."

Ann stared in disbelief at the letter. The shock and the hurt had left her speechless.

Bruner wanted to say something. She saw the callousness in the entire situation. But she stood by, feeling helpless. The girls weren't supposed to get news like this.

Ann resumed reading. "You are consequently invited to a memorial service on November twentieth."

"I'm so sorry, Miss Hardy."

Ann opened the second letter. "This one's from Mama," she said. "Dated November ninth."

"Then everybody knew for a week. Nobody called here, Miss Hardy. I never heard of such a thing."

"Royce must have sat on everything until the memorial service was set."

Ann quietly read her mother's letter. Short sentences. Words in disconnected bursts.

"Your grandma died of a heart attack...The circumstances here at the manor were the cause, we are sure...Broken heart...So sad...So upset that Royce sold three of the farms...He claimed the money was going for investments to finance the estate...At the same time, he's been talking about a water and power company to the north...Since we're near Thanksgiving recess, I am asking the school if you can come home for an extra week. To attend the service."

Ann looked up from the page. "Mama's asking if I can come home early to attend the service."

"Nadia will grant it, I'm sure."

Outside, the bell rang for change of classes.

"I just have to say I have never heard of anything so cruel, Miss Hardy. Surely it's a misunderstanding."

"It's a cruel world out there," Ann said.

"But people just aren't that way. They can't be."

"Some of them are. And they got me where they want me...for now at least," Ann said.

25

ON THE MORNING OF NOVEMBER 17 Ann left Clearwater to catch the train home.

By the afternoon, the train was pulling into Winfield. From her seat, she saw Lucille and Olga, as well as her friends Ellen and Judy, on the platform.

"Everyone's there, as if nothing happened," she said to herself. "I miss Grandma, too, but I've got some issues to settle with them."

As Ann gathered her bags, she saw that both Olga and her mother were red-cheeked from mourning their loss.

"I can see they're upset about Grandma," she thought. "Mama looks devastated...I forget how much this must hurt her. She just lost her mother. I have to ask myself how I'd feel if Mama died...I don't even want to think about it."

Ann was greeted by open arms.

"There's my girl. There's my girl," Lucille said tearfully. "My little girl is growing up."

"I've missed you, Mama."

"You're home now," Lucille said.

"Oh, child, you're back," Olga said. "Look at her. She's a young woman now."

"We're sorry about your grandma," Ellen said. "We all loved her."

Mr. Dobbs, the stationmaster, came out of the office. "Miss Ann, welcome back. I just want to say that I'm sorry about your grandmother. We all miss her a great deal."

"Thank you, Mr. Dobbs. I miss her, too."

Dobbs gave a signal to the engineer. There was a loud puff and then another from the engine. The train slowly moved forward.

"Great lady, she was. Great lady."

He started back into the office. "Say, you haven't seen Doss Claypool, have you?"

"No," Lucille said.

"He's never around when you need him."

"Nothing changes," Lucille said.

"Is Papa coming?" Ann asked.

"He has the car. He went over to Doc Powell's for a minute."

"He's all right, isn't he?"

"We'll explain on our way home," Lucille said. "Around here the walls have ears."

As they started around to the front of the station, the side door opened, and Warren Hyatt stepped outside, rumpled and disorganized.

"Like a bad penny," Lucille muttered. "Try to ignore him."

"Hello, Mrs. Hardy...Hello, Miss Hardy," Hyatt said with exaggerated formality.

"Good afternoon," Ann answered, looking ahead as they passed him.

"You know, Miss Hardy," he chided. "Uh, Miss Hardy, it would be much happier for all of us if we talked openly. You seem to be holding a grudge of some kind."

"Not today, Mr. Hyatt," Ann said.

Hyatt began to follow them, haranguing them with every step. "Of course, we have to remember what it's like to be born in privilege...to be Colonel Carson's granddaughter."

"Some other time, Mr. Hyatt," Lucille stated.

"I think not. I know you want to judge me for what happened...You're judging me right now. It wasn't my fault, by the way."

Lucille spun around angrily. "Mr. Hyatt, I just lost my mother and Ann just lost her grandmother. Your intrusions are neither wanted nor appreciated."

"I'm not intruding. This is a public place," Hyatt whined. "I have just as much right to speak out as you do."

Ann had had enough of his petulant posturing. "Then go speak out somewhere else. I'm tired of looking at your face."

"What did you say?"

"Get out of our way. Move."

With his nose in the air, Warren Hyatt started for the alley to Market Street. "You Carsons need to learn some manners." He sniffed.

"Nothing changes," Lucille said.

"Warren Hyatt's like fruit left on a tree at harvest time," Olga said. "Sooner or later, it begins to rot."

Hyatt entered the alley, twitching and zigzagging, as if pursued by a hoard of gnats.

"There's your papa," Lucille said. An older model car was puttering toward them. He put on the brake and jumped out of the car, running around to hug his daughter.

Ann felt relieved. He seemed full of energy and happy to be alive. It was like the old Jack had returned.

"Look at my daughter. Look at my girl."

Within seconds, hurt and disappointment enveloped Ann, and she pushed away from her father. His breath reeked of alcohol, a smell that she hated. In her mind, every time he drank, he was letting the family down. She was doing her share at Clearwater, and her father couldn't even do his at home.

"What? What's wrong?" Jack exclaimed, unsure of what had happened.

It was not lost on Lucille. She'd gotten used to Jack's drinking and even pretended it was part of their lives and didn't matter anymore.

"This is our car now," Jack said rapidly. "Royce let us buy it, since he controls the purse strings. But it won't be forever. Oh no. It won't be forever, Ann. We didn't find someone like that Arabella Mansfield you admire, but we found a good one."

"What? You found a lawyer?" Ann said in surprise.

"We did. You can be proud of your papa."

Ann had heard correctly. They had found a lawyer, but the wait had been so long. Ann still wanted to find out why nobody had told her about Lady Ann's death and funeral, but the sadness on the faces around her made it impossible. All she could feel was the pressure building again.

"I'll take us home, Jack," Lucille said quietly.

"I can do it," Jack answered.

"I know that. But you drove us in."

Jack turned away, hurt and defensive. "You know . . . I'm doing the best I can here."

There it was again: the same tone, the same refrain. Ann tried not to listen.

"Of course you have," Lucille said.

"I've been trying to deal with this situation as much as anybody in the family. You know that. I've found our outside help. We're not giving up."

"No, we're not," Lucille echoed.

"We're going to stand solid, Mr. Jack," Olga said.

"That's right, Papa," Ann said bitterly. "We're all going to stand real tall."

Everyone turned to Ann in surprise. Her mocking tone had cut through everything and brought the family pain to the surface.

Jack attempted a weak smile. "Maybe Ann doesn't know all the news," he said. "We'll tell her on the way back."

"Let's go, dear," Lucille said.

Ann said good-bye to Ellen and Judy. They both looked uncomfortable, disturbed by the family outburst. Ann knew she would see her friends again before she left. She could talk it over with them.

Ann got into the backseat with Olga.

"I made a mess with that one," she thought. "Grandpa was sure right about anger. Let it out and people can get hurt, but try to hold it inside, and it'll pop out in ways you don't expect. It's a bad deal all the way around."

26

LUCILLE DROVE. ALL AROUND THEM WERE the barren fields and hillsides whose gray desolation made them blend into one another. Every one featured the same furrowed rows in the soil where the harvested stalks once stood. Here and there were the remains of the plants, rapidly assuming the color of the soil beneath them.

Lucille looked over at Jack. "Did you find out anything?"

"Doc says she's in Omaha visiting a niece who's having a baby."

"I didn't know she had a niece."

"First I heard of it," Olga said.

"We're talking about Beulah Jensen," Lucille said to Ann.

"The nurse at the hospital. Why are you looking for her?"

"When your grandma took ill, Royce had her moved to the hospital. She was in a room there for a day before she died. Beulah had just come on for night duty, and she said that around eight p.m., Royce and Fred Brubaker showed up to see Mama. They went into her room and closed the door. Beulah didn't think too much of it at first, but later, when she started to make her rounds, she heard a commotion from Mama's room. She went over and opened the door. Inside, she saw Brubaker holding a paper in front of Mama and Royce telling her to sign it. She was saying no over and over, and then Royce grabbed her arm and tried to force her to do it."

"My God," Ann said. The image seemed to burn into her memory as an example of human cruelty that she couldn't put out of her mind. It was shocking, but considering the participants, not at all surprising.

"When they saw her, Royce let out a yell. Brubaker rushed over, shoved Beulah outside, and slammed the door in her face."

"Did Beulah tell you this?"

"She told me, Miss Ann," Olga said. "Beulah came to me day before yesterday. Said she'd been keeping it a secret because she was scared."

"And now, when we want to talk to her about it, she's disappeared," Lucille said.

"Miss Ann, she was scared of what Mr. Royce might do to her."

"We're sure they were trying to force Mama to change her will," Lucille said.

The car was bumping along the dirt road. Ann noticed how the surrounding emptiness affected their voices. The silence seemed to smother the sound of their words and make everything in the car seem smaller. Ann had not noticed silence so clearly in a long time.

"So we've been checking," Lucille continued. "Both Royce and Fred Brubaker have alibis that place them away from the hospital at the time. Brubaker says he was in Exira."

"And Royce claims he was at the bank," Jack said.

"At eight p.m.?" Ann exclaimed. "What did Grandma say?"

"She never mentioned it," Lucille said. "When we saw her that night, there was no evidence anywhere that there had been a struggle. All she said to us was, 'Whatever happens, save the Northeast Quarter.'"

"That should have signaled something, but we didn't catch it," Jack said.

"And nobody else saw them at the hospital?" Ann asked.

"They planned it pretty well," Olga said.

Lucille maneuvered the car around a hole and continued over some frozen ruts in the road.

"Brubaker's already had a reading of the will," Jack said. "We have fourteen farms left. Royce and the girls get seven. You, your Mama, Zachary, and I get the other seven."

"Was he forcing her to sign over half the estate?"

"We thought so at first," Lucille said. "But Mama had been planning to do this for about a year. She was scared of Royce. She thought if she deeded him half, it would preserve the rest of the estate for us."

They reached a crossroads where four farms intersected. There were no people or vehicles in any direction.

Ann had been waiting for the proper moment, but there didn't seem to be any. She still had something to settle. "Why wasn't I told about Grandma?"

"Royce telephoned the school the night she passed away," Lucille said. "They said they would notify you."

"Nobody told me. Not till the day before yesterday. They held your mail."

"Maybe Royce thought it was for the best."

This was what Ann had feared. Total acquiescence to Royce.

"Then you went along with him. Why, Mama?"

"We didn't want to," Lucille replied.

"Couldn't you have sent me another letter? Or called me from town? Something at least."

"Our hands were tied."

Ann was trying to control the rage churning inside, but she was fighting a losing battle. "Who tied your hands, Mama?"

"Nobody tied them," Jack declared. "We had other things to consider. We're making our move here."

"Thanks to him, I missed my grandma's funeral. I wasn't even told about her death until a week later."

Everyone knew Ann was right, but it was difficult for any of them to talk.

"Ann, I know it was a terrible thing," Jack said. "Bear with us."

"What's he got on you?" Ann cried. "What are you all afraid of? You won't stand up to him face-to-face, and you won't make a move behind his back. What are you afraid of?"

"She doesn't understand," Jack said to Lucille.

"I sure as hell don't, but I'm trying to," Ann said. "What was he thinking of? What did he hope to show other than pure meanness? Was he trying to teach me a lesson?"

"Maybe he just wants to show you who's boss," Lucille replied.

"He's been trying to do that since the day I met him," Ann said.

"Everybody's scared, Miss Ann," Olga said.

"You don't live with him. We do," Lucille echoed.

"Ann, we're sorry," Jack said. "You mean the world to us. We let you down."

"I know you don't understand, Miss Ann," Olga said. "But it's how things are."

Ann could see their distress. It was true she didn't understand. But they were her parents, and in spite of everything, she loved them.

"How was Grandma's funeral?" she asked, in an effort to change the subject.

"A beautiful ceremony," Lucille said. "The whole town turned out for Mama. Hundreds of people, some we didn't even know, covered the entire hill at Riverside."

"Reverend Bidwell went off on a tangent during the eulogy," Jack said. "He started out praising Mother Carson and wound up saying that Royce and the girls had ushered in a new era in Winfield."

"A new era of what?"

"That's Bidwell for you," Jack said. "Maybe he can rein it in during the memorial service."

"What about this lawyer?" Ann said

"Before we get to that, I want to share something with you," Jack said. "I know you don't think so much of your papa right now. But I've got to tell you."

Ann wasn't as angry at Jack as she had been when they left town. She felt more sorry for him.

"Your letter. That was a very nice thing you did for Mother Carson."

"What letter? What are you talking about?"

"The one you wrote to her your first year at school. Where you told her 'if you're feeling sad, think of me. I am always here for you.'"

Ann had almost forgotten the note she had written to give Lady Ann some momentary reassurance two years ago.

"It was a beautiful thing. That letter meant the world to her."

Ann remembered the conversation with Lady Ann beside the front window. She had wanted to reach out to her grandmother and hadn't, so she then wrote the note and mailed it from Coon Falls.

"She carried that letter with her every day," Lucille said. "In her purse. Then in her pocket till it got ragged around the edges."

"She loved that letter, Miss Ann," Olga said. "I'd find her sitting in her chair reading it when Royce was out of the house."

"When she died, we put it in the coffin," Jack said. "Wherever your grandma is right now, she's still got that letter with her."

"I'm glad," Ann said. "Thank you." She was touched by what Jack had told her. She wanted to feel something more, but she couldn't.

"We're keeping on top of things back here," Jack said. "Don't you worry about us."

"Who is this lawyer, Papa?"

"His name's Collinsen. Edward Collinsen. Fine young man. He tells us we may have a case if we can find Beulah Jensen. If we can persuade her to talk, we might be able to prove that Mother Carson signed the will and even the power of attorney under duress."

"Do you think that would work?" Ann asked. "You're putting a lot of hope in one suggestion."

"It's all we've got," Lucille said. "At least we've found a lawyer who's not afraid to go up against Royce."

"He's not afraid. We can make book on that," Jack said.

"How do you know for sure, Papa?"

"He told us so. Arabella Mansfield couldn't have done better herself."

"But who is he?"

"A young man, as I mentioned. High ethical standards. Good attorney. Sings in the choir on Sunday. At Lutheran Church in Council Bluffs, he's considered an extraordinary human being."

"That's good for the choir. But what about the courtroom?"

Jack didn't seem to hear. The words kept pouring out. "When I met him, he listened to my every word. Weighed every thought. And when I gave him a five-hundred-dollar deposit to take our case, he said, 'It's a privilege to take your case.' You hear, Ann? He said it was a privilege. We're going to be just fine."

As Ann listened to her father's assurances, she was increasingly disappointed. The family's inner fortitude seemed to be eroding—that same fortitude in which she had put so much faith. Their entire case was based on accusing Royce of something they thought he might have done. And their legal champion was considered an extraordinary human being by his church choir. Ann found herself wondering how Arabella Mansfield really would have handled it.

"So far, I've managed to meet Collinsen at his office. Tomorrow he's coming to Winfield."

"We've been trying to figure out some place private where we could meet with him," Lucille said. "We settled on the county farm."

"Why the county farm?" Ann asked.

"He can't come to Carson Manor. And there are eyes and ears all over in town. The county farm is the last place anyone would think of."

"I suppose." Somehow Ann couldn't share their optimism.

"We'll go visit Zachary this afternoon," Lucille said. "We'll tell the folks out there we're coming back in the morning."

"That's good. I missed a visit the last time I was here," Ann said.

They reached another crossroads. Lucille turned right onto a rougher dirt road.

"I want to show you something," she said to Ann. "I want you to see what else is going on."

Ann recognized the passing landscape. Wire fences, drab brown soil, and a gun-metal sky. She knew where they were headed.

"Are we going to the Northeast Quarter, Mama?"

"That, and something else."

They continued driving for a few minutes and soon were approaching the houses of a small farm on the left. Lucille slowed down.

"This is Section Two," Ann said.

"Or what's left of it," Jack said.

"Royce moved the Hudsens in here to become gentlemen farmers," Lucille said. "If that's the case, somebody fell off the train."

"Look at that, Miss Ann. Just look at that," Olga said.

Across the road was a section of land with a one-story house and a barn. Both buildings were chipped and worn down—the result of little upkeep and less use. The yard around it was overrun with weeds. Scattered in the strands of decaying foliage was a collection of scraps and junk—a rusted cart here, a couple of broken wagon wheels there—jutting out of the cold ground like some skeletal decoration. Beyond were several open crates and neglected farm implements.

"It looks like a riverbank after a flood," Ann said.

Beyond the house and barn, the field had an equally strange appearance. It was half harvested and then deserted—as if the owners had abandoned their efforts, letting the entire property slide into ruin.

"It's terrible, Miss Ann," Olga said. "They don't do a thing out here."

"They're ruining the land," Ann said.

"They're on the property, and there's nothing we can do," Lucille said.

"Collinsen will get them off," Jack interjected.

"Amazing," Ann said. "Grandpa wouldn't have believed it."

"He sure wouldn't, Miss Ann."

"Have a little faith in our plan," Jack said. "To get this far, we've had to compromise. We didn't like it, but all that's going to change. Have a little faith in your papa."

She was taking in the decay of the property when she spotted some movement at the corner of the drive. Goliath, the bull terrier, looked at her from the weeds. He was scuffed and dirty and shivering in the cold.

"That poor little dog," Olga said. "I'm surprised he's still alive, the way they treat him. I saw that Jago boy throw a shovel at him the other day."

Ann was out of the car and crossing over to the dog.

"Ann," Lucille cautioned.

"Don't go on the property. It's dangerous," Jack said.

Ann moved cautiously toward the little terrier. He stepped out of the weeds timidly and looked at her. He was shivering all over, but curious to see what Ann was up to. As Ann drew closer, he scuttled a few feet up the drive and stood to stare back at her.

"It's OK. I'm not going to hit you," Ann said.

Ann crouched down and extended her hand.

"Miss Ann!"

"Ann! Get back in the car!"

Ann held out her hand. "It's OK... It's OK... I'm not going to hurt you."

The little dog stopped.

"It's OK. It's OK."

"Ann!"

"That's not right to do to a dog. Lock you out of the house on a cold day. It's not right."

Ann stepped forward with her hand extended. In a flash, Goliath bolted and ran for the house, scrunching low and disappearing beneath the porch.

Ann watched where the terrier vanished. He never showed himself again.

"Ann, you shouldn't have done that," Lucille said. "You don't know if those people were home or not. That Kurt and his crazy son."

"They weren't home," Ann said. "There's nobody but that little dog."

Ann got back in the car. Lucille drove about a hundred feet up the road before she stopped again. Already the soil was darker and richer—even in the drab fall weather. All the corn had been harvested, and the furrows seemed to have retained their moisture and richness—just waiting for the warmer seasons to arrive.

"The Northeast Quarter," Ann said in a whisper.

Nobody spoke for several minutes. They were regarding this spot of land with the hushed reverence of visitors to a cathedral.

"Sometimes we just drive out here and look at it," Lucille said. "It gives us strength and perseverance."

Even in the winter chill, the quarter had more life in it than all the other fields around.

"I had forgotten its majesty," Ann said.

"Majesty?" Jack asked with a quizzical smile. "That's a good word for it."

"Grandpa knew what he was doing when he started here."

"A field. A farm. A town. An empire, Miss Ann...It all started here," Olga said.

They sat in silence. A breeze was blowing through the stalks, but nobody noticed.

Jack glanced at his pocket watch. "We better get back."

"We've had a nice little side trip," Lucille said. "Now it's back to the grim realities."

"Lord, deliver us," muttered Olga.

27

Twenty minutes later, they were pulling into the driveway of Carson Manor. The first thing they noticed was Kurt Hudsen's dilapidated car sprawled diagonally across the front parking area. Jago was standing alongside the car holding a bouquet that had already withered in the cold. Ever the odd man out, he was staring wistfully at the front door of the house.

"Oh Lord, they're here," Lucille murmured.

The front door opened, and Carol appeared: cool, efficient, emotionless. She was in her twenties now, but already she seemed middle-aged.

"Olga!" she bellowed. "Where were you?" She sounded like a miniature Fairchild.

"She was with us, Carol," Lucille replied.

"Her services were required here."

"I'm sorry, Miss Carol," Olga said.

"Just so you know, I had to fix tea myself."

"That's mighty unfortunate, Carol." Jack said. Ann was pleased her papa still had some wit about him.

"Miss Carol?" Jago ventured tentatively, clutching the bouquet.

"Ann, just so you know, there isn't room for you in the manor," Carol announced. "You will be residing in the gatehouse."

"Why is that?" Ann inquired.

"New arrangements."

"Couldn't we be a little more flexible?" Lucille asked.

"I'll be fine, Mama," Ann said.

Jago held out the limp bouquet again. "Miss Carol?"

"What?"

"Does Miss Cassie know I'm out here?"

"Of course she knows, Jago. Why do you think she's staying in the house?"

The front door opened again. Chamberlin stepped out, followed by Kurt Hudsen and a very uneasy Cassie.

Jago brightened at the sight of her.

"So you're here," Chamberlin said, gesturing to the arrivals.

Ann studied the Chamberlins. During her time away, she had placed her true feelings for them in the back of her mind, but now that they were in front of her, she was determined to keep her temper under control.

"Hello, girlie," Kurt drawled. "Haven't see you lately."

Jago waited until he could stand it no longer and then darted straight for Cassie, who recoiled in disgust.

"Miss Cassie," Jago said expectantly, holding out the flowers.

"What...what is it?" Cassie said, leaning away as if they were putrid.

"I tried to discourage him," Carol said.

"I brought you these, Miss Cassie," Jago said, thrusting the flowers at her again.

A look of revulsion crossed Cassie's face. "What am I supposed to do with that?" She took the flowers and searched frantically for a place to drop them.

"Oh, they're cold...and clammy. They're awful."

"Olga, take that...wilted clump and do something with it," Carol snapped.

"Yes, Miss Carol," Olga said, taking the flowers and going into the house.

Ann found the scene grotesquely funny, but she couldn't laugh because Cassie was genuinely terrified and Jago's devotion had shut out any sense of the reality around them.

"I want to say something, Miss Cassie," Jago began.

"Please don't..."

"I know you're a great lady and all..."

"Face it, Jago," Carol declared loudly. "Before you make a bigger fool of yourself. You're a field hand. You're outside help. Unless you're master of the house, my sister has no time for you."

"No time." Cassie gasped as though she were breathing polluted air. "No time..."

"I know, but I gotta say this," he continued urgently. "Miss Cassie. I'm not much now, but I got a bright future. I can get a job in Kansas City. In the stockyards. I know some days I'd be shovelin' cow dung, but not on weekends. I know the dung gets in your boots, but I'm not that kind of man..."

Carol burst out laughing. Jago appeared stricken.

"Why are you laughin' at me, Miss Carol? Why?"

The mocking and raucous laughter continued.

"I suppose I'm funny to a great lady like you."

"We better go, boy," Kurt said.

"Why is she laughin' at me, Papa?"

As he stood there, hearing Carol's boisterous cackle, his hurt suddenly exploded.

"It's them, ain't it?" he said, glaring at Ann and her parents. "It's because of her comin' home. Colonel's granddaughter comes home, and they got your thinkin' all confused. That's what it is."

"We haven't said a thing, Jago," Jack said.

"You think this is funny?" he snarled at Ann. "You think I'm funny?"

"Don't yell at me. I just got here," Ann said.

"Well, you damn well shoulda stayed away."

With a look of desperation, he turned back to Chamberlin.

"Mr. Royce. Please, I want to ask permission. Official permission. My intentions are honorable and true, and I brought flowers to prove it. I'm...I'm askin' permission to call on Miss Cassie."

"Nope," Carol said sternly. "Nope. Nope. Nope...none of that."

"Please say no, Papa," Cassie wailed. "Please say no."

Chamberlin was amused at Jago's pigheadedness, but he also had his interests to protect. "Jago, you've got to face facts here. Both my daughters said no."

"They don't know what they're sayin'..."

"Don't interrupt me. You're a good man in the field—even parts of the back yard. But among people of class and culture, you couldn't tell a fingerbowl from a spittoon."

Jago was crushed. He had not expected to feel such hurt. "I'm better than that, Mr. Royce. You know I'm better than that."

"You asked. I'm telling you."

"Got your answer now?" Kurt asked.

"It sure ain't the one I wanted."

"Son, it's time we leave." It was one of the few times he had called Jago "son" instead of "boy."

Kurt and Jago started for the car. Kurt cupped his hands around his mouth and let loose his cry of "Maaww!"

The sound of a multitude of paws hitting the soil came from one end of the manor house as the three hounds converged on the car. Kurt held the door open so they could pile into the backseat.

"Everybody on board?" Chamberlin asked.

Ann watched the car back out of the driveway. She wondered what Chamberlin was thinking. He certainly wouldn't ban them from Carson Manor because Jago terrified his daughter. He would always need them to enforce his transactions around Franklin County. Everything he did had a reason. Everything was part of a long-term plan. This thought reminded Ann that she had some questions of her own.

"Why didn't you notify me of Grandma's death?" she demanded.

"What?" Royce said, startled at her tone.

"Why didn't you notify me?"

"I notified you at the proper time."

"I missed her funeral. I'd like to know why."

Lucille and Jack were regarding the growing tension with some unease. They had not expected the situation to heat up so quickly.

"Ann, maybe we can talk about this later," Jack said.

Ann knew she would have to watch herself. The adults had their strategies, and she had a knack for speaking up without thinking. Then she noted Royce's familiar expression: the cold half smile that appeared when he was about to make a move. Something was starting up.

"Uh, Jack," he purred, "we have some time now."

"For what?" Jack heard the solicitous tone in his voice. "What is it, Royce?"

"You wanted to talk," he said, as Cassie disappeared into the house. "About the estate, Jack. Soil enrichment next year. You said you wanted to talk."

Ann saw the power game immediately. Jack was fine alone with his family, but with Royce, it was another matter.

"Papa, you can talk to him later," she said.

"Yes, we'll do it another time, Royce," Jack said.

"But it was so important to you," Royce said.

Ann saw that Royce's eyes were on her and not Jack. The battle lines had been drawn long ago. This demonstration was for her benefit, and Jack was the pawn. Royce was planning to get him drunk.

"I want to spend some time with my family," Jack said.

"You can do that later," Royce countered. "I insist."

"I'm real sorry to hear that, Royce. But my daughter's home."

Ann saw her father smiling back at Royce. He was hesitant but standing his ground, and he was even returning the same half smile. Ann felt a spark of encouragement because someone on her side was finally standing up to Royce.

Cassie appeared in the doorway with the bottle.

"You'll have my undivided attention, right there in the study," Royce offered.

There was a silence. The Chamberlins had not expected this.

"I have an idea," Jack said. "Instead of tonight, I'd like to have our talk tomorrow at the bank."

"Why?"

"I'd like to include Fred and Patrick. I value their opinion. We'll use the big map in your office."

Royce was staring questioningly at Jack. This show of confidence was something new.

"It's important for the estate," Jack said. "They're available tomorrow afternoon, and if I'm not mistaken, so are you."

"You've been busy," Royce said.

Jack glanced over at his daughter with a twinkle in his eye. "I'll see you at dinner. I'm spending some time with my family."

Ann took her suitcase and started for the gatehouse. She had not been this proud of her father for many years.

28

THE GATEHOUSE HAD BEEN CONSTRUCTED A long time ago as residence for a carriage driver and was essentially a glorified shack—a bedroom the size of a closet and a cramped sitting room with a front door. With a single light in the sitting room, it had minimal electricity that fed off the main current to the manor house.

Ann missed her grandmother. If Colonel Wallace had provided the life-force for Carson Manor, Lady Ann had been its heart. Ann had not realized how much she'd missed her until this visit.

Late that afternoon she and her parents bundled up with scarves and top-coats and drove over to the county farm to see Zachary. The sky was dark and cloudy, as if it were about to snow. A gloom seemed to hang over the drab landscape like a mist.

Ann was still proud of the way Jack had handled Royce. She hoped this was a new beginning. It was as if some of her grandmother's courage and spirit were still alive at Carson Manor.

"Have a little faith in your old man," Jack had said. "I'll be ready for Royce at the bank tomorrow afternoon. Give you time out here with Collinsen."

"We're almost forgetting about Zachary," Ann said. "How's he taking Grandma being gone?"

"Same as the rest of us."

"How did he handle the funeral?"

Lucille slowly shook her head.

"He went to the funeral, didn't he?" Ann was incredulous. "You mean, he didn't go?"

"Royce decided he should stay out at the farm."

"What's he got to say about it?"

"Carol and Cassie felt that Zachary's grief would upset the well-wishers."

"How is Zachary now?"

"Confused...hurt."

"Poor Zachary."

⁓

Ann could not stay angry at her parents for very long. A return home to Carson Manor reminded her that Jack and Lucille were coping with the situation the best way they could.

The county farm was an old three-story building set in the middle of what was once working farmland. Back then it was known as the Browning place. Browning was one of Winfield's original founders—along with Colonel Carson. But decades ago, Browning had died and his family donated the farm and property to Franklin County. It was managed by a man named Horace Hester who visited the premises once a month.

The building itself was bleached and worn by time and the elements. There were five wooden armchairs scattered about in front of the building. The curtains in every smudged and unwashed window were white—the sort of functional material found in hospital. A faded sign in front read HARVEST HORIZONS.

The icy breeze stung their cheeks as they drove up. They got out of the car and into the building as quickly as they could. Once inside, a rush of humidity and heat immediately enveloped them, so they removed their coats.

Down the hallway, there was a muffled cry of one of the residents.

"Poor soul," Lucille said.

They were in the middle of the waiting area that had a few chairs and a sofa off to their left and a reception desk directly in front of them. The walls were a functional knotted pine. Sitting on the chairs were two old women in hospital dressing gowns. One was staring vacantly into space while the other looked absently over at Ann and Lucille and then turned straight ahead.

Ann recognized the second woman. "It's Mrs. Sloat," she said.

She ventured forward a few steps. "Hello, Mrs. Sloat."

The woman glanced absently at Ann.

"It's me. Ann Hardy."

"She don't know you no more," said a voice from the sofa. Ann looked over just as Bonnie, one of the attendants, was sitting up sleepily. She had been dozing, and until she spoke, Ann had not noticed her.

"Fact is, she don't know nobody no more," Bonnie said. "Nobody at all."

Tracy Stabb, a nurse and acting receptionist, entered from the hallway.

"Hello, Tracy," Jack said. "We've come to see Zachary."

"I'll get him," Bonnie said.

Bonnie stood up and stretched. She shuffled drowsily up the hallway. Again, there was the same muffled cry from the residents' area.

"That's Old Mrs. Schrader," Tracy said. "Somebody needs to sit her down and give her a good stern talking to. Tell her to quit fussin' and stop that yellin'."

"How's Zachary?" Lucille asked.

"Fine," Tracy said. "I just wish he'd mingle with the other residents. Every time I look around, he's always sitting over here or over there, just like a wallflower."

For a third time, the muffled cry floated out into the lobby.

"He doesn't enter in. Why, the other afternoon at tea time, everyone was sitting over there being as sociable as can be, and there was Zachary over here, all by his lonesome. So I went over to him and I said, 'Zachary, there's all kinds of people you could talk to, but you don't. You just sit on the side all by yourself. Don't be such a wallflower, Zachary.'"

"He's been mourning his mother's death," Jack said.

"Oh no. He's been standoffish ever since he got here—just sits there all the time."

"He'll join in when he's ready," Ann said.

"And when's that gonna be?" Tracy retorted. "Five years from now?"

"He may think you're criticizing him."

"I'm not criticizing anyone," Tracy said. "I'm just trying to help him."

"Here we are" came Bonnie's voice from the hallway. She and Zachary walked over to them. Zachary was clad in the same hospital gown as the other residents. He seemed haggard and dazed. His eyes were fixed on the floor ahead of him, but when he saw Lucille and Jack, his expression brightened.

"Hello, Zachary. I told you we'd come to see you," Jack said.

"Lucille…Jack."

"And you've got a visitor."

His eyes moved over to Ann. "Ann?"

"It's me, Zachary," Ann said, crossing to him.

He opened his arms and gave her a hug.

"Ann," he said with a full smile. "It's Ann."

"It's me. I've missed you, Zachary," Ann said.

"Everyone came. Jack and Lucille and Ann, but no Mama."

"Awww, that's sweet," Tracy drawled. "He misses his mama."

"How's everything been, Zachary?" Ann asked.

"Everything's been fine, hasn't it, Zachary?" Tracy replied enthusiastically.

"Uh-huh," Zachary said lethargically.

"Are you happy here?" Ann asked.

"Of course he's happy," Tracy announced. "Happy as Christmas morning, aren't you, Zachary? Remember what we say? Happy is as happy does." She seemed determined to be part of the family visit.

Lucille cast a quick glance at Ann. Ann caught on right away. Nurse Stabb would have to be worked out of the conversation.

"How's the family, Tracy?" Lucille asked.

"What? I don't have a family. You know that."

"Don't mind them," Ann said quietly to Zachary. "Let's go over here to the window."

They started across the lobby. "How have you been?"

"I miss Mama."

"She knows we love her, Zachary."

"I wanted to say good-bye."

Lucille had positioned herself between Tracy and her view of Ann and Zachary. Tracy was attempting to see around Lucille, while carrying on a conversation with her.

"What are they talking about over there?" Tracy inquired.

"You know with your cousin in Chicago now, you ought to come to tea at the Winfield Women's Club," Lucille said.

"Why would I want to do that?"

"Expand your horizons," Jack said.

Tracy was squirming now, determined to see around Lucille or Jack one way or another.

"My horizons are just fine," she said.

"Ann," Zachary was saying, "when can I come home?"

"What's he say?" Tracy cried. "What's he say about home?"

"He's saying how this place has become a home away from home," Lucille said.

"He wasn't saying that." Suddenly, a half decibel louder, Tracy said, "What were you saying, Zachary?"

"They're just talking, Tracy," Jack said. "Take it easy."

"I'm asking what they were saying."

"Let's go see your room," Ann said, taking Zachary by the hand. They started out of the lobby and up the hallway.

"Where are they going?" Tracy exclaimed.

Ann and Zachary were out of the lobby and starting down the hallway. It seemed dank and humid.

"I try to get along, Ann," he said. "I try to do my share."

"I know you do."

"I want to come home, Ann."

Ann stopped and took Zachary by the arm. "I know you do. And I know you're doing your share here."

Zachary seemed amazed. "You do?"

"Yes, I do. Let's make a promise, you and me, that someday we'll both come home."

"Yeah, yeah, we'll both come home, Ann."

"Someday, Zachary. That'll be our promise."

"Zachary?" a familiar voice called down the hallway. "Where's Zachary?"

Ann heard her parents' voices trying to placate Tracy Stabb.

"Zachary?" Zachary?" the voice called once again, louder and louder. Tracy stood at the head of the hallway. "Oh, there you are. I thought you'd run off."

"We were socializing," Ann said.

"It's not the same thing. Socializing with family and being sociable." Tracy looked to Zachary. "Zachary, we're about to get ready for tea. I hope you'll join in with the others. We don't want you to be a wallflower."

Tracy extended her hand. Zachary had a pained expression.

"Better go with her," Ann said.

Ann followed Tracy and Zachary up the hall. When they were back in the lobby, Lucille gave Zachary a hug. "We'll be out to see you again tomorrow. You take care now."

Zachary watched Ann and her parents as they put on their coats and scarves. Ann looked back at him. He was grinning.

"Someday, Ann," he said.

29

DINNER WAS ALWAYS UNCOMFORTABLE AT THE Carson Manor. Usually, Royce and his daughters would talk while Ann and her family answered when spoken to.

Ann rarely entered into the discourse. Whenever she did, Carol was always ready with a correction or a snide remark.

Tonight's dinner was chicken, mashed potatoes, a side serving of biscuits, and the traditional starter of cream of barley soup, one of Ann's favorites. It reminded her of happier times at the manor house before the colonel died.

The conversation began without much ceremony. Then it began to change.

"How are your studies, Ann?" Royce asked.

"Good enough."

"Is that all?"

"It's school, Royce."

Royce stared at Ann, and Ann looked back at him. They seemed to have this conversation every time she came home.

"What are they teaching you?" he continued.

To Ann this always seemed like a strange question given that both his daughters were products of a Clearwater education.

"Didn't they tell you?" Ann answered, gesturing to the girls.

"I'm interested in what you have to say."

"This isn't about school. It never has been," Ann thought. "Typical of Royce, he asks one thing, but he's listening for something else."

"At Clearwater they teach us to be proper maidens who know their place in the world," she said.

"I'm sure there's more than that," Jack said.

"There is, Papa. But that's what we're left with at the end of the day."

"But Royce has gone to considerable expense to send you there. You must have some kind of book learning, like the three Rs. Don't you learn the three Rs?"

"Actually, I don't feel like talking about it," Ann said. "It's been a long day. I missed my grandma's funeral. All this takes some getting used to."

"I've been thinking about that," Royce said. "Maybe I can make it up to you in some way."

Both Lucille and Jack glanced up from their plates. Making amends was out of character for Royce Chamberlin.

"How?" Ann asked.

"Indulge me first. I was asking about your studies."

"We have English," Ann began. "French conversation, feminine ethics, feminine thought, discourse on arts within the home, posture class, and nature walks. Just the sort of things that prepare a woman for the rigors of life."

"How do you feel about that?"

"I don't have much choice in the matter," she said.

"If you did have a choice, what would you do? Would you want to study something that interested you?"

"Anybody would want to do that."

"I spoke with Nadia Fairchild. She shared some of your responses on the Necessities for Life examinations."

"You mean the Necessaries for Living exercises," Cassie said.

"Oh, those things," Ann said, trying to conceal a laugh. "We just write what we feel. Whatever pops into our heads. We come back from the holiday, and they shove those questions in our faces before we're even unpacked."

"I hated them, Papa," Cassie continued. "I have no use for them. All those questions about adding and subtracting in situations we'd never encounter in real life. For every question, I'd answer, 'Ask my Papa.' That's exactly what I said. 'Ask my Papa.'"

Cassie seemed unusually giddy tonight. Ann couldn't tell if she was tipsy or not.

"And what did you do?" Royce asked Ann.

"I answered them the best I could," Ann said.

"According to Nadia Fairchild, your responses showed you have an aptitude for business," Royce said. "Some interest in farming as well. That you're independent. A leader, not a follower. A manager, not a worker. That in the scheme of life, you want to run things."

"They showed all that?" Ann asked innocently. "Who'd have known?"

"They also showed you want to have a say in how things work."

"I don't want to run things," Ann said. "I just like to know how things are run."

"And that is what sets you apart from the other girls at Clearwater."

"Is that a bad thing?" Lucille asked. "What's this about?"

Ann knew her parents were trying to make sense of the conversation. They were curious but maintaining their reserve.

"It isn't that we don't want to know anything," Cassie trilled. "We just feel that the thinking and doing should be left to others."

"So I have an aptitude," Ann said. "What does that mean?"

"A few years ago your grandmother gave me a chance. Perhaps now I can return the favor."

"In what way?" Lucille asked.

"I'm wondering if there isn't some way to develop Ann's aptitudes and interests. Special talents should not be ignored. With proper education, we could put them to use right here.

"You mean another school?"

Ann noticed her parents were affected by this display of generosity. The words were persuasive. She hoped they were not being taken in, especially right before the meeting tomorrow.

Royce assumed the humble mien he had used when he was courting Lady Ann.

"When Lady Ann left us, I realized something very important and so obvious I blame myself for not seeing it sooner. Sitting here at the table, we're no longer two families. We're one family now."

All at once, an image flashed in Ann's mind. Royce Chamberlin and Brubaker hovering over Lady Ann's death bed, clutching her arm, and trying to force her to sign a change in the will before she died.

"We've had our share of disagreements, but the estate is bigger than all of us. We should realize that. We're one family with one purpose. The times are changing, and we need to keep up."

"So where does that put me?"

"It would put you in a position of responsibility—managerial and custodial responsibility."

The word *custodial* stuck out to Ann. At Clearwater, the handyman was called the custodian. With Royce's soothing tone and that word, a picture was beginning to form in Ann's mind.

"Custodial?" Ann asked.

"Yes."

"What about Carol and Cassie?"

"What about us?" Carol fired back.

"While I'm being educated, what are they going to do?"

"They will be taken care of. The offer is for you."

The expression *taken care of* offered Ann another clue; it meant leaving the work to others.

"We should develop your natural talents, Ann."

"I appreciate that," Ann said, still sizing up the situation.

"She does," Jack said. "She certainly does."

"If I do this, I'd like to include some study of law."

Royce stiffened. He had not expected this. "Why?"

"I should learn about the legalities of what I'm doing, shouldn't I?"

"Are you implying that what I do is not legal?"

"No, nobody's saying anything like that, Royce," Jack said. "Are you, Ann?"

Ann smiled. "I'm saying that if you're offering to further my education, I'd like a little legal development as well. You never know when it might come in handy."

"And my answer is when you have a good offer, don't let it become a missed opportunity," Royce stated firmly.

"She's not questioning you, Royce," Lucille said.

Ann put her fork on her plate. "I do want to ask again. What about Carol and Cassie?"

"And I said you leave that to me."

"You're supposed to support us in our old age," Cassie said with a giggle.

"That's what I thought it was," Ann said.

Everyone sat in embarrassed silence. Royce was scowling at Cassie, and Carol's jaw was clenched in indignation. Cassie maintained her gay expression until she noticed all eyes were upon her. Jack and Lucille were stunned at how easily Ann had pulled the scheme out into the open. It was an explosive situation at a delicate time—right before the meeting tomorrow afternoon. Everything depended on what Ann would say next.

Ann maintained her smile. "Well, now we're all clear on what we're talking about. I'll just say that I'll think on it, Royce."

She placed her napkin beside her plate. "As I said, it's been a long trip. I think I'll call it a day. Good night, everyone."

She stood up and walked out of the room.

Royce watched her leave. She was an enemy, but she had the qualities of honesty and strength he had hoped his daughters might learn, and which he knew now they would never possess. What hurt him most at that moment was that he knew there was nothing he could do about it.

30

ANN THOUGHT SHE WAS TIRED ENOUGH to fall asleep right away. Instead, she drifted in and out of periods of drowsiness, her thoughts focused on what had happened at dinner and anticipation of the events that would occur tomorrow.

Her mind kept returning to the image of Royce and Brubaker in Lady Ann's room at the hospital.

"I'm going to have a look at that will," she said to herself. "I'll do it tomorrow morning. Mama and I have some errands in town, followed by an appointment with Brubaker. While Mama's at the dry goods, I'll slip away and see Brubaker first." She shut her eyes and hoped she would get some rest.

She was awakened by a noise. It was quick and it was over. Ann sat up to listen. There was no commotion from the yard or the road out front. The only sound was a tapping from the stove as the embers died. Outside, there was a soft breeze and the scratching of a tree branch on the roof. Whatever it was, it had been loud enough to startle her.

She got up to look out the window. In the moonlight, the manor house looked like a caricature of itself etched in charcoal.

"Everything looks still out there," Ann said to herself. "Maybe I was dreaming about being awakened and that woke me up."

She saw a shaft of light appear along one side of the front door of the house that began as a tiny amber slit and slowly became wider. Ann could make out the silhouette of one the girls hovering just inside the doorway—Carol.

"What's she doing?" Ann thought. "Maybe she heard it, too."

Carol appeared to be looking beyond the gatehouse in the direction of the road. She didn't appear curious—just watchful, like a sentry on guard duty.

"She opens the door and just stands there waiting—waiting for what? What could she be looking at?" Ann wondered.

Ann crossed the sitting room to the window in the bedroom. She pulled the curtain and looked out at the road and fields beyond. Across the road the ghostly furrows and scraggly remnants of the harvest stood out against the black sky.

All at once, she felt a chill. On the edge of the road beside the field were Royce Chamberlin and Cassie. Standing side by side in the night air, their eyes were riveted on the gatehouse. They were not smiling, or talking, or even moving; they were just looking.

Ann pulled the curtain closed and watched through a crack. In the cold night air, Chamberlin appeared like a stone statue in a cemetery, impervious to the elements. With her topcoat and scarf around her face, Cassie was like a wraith—more wispy than flesh and blood, but sharing her father's interest in what was in front of them. They remained in position for what seemed like minutes.

"What in the world are they doing?" Ann thought. "Olga says nighttime is when the creepy-crawlies come out. They look right at home."

Finally, Royce took Cassie's arm, and they began to walk in a leisurely manner up the road. From all appearances, they might have been taking a promenade in Pomphrey Park on a Sunday afternoon.

"It's the middle of the night, and they're out for a stroll," Ann said to herself. "It must be thirty degrees out there. Don't they even feel the cold?"

They walked several steps more and turned to start back. Ann remembered Carol. She crossed back into the sitting room. As she peered around the curtain, she saw that Carol was still waiting in the doorway.

"There they are, walking arm in arm, and here's Carol, holding the door for them. Whatever they're doing, Carol's not a part of it. She never is. No wonder she's angry all the time. I could almost feel sorry for her if she weren't so mean."

The stove tapped again.

Ann noticed that Carol's attention had turned to the window where she was standing. Suddenly, Carol went out the front door and headed across the yard to the gatehouse.

Ann immediately checked the door. It was locked. As Carol's footsteps grew louder, Ann backed across the room into the shadows. A few seconds later, Carol stood in front of the window. She pressed her face against the glass in an effort to pick up any noise or movement inside.

"She's not here because she saw me," Ann thought. "She's looking to see if I'm up."

Carol continued to peer into the window. Her pudgy features were distorted against the glass. Finally she stalked back across the yard to the manor house.

"That midnight stroll... I guess I wasn't supposed to see it," Ann thought.

Carol opened the front door and disappeared inside.

Ann moved away from the window and across the sitting room, where she picked up a tiny clock on the table. She held it up in the light from outside. It was 1:45 a.m.

"Sheez, it'll be dawn in a few hours."

Ann returned to the bedroom. Looking outside, she saw that Chamberlin and Cassie were gone. She returned to the sitting room to look. The front door of the manor house was closed. Everything outside was still.

Ann waited for a long time without hearing anything—no footsteps, no sound, nothing. She finally took a chair and placed it under the door handle, which she hoped would prevent anyone from opening the door. Then she sat down in the sitting-room chair and tried to go sleep.

31

THE FOLLOWING MORNING, ANN AND LUCILLE began the drive into town. After they had been away from Carson Manor for a few minutes, Ann related her experience during the night.

"How bizarre. They're a really strange family," Lucille said.

"Doesn't Cassie have any boyfriends?"

"Neither girl does. It's just them and Royce, tied together in a knot. Of the two, Royce seems to favor Cassie, but Carol's devoted to him just the same."

"You'd think with them living in Carson Manor, we'd have no end of balls and soirees."

"Nope."

"Maybe Royce scares away any potential suitors."

"I don't think so," Lucille said. "It's not for lack of opportunity. I don't think they're interested."

Ann pictured Royce and Cassie strolling in the dark of night out in front of the house.

"It's like they're only interested in each other. I think it's peculiar, Mama."

"How about you?" Lucille asked. "Do you have any gentleman callers?"

Ann laughed. "Not around Clearwater. School says it's preparing us for womanhood. I say they're teaching us to be old maids. They're having a little trouble with me."

"It won't be much longer, Ann."

"I hope not. I'm not working for the girls after he's gone."

"No one's asking you to."

"He did. Where did he get the gall to come up with that idea?"

Lucille glanced over with a worried expression. "Try to hang on, Ann. It's only a little while longer. Try not to antagonize him."

Ann wondered how a person could win a fight if she were worried all the time about angering or offending her opponent.

Shortly after, they were driving up Market Street. Ann felt at home—if only for a few minutes. Nothing had changed. The only difference she noticed was the presence of more cars. There seemed to be an even distribution of wagons and automobiles—even though the total number of both for each side of the thoroughfare was a single-digit number.

They had an appointment with Fred Brubaker at ten. Lucille thought with a routine appointment at the bank and lawyers, nobody would suspect a meeting with a second attorney that afternoon. Ann went along with the scheme, but she had her own plan. Ann told her mother she was going to Sidford's Flowers, and while Lucille went to the dry goods store, Ann walked over to the bank.

Sonya the teller glanced up impassively from her seat in the cage.

"Good morning. May I help you?"

"I'm here to see Fred Brubaker. I'm a little early."

"Do you have an account here?" Sonya asked.

"Yes, I do."

"I don't believe I know you."

"I'm Ann Hardy."

"Has Mr. Brubaker ever made your acquaintance?"

Before Ann could answer, the door to the spare room opened, and Van Burin squeezed out. His self-generated vivacity seemed more forced than usual. Ann also noticed his hair. Over the years it had grown darker. It hadn't changed colors exactly, but the flaming red was easing into a grubby brown.

"Ann, Ann," he said. "How good to see you."

"Mr. Van Burin."

"Sonya, this is Ann Hardy. She's a longtime customer," Van Burin said. "Almost family. Ann left us to go to the same exclusive private school that Royce's daughters attended. She grew up here, but now she's out hobnobbing with the rich and famous. Isn't that right, Ann?"

"We don't hobnob at Clearwater," Ann said.

Ann noticed another change. There was an edge in Van Burin's voice—a little resentment, a little condescension. It was as if he had swallowed all of Royce's elaborations of the many virtues of Clearwater School and had begun to hold it against Ann.

"We missed you at your grandmother's funeral," Van Burin said.

"I missed being there," Ann replied.

"Oh. Uh. Well, about your grandmother. You knew it was bound to happen,

Ann. She was getting along in years. You knew that. You knew it was bound to happen."

As Van Burin prattled on, he offered no words of sympathy for Ann's loss. In fact, he hadn't even asked how she was feeling. Something was definitely different.

"You here to see Fred? He said you and Lucille had an appointment."

At that moment, Brubaker appeared in the doorway from the street.

"I hear it, Patrick," Brubaker said. "I hear a familiar voice."

Brubaker's suit was more expensive, and he looked more prosperous than he had the last time she had seen him.

"Ann, it's so good to see you. I thought Lucille was coming."

"She is, but I was hoping to see you for a moment before the meeting."

"Of course, come in."

Ann followed Brubaker to his office. The interior was almost a duplicate of Royce Chamberlin's office at the bank—same style desk, same style leather armchair for the attorney and two lesser armchairs across the desk for the clients. Ann and Brubaker sat down in their respective places. Van Burin hovered in the doorway like an expectant puppy.

"How's school?" Brubaker asked. "I always wanted to send my children to boarding school. Get a real first-class education. But with the economy after the war and assorted humanitarian efforts, that was not to be."

Ann noticed Brubaker's diamond stickpin. She understood why it "was not to be."

"By the way, they're auctioning off some of your grandmother's personal possessions at Chaynie House in Des Moines. You might want to go over there and bid on something."

Ann was surprised—as well as insulted and angry—that Lady Ann's possessions were being placed on an auction block. She had promised to hold her temper, but it was going to be difficult. "I have to bid on my grandmother's property?" she said slowly.

"Well, yes, it's an auction."

"How did this get started?"

"Patrick here. He got himself involved with Chaynie House. It's a distinguished and reputable establishment that serves all the big Midwest families. They even appointed him an officer. Didn't they, Patrick?"

"I'm honorary facilitator of estate planning," Van Burin said proudly.

"Chaynie's opened a bureau here in Winfield. Auctions to be held at the meeting hall. These are tough times. We're all in it together. An auction's a good way to convert estate property into assets for the family."

Brubaker's enthusiasm made the whole thing seem slightly queasy. "It's still an auction, isn't it?" Ann asked.

"It helps the family plan for the future, Ann."

"And now it's my grandma's turn."

"The invitation's open," Brubaker said.

"No, thanks," Ann said. "Anything my grandmother wanted me to have, she already gave me."

A tiny gasp from Van Burin.

"Oh?" Brubaker said uneasily. "What things? Like what for instance?"

"Personal things."

"But what things? Were there any items we missed?"

"We wanted to be thorough," Van Burin echoed.

"Memories," Ann said directly.

"Ah, memories," Brubaker said warmly. "Of course. We all have memories."

"Yes, we do," Van Burin burbled. "We all remember our memories."

"Nothing else?" Brubaker inquired. "Nothing tangible?"

"Memories," Ann repeated. "Now I'd like to see Grandma's will."

Brubaker was surprised. "You what?"

"Now, why would a little girl like you ask a big question like that?" Van Burin said.

"Because this little girl is Lady Ann Carson's granddaughter and I'm asking."

"The will...the will." Brubaker muttered. "I'm not sure if we have it right here. We were sending it over to the courthouse."

"It's not at the courthouse. Papa was there on Friday."

"You know, Jack's coming this afternoon..."

"Maybe it's in the file cabinet, Mr. Brubaker."

"Yes, yes, I suppose it must be," Brubaker said. "You're mighty determined."

Brubaker turned in his chair to face the file cabinets behind him. His heart was definitely not in the search.

"I don't know why you need to see it," Van Burin said. "We're all friends here. We're like family."

"It's usually in the upper drawer behind you," Ann said.

Brubaker opened the top drawer of the file cabinet and took out a folder. "Here it is. I don't know what I could have been thinking."

As he was handing it to Ann, Lucille entered the office.

Van Burin sighed in relief. "Lucille, we were wondering where you were."

"I hope I'm not late."

"No, you're on time, Mama," Ann said, examining the pages.

"Ann here wanted to see a copy of her grandmother's will," Brubaker said.

"And we were telling her we're all friends here," Van Burin added.

"But why are you looking at the will?" Lucille said nervously.

"I haven't seen it," Ann said. She glanced up in time to see Brubaker shrugging his shoulders, as if to say, "I don't know any more than you do."

"I was wondering," Ann said. "Were you out at the hospital the day before Grandma died?"

"Why do you ask?" Brubaker said.

"I was just wondering if Grandma had any visitors."

"No, Royce was very adamant about that."

"We'd better be going, dear," Lucille said. "We have to go back to the printer's."

"What about our meeting, Lucille?" Brubaker asked.

"We can reschedule it. Perhaps after the memorial service. We're on our way to pick up the programs."

Ann saw that Lucille was nervous. But with the will in her hands, she had gone too far to stop. Her eyes went back to the bequests and codicils in front of her.

"You see, Ann?" Brubaker said. "Your grandma was quite clear in her wishes. She wanted Royce and his girls to have a half share of the estate."

"And she signed it," Ann said, examining the bottom of the page. There was Lady Ann's signature—all done very neatly and legibly. Nothing anywhere suggested that it had been forced.

"Of course she signed it," Brubaker said. "Right here in the office...six months before she passed away."

"Lucille was present, too, if I'm not mistaken," Van Burin said. "Sitting right there."

This was another jolt to Ann, but by now she was used to them. She wondered why her parents had never mentioned this to her.

"Yes," Lucille said quietly. "I was here."

"Everybody," Brubaker declared triumphantly. "Everyone right here in the office. Lady Ann was in full command of her faculties."

"Straight as a dye and sharp as a tack," Van Burin echoed. "All of us present and in full command of our faculties."

Ann placed the will back on Brubaker's desk.

"Have you been out to the grave site?" Van Burin asked, in an effort to redirect the conversation.

"Not yet," Ann said.

"But you are going to be in town for the memorial service."

"I plan to be."

"Sadly, I can't be there. Royce wants me to attend a business meeting with Pheasant Valley Power Company tomorrow. It's important for the town…"

"You do what you have to do," Ann said.

"While you're at Dooley's, I'd like you to order a personal tribute program for me from me and my family. Make it something about two feet square with graceful writing against ebony. From me, my wife, my son Patrick Junior, and my daughter Camille. Pick it up when it's done, and then take it to the service and make sure it's right beside Lady Ann's headstone. Put it in a prominent position, so nobody will miss it. Take care of it, and I'll deposit the money in your account."

Ann was stunned. Van Burin was asking a bereaved person to order and pick up an item for her grandmother's memorial service. The real Van Burin had emerged from behind his jovial façade for the first time, and she was seeing what he really thought of her. Her contempt for him was growing by the second. She wanted to act on it, but she had made a promise to Lucille.

"Pardon me?" she asked.

"Order a personal tribute program, if it's not too difficult for you," Van Burin said.

"No, no," Ann said. "I can order it."

"Of course, you can order it. It's not too much. Work it into that busy social schedule of yours."

"What schedule?" Ann was trying not to rise to the bait, but Van Burin never knew when to stop.

"You should know, Ann. You're so busy. You're a regular social butterfly."

"I'm at school, Mr. Van Burin."

"No, you're not. You're back and forth from here to school…hobnobbing with the Minnesota high society. It keeps you so engaged you missed your grandmother's funeral."

That did it.

"Order it yourself," Ann said.

Van Burin gasped in shock. "What?"

"Order it yourself. Or send Sonya in there."

"You mean you won't make a little trip over to the printer's?"

"You do it."

"I'll go," Lucille blurted out. "I'll do it. We were going there anyway."

Ann's heart began to sink. "Not now," she thought. "Why now?"

"Don't worry, Patrick. We'll take care of it. We'll do it right away."

Van Burin saw Lucille's disappointment. Here was a chance to rub it in.

"I'm not asking very much, am I, Lucille?"

"No, of course not. It'll be our pleasure."

"It isn't so much to ask…Since you were going there anyway."

Ann watched as another chunk of familial support slipped away. It seemed her family was incapable of maintaining a united front for very long.

"We'll be glad to do it."

"Thank you, Lucille," Van Burin answered, once again eyeing Ann. "If it's not an imposition for you."

"She said she'd do it, Patrick," Brubaker said impatiently. "How many times do you need to hear it?"

"We have to go," Lucille stammered. "We'll have to make it later, Fred. I'm so sorry."

"Always a pleasure to see you," Brubaker said. "Sorry for the mix-up. Tell Jack we'll see him this afternoon."

Ann and Lucille were on the sidewalk in seconds. Ann's eyes were stinging. Neither of them spoke. They got in the car and began the drive up Market Street.

"Why, Mama?" Ann exclaimed.

"When will you understand that there are some things you have to do for people?"

"It depends on who's asking," Ann answered.

"Friendships need tending."

"He's no friend. He never has been. You heard him in there."

"It doesn't matter what he asked. Friendships need tending," Lucille said urgently. "Business friendships. Social friendships. There's some things you have to do for people. We'll pick up the programs, and then we'll order whatever this thing is for Patrick Van Burin."

Ann could not tell which hurt worse—the disappointment or the anger. Once again, they had acquiesced to the forces around them.

"The longer they give in, the tougher the fight at the end," she said to herself. "Why can't they see it?"

Lucille pulled the car up along the sidewalk in front of the shop marked Dooley and Sons. Her voice was quiet and firm.

"Today of all days, we don't want to upset anything. What's the matter with you?"

"You heard him. How am I supposed to answer that, Mama?"

"You're not. You're supposed to take it. You take it off him, and you live with it."

"Well, I don't think I can do that," Ann said angrily.

"Coming in and demanding to see the will. And then this set-to with Patrick Van Burin."

"Can't I ask to see Grandma's will?"

"This isn't about you, Ann. Jack's going to be there this afternoon. He's going to have to deal with the mess you made."

"There's no mess that wasn't there before. Besides, we're running his errand for him, aren't we?"

Lucille turned away from Ann. "I don't want to discuss it anymore."

"Mama…"

"No, no. It's over. I don't want to discuss it."

There was no talking to Lucille. Ann could only hope the afternoon meeting would prove fruitful, but her doubts were growing.

"Now let's go in there and get this over with," Lucille said.

Back at the office, Van Burin and Brubaker watched them enter the print shop.

"Spoiled brat," Van Burin fumed. "I knew she'd turn out that way. Knew it from way back. Born into wealth and she acts like she fell off the peanut wagon."

"Careful now. You're starting to sound like Warren Hyatt."

"You saw it. Wouldn't even buy a tribute for her own grandmother. Didn't even bother to come home for the funeral. All that money and she can't tell if it's tea time or pee time."

Brubaker shook his head in mock bewilderment. "It's terrible, Patrick. Simply terrible. What's the world coming to?"

"I mean it, Fred."

"I know."

Van Burin became pensive.

"Why did she want to see the will?" he asked.

32

When the time came, Jack left for town. He even gave them a thumbs-up as he got into his car. A few minutes later, Ann and Lucille drove out to the county farm.

A steady curl of white smoke was coming out of the chimney. A smaller series of puffs was emerging from a stovepipe to one side.

A dusty gray Packard was parked beside the garage. A young man was seated inside behind the steering wheel, an open newspaper in front of him. The glass on the windows had not steamed up, leading Ann to suspect he had not been there long.

"If that's him, he's early," Lucille said.

They pulled to a stop beside the other car. The man put down his newspaper and opened the door to step out. He was in his late twenties and clad in a heavy topcoat that covered his suit. His wire-rimmed spectacles and concerned expression made him look like an anxious clerk.

"Mrs. Hardy? I'm Edward Collinsen. From Council Bluffs."

"Glad to meet you," Lucille replied. "This is my daughter Ann."

They started for the front door. It was cold enough that they could see the steam from their breath every time they spoke. Ann looked ahead to the steamy windows of the building. She could make out the silhouette of a person watching them through a clear circular spot on the glass.

"I hope you don't mind coming all the way out here," Lucille said.

"Not at all. I understand the situation."

Ann opened the door, and they entered the lobby, where the heat and humidity immediately engulfed them. They took off their coats and scarves. Bonnie was at the reception desk. Tracy was awkwardly positioned in the center of the lobby, as if she had been caught scurrying away from the window.

"Hello, Tracy," Lucille said. "We've come to see Zachary. Is he in his room?"

"He certainly is," Tracy answered. "You want me to bring him out?"

"Don't trouble yourself."

Tracy was eyeing Collinsen in a suspicious manner.

"This gentleman is a friend of the family," Lucille explained.

The three passed the front desk and continued up the hall to Zachary's room. Lucille handed Ann a small book of pictures to occupy Zachary's attention.

"Who do you suppose that was? He don't look like nobody from around here," Bonnie said.

"If he's a family friend, she might have introduced him," Tracy added.

Ann reached Zachary's door first. The heat throughout the building gave its wooden surface a peculiar shine, as if it were perspiring.

She knocked and opened the door. Zachary grinned when he saw them.

"I told you we'd come," Lucille said.

Zachary was looking questioningly at Collinsen. "Zachary, this is Mr. Collinsen," Lucille said. "We're going to be discussing a few things, and if there's time, we'll show him around."

"Hello, Zachary," Collinsen said.

Ann and Zachary sat on the foot of Zachary's bed. Lucille and Collinsen took seats in the two chairs in the room. Ann kept her attention on the discussion while Zachary looked at the drawings in the book.

Collinsen cleared his throat. "To get started, as you know, I've had several discussions with Jack. I think we have a case. A very good case in every sense of the word, except we need evidence."

Ann looked up from the booklet. "A good case in every sense of the word without evidence? What kind of case is that?" she thought.

"What about Mama's will?" Lucille asked.

"According to Jack, there were no signs of duress. He's seen the will several times. If I'm not mistaken, you were in the office for the original signing."

"I was. It was signed in an orderly manner in an office in front of witnesses."

"And it's the same story with the power of attorney."

"An orderly manner in front of witnesses. That's the way Royce does things."

"What about Beulah Jensen?" Ann asked. "She said Royce and Brubaker were in Grandma's room?"

Collinsen's eyebrows seemed to pull together about his nose. "It's hearsay. Beulah telling Olga and Olga telling you. Besides, Beulah has fled the state."

"It's pretty obvious what they were up to."

"Definitely. But there were no changes in the will. Whatever Royce and Brubaker intended, they didn't accomplish."

Zachary had started listening when Ann entered the conversation. "Royce and Fred? Did they do something?"

"It's a misunderstanding," Ann said.

"Do they know where Beulah is?" Lucille asked.

"Her family says she left on the first train to California."

"She's terrified of what Royce might do to her."

"A lot of people are afraid of him," Collinsen said.

Ann heard a creak from Zachary's door. Slow and drawn out, as if someone were leaning against the other side. Ann was off the bed and across the room. She opened the door. Up the hall Tracy was stacking cups on a cart.

"Is everything all right?" Tracy asked.

"Just fine," Ann answered.

"Let me know if you need anything."

Ann stepped inside and closed the door. "Tracy," she whispered.

"You think she was listening?" Lucille asked

"It's hard to say."

"We're all a little jumpy," Lucille said.

"It's understandable. You're taking a big step," Collinsen said.

Outside, Tracy was hurrying down the hall to the lobby. "Shame on them," she muttered angrily. "Shame on them."

"What's wrong?" Bonnie asked.

When she reached the desk, she snatched up the telephone. "I would never have believed it. How dare they?"

"What are you doing? What happened?"

"Putting a stop to something right quick." She moved her mouth up to the receiver. "Tessa, this is Tracy out at the county farm. I need to talk to Royce Chamberlin at the bank. It's an emergency."

"Tracy, what's going on?" Bonnie asked again.

"The way they're talking about Mr. Royce—shame on them."

"What? Who?"

"That man is some lawyer they hired behind Mr. Royce's back. Imagine they would do that."

She pulled the receiver closer to her mouth and spoke in a raspy whisper. "Mr. Royce. This is Tracy Stabb. Yes, I'm whispering for a reason, a very good reason. Listen, there's something going on out here you should know about."

Back in the room, Collinsen was adjusting his spectacles.

"You have to understand the caliber of the opposition. He may have started as a humble bank teller, but now he has his hands in just about everything: property, finances, people's lives. Everything Royce has done involving the Carson estate is within the law. It doesn't make it right, and it doesn't make life easier for you, but technically it's legal. Even the personal selection of certain family members to be at the funeral. It was cruel and insensitive but not illegal. He's head of the family now."

"Yes."

"I have a tidbit that might interest you. You know Buddy Brenner and Bob Ishie?"

"Brenner and Ishie. They used to work for us," Lucille said. "Mama fired them. Royce lent them money. A few weeks later they purchased their own farms in Albert Mill. If only we knew then what we know now," Lucille said.

"It didn't work for long," Collinsen said. "Neither Brenner nor Ishie could make a go of it as farmers. Both places went under."

"That doesn't surprise me one bit."

Ann was still amazed at the ingenuity of the transaction. "He pays them. They convert the money to land. They fail. Royce takes back the land and puts it up for sale at a higher price. He's made a profit in the long run."

Collinsen continued. "Speaking of land, I've heard rumors about the bank using force to evict people who default on their mortgages. A couple of people were hospitalized; one man was in a coma for a week."

"Not a rumor," Lucille said. "It's the Hudsens on section two."

"Has anyone gone to the authorities?"

"No, they just pack up and leave."

Ann was growing impatient. It had been an interesting discussion so far, but she wondered how any of this would affect their case.

"What about you, Zachary?" Collinsen asked. "Are you happy here?"

Zachary was silent.

"Are they treating you well? Do you have any friends here?"

"Yeah, yeah, I have friends. Lucille and Jack and Ann."

"They're family, Zachary."

"They come and see me," Zachary said proudly.

"What about going home? Do you want to go home?"

"Oh yes. Oh yes. Someday…someday, Ann and I are going home. We're going home. That's our promise."

"We certainly hope so," Lucille said.

"Where does this leave us? What about our case?" Ann asked.

"I thought we had something," Lucille echoed.

"We do. We have a very good case," Collinsen said. "Seen from the proper perspective."

"And what perspective is that?"

"The perspective of moral strength—the knowledge that it will succeed in court before a jury of our peers."

Collinsen's expression became more serious. "This is a David-and-Goliath situation. If we consider it through the prism of moral truth against material force, we have a very good case."

"I still don't understand," Ann said.

"David and Goliath. Moral strength versus material force. On one side, there's David and the Israelites. On the other, Goliath and the Philistines. The Philistines were a mighty army that everyone feared. When David strode out to meet Goliath, they all laughed. He looked unprepared for battle, but he wasn't in the least. He had spiritual and moral strength on his side."

"I thought he had a slingshot," Ann said.

"What does this have to do with Winfield, Iowa?" Lucille asked.

"Everything. You see, God gave David everything he needed to slay the giant. David had the weapons of the angels on his side. Although he seemed unprepared from the point of view of everyone around, he emerged victorious. Just as we can. Of course, we have to do some preparation first."

"No, no," Ann thought. "Take away the scripture, and David was a shrewd kid against an overconfident blowhard who'd let success go to his head. What we have here is an overconfident kid against an opponent who can see you coming before you ever decide to leave."

"There's no argument they can make and no tactic they can use," Collinsen continued. "Just ask my father. He faced men like Royce Chamberlin on a daily basis when he worked in New York."

"Your father was in law?" Lucille inquired.

"Wendell Collinsen. Worked with the district attorney's office in Brooklyn. He took on the toughest characters imaginable on the Brooklyn docks. And he won because he had right on his side. All it takes is moral courage and the integrity to stand up for what you believe in."

"You need evidence," Ann said. "Do you think you can win this?"

"Yes. We have dedication and moral strength. And you're right—what we need is evidence."

Ann felt discouraged. And they had not even filed their lawsuit.

"Ann, to reassure you, my father would face characters like Chamberlin and his bullyboys in court on a daily basis. Our family is used to trouble. All you need is the right person to represent you, and I hope, in my humble way, that I can do that."

"How did he persuade Papa he was the right man?" Ann thought. "Probably because he was the only lawyer who would take our case. When you're thirsty in the desert, any kind of water looks like a lifesaver. Here it's been doubled: a desperate client and a needy lawyer. What the hell have we gotten into?"

"The best thing I can recommend is to stay the course," Collinsen said. "Keep in touch with me through Jack. We do have a very good case."

"Thank you for taking us on," Lucille said. "A lot of attorneys were afraid to talk to us."

The conversation did not conclude so much as slowly devolve into small talk. It touched on such topics as Carson family history, the founding of Winfield, and Ann at Clearwater.

Fifteen minutes later they said good-bye to Zachary and were out in the hallway. They arrived in the lobby to find Tracy and Bonnie at the reception desk. Bonnie appeared uneasy. Tracy was glaring at them.

"Did you have a nice visit?" she called out in what was almost a jeer.

"We got some things settled," Lucille answered.

"Will we be seeing more of you?" Tracy asked Collinsen.

"It's possible."

"Are you trying to tell us something?" Ann asked.

"Yes, I am," Tracy stated. "Mr. Royce is a hard-working husband and father. A pillar of the community. You have no business going behind his back. And I told him so."

"You what?"

Lucille winced. The very thing they had hoped to avoid had just occurred. "Why in the world did you do that, Tracy?"

"Mr. Royce thinks only of his family and the people in our wonderful town. And this is how you repay him? Shame on you."

"You should have stayed out of it," Ann said. "You should have minded your own business."

"Will you be all right?" Collinsen asked Lucille.

"We'll get through it one way or another. I'm sorry. I sure didn't expect this."

"Look," Ann said.

In the distance a car was speeding through the empty fields. It bounced and swayed along until it swerved into the driveway of the county farm. Even then, it did not slow down.

"That's Royce's car," Lucille said.

"You brought this on yourselves," Tracy said. "You should never have gone behind Mr. Royce's back."

Kurt Hudsen was the driver. In the backseat Royce and Jack were in the middle of a heated argument.

The car stopped in the front yard. Chamberlin was more furious than Ann had ever seen. Jack was attempting to mediate, but under the onslaught of Royce's tirade, he could barely say a word.

Kurt got out of the car to open the door for the passengers, but Royce was already heading for the entrance. With Jack and Kurt behind him, he stormed into the lobby.

"You betrayed me, Jack," he snarled. "You betrayed me."

"Please. Calm down, Royce. We can talk about this."

"You got the four of us together under false pretenses. You lied to me." His attention turned to Lucille. "What are you doing here?"

"I think you already know," Lucille answered.

Tracy was watching eagerly. "I hope I did the right thing, Mr. Royce," she ventured. "I was thinking of what's best for everyone..."

Ignoring her, his gaze found Collinsen. "I don't believe we've met," he said.

"I'm Edward Collinsen."

The cold eyes twinkled. "Collinsen...Edward Collinsen...the Collinsens of Council Bluffs. You're a long way from home."

"I really hope I did the right thing, Mr. Royce. I was only..."

"Shut up," Royce snapped at Tracy, his eyes never leaving the young man. "You work for Pine and Hall. You're their new boy. Are you the best they could come up with?"

Royce shot a glance over to Jack and Lucille. "Of course I knew. I've known for some time. I was waiting to see who you plucked out of the wood box."

For the next few seconds, Royce stared blankly at Collinsen.

"I'm not afraid of you, Mr. Chamberlin," Collinsen said uneasily.

Kurt snickered from the doorway. Ann's heart was sinking further. Collinsen's response was intended to show courage and resolve. Instead, it revealed the opposite.

"First big case?" Chamberlin asked Collinsen.

"I'm not at liberty to say."

"Well, I'll take the liberty for you. You're young. Starting out. Want to make a name for yourself. You represent them and you take me to court."

"If that's what it takes."

"I'll tell you what'll happen. You file your suit, and we go to court. I'll drag the case out for months. For years. Pine and Hall will ask you, 'What's going on here? You said you'd wrap this up. You're spending all this time and money and you're not getting anywhere.' And you'll answer, 'I can handle it. I know what I'm doing. Trust me.' And it goes on. They'll come back to you—on their knees this time: 'What are you doing to us? We're losing all our assets in delays and appeals.' But you press on and on. Finally, you'll just get bogged down. Your firm will go bankrupt. And there you'll be, out on the street."

"That won't happen."

"No one will touch you. No one will hire you because the whole time you're suing me, I'll put the word out that you're incompetent. You bankrupted your firm. You'll look for work. Here. There. Left and right. And one day you'll wake up all alone on the shores of Lake Erie, wondering how the hell you got there."

"That's not going to deter me..."

"You better let it deter you, boy," Kurt drawled. "He just painted your future."

"In a court of law, this family has rights..."

"Let's take the family view," Royce said. "That's what this boils down to. Dissension among the relatives. Jack and Lucille are my family now. If they weren't, you wouldn't be here. What about your family?"

"What about them?"

"You're Wendell Collinsen's boy. Your father's living in a residence for retired jurists in Chicago. You have a wife and baby daughter at home. How are you going to support them?"

Collinsen appeared shocked. "How do you know about my family? You leave my family out of this."

"I'm going to rephrase it as a simple offer: my family or your family."

"If you're not workin', you can't provide for 'em," Kurt said.

"My family or your family."

"It...it's a question of truth and human decency," Collinsen stammered.

"My family...or your family," Chamberlin repeated slowly. "And we can start right now."

Collinsen was frozen. His expression had moved from somber to perplexed to stricken. Whether Royce could do what he said was not important. He had made Collinsen believe that he could do it.

"Someone's going to stop you," he declared, his voice shaking.

"But not today," Chamberlin said. "Go home. Give your wife and daughter a hug. We'll forget the whole thing."

Collinsen looked desperately to Jack and Lucille. He seemed to be shrinking by the second.

"I don't know what to do."

"Yes, you do," Kurt said.

"I'm sorry," he said finally. "I can't do this...I wanted to...but I can't."

"Then why did you say you'd take our case?" Lucille cried.

"I have to think of my family. Don't you see? I have to think of them."

Ann clenched her fist in anger. It had been slowly building all day. She saw exactly how this sad excuse for a lawyer would have conducted himself in a courtroom. One objection and the extraordinary human being would concede everything.

"It's my family. Don't you see?" Collinsen implored.

"Yes, yes," Lucille said disgustedly. "We see. We've seen it all before. Different excuse. Same message. Go on. Get out of here."

"Please to try to understand."

"Go home. It's not your fight anyway."

Collinsen rushed out the front door. He appeared dazed, unsure of where he was and stumbling for his car as fast as he could go. Within seconds the engine started and the car was weaving down the driveway to the road.

Royce watched the car vanish in the distance. If this was a personal triumph, he was not feeling it. Everything around him seemed sour and empty.

"What do you have to say for yourselves?" he said to Jack and Lucille.

"We were investigating our options. That's all we were doing," Lucille said.

As always, Jack felt the pressure of the moment building all around him. He felt the need to speak out or take action, but by now his choices were limited.

"All right, Royce," he said. "We have to get along here. I realize that. We were wrong. We made a mistake. We should have talked first. I admit it."

"No, Papa. We weren't wrong," Ann said clearly.

Royce turned to face Ann. Her declaration affected him more than any protestations from her parents. "Ann, for your sake, you better not mean that. I have plans for you."

"What plans?" Ann retorted. "Working as a drudge for Cassie and Carol? I'm not going to work for your girls. Not now. Not ever."

"Ann! Stop it!" Jack cried. Whatever spark of defiance he had manifested earlier had been snuffed out. "Don't listen to her," he pleaded. "We can work this out. I'll take full responsibility"

"Jack, please," Lucille said.

"Stay out of this," he said. "I'll handle this. I'll take responsibility. Let me take responsibility."

"You take responsibility?" Royce snarled. "How can you take responsibility when you can't take care of yourself?"

With a sudden lunge, Chamberlin raised his fist to smash Jack in the face. Instinctively, Jack reeled backward to avoid the blow. He tripped over his feet and staggered to the floor.

"Don't hit me," he whispered.

Royce looked down at him. "Hit you? You know me. I never get my hands dirty..."

"I'm calling the sheriff," Bonnie said.

"What for?" Tracy asked.

Bonnie was out of her seat and scurrying into the hallway.

"Don't you ever say a word against me again," Chamberlin said.

"I won't, Royce. I'm sorry," Jack murmured.

Ann wanted to feel angry at Jack, but her hatred was directed at everyone around her. Tracy. Collinsen. Royce for breaking Jack's spirit. And Jack for not fighting back.

Ann leaned over Jack. "Come on, Papa. Try to get up."

"I was out of line," Jack was whispering. "I should never have done this."

Chamberlin was regarding the scene with a grim expression. The scene was affecting him more than he cared to admit. Ann looked up at him from where she was beside Jack.

"You can stuff your plans. Every one of them," she said. "You can go straight to hell."

"Whooo!" Kurt chuckled. "She looks like she'd cut your throat if she had the chance."

"Then we'll see that she never gets the chance," Royce said. "Ann, choices have consequences. You are going back to school. You leave on the four o'clock train."

"Come again?" Ann said.

"You shall remain there until I see fit for you to return to Winfield."

"So I'm being banished."

Ann was ready to lash out at anything that moved. Then she remembered what the colonel had said. When the argument can't be resolved, let the other side win their point. Make your own move later.

"You do what you have to do," she said.

Lucille was fighting back tears. "Jack, please get up."

Jack began to stir. "I know what you think. I know what you think of me."

Ann and Lucille moved to help him up. With a shudder, Jack pushed away from them and scrambled to his feet.

"See? I got off the floor. I got something left in me."

Somewhere in the back of his mind, Royce wondered if he really wanted to be rid of Ann. He returned her hate, but her courage and independence gave him a strange kind of sustenance. There was certainly none of it emanating from anybody else.

"Trust your papa here," Jack was saying. "I know how to get along in the world. That's something you'll have to learn someday."

Lucille put her arm around her husband, wanting to comfort him. They all knew this was more than a mere scuffle.

"You go back to school like Royce says. Don't you worry about us," Jack said. "We'll be fine."

"We're leaving for town," Royce said to the group. "Jack, you ride in the car with them. I don't want to look at you."

When they were outside, Chamberlin and Kurt got into one car, Ann and her parents into the other. Lucille drove with Jack beside her and Ann in the backseat. With Royce's car in the lead, they began the journey into Winfield.

Ann's mind raced through all the unresolved problems she had encountered recently. Anger. Banishment. Hopes dashed and love for her parents. They were all colliding in her mind. All that mattered now was her family.

"I pray and I pray for some relief, and nothing happens," Lucille said. "I know God hears us, or I certainly hope He does, but nothing ever happens. Sometimes it gets worse."

"I don't know the answer, Mama," Ann replied. "I don't know any answer. You had faith…no, we had faith in our plan. We had faith in Collinsen, and Royce blew him away like a leaf. That ought to be enough to knock us out for good. But I won't let it."

"What can you do?" Jack said.

"Forget Royce. I'm talking about us. I may not see you two for a while."

"Don't say that, Ann."

"Listen to me," Ann said urgently. "We don't have much time. There's them and there's us. If we argue about how we got here and what he can do to us, then he's won."

"That's right. He's won," Jack said.

"No! He hasn't won!" Ann shouted. "We've been pushed. We've been crushed. We've been pulled apart, but we're still here. No matter what Royce Chamberlin has done, we're still here. We're family. If we stay a team behind his back, we're still together. We can break this thing. We have to work as a team. You understand?"

Neither Jack nor Lucille spoke. The purr of the car engine was the only sound.

"Do either of you understand?"

Ahead of them was the last hillside before the road turned downward into town.

33

When they arrived in town, Lucille drove straight to the depot. Royce and Kurt parked a short distance away to observe. Ann and her parents crossed the platform to a bench. The air was chilly, but nobody seemed to notice.

After a few minutes, Cyrus, the hired hand, appeared in a buckboard. He carried Ann's bags over to her.

"Sorry, Miss Ann. Just following orders," he said. "You know, this sure ain't the way it was when the colonel was around."

"No, it's not," Ann replied, trying not to remember. "Thank you."

In the baggage room, Doss Claypool slid the door open a crack and spied on the scene with a curious smirk. Old Dawz guessed something unfortunate had happened to Ann and her parents. He didn't know what it was, but it didn't prevent him from relishing the spectacle from a safe spot.

With the arrival of the luggage, Royce and Kurt were satisfied. Ann would be gone in a few minutes. Their car turned into an alley that opened on Market Street.

Ann and her parents waited on the platform. The train was due in twenty minutes.

"I've got to think of something," Ann thought. "I don't want to lose it this time."

They heard hoofbeats. It was Sheriff Dierkes on horseback, approaching at a fast trot. In what seemed like a single fluid movement, he halted, dismounted, and was walking toward them.

"What happened, Jack?"

Ann guessed he had just been to the county farm.

"Just a misunderstanding," Jack said.

"That's not what I heard."

"It's a family matter."

"It was Royce," Ann said. "Royce did it."

"Tell me, Miss Ann."

"We hired a lawyer. Royce found out. We were having a meeting. Tracy called him at the bank."

Dierkes nodded slowly. "I knew one day Royce'd go too far."

"That's not what happened, Sheriff," Jack said. "It's not what happened. It wasn't that way."

"Papa, he's trying to help."

"I don't care. It was me, Sheriff. I'm to blame."

"I don't believe that for a minute," Dierkes said.

"He can help us, Papa."

"But your mother and I have to go home tonight. We have to pick up the pieces of what happened today."

"What did happen, Jack?" Dierkes asked again.

"Nothing to file a complaint about."

Ann could see the frustration building inside Dierkes, trying to help and getting nowhere. "You say you hired a lawyer. Royce found out and scared him off. From what I hear, he threatened you. You can bring charges against him."

"No, we're not doing that."

"Then file charges with me. I can do something," Dierkes said.

"Who says you can?" Jack answered. "Who says any of it would stick? Royce is too big. Too powerful. Anyone who looks at him the wrong way gets hurt." Jack was staring down at the boards on the platform, as if trying to escape the conversation. "We took a chance, and we failed. That's all there is to it. If you brought me a Bible and asked me to swear on it, I'd tell you I slipped on the stairs or tripped over some baling wire."

"We all know what kind of man he is, Jack."

Jack raised his eyes to face Dierkes. "And that's exactly why I will not do this. This is a family matter. We'll deal with it in our own way."

"I'm sorry to hear that," Dierkes said.

"And I'm sorry, too—more than you realize. But that's how it is."

Dierkes turned to go.

"Thank you, Sheriff," Lucille said.

Dierkes was walking back to his horse when he noticed Ann behind him.

"What is it, Miss Ann?"

"This is what we've been living with since Grandpa died. Papa's afraid, and I suppose he has reason. You're the law here. What can we do?"

Dierkes was touched that Ann had such a high regard for what was right. But he also knew the ideals of the world were constrained by the realities.

"It's up to your papa. He's bound and determined. If he'd only change his mind."

"He's right about one thing. If he brought charges, Royce would be in and out of that courtroom like a trip to the barbershop."

"There's that possibility."

Ann looked at her parents huddled on the bench. She was feeling protective of them. She had not felt that way before.

"I'm angry. I'm so very angry," she said.

"I can understand, Miss Ann."

"What can I do? Sure, I'm afraid of Royce. But I'm not afraid to take him on. There's got to be a way I can do it."

Dierkes admired her determination, but he could also see that her declaration was based on raw emotion, not careful planning.

"I can give you an answer, but you're not going to like it," he said. "You're fourteen, dependent, and underage. There's nothing you can do."

"There has to be something."

"Right now adults make the decisions. The only thing you can do is keep your eyes open and hang on until you're of age."

"Which is eighteen. What if I can't wait that long?"

"What do you propose to do, Miss Ann?"

"Well, to start with, I could run away."

"That's one solution."

"Yeah, I could run away."

"What would you do then?"

"I'd get a job somewhere."

"And what then? You're fourteen."

"I'd find something," Ann said. "I've seen fourteen-year-olds working."

"Doing what?" Dierkes asked.

"What do you mean, doing what?"

"What kind of work do fourteen-year-olds do?"

"Whose side are you on?" Ann asked.

She was trying to imagine what she would do next. Dierkes's questions were providing their own answers. She was irritated, but she saw that Dierkes was on her side.

"I wish I weren't fourteen," Ann finally said.

"And that's the hard fact."

"What should I do?"

"I want you to promise me something. A rock-solid promise. Right here. Right now."

"What?"

"Go back to school. Ride it out. If you stay near your folks—even if it's through school—you can see what the other side's up to. Learn their strengths. Find their weaknesses. When you're old enough, then make your move."

"That sounds like my grandpa's advice."

"I can tell you this: Royce Chamberlin's snookered a lot of people in this town. But he hasn't fooled me. Keep your eyes open and gather your facts."

"Hang on and don't fall off."

"You won't fall. You're the colonel's granddaughter."

Even though the message was not the one Ann had hoped for, she felt better. She felt a strength building inside. It was not necessarily hope, but a feeling of resolve. She could wait a little longer.

"At the right time, you make your move," Dierkes said. "Do we have a promise?"

"We have a promise. Thank you, Sheriff."

"I'll be heading off," Dierkes said. He led his horse a few paces away from the depot. He mounted up and rode away along the backs of the buildings that lined Market Street.

Ann heard the sound of a train whistle in the far distance. "My life's full of promises to a lot of people," she thought. "To Grandpa. To Zachary. And now to Sheriff Dierkes. Maybe promises are all we have to hold everything together."

She saw her parents huddled on the bench, watching her. "I'm going to make another one."

Ann went over to Jack and Lucille and took each of them by the hand. "Mama. Papa," she said. "Royce is sending me away. But one of these days, I'll be back. Not for a visit. I'll be back for keeps. I made a promise to Grandpa. I'm going to make one to you now: I *will* be back."

"We're a family," Jack said. "We're still a family."

"That's right. And I will be back," Ann said.

The train was nearing Winfield Station. Jack and Ann picked up her bags to start across the platform.

The train pulled in. Ann hugged her parents one more time and boarded the second car.

After a few minutes, the four o'clock left Winfield.

34

By now Ann had made the trip from Winfield to Clearwater several times, and she looked for certain landmarks along the way. Watching for familiar barns and railroad crossings kept her mind off her own problems. However, as it became darker outside, the scenery and the night began to blur until she found herself looking at her own reflection in the window.

The memory of her father being beaten down by Royce Chamberlin would stay with her for the rest of her life.

Ann got off the train in Minneapolis and took a taxi to Clearwater. She had not made the trip to school in the dark, and after they passed through the shadowy buildings of Coon Falls, Ann noticed there were hardly any lights on the road between the town and the school. Sometime during the day, it had rained. The road was dark, and every now and then, the puddles would pick up a reflection from the moonlight.

Clearwater stood out against the hillside like a ghost fortress in a gothic novel. The sky was spotted with clear areas in the middle of the clouds from the earlier storm. The moon, shining through, reflected off the wet portions of the field and roof of the building. As they approached, Ann could see how the more susceptible of the faculty and student body might think the place was haunted since it seemed completely abandoned.

Ann paid the taxi, took her bags, and walked into the building. Since this was still Thanksgiving recess, the place was vacant except for a few staff, and there was not a single light inside. Only the moonlight through the windows provided the illumination to keep her from bumping into a chair or tripping on the steps. She heard the taxi as it disappeared into the night.

She began the long journey to her room. She had only taken a few steps when suddenly she heard a sound. She stopped to listen. It was a voice—muted yet clear enough to identify as more of a prolonged sobbing than any attempt at speech. Ann listened. Then, just as unexpectedly, the sobbing stopped, and there was nothing but silence and a breeze outside. The old building had its share of creaks, groans, and whispers, but this was most definitely a human in great distress. It reminded Ann of Mrs. Schrader at the county farm. What was going on?

Ann waited. She was sure she had heard it. The rumors about ghosts roaming the halls after bedtime popped into her mind, but she shrugged them off. Maybe this was a ghost, but she wanted to see it first. The sound had been real.

She heard it again. It was coming from the other hallway—the one leading to the teacher's offices and classrooms. It was very faint, but the more closely Ann listened, the better she could make it out. The sound was the uninterrupted sobbing of a child about four or five, all alone and in pain. A sudden shriek was followed by hysterical weeping and then quiet sobbing. She had heard children crying, but something was indeed different here. There were no other voices—no adult voice was attempting to calm or comfort this child. No other children were around either. This child was all alone screaming in the dark.

Ann put down her bags and followed the sound. It stopped. "This is quite bizarre—even for this school," Ann thought. "We don't have any little ones in Clearwater. No one that young. And why would they be all alone here when everyone else is away?"

Ahead of Ann was a shadowy black hallway lined with closed doors. The cries started up again. A child weeping in the dark. Ann quickly noticed that the sound came from a different child. This weeping was shriller and hysterical. It had a metallic quality, as if it were coming through a telephone. Yet Ann had never heard a telephone receiver that projected sound as loudly as this.

As Ann walked toward the sound, she remembered way back to when she was younger. The crying of one infant was contagious to other children in the vicinity. One started and soon there was a chorus. She felt a stirring inside herself. Images of Grandpa, Lady Ann, and her parents began to crowd the edges of her mind. The sound seemed to poke into her and unlock her most vulnerable feelings. She didn't want to get sucked into that kind of crying. She wasn't going to cry today. Sometime down the line, but not today.

She followed the noise down the hallway, door by door, office by office. The cries were coming from inside one of the teachers' offices. She knew immediately whose office it was. The large print on the door read, NADIA FAIRCHILD, HEADMISTRESS. Along the bottom of the door, there was dim sliver of light. A lamp of some sort was on inside the office. Whoever these children were, they had come to Miss Fairchild's office.

Ann arrived at the door, reached up to touch the handle, and paused. This was Miss Fairchild's office. The weeping had ceased. There was no sound from inside. A few seconds went by, and then it started up again. Another child. A third child crying softly and murmuring.

She slowly opened the door until she could see inside. When she did, she froze.

On the other side of the room, Miss Fairchild was seated in her office chair. She was leaning forward on her desk like a walrus basking on an ice floe. Her eyes were closed. She was listening to a circular recording on a machine beside her desk. Upon the desk—arranged like dinnerware waiting to be polished were eight other recording cylinders. She had been listening to them at random as if they were musical selections—only these were recordings of children crying. The weeping was coming out of the speaker of the machine, and Fairchild seemed to be absorbing the sound and letting the waves of emotion touch some space within her.

Ann had never anticipated this. She had intruded on a private moment. What was more startling than Fairchild's choice of listening material was her closed eyes and dreamy smile. The sound of suffering children seemed to be providing her a strange sense of comfort.

"Who is that?" Miss Fairchild had opened her eyes. She had seen Ann standing in the shadows. "What are you doing out of your room at this hour?" she bellowed. "You shouldn't be wandering about after dark. You shall receive demerits."

"It's me, ma'am. Ann Hardy. I just got here."

"From where? Oh, it's you."

"Yes, ma'am."

"Yes, ma'am. How could I forget that discordant rural twang?"

"I arrived on the train."

"Yes. Yes." The old Fairchild was back. "Mr. Royce told me you were returning. You upset a lot of people."

"I did. Yes."

"You enraged Mr. Royce."

"That's about the size of it, ma'am."

"That's unfortunate for you. There will be some supplementary discipline, Miss Hardy."

An awkward silence.

"You probably wonder what I was doing in here."

"No, ma'am, not at all."

"Earlier today we had rain. We should have had snow, but instead we had rain. Raindrops are nature's tears."

Ann felt embarrassed. She was beginning to wish she had left the door closed. "That's perfectly all right, Miss Fairchild."

"Drops from the sky become brooklets and then rivers. They are the tears of the Virgin Mary—weeping for us here on earth."

"Ma'am, I've had a long trip."

"Mary is the most exalted maiden of all. She sees the world as it is. She sees women for what we are—poor banished children of Eve seeking redemption in the peaks and in the valleys. Mary witnesses the nobility of our efforts, and she feels the agony of our failures. She weeps for us, Miss Hardy."

Now Fairchild was bringing Ann into the scenario, which increased her discomfort.

"Perhaps I should get to my room," Ann said.

"She weeps, and her tears become raindrops. Her Son bore the sins of the world. She bears the woe. She bears the pain and tribulation that we as maidens must all endure in our worldly existence. Did you know that?"

"I never thought of it that way."

"How unfortunate for you, Miss Hardy. We had rain today. And Mary wept for us. Remember that."

"Miss Fairchild, why wasn't I told about my grandmother's death?"

Fairchild was irritated. She had intended the conversation to reiterate a life lesson. As usual, Ann was being difficult. "You were informed. I told you as soon as the letter came."

"Actually, I wasn't told for quite a while. Royce said he called you the day after it happened."

"We thought you should be told in due time. Your mother was in complete agreement."

"My mother?"

"Yes, she called me many times. We talked about it at great length. In fact, she called me early this morning. Twice, as a matter of fact."

Ann was incredulous. Fairchild was more than a compulsive liar. She appeared to make up the facts as she went along.

"My mother never called you," Ann said.

"She most certainly did."

"This morning she was with me in Winfield. We were together all morning, and she never called you."

Miss Fairchild glared at Ann. As always, she resented the intrusion of such inconveniences as the truth.

"Miss Hardy, I had hoped your trip home might have taught you something."

"It did, ma'am."

"Actions have consequences. Far-reaching consequences. In your case, demerits," Fairchild blared. "Now go to your room. Go on. Get out of here. Go."

Ann left the office and began the long trek to her room. She wondered who the children were. Why was Fairchild sitting in the dark listening to their tears? She seemed to derive satisfaction from their sorrow. Who were they?

35

One Month Later

Having received five demerits for raising her voice in the dining room, Ann was working them off with a bucket and scrub brush in the hallway in front of her room. She had learned long ago that the stains had been so well trod into the surface that cleaning was impossible.

Ann didn't mind the work. She was alone, and she could think about home. It was also an escape from the classwork, although sometimes the classwork seemed to follow her.

She heard the sound of footsteps on the floor above. The heating had gone out in some of the classrooms, and a small group was using an empty room in the students' quarters. The steps and voices carried clearly through the vent along the wall.

It was Fairchild. "All right, ladies...young ladies. I hope the temperature in this temporary *salle de classe* is more accommodating to you."

"Yes, Miss Fairchild," the young voices responded unanimously. This was a class of twelve-year-olds.

"Take out your notebooks and pencils," Ann whispered.

"Take out your notebooks and pencils," Fairchild bellowed. "In the professional world, should you decide to venture into it, you may be required to take dictation. Just remember that the thinking and the running of the business are better left to those who can. It is a man's world after all."

Ann stopped scrubbing and sat back to listen.

"Sentence one. 'Dearest Randall. Thank you for the violets. Dearest Randall.'"

"Dearest Randall...the poor sap," Ann thought.

"'You are a gentleman to bring me such a lovely bouquet. You are…a gentleman to bring…'"

"You may put them in a vahzz," Ann muttered.

"'You may put them in a vahzz…'"

Ann wondered how many of the students had bought into the thinking the school was trying to instill. She wanted to believe that most of the girls saw through it, but from what she had observed, that was not the case. Clearwater caught them at an early age.

"'You must have gone out of your way to find them. You must have…gone out of…'"

"Have I been here two years?" Ann thought. "They started drumming this one into us a month after I arrived."

"'I have always admired the brouhaha of the business world. I have always admired the brouhaha. I am thankful that you allow me to be part of it.'"

Ann smiled. "Here it comes," she thought.

"'I shall refer your order to Mr. Hortense,'" Miss Fairchild continued.

"Mr. Hortense. I haven't heard one of these for a while."

"'In our company we sell by the bushel, but the final decisions are left to Mr. Hortense.'"

In the distance Ann could make out some footsteps. They were approaching the stairs that led down to her level. The familiar scuffling sound told Ann it was Miss Bruner.

Miss Fairchild's voice continued to drone on. "All the thinking is left to Mr. Hortense.'"

The footsteps continued. As they neared the staircase, they slowed down and then stopped.

"Uh, Miss Hardy?"

"Down here, ma'am."

With one hand on the railing, Miss Bruner cautiously came down the stairs. She was carrying a package about the size of a cigar box.

Ann slid the bucket over to the wall and stood up to greet her.

"Have you learned your lesson, Miss Hardy? Have you searched your heart of hearts?"

"I think so."

"Could you tell me what you've learned?"

"Well, I learned that some days are better than others, just as some stains are tougher than others."

Miss Bruner saw that Ann was not being serious, but being in the dark hall made her nervous.

"I don't think that was the lesson, Miss Hardy."

"It wasn't," Ann said. "But I have been doing some thinking. I'll try to do better."

"Very good."

"'A perfect household,'" Miss Fairchild intoned above them. "'The children in their rooms...the kettle in the kitchen...and my wife beside the stove.'"

"She's giving a Mr. Hortense talk," Ann said to Bruner.

"Yes. That is Nadia's class. She enjoys working with the young ones."

Something had been on Ann's mind ever since her return to school.

"Miss Bruner, I said I learned my lesson, but I'm not really sure why I got these demerits. I think it was for arriving late and disturbing Miss Fairchild."

"I don't know about that."

"About a month ago. When I returned, I wanted to report in. I found Miss Fairchild in her office. She was listening to some recordings."

"Recordings?"

"It wasn't music. I know it sounds strange, but they seemed like voices of little children."

Bruner's hand went up to her mouth in a silent gasp.

"I guess I wasn't supposed to see it, but I had to report my arrival."

"Oh dear, oh dear," Bruner murmured.

"You see, I got here late on the last train. I had to check in with somebody, so I went to Miss Fairchild's office, and there she was."

"Oh, Miss Hardy." Bruner's hand was still over her mouth, her eyes wide.

"It was either report in or get demerits. In this case, I got both."

"You have to understand. She cares so much, Miss Hardy."

"Do you know anything about this?"

"She's an inspired educator, Miss Hardy. She puts her entire soul into her work. She cares so much, and she suffers because she cares."

"What about the children?"

"You shouldn't have intruded. It was a private moment."

"It's too late now, Miss Bruner. Who are they?"

Bruner saw that Ann was not going to give up.

"All right, Miss Hardy. I'll tell you, but this must be in the strictest confidence."

"All right."

"The strictest."

"I understand."

Miss Bruner's mouth moved, as if she were trying to formulate the opening words. "Before Miss Fairchild came to Clearwater, she worked at an orphanage."

"Where?"

"The point is she was dedicated. Truly inspired. She gave of herself and worked like a saint. The children knew it, and they loved her. When she left, all the children cried. They wept, Miss Hardy. Their tears have haunted Nadia Fairchild her whole life. They live inside her. And when she sits in her office and listens to their voices, it is her way of going back to them. She's visiting the children. Don't you see? That one moment in her life which was so special…when she and the children were together."

"Then why did she give me demerits?"

"With Nadia Fairchild, certain allowances must be made. It was only demerits. And demerits allow you to work."

Ann wondered now if she should have asked. The explanation was as bizarre as the original event.

"By the way, you have some mail." Miss Bruner handed Ann the box and a letter.

"Put them in your room and join the others in the auditorium for supplementary posture class."

"Do I have to?"

"You don't want more demerits."

Miss Bruner started back up the hall to the stairs.

Ann quickly opened the letter. It was from Lucille. It read, "Dearest Ann: Things have settled down now. The memorial service was cancelled, which came as no surprise. It makes me wonder if there was ever supposed to be one. Your father is fine. A lot of colds are going around. Doc Powell examined everyone out at the county farm. For the third year now, Zachary has had a clean checkup. Since he started living there, he has not been sick once. He was so happy about it, he made you a present, which we are sending to you. We'll discuss our Christmas visit in the next letter."

Ann tore open the package. Inside was a small wooden box. On it were scrawled the words "For Ann." It was almost identical to the one Zachary presented to the colonel just before he died. Ann smiled. Zachary's spirits were still high in spite of everything.

"Good for you, Zachary," Ann said.

"Was it made by a child?" Miss Bruner was on the steps, waiting for Ann.

"No, but he's pretty special," Ann said.

"It looks as if he made it especially for you."

"He made one for my grandpa, too."

"When?"

"A long time ago."

"We should be going, Miss Hardy."

Ann placed the gifts on her bed and followed Miss Bruner up the stairs.

36

WHEN CHRISTMAS ARRIVED, JACK AND LUCILLE came to Coon Falls and stayed at the Old River Hotel, the only hotel in town.

Jack and Lucille didn't speak much about Winfield—except to say that the bank was foreclosing on more farms. Royce had directed all his attention to persuading investors to join Pheasant Valley Power and Electric. Ann saw that her father was drinking again. He was always describing that one big deed he was going to perform to make their lives better. It was always plans, but never accomplishments. This made Ann sad. The fight seemed to have gone out of both her parents.

The months began to pass. The incident in Miss Fairchild's office and Miss Bruner's explanation faded into memory. Everything became part of a larger tapestry. Finally, it was another year since Ann had been home.

By spring the snow had melted, and the green was beginning to appear on the trees and hillside around the school. The river and rapids had become higher and more boisterous, filling with melting snow from more northern regions. Ann noticed the natural beauty, but she treated any admiration of it as a test of her loyalty. "This is not home," she would say to herself. "It's easy to say that home is wherever I am at the moment, but this is not home. Winfield is home."

Classwork kept Ann from worrying about her family, yet at the same time, it depressed her. Each course was a dreary recitation of the same theme—a woman's subservient place in the world. And each one required an essay or a test on how well the student understood and appreciated what she had been taught.

"You can laugh at this garbage for a while, but the constant repetition wears you down," Ann thought. "At the same time, I'm stuck here. I've got to play along without letting it get to me. How the hell do I do that? There's got to be an answer—some formulaic response I can provide for every assignment that will get the grade without giving me a headache. Something simple and stupid. That shouldn't be too difficult to find."

The solution to Ann's dilemma presented itself in an afternoon class called Literature for Our Daily Lives, taught by Miss Nadia Fairchild, who would ransack assorted literary classics and attempt to apply parts of them to the lives of students at her school. They had already turned *Ivanhoe* on its head. To Miss Fairchild, it was a story of women who behaved as women should: when they found themselves in trouble, the noble knight came riding to the rescue.

Her current target was *Hamlet*. From Fairchild's point of view, the play might as well have been called *The Tragedy of Ophelia*. Each week a student was selected at random to present an oral report on what she had learned.

When Miss Fairchild arrived, the students all curtsied in unison.

"Today, we will discuss an important issue in an important play, *Hamlet* by William Shakespeare. *Hamlet* is analyzed and discussed by scholars the world over for the complexity of its hero. But because it is a man's world, another character is completely overlooked. What character is that?"

A hand went up.

"Miss Pucco, you may tell me."

"Ophelia."

"Who can tell me where the play is set?"

Another hand.

"Miss Cannon, you may tell me."

"Wasn't the play set somewhere in Ireland?"

"Oh no. No. No. How can it be in Ireland when the play's title includes the words *Prince of Denmark*?"

"Oh, then it was in Denmark?"

"I hope you shall be more prepared when it is your turn."

"Yes, Miss Fairchild."

"And now, Ophelia," Fairchild began grandly. "Ophelia is a maiden whose fate echoes down through the ages. She is a maiden in a court whose activities are a mirror of our existence. Her tragedy is as great as that of Hamlet. And what is that? She does not know herself. She enters the intrigue misjudging her strengths and not knowing her limitations. And she is destroyed. At least Hamlet knew the risks. True, he couldn't make up his mind, but he knew the risks. And Ophelia? Sadly, she does not."

Miss Fairchild allowed her gaze to roam around among the faces. It settled on Ann.

"And with that, we will hear our weekly reportage, 'What Ophelia Means to Me.' Miss Hardy, you may begin."

"Me?"

"You have been called, Miss Hardy."

Miss Fairchild lumbered over to her desk.

Ann stood up. She heard a snickering from the back of the room.

Ann could have been flustered, but she stood her ground. What could she say? The course content was ridiculous, but she had to answer something.

Everyone was waiting.

"You may begin, Miss Hardy."

Ann remained cool. There was nothing to lose here. Some words of advice from her grandpa popped into her head. "When they got you on the spot, give them what they want to hear."

"Miss Hardy, we do not have all day."

"Yes, ma'am," Ann said. "We have been studying *Hamlet* and the character of Ophelia. But more importantly, we have been focusing on how the play applies to us. To us…as young women of the twentieth century. Before class I examined the text…all the intrigue…I did some real digging, but the more I dug, the more I realized that what is really important here or in any play we study…is how we think. How we choose. How well we know ourselves."

The hulking frame sat forward with evident interest.

"I came to this realization because of my own personal background, especially my own misunderstanding of my family's efforts to educate me, and my own misinterpretation of all that is being done for my benefit."

"Yes," Fairchild nodded. "Very good."

The words were coming easier now.

"We know that Ophelia had all the qualifications for a perfect maiden. Miss Fairchild tells us so. But Ophelia's big mistake was that she jumped into the brouhaha. The court was ruled by a king. Therefore, it was a man's world. Ophelia should have realized this. She should have stayed back…like a wallflower. She should have let Hamlet finish the business he set out to accomplish. When he told her to go to a nunnery, she should have gone. It wouldn't have been so bad there. She might have been the only character left at the end of the play, but she would have been alive. If she wept a little, she could have looked out at the rain and felt the consolation that our Heavenly Mother was crying, too. She wouldn't have been alone."

Fairchild was listening in amazement. The other students were shocked or bewildered.

"Don't you see?" Ann said. "A maiden today faces tremendous challenges, challenges that come in all shapes and sizes. A maiden must make a stand—within reason. She must decide how she is going to respond to each challenge. And more importantly, she must decide how she will live her life—within proper limits, of course. We know the loss if she chooses incorrectly, as Ophelia did. But if she chooses with enlightenment, she will know her place in the world. She will know the freedom she finds in that place...And she will live a long and happy life. Thank you."

"Miss Hardy," Fairchild said, "I would never have expected this of you. I am not sure if you truly believe what you are saying, but I sense a soul groping in the dark, a soul seeking the light at the end of the tunnel. May I see your notes?"

"My notes?"

"Yes. A speech like that had to have notes."

"I'm sorry, ma'am, but I don't have any notes."

"No notes?"

"I wanted to say what I felt. What I gathered from the text, not the text itself. I was speaking from the heart."

Miss Fairchild scrutinized Ann again. The maiden had given a good speech. But there was that damned attitude. Fairchild decided to let it go this time.

"Very well. You were honestly seeking that nugget of truth. We will know soon enough the honesty of your search. A maiden must choose. A maiden must decide. You are correct in that respect. Sit down, Miss Hardy."

Ann had found what she was seeking. On every assignment or every test in every subject—be it English, history, or maiden ethics—she worked variations of the same theme into every final paragraph: "A maiden today faces tremendous challenges. A maiden must confront these challenges and make a choice. She must do it honestly. She must decide where she stands in the world." The subject discussed was irrelevant—as long as she gave it the same conclusion. For the rest of her days at Clearwater, Ann maintained a passing grade.

37

IN TIME ANN WAS FIFTEEN.

By now she knew that nothing would ever be done to challenge the conditions at home. She herself would have to make any changes when the time came. Royce Chamberlin had chalked up quite a list of transgressions. "I wonder how many laws he's really broken. I'm going to look into this," Ann thought.

She began with the Clearwater Library. The only volumes that mentioned law at all were the dictionary and the encyclopedia, and these only gave brief descriptions and definitions. There was nothing to trouble the head of any pure-minded maiden enrolled at the school.

The Coon Falls Library was no better. Located in a single room on a side street, it featured a smattering of novels, cookbooks, children's books, and Minnesota history—arranged by author rather than subject.

She made another attempt during a rare school field trip into Minneapolis. The girls were given an hour of free time, so Ann went to a bookstore they had passed a few minutes earlier. There was no law section at all. "Why don't you let a lawyer handle it?" the owner suggested.

When Jack and Lucille came for a visit in March, Ann asked them if they would order a book on basic law. It immediately produced an uproar from Jack. "Don't do this," he cried. "My God. Don't tell anyone you're doing this." When Lucille offered to see what she could find at the Winfield library, Jack pleaded with her, saying that the librarian would tell Fred Brubaker and Brubaker would tell Royce. "We have to live with him, Lucille. Please don't do this." On hearing this argument for appeasement and surrender, Ann thought of her grandpa. The colonel would have saddled up, ridden into town, and ransacked the courthouse library till he found the right book.

A week after her parents returned to Winfield, Ann received a note from Lucille: "I will have a look in the library in town. I don't see how I can get into any trouble with a simple question. If I find something, we can order it for you from the publisher or one of the big stores in Chicago or Minneapolis. Love, Mama."

This was heartening news. It might take some time, but Ann was prepared to wait.

In April the weather was pleasant, although a little warm for spring. This year everything seemed early—including what Ann called the Summer Letter from Royce: "For reasons of which we are both well aware, you will not be coming home for the summer recess. Your parents are in agreement with my opinion. However, they will be visiting you at Clearwater."

Late afternoon a few days later, Ann was on a nature walk with Miss Fairchild and some of the older girls. On this particular occasion, they had ventured beyond the sport field and down to the riverbank. They were walking along the rushing, wave-strewn water that ran between school and the hill on the other side.

Ann liked the river. She would pick a whitecap and picture it bobbing along in the current until it finally disappeared. She would imagine hopping on it and riding down to the nearest town or city—anything to escape the monotony of Clearwater and Coon Falls.

"Ah, the wonder of nature," Miss Fairchild bawled. "A walk with Mother Nature is exhilarating, is it not? Do you appreciate the harmony of the waters and the vegetation?"

"Yes, Miss Fairchild. Oh yes, Miss Fairchild," the students eagerly responded.

"The rivulets. The eddies. And the cataracts. Ah, the wonder of it all."

It was a beautiful scene—except for the four support pillars that lay ahead of them. They reached up from the earth and the water to the bridge that linked the road that passed the school to the shore on the other side.

"Onward! There is much to explore! More to appreciate!" Fairchild resumed her position at the head of the line. The girls followed.

Finally Miss Fairchild stopped. "We will have ten minutes to repose and meditate, after which we shall return to school."

Fairchild began to wander along the water's edge. Most of the girls followed her, eager to soak up any tidbits of wisdom. A few remained apart to chat among themselves.

Ann noticed one girl regarding an area on the hillside across the river. At the top of the incline and near the bridge was a one-story structure, rectangular and olive green. It ran about seventy to eighty feet long and had no apparent windows on the side facing the river.

"What's that building?" she said to Ann.

Ann had never seen it before.

"I don't remember it being there last week," said another girl.

"I don't think it was," Ann said.

"It's new," the first girl said. "Like it sprang up overnight."

"Looks like a tent. Maybe it's a chautauqua," the second said. "A place for a revival meeting."

"Not out here," Ann said. "They usually go for fairgrounds—where they can bring in the multitudes and save their souls. This isn't the place for it."

"This morning I heard Estelle talking," the first said. "She says some of the girls on her floor thought they heard music over there."

"Doesn't look very musical to me," Ann said with a laugh. "Looks more deserted. Sort of like our school."

"Shh, don't say that, Ann Hardy," the second cautioned. "You could be reported."

"Shame, Ann Hardy, shame," added the first.

Miss Fairchild and the girls were soon on their way back to school. The mail was in. For Ann there was a letter from her parents—a little thicker than her usual correspondence from home. She had seen Lucille and Jack only a short time before, so she decided to read it when she got back to her room.

Ann sat down on her bed and opened the letter. It was from Lucille and written three days ago: "Dearest Ann, We both miss you dearly, and it is with great regret that we send the following news. Our beloved Zachary is dead."

Ann couldn't believe it. She had grown accustomed to the repetition of bad news from Winfield, but this was something she had not foreseen. Dead. Zachary was dead.

She continued to read: "Sheriff Dierkes informed us yesterday morning. Zachary was found in his room. They said it was pneumonia. Came on very sudden. We shall miss him terribly."

The words were beginning to sink in. Ann felt tears in her eyes, but she had to focus on the letter. Grief would come later.

"What is strange is that we saw Zachary just the day before, and he looked fine. Doc Powell had done his annual checkup a week ago, and Zachary was fit and healthy. We know there is a type of pneumonia people can catch and walk around with for weeks without knowing it. We asked Doc Powell to have another look at Zachary. Even though he had filled out the medical report and death certificate, he said he would do it."

"Who said it was pneumonia in the first place?" Ann thought. "And why didn't they call me about it? It's like they wait for days to gather up the nerve to tell me."

She returned to the letter. "Our troubles were not over. When Doc Powell returned to the county farm the following morning, Zachary's death certificate and medical report were missing from the file. On top of that, Royce had given orders that Zachary's body be cremated immediately. The body had been moved to the funeral home during the night. There would be no funeral, as Zachary would only be missed by the few people who knew him."

"That son of a bitch," Ann said.

"Royce's actions were suspicious to say the least," the letter continued. "But when Doc arrived at the county farm, he discovered Sheriff Dierkes already there investigating a burglary. Seems that the place had been broken into by a couple of hobos who came through the office window on their way to the kitchen. It is curious that nobody heard them. It is also curious that they would stop in the office if they were hungry for food. Everybody is at loose ends here. Our thoughts and prayers are with Zachary. I feel we let him down."

The next page was shorter. "Jack has talked to Sheriff Dierkes. Royce, as head of the family, has the legal power to make Zachary's funeral arrangements. Doc Powell made out a new medical report and death certificate, and he made copies for us and Dierkes. Dierkes said he would investigate further. He told us that he spent the morning going all over the county farm, inside and out. So far there's no evidence of any kind, only suspicions."

Then the writing became more sharp and jagged, as if scribbled on her lap in a rush. "I do think we should all be very careful. Three of us are dead now. Your grandpa. Your grandma. And now Zachary. I am not saying Zachary was murdered, but as we have seen, there are many ways to kill someone. Perhaps we were unwise to try to buck circumstances that overwhelm us. Perhaps we are responsible for what happened to Zachary. Perhaps I am to blame. When I went to the library about your book, that awful Sonya, the teller from the bank, was there. She heard me ask about the law book. I don't know who to trust. It is why I took so long to mail this to you. You have to understand. I hope you forgive us. Love, Mama."

Ann was boiling. She wanted to hit something. It didn't matter what. She swore if someone walked in on her at that moment, she would hit them. Suddenly she grabbed her pillow, pressed it over her mouth, and screamed. The sound was muffled, but it lasted until her lungs were empty and her ribs ached. She took a breath and did it again. Her eyes were stinging. She was not going to cry. That would come later.

She did not go to dinner. She sat in her room, thinking of Zachary's cheerfulness and the empty place in her world now that he was gone. Everything was churning inside, and there was no way to release it. All she could do was scream into her pillow over and over again until she was exhausted.

It wasn't enough. She couldn't share her feelings with anyone, and she couldn't release them. She felt as though the walls were pressing in on her. She had to get out. She didn't care about the consequences. She had to be free.

The window along the ceiling was large enough for her squeeze through. She would go out through the window. She would wait.

When all the girls were asleep, Ann placed the chair on top of her desk and climbed up until she was standing next to it just below the window. Slowly she eased up onto the chair. The furniture wobbled as she shifted her weight. She carefully pulled herself up to the window and opened it. The ground was at eye level on the other side. She pressed herself through the space until she was outside.

She had never seen the school from this side before. It still looked like a bunker in the moonlight. Between the tree branches was a clear sky. She could see around her well enough. Without a sound, she began to run. She raced away from the building and into the woods. She went faster and faster, going as far as she could. She dodged branches and shrubbery. It was a wonder she didn't trip on a rock or a root. She had no thought of getting lost—only of running.

After several minutes, Ann stopped. She sat on a tree stump to listen to the sound of crickets somewhere nearby. She felt better. "I had to do this," she thought. "I'll look a mess when I get back, but it was worth it." The events at home were still with her, but now it wasn't out of proportion.

Up ahead she heard a noise. She listened to see if she would hear it again. There it was. A melody mixed with the breeze and the passing river. Music and laughter that were so far off they seemed distorted but were clear enough to identify. Somewhere out there some people were having a good time.

Ann followed the notes of the melody through the woods until she emerged on the riverbank. She was downriver from the bridge.

"I know where I am," she thought. "All that running, and I only got this far."

The river was flowing and lapping along nearby. The sky was clear and dotted with stars. Across the water and up above, the noise was coming from the new building. Laughter and music. Ann could see tiny shards of light here and there in the walls.

A melody flowed from a piano, followed by a round of applause. Then a drum and a xylophone joined in, playing big-city jazz.

"I think it's a speakeasy," Ann thought. "In the middle of nowhere. Who's going to raid a place way out here?"

Ann looked up the river to the bridge. There was a trail that began close to the abutment on her side that zigzagged upward to where the road met the bridge.

"I bet that'll take me up there."

She moved carefully down the riverbank, stepping over rocks and around clumps of shore vegetation, and started up the path.

When she reached the top, she paused at the edge of the road to get an idea of what lay ahead. From where she stood all the way to the other side, the bridge had a three-foot railing along each side. It was so low it couldn't be seen from the riverbank.

There was a commotion at the other end of the bridge. A car's engine started up. As the vehicle pulled away from the building, the driver gave a single tap on his horn. In response, there was a signal from another person holding a lantern on the other side of the road. Then the car started across the bridge toward them, turning on its headlights as it approached. Ann scurried back down the trail a few steps and ducked. She waited as the car drew near and passed.

"Amazing. They've got a lookout and everything."

Ann returned to the road. She was looking across the bridge at the building on the other side. She scurried quickly along the rail and stopped when she reached the edge of the building.

Up close she saw that the structure was made from a mixture of burlap and wood. Across the road on the hillside, she could make out the silhouette of a man with a pair of binoculars. He was seated, smoking a cigarette and watching the road in the other direction.

She remained in the shadows along the wall, taking in as much as she could. The walls were actually like canvas drapes that extended from the roof to the floor. Occasionally they moved, pressed by a slight breeze from the other side. Ann peered through a crack between two strips of canvas.

Across the room was the door, and the wall featured a series of large open windows. The other two on the sides were made of the same covered canvas. The entire place looked like it was set up on the fly—quickly assembled and ready to be torn down at a minute's notice.

The room was full of couples who were either dancing or seated at one of eight tables. Others stood along the open windows. Most of the customers were dressed for a social occasion—they all seemed to have stopped off on their way from another gathering. The lamps gave everything a yellow tint. Ann could make out a group of cars parked outside along the road or beside the building. She heard the music, but she could not see where it was coming from.

She crept around the building to the first open window. Along the wall was the bar, essentially a long plank extending over three rain barrels. Behind it was a makeshift shelf for the liquor—eight crates turned on their sides. Only the bottle tops were visible. Beside them were two beer kegs with spigots. The bartender reflected the temporary quality of the establishment—dressed casually in an open white shirt and canvas trousers.

To the left of the bar was a small raised platform, just big enough to accommodate the trio of musicians. They were all clean-cut and appeared to be of college age. The piano player was a darkly handsome young man with slender features and black hair. He was accompanied by a chubby drummer and a studious man on the xylophone. They had arrived wearing suits but had removed their coats.

All at once, a group of voices began to cry out from various parts of the room.

"'Tiger Rag'! Hey, Ben! 'Tiger Rag'! Play it, Ben!"

Ben, the piano player, grinned at the crowd. He started to play "Tiger Rag" on the piano, the others musicians joining in. Within seconds the rhythm of the number had the whole place cheering and clapping. Couples were out on the dance floor, and everyone was waiting to join in the chorus: "Hold that tiger! Hold that tiger!"

Once Ann saw the piano player, she couldn't take her eyes off him. She felt good all over. She was excited. At that moment there was no one else around except her and the young man pounding the keys of the piano. She felt as if she were floating, yet her feet were solidly planted on the ground.

She wanted a closer look. She saw a spot where the canvas opened right behind the stage. She was about halfway to the opening when the trio finished "Tiger Rag." There was a roar of applause and cheers from the clientele. Ann reached the opening. It was about three feet wide and clamped together at the top, less an entryway than an air vent for the band.

The trio began a slow number. Ann stepped up to the opening, about ten feet from the piano and quite visible to Ben. She watched him as he played. His assurance at the keyboard was as enchanting as his looks. She was amazed at how she felt inside. She found herself wondering about the texture of his skin. His face. His eyes. She had seen boys and young men around Winfield, but none of them made her feel this way.

Ben's fingers touched the keys, sending mood and atmosphere around the room. He raised his eyes, and then he saw her. This young woman seemed to have been watching him for some time. He was dealing with that surprise when he hit a wrong note. Clark and Lee glanced up from their instruments.

Ben's eyes kept moving to the girl in the passageway. This had never happened before. As he continued playing and glancing over to her, he hit another bad note.

"Ben?" Lee inquired.

They played the tune all the way till the end. There was applause.

Clark looked over at Ben with a puzzled expression. "What happened?" he asked.

"Just a couple of off ones," Ben said.

"You don't hit off ones," Lee said.

"Let's take five," Clark said.

"I'm OK," Ben said.

"We're taking five, partner," Lee said and then announced to the crowd, "We're taking five. Thank you, everybody."

"There was a girl," Ben said.

"What?"

"There."

They had spotted her. Ann backed away from the opening and ran. The reality of the situation hit her. She had snuck out of school to visit a speakeasy, and she would be in big trouble if she were caught. Ann was racing away from the building and down the road to the bridge.

"Hey! Hey!" came a man's voice from the dark.

"What? What happened?" the lookout yelled.

Ann dashed across the bridge, reached the end, and started down the to the riverbank. She would be back to her room in no time.

Ben had gotten up from the piano and was looking out into the night.

"What are you looking for?" Lee asked. "You see someone there?"

"A girl."

"Where?"

"Out there."

Ben left the stage and crossed to the door. A number of customers said, "Ben. Hey, Ben," as he passed. Lee followed. Ben looked out the door.

"Did you see somebody or didn't you?" Lee asked.

"I did, but I'll be damned if I know where she went."

"Hell, girls come and go around here."

"Not like this one," Ben said. "This one was special."

38

ANN SLIPPED BACK INTO HER ROOM with no problem, but she was unable to get to sleep because she could not stop thinking about Ben. She knew she liked him a lot, but who was he? He wasn't much older than Ann, but he was calm and assured, and he seemed completely at home in an illegal operation most likely run by gangsters. Still, he'd hit some off notes the second he'd seen Ann. Did that mean anything? Ann hoped it did. What did he think of her? Was he thinking of her at all? Why did wondering if he was thinking of her make Ann so self-conscious? If this was the beginning of a romantic feeling, then why were there so many doubts and anxieties?

There was only one thing to do: go back.

The following night at 11:00 p.m., Ann was out the window and making her way to the river. She hurried across the bridge without alerting the lookout to her presence. In no time, she was moving along the building to the open spot near the band.

There were not as many customers this time. The trio was playing while two couples danced in the area in front of the stage.

The manager, a middle-aged balding man named Gus, was positioned behind the bar. Pleasant, sociable, and tough, he was watching everything and missing nothing. At a place like this, no one knew who the actual owner was. There was money. There was illegal booze and music. Somebody up the business ladder had chosen a manager to run the place. The establishment ran until it was closed down or the bosses decided it was time to move it somewhere else.

Onstage, the trio was in the middle of the number. Ben provided the melody on the piano. Now and then his eyes would glance over to the opening where he had seen Ann earlier, so once Ann was in place, he saw her immediately. This time he smiled at her and continued to play without a flaw.

"Look who's back," Lee said.

With a flourish on the piano, the trio brought the number to a close. Again, there was applause and cheers.

"Want to take five, Ben?" Lee asked.

"What do you think?" Clark said with a laugh.

Ben stood up from the piano. "Thank you. Thank you," he said to the customers. "Be right back."

Ben pointed to the doorway across the room. Ann disappeared from the opening. Gus looked up questioningly from the bar.

"Whatsa matter, you boys? You just took five an hour ago," he said.

When he saw Ann outside the doorway, he raced around the bar to confront her.

"Whoa! Whoa!" Gus shouted. "Get away from there. Scat! Scat!"

"It's OK, Gus," Ben said as he arrived at the doorway.

"What's this?" Gus said to Ann. "Who are you? What are you doin' there?"

"I heard the music," Ann said.

"You're a kid. Get outta here!"

"I was just stopping by."

"Stoppin' by? You're from that school over there, ain't you? That old place by the river."

"I didn't know it was a school," Ann said. "I thought it was a hospital."

"She just stopped to hear the music," Ben said.

"Music, hell…She's underage, Ben. Jailbait. We serve booze here. We got enough trouble without some kid stirrin' things up."

"She'll stay outside, Gus."

"I will, Mister. I promise," Ann said.

Gus looked her over. She seemed too innocent to cause trouble.

"You don't drink nuthin'. You don't even sniff the cork, and I mean that."

"I won't," Ann said.

"I'll take responsibility," Ben said.

"You better. We got a business operation here. You know the Gandolfo brothers ain't gonna like this."

Ben was intrigued by Ann. She was younger than he had thought, but in many ways she seemed like an adult. She was polite, yet she held her own with Gus. She had the most direct eyes of any girl he'd ever seen.

"This is walkin' the thin line, Ben," Gus said.

"She won't cause trouble."

"Just keep her outside. I mean that." Gus started back to the bar. He turned once more to reemphasize his point. "I mean that."

"You see his point, don't you?" Ben said to Ann.

"What is this place?" Ann asked.

"It's what you'd call a movable entertainment venture. A sign of the times."

"It's a speakeasy," Ann said.

"That's one way to describe it," Ben said. "You want some root beer?"

"Root beer is fine," Ann said.

"I'll get our drinks," Ben said, moving to the bar.

Ann watched him crossing to the bar. She liked everything about him, even the way he walked across a room. No other boy had made her feel that way.

Ben returned with two bottles of root beer. "You are from the school, right?"

"Yes," Ann said.

"And you snuck over here?"

"I heard the piano," Ann said.

Ben laughed. "You've got nerve."

"Is playing the piano your job?"

"Part-time. I'm a sophomore at Illinois Tech. We all are. Lee, Clark, and myself. We do this on the side for extra money."

"So you're at the university?"

"I want to go into business. Insurance. But I like music. Times are tough, so we do this."

"How did you end up out here?"

"Gus over there heard us playing at his niece's wedding. He offered us a job for the summer. By the way, I'm Ben."

"I'm Ann."

They were so involved in their conversation that everything else in the room seemed far away. Each was captivated by the other.

Although Ann felt tongue-tied, she felt compelled to say something. "I took a chance coming here. I'm glad I did."

"Listen," Ben said, "if there's a risk of you getting into trouble..."

"I can stay a little longer. Are you from Minneapolis?"

"Chicago. What about you?"

"Iowa. A little town called Winfield."

Lee and Clark were waiting at the front of the stage.

"Ben?" It was Lee calling and gesturing to the piano.

"It isn't even five minutes," Ben called back. "How did you get over here from Clearwater?" he said to Ann.

"Climbed out a window."

"Just like that? You're an enterprising girl."

"If I set out to do something, I try to do it. A little trait I picked up from my grandpa."

"Time for music, Ben," Gus said from the bar.

"I better go," Ben said.

"Me, too."

"You be careful on the way back now."

As Ann watched Ben walking back to the stage, a battered and dirty black sedan turned off the road and pulled in behind her.

The arrivals were a decidedly seedy bunch—two men and two women. The men were dressed in stained and wrinkled suits, and the women looked like flappers who had spent a week sleeping on a park bench. They clambered out of the car and made straight for the entrance. Ann didn't notice them until the stench of alcohol and sweat wafted over her.

The central figure in the group was a bloated, overweight man named Varnesto Henchawz. The other man, Ricardo by name, was in a constant state of motion—scurrying around Henchawz, always obsequious, always checking, and always managing the life of his boss.

Gus reacted with alarm. "Oh jeez. Jeez Louise. Not them." He was out from behind the bar and crossing the room. "Whoa, no! Whoa, no! Not tonight!"

Henchawz squinted through bloodshot eyes. *"Buenos noches, amigo. Su casa es mi casa."*

"No. No *casa* crap. I know you. We've had trouble before."

Henchawz slowly pointed a greasy finger to his ear. "I don't *hear* you!" he shouted gaily.

Ricardo slid up to Gus. "A little hospitality. One drink. That's all."

"No. You're trouble. You better go."

"We don't want no trouble. A little hospitality. Please? We're askin' nice."

Henchawz sauntered over to the bar. Ricardo scuttled away from Gus and over to Henchawz.

"What do you want, boss? What do you need?"

The big man was massaging his right temple. "I want a drink."

"See? He just wants a drink. Anything you got. He needs to relax."

"I need to relax," the big man said.

"One drink, please," Ricardo said.

"Just one drink now," Gus said, moving back to the bar.

"One drink. No trouble."

Gus poured a drink and handed it to Henchawz. The big man downed it in a single motion.

"More."

Gus poured a second shot. Henchawz downed it.

"See?" Ricardo said to Gus. "He's happy now. Are you happy, boss?"

"I'm happy," the big man mumbled. "Pay him."

Ricardo put some money on the bar.

From the stage, Ben and the other band members were observing Gus and the intruders.

"Who the hell is that?" Lee said.

"Three hundred pounds of trouble," Clark answered. "The big one ran a dance studio till the law shut him down. Now they roam like a pack of animals."

"I've never seen him before," Ben said.

"He's a mean drunk."

"Anything else we can do for you?" Gus was asking.

"Don't rush us. We're starting to like the place," Ricardo said.

"Let's cut it," Ben said. The trio stopped playing. When the music stopped, Henchawz looked up from his drink in a bleary manner.

"They stopped the music."

"What is it, boss?" Ricardo asked.

"I don't hear no music."

"What is it? What do you need?"

"Why they stop the music?" Henchawz began to gaze around the room, sizing up the other customers one by one.

"What is it, boss?"

Henchawz spoke slowly, still looking around the room. "I want it to be different tonight. I remember how it was when we had the studio. Music in the air, booze around. A man could feel alive. Just get lost in the music and the motion and the booze. Leave all his troubles at the door. Remember?"

"I remember," Ricardo said.

"Look at us. Now we have to beg for it."

Henchawz's gaze stopped when he landed on Ann.

"I'm tired of beggin' for it, Ricardo."

"You're looking at the girl. What is it, boss?"

One of the women edged over to Ann. "You bring your dancing shoes?" she asked knowingly.

"Excuse me?" Ann said.

"What is it, boss? What do you need?" Ricardo repeated.

"I want to dance."

"The boss wants to dance," Ricardo said to Gus.

"Wait a minute now. You got your drinks." Gus said.

"Varnesto Henchawz is a very great man. He wants a dance. Just one dance."

"Tonight I am gonna indulge myself," Henchawz stated proudly. "Wine, women, and dance—all right here. Tonight, this is my dance floor."

Already one couple was slipping out the door, anticipating a problem.

"Just one dance. Be a sport," Ricardo said to Gus.

"All right. One dance and that's it," Gus answered.

Ann sensed trouble brewing beneath the surface. The entire situation reminded her of home. A bully starts making demands, and his victim keeps giving in until it is too late. Different characters and props, but the same scenario.

Henchawz waddled onto the dance floor. The remaining customers observed—either in embarrassment or shocked silence. Perhaps it was the sudden appearance of the degenerate quartet that paralyzed them. Or perhaps the knowledge that they were all on their own. In a place that operates outside the law, no one can call the police.

The two women, Wendy and Alayna, watched his every move. "Amazing how he takes control of the room," Wendy said appreciatively.

"Knows who's here and who isn't," Alayna said in agreement.

"He did promise us an evening of dance and song."

"You play tango?" Ricardo said to Ben.

"We know a few."

"Play one."

"'Monte in Moonlight,'" Ben said to the others. The trio began to play.

Henchawz began swaying in time with the music. Wobbling in place with eyes closed, he lost himself in the music.

Ricardo's attention kept returning to Ben. The piano player bothered him. There was something about Ben. He didn't look like he belonged in this crowd. Was he pampered and privileged or did he just seem that way? In Ricardo's mind, Ben was an easy mark. Too good to pass up. He needed a butt for their jokes that night. He went over to the piano and hovered over Ben's shoulder.

"You better watch it, boy. He's a tomcat tonight," Ricardo murmured.

"Excuse me?"

"That little girl over there. I see you like her."

"I just met her," Ben said.

"I see you like her. But you got to face up. He wants her."

"Get away. We're playing," Lee said to Ricardo.

"I'm talking to piano boy. Don't interrupt me," Ricardo fired back. He pressed up to Ben's ear. "You man up now and let him have her."

With a dreamy expression Henchawz attempted the arrogant pose of a flamenco dancer. He put one foot up and down and then the other. With a rapid lunge, he grabbed Ann and pulled her out onto the dance floor.

"Hey!" Ann cried.

Henchawz pushed and shoved Ann about as he danced the tango. With his weight and his drunken condition, it was a grotesque parody of the dance.

"Stay out of it, boy," Ricardo crooned. "This is a man's dance. Let it happen. Let it go."

Ben had not said anything. He may have looked like a target to the unimaginative, but he did not appear perturbed at all. He was playing the notes and keeping his eye on Ann.

"OK, Ann?" Ben called.

"I'm OK."

"Of course she's OK," Ricardo whispered. "Don't you worry now. He wants your girl. Take it like a man."

"I'll keep it in mind," Ben said.

Ricardo snickered again. "Good boy. Bet your mama tells you that."

Ann was watching Ben. She saw Ricardo jabbering into Ben's ear. He was trying to rile him but was not succeeding. Ben was preparing to take some kind of action. She was sure of it. He seemed totally cooperative until she saw his eyes. Cool and calculating, he was planning something.

Huffing and puffing, Henchawz held Ann against him. He leaned forward and began to whisper in her ear. His breath was humid and sour.

"He's a master of the dance," Wendy said.

"More than a master," Alayna added. "He's a maestro. A master and a maestro."

"Then why won't he dance with us?"

"Watch them, boy," Ricardo whispered. "Watch him hold her. Watch him now. You must have this happen all the time. Losing your girl to the stronger man. You hear what I'm saying, don't you?"

"I am not obese," Henchawz wheezed into Ann's ear. "I am pwattly. Pwattly is not obese."

"You don't say," Ann replied.

Henchawz leaned forward. "There is an intense connection between us. The connection between the man and the woman, the older man and the young girl. Do you feel it?"

He leaned forward and stuck his tongue in her ear.

"Hey!" Ann cried. "Get your tongue out of my ear!"

"That did it," Ben announced. The trio stopped. Ann broke away from Henchawz and ran over to Ben.

"Come back here!" Henchawz bellowed. "Come back here!"

"You're crazy," Ann said. "You stay away from me!"

"All over," Gus said loudly. "You're finished! You're out!"

"What? Why you have to butt in?" Ricardo screamed from the stage.

"It's over and you're leaving."

He raced over to Gus. "Why'd you have to break the mood? Why'd you have to spoil it?"

"Because I run this place and I'm telling you."

"You're telling us?" Ricardo was grinning. Suddenly, he punched Gus in the face, sending him reeling across the room.

"Your boss just got outvoted," Ricardo said to Ben.

Ben was beside Gus. Lee and Clark joined him.

"I'm OK. I'm OK," Gus said.

"I thought they were gonna be nice. *Su casa es mi casa* and all that," Henchawz growled. "I was feeling alive there. Then they ruined it."

"What is it, boss?"

"I shouldn't have to beg."

"No, boss."

"I'm tired of begging. Now I take."

"Yes, you take. You want to dance some more?"

"I want the girl."

"You want the girl, boss?" Ricardo asked, partly to confirm the outlandish suggestion.

"I want the girl, Ricardo." He was glowering at Ann. "You...come here."

"I'm not going with you," Ann said.

"I didn't hear you," Henchawz chanted. "Don't you want to go with an older man with experience?"

"No. You're fat. You're drunk. And you smell like you just threw up."

"You don't have a choice. You're coming with us."

Ricardo smiled at Ben. "Looks like he's going to get your girl anyway."

"I don't think so," Ben said.

"Oh, you don't?"

"My boss told you to leave."

Henchawz was huffing and puffing. "You give me the girl."

"I said no," Ben said.

"You give her to me, or we'll wreck the place."

"That's not going to happen either," Ben said.

Ricardo roared with laughter. Henchawz finally joined in.

"My boss told you to leave. And I'm asking you, too."

More laughter.

"Oh, you are? Listen to him, boss. He's asking us."

"I am trying to be nice about this," Ben said.

Ann was mystified. The words were solicitous, but his eyes were cold. Ben was playing them, and they were walking right into it.

"What if we take the girl and wreck the place anyway? What do you think of that?"

"You're not a very good listener."

"You hear that, boss?" Ricardo said, still laughing. "What are you going to do about it?"

"What am I going to do about it?"

"Yes, boss. What are you going to do?"

"I'm gonna bust him." With a roar, Henchawz swung at Ben, who dodged the blow and moved away to engage his next attack.

"Get him, boss!" Ricardo yelled.

Henchawz swung wildly a second time. Ben ducked. Henchawz staggered into one of the tables. Looking around wildly, he grabbed a chair.

"Watch it, Ben!" Ann cried.

Henchawz brought the chair down at Ben. Ben jumped to one side and drove his fist into the big man's stomach. Henchawz staggered backward. The expression on Ben's face was cold and determined. Ben advanced on him. His fists were a blur as he pummeled the big man, knocking him onto a table.

With his boss in trouble, Ricardo was shrieking now. "Kill him! Kill him!"

Henchawz spun around, his fists raised. Ben waded into him, knocking him back with one blow after another. Henchawz was rocking on his feet when Ben flattened him.

"Take this piece of blubber out of here," Ben said to Ricardo.

Ricardo was stunned. This hadn't turn out the way he had expected at all. "You shouldna done that, boy," he said to Ben. "You tricked and humiliated a great man. The Tango King of Goose Back, Ontario."

"It was your choice."

"That don't matter. You played us."

Ricardo and the two women were helping a dazed Henchawz to his feet.

"That's what you did. You played us. That ain't right."

Ben crossed the dance floor to Ricardo. Ricardo was grinning sheepishly. "Hey, about what I said. No offense, you know?"

"None taken," Ben said. He punched Ricardo, sending him reeling into the bar and onto the floor.

Gus was looking down at Ricardo. "Show your face here again, I will call the police."

Ricardo scrambled to his feet and scurried over to his companions. "He don't forget," he was mumbling. "Tango King. He don't forget. And I don't forget either."

"That wasn't fair," Alayna whined. "That wasn't fair at all."

"Some evening we had," Wendy echoed.

The four reached the entrance. They had the same disheveled appearance as when they arrived, but they were limping now.

"We don't forget!" Ricardo yelled. "We don't forget!"

Ann was transfixed. She was flooded with emotions: anger, vindication, and a growing attraction to Ben. Here was someone who stood up to a bully, tricked him, and then beat him on his own terms. He even seemed to derive pleasure in watching their own stupidity lead them into the trap. For the past five years, she had dreamed of using the same strategy on the forces at home. Ben had just done it. It was a vicarious triumph for Ann. She felt terrific.

"OK, Ben?" Gus asked.

"Yeah."

"Thanks for steppin' in. Better see to the girl."

Gus was in the center of the room. "All right, people. Back to normal! Drinks on the house!"

Ann rushed over to Ben. "Are you all right?" she asked.

"Yeah, what about you?" said Ben.

"No one's ever come to my rescue before."

"No one?"

"You're the first."

From outside came the sound of the sedan driving away. There was a final cry from Ricardo and then silence.

Ann and Ben smiled at each other for what seemed like minutes. They had just met, but already they felt like they had known each other for a long time.

One of the customers was checking his watch. "Twelve fifteen. We're late."

This brought Ann back to reality. She had to get back to Clearwater. "Ben, I think I better go. I don't want to, but I think I better. I'd like to talk some more."

"Do they ever allow the girls to go into Coon Falls?" Ben said.

"Sure."

"Maybe we could meet at the Igloo. You know, the ice cream parlor."

"I'd like that," Ann replied. "I better tell you something, though. I'll be sixteen on July fourth."

"OK, I'll be twenty on January twenty-ninth."

Ben was watching her leave. He had to say something more. "I guess we're set then. Ann, I really liked meeting you."

Ann smiled. "In spring and summer we have afternoons free in town. Three to five."

"How about Tuesday at the Igloo?"

"It's a deal," Ann said.

"Good night, Ann from Winfield."

"Good night, Ben."

As Ann crossed the bridge on her way back to school, she knew she would remember this night for the rest of her life.

39

THE IGLOO WAS COON FALLS'S ONLY ice cream parlor. At one time it had been the Green Frog, a local tavern, but when Prohibition had arrived, the owners had changed their line of work to accommodate the changing times. Due to a limited budget, they'd ended up using almost the same décor. The bar remained along one wall, converted into a counter. The chunky black furniture did not match the cheery light blue of the walls.

Ann and Ben began to meet there every Tuesday. They usually found a seat by the window. Each would have a soda or a sundae. Ann told him about her family and the troubles back in Winfield. Ben was drawn more and more by her strength and determination.

"Sounds like you're outnumbered back there," he said.

"It won't be forever."

"How long has it been? Five years?"

Ann dabbed her spoon in her chocolate sundae. "Going on six."

"A long time. That's rough, Ann."

"One day I'm going home—for keeps. When I do, I'm going to make some changes."

"Good luck to you."

"Whatever it is, I'll have to do it alone. No one else there will lift a finger."

He seemed concerned about her plight. But who was he? She ran through the sequence of events at the speakeasy, from their initial meeting to the fight. She could identify with standing up to a bully, but Ben had done it in a way she had never seen before. He seemed to lure them in by projecting a nonassertive front that drew out their cruelty and overconfidence and then throttling them before they realized they had been duped. As Ben had said afterward, "It was your choice." He was doing what she had wanted to do to all her opponents in

Winfield. It was a vicarious thrill for Ann. But then why was she questioning the tactic when she wanted to do it herself?

"Ben, I'll always appreciate what you did, taking on that Henchawz and all."

"He was a bad one," Ben said.

"It seemed like you suckered him into attacking you."

"I thought you liked the idea."

"I do. I'd love to pull that strategy on a whole list of people back home. When you knock a bully off his perch, it's a cause for celebration."

"It can be."

"What do mean it can be?"

"I didn't do it for any celebration. I did it because we were in trouble."

"People aren't made to be walked on, Ben. It's not our nature to be victims."

Ben was puzzled. "I agree one hundred percent. So why are we talking about this?"

Ann smiled. "I'm not sure now. I wanted to question it, and I wound up in the cheering section."

"Henchawz was a mean drunk. He grabbed you. Punched Gus. He was being controlled by that little rodent. There was no reasoning with either of them."

Ben took a bite from his sundae. "You're asking me if I could have handled it another way."

"I guess."

"Maybe, but it would have still ended with a fight."

"I take it you're not a pacifist, Ben."

"Pacifism's a fine theory," Ben said. "Lots of times it works. If you can talk it out, all the better for everybody."

"But…"

"Sometimes it sends the wrong message. Some people take it as a sign of weakness. You don't want to fight, but they force you into it. And when that happens, you fight to win."

"I'm not saying I didn't appreciate it," Ann said.

"I know."

"Do you mind talking about it?" Ann asked.

"Hell, no. We're taking inventory."

"You know, my grandpa used to say, 'If you defeat an enemy and find yourself wondering if you did it the proper way, then you've got too much time on your hands.'"

"A wise man."

"Why are you smiling?"

"Nothing. I've never met a girl like you before."

With every meeting, Ann was more drawn to Ben. He had been a complete gentleman. He'd never tried to kiss her, although she swore there were moments when they'd exchange glances and seemed ready to kiss. "I like him a lot," she said to herself. "I think about him all the time. I imagine Ben and me together in town. In the city. Even in Winfield. Holding hands. Kissing. Everything. I want this relationship to go further, but something is holding me back. It's not that I'm afraid or anything. But there's only so much of me to go around. I'm tied up in Winfield—with Mama and Papa and my promise to Grandpa. Till that's settled, I'm no good for anybody."

❧

The weeks passed. On the Fourth of July, 1924, Ann Hardy was sixteen.

Except for five other girls, Ann was alone at Clearwater. She had received a card from Lucille and Jack as well as a new summer blouse for a birthday gift. There was no mention of their coming to celebrate with her as they had done in years past. Ann had written to them twice, specifically inviting them so they could meet Ben. Their replies had been a recitation of the latest gossip around Winfield.

Ann was sitting alone on the wooden bench in front of the Igloo. It was mid-morning. The town was having its yearly holiday picnic, and most of the businesses were shut. The girls at Clearwater were given the morning free in town. Every now and then a cluster of locals would pass on their way to the festivities at the edge of town. Ann had not realized how many people there were living around Coon Falls. Most of the time, they seemed to avoid coming to town.

Ben arrived in the gray Packard he always drove. Actually, it was one-third his car. He and the others in the trio had pooled their money and bought it so they could get to and from their engagements. He got out of the car with a bouquet of roses.

"Happy birthday," he called as he came over. He handed her the flowers—one dozen red roses.

"Thank you. Oh, Ben, they're beautiful!"

Ann was looking joyfully from the flowers to Ben and back again. She did not tell him, but these were the first flowers she had ever received from a boy she could call a serious beau.

"There's a pastry booth at the picnic," he said. "We can find a seat along the riverbank."

Ann was still taking in the beauty of her gift. Real roses. And for her. "Let me look at these," she said. "It's a beautiful present." She gave him a peck on the cheek.

She realized it was the first time they had approached a kiss. She wanted to give him one right on the mouth. She felt her heart stop. She could right now.

The moment was slipping away. She put her arm in his, and they began to stroll down the nearly deserted street.

"Did you hear from your family?" he asked.

"Only a card. Usually Mama and Papa come here. I had asked them to come this year so you could meet them."

"I'd have liked that."

They walked along in the center of the street. There was no traffic in either direction. Somewhere in the distance was the pop of a firecracker. The church bell began tolling ten o'clock.

"They could have said, 'We can't come,'" Ann said. "Instead, all I got was town gossip."

"Maybe no news is good news."

Another firecracker popped, and there were shouts and cheers from the riverbank.

"I have some news," Ben said. "Maybe not the best. Gus is closing down at the end of the summer."

"Why?"

"He's been getting threats. He thinks it's from that Henchawz and his bunch."

"They were crazy."

"It just takes one with a grudge," Ben said. "The Gandolfo brothers are cautious. When it comes to business, they like to move around. It was time anyway."

"What'll Gus do?"

"Simple. The place can be pulled down in one night. Floor goes back to the lumberyard. Bar's returned to the YMCA. Piano, lamps, and tables go to a warehouse. Only thing left is the flat area overlooking the river."

"Everything changes but the land," Ann said pensively.

"What?"

"Something my grandpa used to say. After Gus closes, we'll still see each other, won't we?"

"Of course we will," Ben said. "I think it's better that we meet here in town. Safer for you."

"Sneaking out was fun."

"You could have been caught, and we wouldn't be sitting here now."

"That's true."

"I have to say this," Ben said. "I feel good every time I talk to you. Just talking with you is an amazing feeling."

Ben was leaning forward to kiss her when they heard a car approaching rapidly with its horn beeping frantically. The car swerved and weaved from one side of the road to the other.

"What's the matter with them?" Ben said. "Are they drunk?"

"It's the car from school."

The car veered around them and skidded to a stop. Inside was Miss Saypin, a middle-aged woman with a stricken expression and huge black circles under her eyes. Next to her was a nervous passenger, the elderly Miss Webber.

"Miss Hardy," Miss Saypin said, "you were warned about socializing without school permission."

"Socializing with young men," Miss Webber chided.

"You were warned," Saypin repeated.

Ann thought the circles under Saypin's eyes made her look like a worried raccoon.

"We were going to the picnic," Ben said.

"That's not the point," Miss Saypin declared. "I am sure...I am..." Slowly, her mouth opened into a monstrous yawn. "Sure...you are a fine young man."

"He is," Ann said.

"Nevertheless, you are disregarding school policy."

"I'm not disregarding it, Miss Saypin. We're just going down to the riverbank," Ann said.

"Be that as it may, Miss Hardy," Saypin said. "It is not our habit to adopt a fuddy-duddy attitude. We wouldn't do this unless it was dreadfully serious."

"Oh," Miss Webber said, suddenly remembering. "The phone call."

"Oh yes, of course," Miss Saypin said. "We were led astray by this other discussion. A half hour ago we received a call from Winfield."

"What?"

"There's been some sort of accident. Miss Fairchild asked us to return you to school if we found you."

Ann was filled with a clammy dread. Any news from home was always bad news. Not knowing what it was made it worse.

"What sort of accident?"

"I don't know," Saypin said.

"An accident," Webber added.

"Does anybody know what happened?"

"Nadia Fairchild will inform you at school," Miss Saypin said. "We are to drive you back."

Ben saw that Ann was genuinely upset—both at the vagueness of the news and the roundabout way it had been delivered.

"You go on with them," he said. "Is there anything I can do?"

"I'll be all right," Ann said. She leaned forward and they kissed. The two women gasped.

"Thank you for the flowers, Ben," Ann said.

Ann climbed into the backseat with her bouquet. Miss Saypin turned the car around in the direction of Clearwater. She hit the accelerator, and they headed out of town. Ann turned to look out the rear window. She waved at Ben. He was waving back. Rapidly, he became smaller and smaller and then vanished when the car turned a curve.

"Why did you kiss that young man?" Saypin asked.

Ann was frustrated, anxious, and irritated. She knew she would get the news when they arrived, but this did not stop her.

"Do you have any idea what happened? Was somebody hurt?"

Webber was edgily watching Saypin at the wheel. Saypin slowly opened her mouth to yawn.

"Watch the road, Millie," Webber cautioned.

The car swerved, but regained its course.

"Those flowers," Miss Saypin said abruptly. "Did the young man give them to you?"

"It's my birthday." Ann felt her anger mounting. Every announcement from home was always turned into a guessing game. "Does anybody at school know what happened?"

"Kissing him in public. Public osculation, Miss Hardy."

"She means the kiss, Miss Hardy," Webber said.

"Yes, yes. It's my birthday."

They were speeding through the woods. The car lurched from one side of the road to the other. Within minutes, they were pulling into the school driveway.

Miss Fairchild was at the window of her office, looking out over the entrance area to the school. She watched Ann and the two staff members leave the car and start for the entrance door. But most of all, she saw the roses. Beautiful red roses. Her eyes fastened on the bouquet. Fairchild left her office to meet Ann.

Ann was the first into the waiting area. She was starting for the hallway when Fairchild appeared. Miss Bruner was hovering with a suitcase in the hallway to the students' rooms.

"Miss Fairchild, what has happened?" Ann said.

"Those are very nice flowers, Miss Hardy. Who gave them to you?"

"What?"

"A young man gave them to her," Saypin said as she and Webber entered.

"A young man?" Fairchild cried.

"Yes, yes, but I got a call. What happened?" Ann inquired impatiently.

"We will take them and put them in a vahz for you."

"No, please tell me..."

"Beauty must be shared by everyone," Miss Fairchild said, advancing on her. "We shall place them where they may be shared with the other girls."

"No, no, I'll take care of them," Ann said. "You said there was an accident."

Miss Fairchild continued toward Ann. "You may give them to me," she said.

"No."

"You may give them to me."

"I just want to know what happened."

Fairchild grabbed the base of the bouquet. Ann did not let go.

"Give them. Let you give them to me." Miss Fairchild was becoming more and more enraged. With teeth clenched, she was pulling on the bouquet as hard as she could.

"No. They're mine…"

"Let you give them. Let you give them…"

Ann let them go. "OK! Take the goddamn flowers!" she screamed. "I hope you choke on them! Now, what the hell happened?"

Miss Fairchild recoiled in shock.

"I want an answer," Ann demanded.

"All right. An hour ago I received a call from Winfield. There was an accident. Your parents were in an automobile mishap on the outskirts of town. You are to return to Winfield immediately."

"Were they hurt? Are they in the hospital?"

"Your father was driving. He was speeding, and he missed a turn. They were taken to Red Fern Hospital. It is my duty as headmistress to inform you. We've packed your bags and called a taxi. If you leave now, you can catch the noon train in Minneapolis."

Jack and Lucille were the center of Ann's world, and Fairchild's words were throwing her image of that world off balance. But Fairchild was a habitual liar. Maybe the report wasn't that serious. Then again, an announcement like this hurt too much to have been made up.

"When did this happen, Miss Fairchild?"

"This morning. That's what they said."

"Who called?"

"Mr. Royce."

"And when did he call?"

"This morning, Miss Hardy. Surely you don't think we would lie to you."

Inside, Ann was beginning to react. Frustration turned to anger and then to a kind of numbness.

Miss Fairchild was regarding Ann with a blend of resentment and curiosity. Even in grief, this girl had no qualms about standing up for herself.

"Miss Hardy, you don't cry, do you?"

"We all have our own ways of crying."

"But when will you cry?"

"I'll cry when I'm damn well ready," Ann answered. "But not today."

Fairchild took the bouquet and returned to her office. Saypin and Webber followed her. Finally, Ann saw Bruner in the hallway with her suitcase. With a soft scuffing along the floor, Bruner came over.

"I threw some things together for you. The taxi should be here in a few minutes."

"Thank you, Miss Bruner," Ann said.

Everything was whirling around her, yet the lobby was totally still.

"I'm so sorry, Miss Hardy."

Bruner seemed about to say something.

"What is it, Miss Bruner?"

"What happened. I'm sorry, Miss Hardy. A maiden's life should be happy. Free of mishaps and misery."

"Do you know something?" Ann asked anxiously. "Tell me. Please."

"I shouldn't."

"Please, Miss Bruner."

"All right. But don't say I told you."

"What is it?"

"Promise me. Promise you won't say where you heard this." Bruner began to speak with great difficulty. "Your father was killed in the accident. I don't know why Nadia didn't tell you—maybe she thinks she's sparing you grief. I don't understand because you'll have to be told sometime. He was killed, and your mother was seriously injured. She's in the hospital. That's why they want you home."

Images of her parents flooded through her mind. Jack at the banquets. Jack laughing. Lucille's tenderness to her family. Jack and Lucille and Ann together. And the shell Jack had become. Again, she wanted to scream. She wanted to rush out in front of school and scream until there was nothing left inside.

"Thank you for telling me," she said quietly.

Bruner became desperate. "You have to understand, Miss Hardy…about the roses?"

"What?" Her insides were churning.

"About Nadia and the flowers. You have to understand. It's her way. Don't you see? She's an inspired educator. She goes her own way."

"Yes, yes," Ann said, half-understanding.

"It's her way. She walks her own path. Don't you see? The tremendous pressures of running a school."

"I really don't give a damn," Ann said. "If you don't mind, I'd like to be alone."

"Yes, yes, I understand," Bruner said.

"Thank you again for telling me."

Ann walked over to the front door and stared out at the field. Bruner shuffled toward the hallway and was gone.

Ann waited for about ten minutes. She felt an ache deep inside. Her eyes were filling with tears, so she focused on the patterns of grass growth in the field. Some grew one direction while others looked like bushy clumps. She would start counting them and then forget where she started.

In her office Miss Fairchild was seated at the desk with her eyes shut. The top half of the bouquet of roses sat in a chipped green vase on the bookshelf behind her.

When the taxi pulled into the driveway, she went to the window to observe Ann's departure. Fairchild remained alone there long after the taxi had disappeared among the trees.

40

THE TRAIN WAS CHUGGING THROUGH A green and yellow wave of cornfields at the edge of Franklin County. Ann looked out the window. The sight of the cornfields gave her some reassurance. Her thoughts went back to Grandpa's words: everything changes but the land.

Many of the farms had a full bloom of crops that would be ready for harvest in a few months. Others showed undeveloped fields and white signs hammered unceremoniously into the ground in front—foreclosures by the Iowa Trust Bank. There were more of them now.

As the train pulled into Winfield, Ann saw Olga standing with three passengers who were waiting to board. She grabbed her bag and rushed out of the car.

"Miss Ann...Miss Ann," Olga cried as she hugged Ann. "What a calamity."

"What happened? Where's Mama?"

"In Red Fern Hospital."

"And Papa's dead?"

"I'm so sorry, Miss Ann."

Ann still didn't want to believe it, but she knew it was true.

Before they could leave the boarding platform, the baggage door opened and Doss Claypool leaned out.

"Oh jeez," Ann said under her breath.

The Woodchuck hadn't expected to see her. He was on an errand for Mr. Dobbs. But knowing this was a family tragedy for the Carsons, he couldn't resist.

"That's right...that's right, Miss Ann," Doss drawled as an introduction. "Jest Old Dawz here. Just like out at the farm. My condolences on your loss and all that."

"Thank you," Ann said without looking at him.

"But I want to hear all about it. That big expensive school you're going to..."

"Some other time, Doss," Ann said.

"Doss, she just lost her papa. Leave her alone!" Olga exclaimed.

Doss stepped closer. "Oh, I know that, and I paid my sympathies. I'm wondering how it is with those rich people in Minneapolis. Tell Old Dawz here how many big estates you've been invited to and how many debutante's bawls..."

All Ann could feel was contempt. "You're in the way, Doss." She picked up her bag to leave.

"I bet you're wonderin' why Old Dawz is workin' here in town! I bet you're wonderin'!"

Ann's eyes flashed. "I don't give a good goddamn what you're doing here! You were gutter trash at the manor, and you're gutter trash now!"

Ann and Olga brushed past him. "Well, just for that, I won't help you with your bag!" he shouted after them. "You bein' so self-sufficient and all. Enough said! Enough said!"

Ann and Olga reached the front of the depot. The buggy was at the hitch rail directly ahead.

"Some days I just can't hold it in," Ann said.

"You're entitled," Olga said.

Ann placed her suitcase in the back. "Mama's at Red Fern?"

"Yes, Miss Ann."

"I'll take us," Ann said.

Ann and Olga got into the buggy. Ann took the reins and gave a little jerk. "Now tell me what happened," she said.

"Oh, such a calamity. And on your birthday."

"Tell me."

"Your papa'd started drinking late yesterday. Got into a fight with Mr. Royce."

"Did Royce hit him?"

"No, no. It was all words. Angry words. First with Royce. Then your mama. Went on all night. Mr. Jack said he was through being pushed around. Sometime this morning, he and your mama got into his car and started for town. Your papa said he was going to make something right at the bank."

"But it's a holiday. The bank's closed."

"You couldn't tell him that. Your mama went along to try to stop him. From what we heard, they were going way too fast. Made the turn out at Layland's place, but Rudy Sims's wagon had a busted wheel along the right side of the road. Your papa swerved to avoid it, and the car went off the road. Your papa...well...he died. Your mama was thrown when the car turned over."

Ann still felt paralyzed from the shock. When she was younger, she had never really considered her parents' dying. They were always beside her.

"She's really hurt, Miss Ann—all broken up inside. Doc Powell's looking after her. All they can do now is ease the pain. It's terrible."

Ann was trying to imagine her mother dying. She still hadn't accepted that her father was already gone. She knew that one of life's doors was closing—both inside and right in front of her—yet there was nothing she could do to prevent it.

"That's what happened," Olga said. "Poor Mr. Jack. Your mama tried to keep him from drinking, but every time you turned around, Mr. Royce was slipping him a bottle."

"Did he slip him a bottle this time?"

"No, but he was really mad at Mr. Jack."

For a few seconds, Ann was proud of her father. If Jack had gotten Royce angry, then he must have done some damage.

"What got Papa started?"

"I couldn't hear. Something about the county farm. Something about watchdogs out at the county farm."

"There are no watchdogs out there."

They rolled along in silence except for the rapid clop-clop of the horses and the wheels on the street beneath them.

"Are they planning to buy a dog out at the farm?"

"No, this was over something that already happened."

They passed Pomphrey Park on their way to the courthouse. Picnic tables and banners with American flags were scattered here and there. Groups of townspeople were clustered around the park area. Children with balloons and ice cream cones were darting back and forth. Gay shouts abounded, but Ann did not hear them.

In a few minutes, they were among some of the finer homes. Most of these were two- or three-story houses with a lawn and large tree in the front yard. Ann had not been in this part of Winfield for years.

"Don't be surprised at the look of the hospital," Olga said. "It's not Red Fern anymore."

"What is it then?"

"Chamberlin Memorial. Mr. Royce made a donation, so they named it after him."

"So Mama's in Royce's hospital?"

"Doc Powell's right there with her."

"I'm glad," Ann said, feeling relieved.

"But Mr. Royce has hired Tracy Stabb as her private nurse."

"Tracy Stabb? She's the worst nurse in Franklin County."

Ahead of them on the right was the hospital. A brick building two stories tall, in many ways it was a successful version of the county farm. Both had lob-bies in the front, but Winfield's hospital had an extra floor and more knowledge-able staff.

As they pulled up, Ann caught sight of the sign in the front yard. Newly painted and planted in the center of the grass, it resembled a small billboard. The words, in oversized letters, were CHAMBERLIN MEMORIAL HOSPITAL.

"Chamberlin Memorial…who would have thought," Ann scoffed.

"Everybody still calls it Red Fern," Olga said.

They entered the lobby. Unlike the county farm, this place had no problems with the temperature. The couches in the waiting area were smooth and sturdy. Everything was either brand-new or well preserved. There was even a small table with some toys for younger visitors.

On the wall to the left was a large painting of Royce Chamberlin and his daughters. Bathed in a yellow glow that suggested a heavenly light, Royce was seated formally in a huge armchair. The girls were positioned on the floor at his feet, one on each side of him—Cassie on the left and Carol on the right. Each girl had an elbow on one of Chamberlin's knees. Preserved in oil, they seemed like a complete and self-contained family unit.

"There's another one like it on the wall at home," Olga said.

Doc Powell was in the hallway. On seeing Ann, he came right over. He was tired. It looked as if he had been working many hours without a break.

"Ann, I'm glad you're here. Sorry it isn't under better circumstances."

"How is she?"

"Not good. She suffered multiple fractures and internal injuries. It's a mira-cle she's with us."

"Is there any hope?"

Powell shook his head. "We're keeping her as comfortable as possible. That's all we can do."

Ann felt herself reacting, but there was no feeling. Everything was so sudden and so immense that all she could do was await the next bit of news and try to cope with it.

"May I see her?"

"She's in room five down the hall," Powell said.

"Thanks, Doc."

"I'll wait out here, Miss Ann," Olga said.

Ann hurried down the corridor to room five, which was the last one on the right. Part of her dreaded to see what was on the other side of the door. The description of her mother's injuries had created a lump in her chest.

She knocked on the door and slowly opened it. There were voices inside. She recognized them immediately: Lucille and Tracy Stabb.

Tracy was sitting in a chair across from the bed—more interested in a magazine than her patient.

"You know these mail order patterns from Marshall Field's," Tracy prattled. "They can turn out good if you put your mind to it. You should try a pattern when you get better."

Lucille's face was badly bruised in several places. She was in bed with casts on both legs and her left arm. Only her right arm was free. The bed had been elevated slightly, so Lucille could see the door. To her right on the night table were two bottles of pills, a small tray with a hypodermic, and two small containers of serum. There were no other medications around. Alongside was a pitcher of water and a glass.

"Mama?"

On hearing Ann's voice, Lucille smiled. She tried to lift her head to see, but the pain stopped her. Ann was immediately at her side.

"What are you doing here?" Tracy demanded.

"It's all right, Tracy." It was Doc Powell in the doorway. Suspecting some interference from Tracy, he had followed Ann down to the room. "Let's leave them alone for a while."

"I'm not supposed to leave the patient."

"It's all right."

Tracy followed Doc Powell out into the hall. Ann pulled the chair alongside the bed.

"I'm so glad you're here," Lucille said.

"I came as quickly as I could."

Lucille slowly extended her right arm. Ann took her hand. It felt cold.

"My good arm. It's about the only thing I can move," Lucille said.

"You're strong, Mama."

Lucille was still smiling at Ann. "Your mama's all banged up. I sure didn't expect this to happen."

"I know."

Lucille's smile was gone. "I miss him. I miss your papa."

"I miss him, too."

Lucille frowned, as if groping in the dark for a thought or correct word. "He's dead, isn't he?"

"Yes, Mama." As Ann spoke the words, she realized once again that she was talking about her father. It was true. Jack was gone.

"He was a good man."

"Yes. He was."

Lucille suddenly squeezed Ann's hand. Her tone was desperate. "And he loved you. Your father loved you, Ann."

Ann didn't know how to respond to this. She could see her mother was trying to whitewash the memory of Jack's dissolution for as long as she could. For
Ann, it was sad to see. But she was dealing with her own feelings. She didn't
even want to think about it, so she held her mother's hand until Lucille relaxed
her grip.

"I'm sorry, Ann."

"There's nothing to apologize for," Ann said.

"Ever since your grandma died, I started sounding just like her. Saying the
exact same words."

"What do you mean?"

"Oh, I do...I do. When your father started drinking, I began living two
lives...and fearing for three...Fear. Anger. Defeat. Over and over. They eat
away inside of you like a cancer. Your body and your mind can't survive. First
Mama. Then Zachary. Now Jack and me. We're all being pulled under."

"We're going to manage," Ann said.

Ann noticed a new defiance in her mother. The injuries had ravaged her, but
inside she seemed toughened by them. And her eyes were more alive than Ann
had ever seen. It wasn't the pain. It was anger. And it burned out into the room.

"We're leaving you with a hell of a battle."

"Try to get some rest," Ann said.

"No time," Lucille said. "Here's a little perspective from your mama. You
can't live with evil. You have to fight it. And I'm fighting it right now. Right
here...I am. I'm fighting it right here in this room."

"I'm glad, Mama." Ann was not sure how Lucille could conduct a battle
from a hospital bed in her condition, but she appreciated the boldness of her
words and the determination in her voice.

"Maybe a little late. But I'm doing it. First time in my life. They pushed me
around long enough. They're not going to do it anymore."

"Good."

"I can feel them all gathering outside. Royce. Brubaker. Van Burin. They
haven't taken over this room. This is my room."

Ann wanted to hug her mother. She had never seen this kind of audacity
before, and she realized that a lot of her strength must have come from her
mother as well as the colonel. She leaned over very gently and kissed Lucille on
the forehead.

"That's my girl," Lucille whispered. "That's my girl." She winced. The pain
was beginning to return.

Ann stepped away from the bed. "Want me to call Doc Powell?"

"Don't feel much till it hits," Lucille murmured. "Hurts like sin. They come
in here and shoot me up with something. Then I kind of float off."

"I'm calling him," Ann said, starting for the door.

"Wait."

Ann saw the pain, distress, and confusion on her mother's face. She was trying to say something and understand it at the same time.

"Why'd Papa want to go into town? What in the world was he thinking of?"

Lucille's face was contorted. "Wanted to go into town and tear up all the contracts we ever signed...Everything that...put us under Royce's thumb." Another wave of pain shot through her. Lucille screamed.

Ann raced to the door. Doc Powell was already in the hallway, followed by Tracy. He entered and went straight to the medicines.

"I heard her," Powell said. "We'll let her get some rest."

"Maybe you should go outside," Tracy said to Ann.

"I'm staying right here," Ann replied.

Powell was beside the bed. He had taken the syringe and was drawing some serum from one of the tiny bottles. Lucille's entire body was clenched in pain.

Lucille tried to smile. "Was I that loud, Doc?"

"You're a fighter, Lucille," he said.

Powell stepped over to her free arm.

"One of these days, I'm not going to wake up," Lucille said, attempting to laugh.

"We're all right here with you. Look at us. Look at us," he said as he gave her the injection. "We're all here. We're all with you."

In a moment he had finished.

"I'll just drift off to sleep," Lucille said. "I see Ann...I see my girl."

"Thank you, Doc," Ann said.

"She'll get some rest now."

Tracy cast a disapproving glance at Ann. "I really think you should let your mother rest. Why don't go out and take a walk or something?"

Ann turned to Powell. "Could I see you for a minute?"

Tracy watched suspiciously as Ann and Powell stepped out into the hallway.

"Could you take her off the case?" Ann asked.

Powell attempted a serious expression. "I think we can do that. You're going to stay with your mother?"

"Yes."

"I heard that," Tracy said loudly from inside the room. "You can't take me off the case. Mr. Royce assigned me this patient. This is Mr. Royce's hospital. The sign outside says so."

"I'll talk to Mr. Royce," Powell replied. "Thank you, Tracy."

"We'll see what Mr. Royce has to say," Tracy said as she started across the lobby.

"Thank you," Ann said to Doc Powell.

"Call me if you need me."

Ann went back into the room. Lucille was drifting off to sleep. Ann sat down in the chair. She took her mother's hand and watched over her as she slept.

41

After Olga left, Ann spent the rest of the afternoon with her mother. Feelings of pain and loss were pulling at her, but right now she was taking responsibility for Lucille. She thought of her father, but the ache was not as deep. Jack's departure had been sudden, but Ann realized that as he deteriorated, she had been saying good-bye to him for the last few years. She wished she had been home. She might have been able to prevent the accident.

But these were all past considerations. The reality was that Lucille was dying, and she would stay with her mother until the end. Royce and the girls hadn't shown up at the hospital, and she didn't look forward to seeing them.

Around 6:00 p.m., Ann went outside for some air. She was standing on the lawn, listening to the cicadas in the trees across the street, when her eyes focused on the rose garden of a neighboring house. Roses. It was only this morning that Ben had given her the bouquet. It seemed so long ago. Then she remembered it was still her birthday. Everything seemed blurred and indistinct except the yard in front of her.

She heard the sound of hoofbeats. Sheriff Dierkes was riding past. When he saw Ann on the lawn, he rode into the driveway and dismounted.

Ann was glad to see Dierkes. There were questions she wanted to ask him. But there was also comfort in talking with him. He was one of the few people in Winfield who stood for a kind of moral order. Maybe things weren't the way they should have been in Franklin County, but like her grandfather, Dierkes projected the assurance that someday things would return to the way they were.

"My condolences, Miss Ann. Your father was a good man."

"Thank you, Sheriff."

"How's your mother?"

"Hanging on. She's asleep right now."

"I'm sorry. You've been given a heavy load."

Ann knew this wasn't perhaps the right moment to bring up any of what she wanted to discuss, but she might not have another chance. If anyone knew the full story, it was Dierkes.

"Sheriff, what do you know about the accident?"

"Well, your papa'd been drinking, and he was driving too fast. He reached that crazy turn out at Layland's, and he swerved to avoid Rudy Sims's wagon."

"What time was this?"

"About seven thirty. He'd been drinking all night."

"And it was in front of Layland's farm."

"That's right."

"Did anybody see it?"

"Both Sims and Layland. They called the hospital right away."

Ann was thinking of her father and what had started him off the night before.

"Sheriff, Olga said Papa was really upset. Something set him off. Something about a watchdog out at the county farm. Do you know anything about that?"

Dierkes had a grim expression. "A watchdog? No. It was a rumor. A stupid rumor."

"What kind of rumor?"

"One that should never have gotten started."

"What was it? If it got my papa upset, it's important to me."

"There was talk—just talk—that around the time Zachary died, there were dog tracks around the building out there."

"Were there?"

"Not when I looked. The next morning I spent a couple of hours out there. Indoors and out. No tracks anywhere."

"How did you hear about the tracks?"

"In town I heard that Tracy Stabb said she saw them. Then when I talked to her, she said she only heard it from Willie Sloate, who was out there visiting his mother."

"What did Willie say?"

"He says he could have seen something. Now he isn't sure."

Ann wanted this to lead up to something. Some kind of resolution. She was being forced to accept the death of her parents. The facts of what triggered her father didn't make sense, so she wanted to examine and reexamine them until they did.

"That's the order of events, Miss Ann. You also have to remember that nobody at the farm heard or saw anything. Dogs make noise."

It didn't matter. This was a link that might bring some details together.

"Sheriff, you know Kurt and Jago have a pack of hounds."

"I'm aware of that."

"The Hudsens let them run all over the place. They're big, and they leave tracks."

"I'm aware of that too, Miss Ann."

"I see a connection here."

"With your mama in there, maybe this isn't the time..."

"I'm going to say it. We all agree there are a lot of unanswered questions surrounding Zachary's death. How sudden it was, how quickly Royce had him cremated, then the disappearing paperwork. You see where I'm going with this. If there were dog tracks, that might put the Hudsens out at the farm when Zachary died. They might have had something to do with his death. I think it's believable."

"It's connected because there's bad blood between you and Royce. It wouldn't stand up in court. For one thing, there's no proof. We don't know if there ever were any tracks."

"Then why did people wait so long to bring it up? Were they afraid?"

"Miss Ann, when people can't understand something, they look for a reason or an explanation. When they can't find it, sometimes they create a picture instead of sticking to the facts in front of them. I checked the Hudsen's whereabouts that day. They were out of town."

Ann was looking directly at Dierkes. "You know the Hudsens. Kurt and Jago have a list of grievances against them as long as Market Street. You know it as well as I do. They're bad people. I don't like them. I never did."

Dierkes smiled. "A lot of people don't, but I deal in facts. I have to. I've followed up every complaint about Kurt and Jago, but when I get back to the people involved, they refuse to press charges or deny it ever happened."

"That's a sure sign of guilt to me."

"No doubt, but I still need proof."

Ann respected Dierkes's regard for the law. At the same time, she believed the guilty should pay for their wrongdoings.

"Yes," Ann said. She began to prod a small weed with her shoe. "There's a big difference between what's law and what's right."

"And I represent the law."

"Maybe at heart I'm a vigilante."

"No, you're not. You know if we took the law into our own hands, we'd be little better than animals."

"We'd get our revenge."

"We would. But at what cost?"

Ann frowned. Much as she wished otherwise, Dierkes had made his point. In spite of losing the argument, the conversation made her feel better.

"Miss Ann, if it's any consolation, there are a lot of people in Franklin County who feel the same as you. Their numbers are growing. Someday something out there's going to pop."

"Someday," Ann said.

"I'll ask around again," Dierkes said. "See what I come up with."

"Thanks, Sheriff. I haven't forgotten our talk. You said, 'Hang on and don't fall off.'"

"You won't fall…You're the colonel's granddaughter. My condolences once again."

Ann went back inside to sit with her mother.

42

ANN SPENT THE NIGHT AT THE hospital. She tried to rest in the chair in Lucille's room but was unable to sleep. Finally, at 3:00 a.m. she went out into the lobby and lay down on one of the couches. Olivia, the night nurse, said she would watch Lucille and alert Ann if there were any changes.

Ann was asleep at 6:30 a.m. when Royce Chamberlin's car pulled up in front of the hospital. He and Fred Brubaker rushed into the lobby on their way to Lucille's room. As always on these occasions, Brubaker was holding a folder.

Olivia was stepping out of Lucille's room.

"How's she doing?" Brubaker asked with grave concern.

"The same. Ann's right over there."

"Let's not disturb Ann," Chamberlin suggested.

"Let her rest," Brubaker added. "She's been through so much."

"Is Tracy Stabb with Lucille?" Chamberlin inquired.

"Doc Powell took her off the case."

"I'm putting her back on. If she's here, tell her we'll be in Lucille's room."

"I'll get her," Olivia said.

Royce and Brubaker went into the room.

Lucille had awakened. Although the effects of the most recent sedative had not worn off, she was pale and physically drained.

"You're up early," she said mockingly.

"Hello, Lucille. How are we feeling?" Brubaker replied.

"Still here, Fred."

While Brubaker began his speech, Chamberlin scowled impatiently in the background.

"I hope you've had time to reflect, Lucille…"

"Slow down, Fred. Where's the fire?" Lucille shot back.

Brubaker continued in the same gentle manner. "I realize this is an uncomfortable moment, but during the tough times, we have to address the tough questions."

"Listen to him, Lucille," Chamberlin prodded.

"I am, Royce. I've heard this speech before."

"Now, Lucille, you don't want to appear ungrateful," Brubaker said. "Royce has provided you with the best care that money can provide."

Lucille's eyes flashed. "Is this what you said to Mama when she was dying? Which room was it? Was it this room? I don't remember. Was it this room?"

"I don't recall. It was so long ago," Brubaker said. "As your family lawyer, I look after every member of the family—past and present. The fact is, you haven't updated any of your bequests since Little Ann was born."

"Speaking of Ann, where is she?" Lucille said abruptly. "Where's my daughter?"

"She'll be with us in a minute," Brubaker said. "About these bequests..."

"They'll stay as they are, Fred."

"She's not receptive," Chamberlin growled.

"Now it comes out," Lucille declared. "All the care and concern, the private nurse and all the trimmings, that was just a prelude to this."

"And?" Brubaker inquired innocently.

"The answer is no," Lucille said defiantly.

"I know how you've responded to my efforts, Lucille. But I wonder if that's what you really want in the long run. Ann's a big girl now. She's going to be out on her own. You have seven farms to think of, including the Northeast Quarter."

"Where's Ann?" Lucille cried.

"I told you."

"I want her in here now."

"After we've settled our business."

"No. Now!"

There was a tap on the door. Royce opened it a crack. An unkempt and half-awake Tracy Stabb was outside.

"Stay with Ann," he ordered. "Sit on her if you have to."

"What are they saying?" Lucille asked from the bed.

"She's going to find Ann," Brubaker said. "Now about the bequests..."

"My will stays as is."

Chamberlin was back in the room. "Why don't you read it again?" he said.

"I have a copy here with a few minor codicils," Brubaker said in a matter-of-fact tone.

"Like what?"

"A few things here and there. Ease of cash flow considerations between accounts and bequests. Just to clear up a few points."

"The will is perfectly clear as it is," Lucille stated.

Lucille grimaced. The pain started up again. It would come in waves.

"Are you all right, Lucille?" Brubaker inquired.

"She's fine," Chamberlin said.

"Could I have some water?" Lucille asked. "And get Doc or whoever's on duty."

Brubaker took the pitcher and poured her a glass. He extended it to Lucille's free arm.

"Could you help me drink it, Fred?"

As Lucille reached for the glass, Chamberlin seized Brubaker's arm to prevent him from giving it to her.

"I'm not a patient man," Chamberlin said without emotion.

"I just want some water, Royce. Just water. And please call somebody."

Nobody moved. Even Brubaker seemed taken aback by Royce's tactic. "Lucille, I'm appealing to you as your lawyer."

"No," Lucille said.

"Royce wants you to focus on the issue here. Will you just reconsider? I'm asking you," Brubaker continued. He knew Royce would hold his arm for as long as it took.

Thirty seconds passed. Another wave of pain passed through Lucille.

"You win...I'll listen," she finally said.

Chamberlin released Brubaker's arm. He held the glass up to Lucille's mouth. With her hand on the glass, she gulped the contents.

"You've got about five minutes before I start to scream, Fred."

"It so happens I have a revised copy of the will right here," Brubaker said, as if nothing had happened. "It's a simple change in the flow of funds. You sign right here and have a nap. We can go over it later when you wake up."

"What's in it?" Lucille asked.

Brubaker held out the papers, making sure they were too far away for her to see. "Just a few things. Paragraph here. Another one on this page."

"I can't see them, Fred."

"I'll tell you right now. We had to make some changes on this page..."

"What changes?"

"Royce invested some of Lady Ann's share of the estate."

"Then why can't I see them?"

"I'm trying to tell you—to spare you the trouble of reading it."

"Is this the only copy of this revised will?" Lucille asked knowingly.

"Why yes," Brubaker replied. "We wanted you to be the first to see it."

"OK," Lucille sighed. "I'll sign it."

"That's the spirit."

With the will against his folder as an impromptu desk, Brubaker placed the paperwork beside Lucille's free hand. Chamberlin extended a pen.

With the revised will in her hand, Lucille glared up at Chamberlin and Brubaker. Suddenly, she jammed a corner of the will into her mouth and bit down on it. Then, clenching the document in her teeth, she tore the papers in half with her free hand. She let out a scream as the papers ripped. She spit out one half of the will and tossed the other on the floor. The effort was exhausting.

"The old will…stays in effect," she said with a smile.

"Originals can be rewritten," Chamberlin snapped. "We'll be back."

"We'll talk again, Lucille," Brubaker said.

Out in the lobby, Ann had opened her eyes. Tracy Stabb was beside the couch, staring down at her. Ann knew immediately that something was wrong. Tracy's efforts at nonchalance always signaled trouble.

"What's happened? What's going on?" Ann said, trying to wake up as quickly as possible.

"Nothing. Nothing at all," Tracy said.

There was a scream from Lucille's room. Ann saw Olivia and Doc Powell rushing toward the hallway. Powell appeared to be waking up as he moved.

Ann was on her feet. "It's my mother. What's happened in there?"

She saw Chamberlin and Brubaker emerging from the hall and into the lobby. They had to have been in Lucille's room. She pushed around Tracy and started for the hallway.

"Why, Ann," Brubaker said, "this is a surprise."

Ann stopped. "You were with my mother."

"We were checking to see how she is."

"With a folder?"

"Hello, Ann," Chamberlin said.

Ann thought Chamberlin's color had become more ashen—as if corruption had fossilized his features. "I'd like a word with you."

"Not now," Ann said as she headed for the hallway. When she reached the door, she saw Olivia holding Lucille's hand while Doc Powell prepared an injection.

"Doc?"

"When I learned Fred and Royce were here, I figured she needed a rest."

"You spent the night here?"

"Yes," Doc said, putting the tiny bottle on the night table.

"Thank you."

Lucillle attempted to smile when she saw Ann.

"Ann…"

"I'm here, Mama."

Ann watched as Doc Powell gave her the injection. "We're here, Lucille. Look at us. Ann's here, and Olivia. We're all right with you. We're all here..."

"I'm causing a lot of problems, aren't I, Doc?" Lucille said, attempting a smile.

"You're a fighter, Lucille," Powell said. "If you need me, I'll be right outside."

Ann held the door for Powell and Olivia. "Thanks again, Doc."

"I like the way Doc handles this," Lucille said. "He wants me to see everyone standing around when he gives me my shot. If I don't come back, I'll know I didn't die alone."

"He's a good man. Is the pain better now?"

"Where did you sleep?" Lucille asked.

"Out in the lobby."

"The vultures are circling, Ann."

Ann heard a creak behind her. The door was open a sliver. She seized the handle and pulled it open to reveal Tracy crouched outside

"Uh, I was just checking to see if everything was all right," Tracy said

"It is," Ann answered, pushing the door shut.

"She's a skunk," Lucille muttered. "She's the one who called Royce about our meeting with Collinsen..."

"I know, Mama."

Outside, there was a commotion as Carol and Cassie arrived. Cassie rushed over to her father, leaving Carol holding the door.

"Is she dead yet?" Cassie asked.

"Cassie, what an awful thing to say," Powell said from where he was standing at the reception desk.

"She is dying, isn't she?" Carol brayed. "Is Ann here?"

"Yes," Chamberlin said.

"I'd better get back to the office," Brubaker said to Royce.

In Lucille's room, Ann was holding her mother's hand. The injection was beginning to take effect, but this time Lucille seemed determined to remain awake for as long as she could.

"I never got a chance to meet that young man of yours," she said.

"Ben."

"Is it serious? You're so young."

"I've had to grow up pretty fast. Yeah, it's serious."

"There's so much I'm going to miss," Lucille said. She squeezed Ann's hand. "I'm sorry, Ann...I'm so sorry...for leaving you with this. Fear and acquiescence are the curses of our family. They weren't when my papa was alive. A mother's duty is to look after her children. I was too busy thinking of myself and Jack. We let you down."

"You didn't let me down. Neither you nor Papa."

Another creak came from door, which was ajar again. Ann was surprised that Tracy would be back so soon. She got up and crossed straight to the door. Grabbing the handle, she yanked it open and then slammed it shut as hard as she could. There was a dull thud, followed by a loud "Ow! Ow!" on the other side.

Ann opened it. Tracy had her hand on her forehead where the door had hit her.

"You didn't have to do that," Tracy said. "I was just checking."

"Of course you were," Ann said as she shut the door again.

Lucille was grinning. "Serves her right. A good whack."

Ann returned to her mother's side.

"They're out there hovering," Lucille said. "They've been trying to get me to sign a new will, just like they tried with your grandma. But you know what? I've been stronger."

"Good."

"They were sticking something in my face for me to sign."

"And?"

"Look down there."

Ann saw the two strips of paper on the floor. "Good for you, Mama."

Lucille grabbed Ann's arm, a desperate look in her eyes. "You're going to have to fight them someday. You can't now because they control everything. You'll have to depend on them a little more... just a little longer."

"I know," Ann said.

"When the time comes... when you make your move, don't show pity. Don't forgive at the last moment. Don't be talked out of anything. You go for the heart. You drive the blade all the way in, and you hold it there till they've uttered their last cry and drawn their last breath. You hold it there until you've finished the job."

Her eyes seemed to sparkle. All the anger she had held in was released in a single quiet command.

"Get them, Ann. Get them."

"I will."

"Now let me look at you."

Ann sat down on the edge of the bed. "I'm here, Mama."

Slowly, Lucille's expression changed to one of peace.

"I think I'm going to go now," Lucille said dreamily.

Lucille leaned back on her pillow and closed her eyes. Her breathing was slow and gentle. Then it stopped. Ann listened. Lucille did not breathe again.

"Mama?" Ann said.

Lucille was gone. Ann felt the grief building up inside her. She held onto Lucille's hand until it passed. Tears would come later.

Ann sat on the edge of the bed for several minutes, and then she leaned over and kissed Lucille for the last time.

"I'll get them, Mama," she said with the same fierce calm. "I'll get them, all right."

43

THE REST OF THE MORNING WAS a blur. When Ann finally left the room to find Doc Powell, she noticed a few people gathered on the other side of the lobby. She was sure one was Royce, but at this point she didn't want to interact with anyone.

Doc Powell was in the office. They went back to Lucille's room immediately. Ann noticed the door to the room was open. Someone had gone in there after she'd left. Ordinarily, Ann would have been curious, but now it was just another detail. She started to watch Powell examine Lucille but looked away. He would only confirm what she already knew. Her gaze wandered from the bed to the floor, and she noticed that the two strips of paper were gone. Someone had picked up the pieces of the will. Too much had happened that morning for her to nurture any suspicions or draw any conclusions. She didn't think of it again.

Ann accompanied Lucille's body to Lumsden's Funeral Parlor. Judy and Ellen joined her. When she arrived at Lumsden's to make the arrangements, she was told that Royce had already set her parents' funeral for the following day. It was as if she had no say in the matter.

Ann knew she would have to spend the night at Carson Manor. She couldn't avoid it, so she delayed the trip out for as long as she could. She spent the afternoon with her friends. After dinner with Judy and her family at their farm, Olga arrived with the buggy at 7:30 p.m. to take her home.

They were a few minutes away from Judy's, one of those seemingly endless dirt roads that crisscrossed in the middle of the cornfields. Everything around them was a swirl of green and yellow.

"It's good you have some friends, Miss Ann. People you can spend some time with."

"It certainly is."

"You know the funeral's tomorrow," Olga said.

"That's what they told me at Lumsden's. When did Royce make the arrangements?"

"Yesterday before lunch."

Ann felt like she had been slapped, but she was too numb for the pain to register.

"That was before Mama died. Just a ceremony with no reception. Bury them quick and walk away."

"It's terrible, Miss Ann. Your mama and papa deserve better."

They made the rest of the journey without speaking. Ann saw Carson Manor rising above the fields in the distance. Every part of it triggered a memory, but looking at it made her feel alone.

"Right now I may be powerless, but I am not helpless," she thought. "I will not let myself be helpless."

The buggy stopped in front of the manor house. One of the hands took the reins and led the horse and buggy away. Carol and Cassie appeared on the porch.

"So you've finally decided to join us," Carol blared, almost a reprimand.

"Our condolences, I'm sure," Cassie trilled. "It's what we say under the circumstances, isn't it?"

"I'll get settled in," Ann said to Olga. She was reaching for her bag.

"Ann..."

Royce was in the doorway behind the girls. To Ann he seemed more spectre-like than human, and he had a peculiar smile on his face. She couldn't figure out what it was expressing. It seemed to be more relief than triumph.

"We haven't had time to speak. So much has happened," he said. "You know the funeral's tomorrow."

"Rather fast, isn't it?" Ann replied.

"I took charge to spare you unnecessary pain and aggravation," he said to Ann. "I was thinking of you."

"You took charge when Zachary died, too."

"I was doing what's best for everyone."

"You should appreciate what Papa did," Cassie said.

"I think we should have a talk," Chamberlin said with the same smile.

Slowly, he stuck out his right hand. Ann stared at it. Chamberlin wanted to shake hands, like a peace offering. Ann noticed that the hand seemed skeletal now, and the gesture carried a litany of sordid undercurrents. Ann did not budge. If it had to be this way until one of them dropped dead, then so be it.

"I think we should accept the reality and build a common ground, Ann."

"Papa is offering to shake your hand," Cassie said.

"I'm trying to make amends," he said.

"No, you're trying to sweep it under the rug," Ann answered.

The smile was gone. Royce lowered his arm. "All right. If it's going to be that way, you'll be sitting with us at the ceremony tomorrow. I want us together. You're in my family now, symbolically at least."

Inside Ann was tightening into a knot. Torn between grief and trying to keep her temper, she was fighting a losing battle.

"What made Papa so angry?" she demanded. "What were you talking about before he left?"

"I was trying to reason with him."

"It was about dog tracks at the county farm when Zachary died."

"Perhaps."

"Were the Hudsens out there the day Zachary died?"

"Why do you ask?"

"I want to know if they were near the place the day he died."

"They were far away, Ann. And they have witnesses."

"They usually do."

Chamberlin attempted a concerned tone. "Ann, there was no reasoning with Jack. I tried to stop him. I always tried to dissuade him."

"By slipping him a bottle?"

The smile vanished. "We're going to end this conversation right now. Get yourself moved in."

Ann reached for her bag.

"You're going back to school right after the service. On the way to the station, you have an appointment with Fred Brubaker. See that you keep it."

Ann started for the gatehouse. She was halfway there when she noticed that Carol was following her.

"I remember the way," Ann said.

As Ann arrived at the front door and opened it, Carol gave her a vicious shove. Ann staggered inside, dropping her bag. She caught her balance and spun around to confront her attacker.

"Is that a welcome home, Carol?" Ann challenged.

"Your parents are dead, and you've got no one," Carol said.

"You followed me out here to say that?" Ann said. "What's bothering you?"

"Nothing's bothering me at all," Carol bellowed. "Nothing at all. I just want to tell you that there's a rumor going around that Idiot Boy might be your real papa and not Jack. Wouldn't surprise me at all, Idiot Boy being your papa."

Ann saw the torment beneath Carol's anger. Her eyes were puffy and bloodshot, and her face registered pure anguish. It was as if her own spite and vicious nature had infected her.

She remembered all the times Carol had struck her when she was little. Then she thought of Lucille's words about not showing pity.

"What's the matter, Carol? Doesn't Daddy love you anymore?"

With a cry, Carol shoved Ann again. This time Ann caught her balance and drove her fist into Carol's face as hard as she could. Carol screamed and collapsed into a heap along the wall. She spat blood and looked up at Ann.

"I'm letting you know where we stand," Ann said. "Don't you ever touch me again."

"My papa will kill you," Carol cried hoarsely. "He'll kill you!"

"No, he won't because the fight's not over."

Carol's horror and dismay intensified. She had never expected Ann to stand up for herself. None of the others in Ann's family would have dared. And here was Ann, staring down at her with a clenched fist.

"Get out of here," Ann said.

With her hand to her mouth, Carol bolted out the front door. Ann heard her sobbing all the way across the yard to the manor house.

Ann knew that Carol would immediately tell Royce what happened. She was sure to exaggerate it into an unprovoked attack on Ann's part, but that didn't matter much to Ann. Carol's violent behavior had needed a response for a long time.

Just the same, what would happen to her now? She was sixteen and still a dependent. Most likely she would go back to school and stay until she graduated. What about after that?

"I'll have to take this one step at a time," Ann thought. "Right now, it's getting through tomorrow."

She sat down in the armchair, closed her eyes, and attempted to get some sleep. But her mind was racing over all the recent developments as well as their possible consequences. Everything was so fresh and powerful that she remained wide awake.

Although Ann missed her mother, she felt she should be thinking more about Jack. She loved him and would miss him. But somehow in death as well as in life, Jack always had a supporting role. She wanted to give Jack the respect a father deserved, but remembering his deterioration over the past years, she could not. And this made her sad as well.

Ann sat for hours. At 3:45 a.m. she was still restless. It was silent in the main house, so she decided to walk over to where everything started: the Northeast Quarter. She needed to put everything into proper perspective. Her grandpa had always said, "If you have a problem, take it out to the Quarter. A few minutes there'll cut anything down to manageable size."

She dressed and slipped out of the gatehouse. As she moved out of the driveway, she heard the buzzing of the wires that attached the tiny dwelling to the manor house.

Ann started up the road. The only noise was the chirping of an occasional cricket, the clip of her footsteps on the dirt surface beneath her, and, far away, the hoot of an owl.

She was totally alone except for the myriad of night creatures in the fields on either side. She felt at home here—with the sounds, the earth smells, and the cool temperature of the summer night. At the same time, everything felt different now. She recognized many of the familiar landmarks she knew from her childhood, but they seemed remote and indistinct in the half light.

"I'd forgotten this," she thought. "It's a whole different world at night."

Along the horizon, the sky was a shade brighter than the rest of the heavens. The moon was still out, but daylight was coming. Grandpa used to say, "The sun's announcing the changing of the guard."

Ann kept walking for thirty minutes. Finally, she was within sight of her destination. She knew this when found herself across the street from Section Two. The Hudsen place looked deserted. With bottles and wagon parts strewn about, the farm had deteriorated into a local embarrassment. And to top it off, Kurt and Jago had done something no self-respecting farmer could abide: they had not bothered to irrigate their land.

Up the road was the Northeast Quarter. Even at night the tall cornstalks retained a kind of nobility as they stood in formation, every one abundant and perfectly formed. The soil beneath was still dark and rich. Even in these hard times, it had the aura of a special place.

Ann walked along the edge, taking in the majestic stalks row by row. She was far enough from home that she figured now was time for her and the colonel to have a little talk.

"Grandpa," she thought, "I'd pray to God, but He's busy right now, so I'm going to talk to you. What would you have done? I'm the only one left. I feel as alone in life as I do standing here. But alone doesn't mean defeated."

She heard cricket noises all around her. They would stop as she came near and then start up again after she had passed. She took in the sounds and smells of the field. The colonel was right. This field was the mother lode.

"It seems so long ago now that I made a promise to you, but the promise was real. Keep the Northeast Quarter. Protect it. It was a pledge, and I'm going to honor it, not out of obligation, but because it's the right thing. The same blood flows in our veins. People say I have some of your strength, but some days I sure don't feel it."

Somewhere in the distance, a pheasant was scared off by a roaming watchdog. With a rustling and flapping noise, it took off across the landscape. Then there was only the chirping of the crickets again.

"You must have sensed the storm coming at the birthday party. It was important enough that you stopped your speech and made me swear to it. So I'm here now talking to you. I suppose I'm afraid, Grandpa. Not afraid to make a stand. I just don't want to let you down. There's me and there's them. And their side's growing. Someday, I'm going to have to take them all on."

It was a little brighter. The sun was still below the horizon, but the orange glow where the land met the sky was growing bigger.

"I sure wish you could hear me. I miss you and Grandma. Now Papa and Mama are gone, too."

Another bird began to peep off in the cornstalks. Then a warbling began across the road.

"I guess everybody's starting to wake up. I'm glad I came out here. I won't let you down."

Ann was listening to the variety of birdsong when she heard a rustling behind her. It came from the base of one of the rows of corn. She saw a pair of eyes and then the familiar form of a white dog a short distance away. Goliath, the little bull terrier, had been watching her for a long time.

"Look at you," Ann said. "I didn't know you were there."

Goliath was a mess. His face and back had two red streaks across them where he had been beaten. His fur was dirty and ruffled.

Ann squatted down and held out her hand. Goliath scurried back and stopped. He was looking at Ann quizzically. A human who was friendly. This was unusual.

She kept her hand extended, and he watched her intently before taking a few steps toward her.

"I won't hurt you," she said.

He inched forward a little more.

"That's right…That's right…I won't hit you. You look like you've seen the wrong end of a riding crop." Her hand remained out. With head lowered almost in shame, he crept closer.

"We've both seen our share of sonsabitches, haven't we?"

Goliath finally reached her hand and touched it with his nose. Ann let him sniff and explore her hand. When she shifted her weight, the dog jumped back in terror.

"Sorry," Ann said.

Goliath watched her intently for another minute or so and then crossed back to her. Ann's hand was extended again. He approached and began to touch it with his nose.

"Yes, yes," Ann said. "That's it."

She wanted to try to pet him but held back. Having him approach her was a victory in itself.

After several seconds, Goliath moved back from her hand and stared at her. Then suddenly, he darted into the dark air. Ann heard him running through the furrows and crossing the road somewhere up the way. Then there was silence.

Ann smiled. "I thought I was alone out here. I'm not sure if that was your answer, Grandpa, but I'm taking it to heart."

She looked to the horizon. The tip of the sun was barely visible. The birds were warbling here and there. In the far distance, a rooster was crowing.

"I'd better get back. There's a lot to do today."

With a last glance at the Quarter, Ann began the walk back home.

44

ANN WAS ABLE TO SLEEP FOR a few hours. This was more from the lack of sleep the night before than a need to rest. She would drift off, feel two or three seconds of warmth as she recognized home, and then a chill when reality set in.

She had some deeds to accomplish, and with her departure for school immediately after the ceremony, she only had a few hours.

Ann waited until Royce had left. She had a fried egg and biscuits in the kitchen with Olga and then went to the barn to hitch up the buggy. She told everyone she was going for a ride by herself to be alone with her grief. In truth, she was going to see Fred Brubaker.

She left Carson Manor at nine thirty. When she arrived in Winfield, it was midmorning. Market Street was as full of traffic as it would ever get for the day. It looked the same to Ann, only now the car and horse traffic was evenly distributed.

Ann turned the buggy and started up Market Street. People were moving here on the sidewalk, some coming in and out of stores. A few would nod or give a sympathetic smile to Ann. She nodded in return. "Grandpa would know the name of every person I passed. Some of them I know. Some I barely remember. It was a different time back then."

As she was passing the barbershop, there was a commotion at the door. Cecil, the barber, was evicting Warren Hyatt.

"One more thing, Cecil . . ."

"I'm busy. I have customers," Cecil said.

Hyatt was stumbling backward onto the sidewalk. "You're not listening. In the true society . . . in the real society, there are no customers—only comrades."

"No, I'm busy . . ."

"In Russia you'd be calling me comrade . . ."

Cecil grabbed a lollipop from a jar by the door and stuck it in Hyatt's hand.

"I'll give you a lollipop if you leave, Warren."

Hyatt spotted Ann passing in the buggy. She didn't want anything to do with him. With eyes straight ahead, she flicked the reins and continued her journey up the street. Hyatt perked up when he saw her.

"Good morning, Miss Hardy!" he said loudly. "Good morning! Isn't it a wonderful day?"

The buggy was moving away.

"Come back here, Miss Hardy! Don't try to avoid me!"

Ann did not look back. Her mind was on what Royce and Brubaker were up to at the bank. Royce had stipulated an appointment on the way out of town. It seemed like he wanted to force her into a transaction where she would have little time to consider and no time to react. Whatever it was, she was going to find out.

"Miss Hardy! Miss Hardy!"

Warren Hyatt pursued her, staggering and dodging whatever traffic came along.

Up the street on the left was the bank and law office. Pomphrey Park was directly ahead. There was an open spot along the sidewalk just before Brubaker's office. Ann pulled over and got out of the buggy, tying the reins to the hitch rail.

Warren Hyatt had almost caught up with her. He was gasping for breath, but he didn't seem to care. "Miss Hardy! Oh, Miss Hardy!"

Ann started walking. The law office was two doors away.

"Come back here, Miss Hardy! I'm talking to you!"

Ann continued, Hyatt trailing behind.

"You're not so high and mighty now! Dignity and compassion, Miss Hardy!"

Ann kept moving. The door was just ahead.

"Miss Hardy! Sooner or later you'll have to speak with me!"

Ann stopped. "You don't want me to speak with you. You want me to tell you Grandpa's death wasn't your fault."

Hyatt gasped. "How dare you say that?"

"That's all you've ever wanted," Ann said.

"It wasn't my fault! Everybody knows it wasn't my fault!"

"Good day, Mr. Hyatt."

"None of it was! Don't you say that!"

Inside the office, Fred Brubaker crossed to the door to investigate the disturbance. Farther down in the bank, Chamberlin looked up from some paperwork.

"Don't you ever say that!"

Brubaker arrived at the door to find himself facing Ann.

"Mr. Brubaker, may I see you?" she said.

"Come inside," Brubaker replied.

"We'll have this talk again, Miss Hardy. You can't run from the truth."

"Good-bye, Warren. Run along now," Brubaker said to Hyatt.

Ann took a seat at his desk. She saw that they had opened a doorway between the bank lobby and the law office.

"He's gone now," Brubaker said. "What did he want from you, Ann?"

"He wants me to tell him he's not responsible for Grandpa's death."

"Fat chance of that. Everybody there knows what happened." Brubaker smiled.

"What did you want to see me about?" Ann asked.

Brubaker was puzzled. "I thought you were coming in this afternoon."

"I decided to come now."

Chamberlin had crossed the lobby to investigate. "What are you doing here?" he said to Ann. "You were told to come this afternoon."

"I can handle it, Royce," Brubaker said. "It's a matter of formalities. That's all."

"What's this about, Mr. Brubaker?" Ann asked.

For the first time, Fred Brubaker saw the determination behind the smile. This wasn't the little girl who'd accompanied Lady Ann and Lucille after the colonel died. This was someone who was alert and wary—and waiting to consider what he had to say next.

"First of all, as your family attorney, let me offer my condolences for your loss. We all know what it's like to lose a parent."

"Thank you."

"The reason for this meeting," he began. "Ann, you're an orphan—a young lady orphaned at fifteen."

"Sixteen."

"Sixteen. But the fact is that you need a legal guardian."

"I do?" Ann was curious. This didn't seem to be something they needed to rush through at the last moment. Yet here they were.

"Royce is your step-grandfather. He's not your legal guardian."

"I don't understand."

"The law's quite clear on this. At your age, you have to have a guardian. I'd like you to pick one while you're here. Make everything official."

"I don't need a guardian," Ann said. "Do we have to talk about this now? My parents haven't even had their funeral."

"I was hoping we could resolve this before you return to school," Brubaker said. "It's imperative. I say this because I'm the estate lawyer, and I'm in charge of your legal affairs until you're twenty-one."

"So you were waiting until I was on my way out of town?"

"Your mother was quite clear in her wishes that I guide you legally until you're of age."

"Speaking of the will, may I see it?"

"Pardon me?"

"May I see a copy of the will?"

"I don't have a copy of it right now."

"Why not?" Ann asked.

"I didn't know you wanted to see it. We sent it over to Judge Post for formal documentation. I'll have a copy of it sent off to school."

"Were there any changes?"

"Not that I know of."

"Then why did Mama tear it up and throw it on the floor in her room?"

"It was a proposal that Lucille was considering, but it's of no importance now," Chamberlin said.

"What was she considering?"

"Cash flow considerations. It was considered and tabled," Brubaker said. "It's nothing. You'll get a copy of the will. I promise."

Although Brubaker had not admitted anything, Ann was suspicious. More than ever, she wanted to see a copy of the will.

"Right now we have to pick a guardian."

"I'm at school all the time. Why do I need a guardian?"

"It's the law, Ann," he said. "You have to pick one, and that's final."

Before the discussion could escalate, Van Burin entered the lobby of the bank. He was bubbling with good cheer. "Good morning, everyone. Good morning."

His voice trailed off when he saw Ann. "Oh, hello."

"Mr. Van Burin."

Ann saw that his hair was now a drab and muddy gray, which was a far cry from the flaming red of years past.

"They went ahead without you," Chamberlin said.

Van Burin became nervous and fidgety. "This wasn't a morning appointment. It's why I wasn't here," he cried, his voice becoming shriller. "The wife sent me to pick up some favors for the grandchildren's party, and this was supposed to be after the funeral, not before. And after is not before and certainly not now. It's completely unexpected, unprepared for, and unannounced."

Ann noticed that Van Burin's overworked good cheer was approaching hysterical babbling. This was a man living in abject terror.

"We were helping Ann select a guardian," Brubaker said.

"Yes. Of course. That's why we're here."

Ann saw the walls forming around her. With Royce in the doorway, it was three against one. She decided to accept the proposition. This wasn't the time to make a move.

"Patrick, would you begin?" Chamberlin said.

"Yes. Ann, we may have had our differences, but as your banker, I advise you to listen to Fred with both ears. Family. There's something magical in that word. If you're not part of a family, you're not part of anything…"

"My family is gone," Ann said.

"That's what I mean. A person needs a family. With no family, he's like a twig without a tree."

"I won't argue with that."

Van Burin was beaming again. "I knew she'd see. We've had our differences, but you're still the colonel's granddaughter."

Brubaker cleared his throat, no doubt preparing a pithy remark. "As a candidate, I suggest your grandfather here."

"Step-grandfather," Ann corrected.

"Of course. What am I saying? That'll make it official."

"No," Ann stated.

"He's a pillar of the community." Brubaker studied Ann. "You have to pick someone."

"Anyone I want?"

"Yes, anyone you want. And you have to do it before you go back to school."

"All right."

"So who do you pick?"

"I pick Mr. Van Burin," Ann said with a smile.

Van Burin was aghast. "What? Me?" His eyes darted from Chamberlin to Brubaker and back again. "You can't select me. She can't do it. It's not possible."

"Anyone I want, right?"

"Anyone you want," Brubaker said.

"And is the law quite clear on that?"

"Yes."

"Then I choose Mr. Van Burin."

"Now you just wait a minute, missy," Van Burin sputtered. "I am not involved. I am out of this…"

"Family," Ann said.

"Oh no. You can't come into our family…"

"Nobody wants to be a twig without a tree…"

"May I ask why, Ann?" Brubaker ventured delicately.

"Because he's where the money is."

"I am against this," Van Burin grumbled. "I really think we should rethink…"

Ann looked to Brubaker. "Is it settled?"

Brubaker tried to conceal his amusement at Van Burin's reaction. "You're the lucky man, Patrick."

"Nobody asked me. How long does this have to go on?"

"Till she's of age."

"I didn't expect this. It's not fair. I'll have to make arrangements."

"Don't look so downcast, Patrick," Chamberlin said. "She's away at school most of the time. When she's home, she stays in the gatehouse."

"Oh. Just so we know where everybody is."

"Family is a magical thing," Ann said to Van Burin.

"Now you just wait a minute," Van Burin whined. "I didn't ask for this, you know."

"And now that we're family, I'd like a copy of my bank statement sent to school every month."

"What?"

"My bank statement. You can send it."

"You never asked for it before."

"I'm asking now."

"He can do it," Brubaker said.

"I'll have it sent to you." Van Burin sighed.

Ann grinned. "Anything I ask for and don't get, I just call my guardian, right?"

"You're the man, Patrick," Brubaker said grandly. "Now that we're settled, I suggest we adjourn until we see each other out at the cemetery."

Ann stood up. "Now that we're settled, I'll see you all there."

Ann left the office and went into the street. She knew she had not gained anything from the exchange, but she felt good. She had stood up to them.

"I didn't expect this," Van Burin was saying. "Somebody should see it from my side. That girl doesn't respect us. She's a spoiled rotten ingrate."

"Easy, Patrick," Chamberlin crooned. "Put on your sad face. We'll be closing soon. We'll see you at the service."

45

THE FUNERAL WAS SET FOR 2:00 p.m. An hour earlier, Ann dressed for the occasion and slipped out of the gatehouse. She took the buggy and left before anyone noticed she was gone.

Everything changes but the land. She was happy to be out of the household and among the cornfields, where everything seemed timeless.

As the time drew near, she was approaching the green incline of Riverside Cemetery. She could see a small tent over the area where the service would take place. Already, the hill was dotted with the cars and carriages of people starting to arrive. Soon she was passing the first rows of headstones in Riverside. Some had flowers and flags on them from the holiday only a few days before.

Up ahead, Judy and Ellen had just arrived with their families. The two groups approached Ann to offer condolences.

"May I sit with you?" Ann asked. "I'm not exactly welcome in my home right now."

"Of course you can," Judy's father answered. "We're proud to have you."

Ann saw the row of chairs cordoned off for the immediate family. For the moment they were empty. She and her companions took places in the first row of seats on the other side. Slowly, the well-wishers began to arrive.

The ceremony would be a smaller version of the colonel's funeral years before. The flower-covered caskets were on a pallet next to the green canvas that was spread over the final resting places for Jack and Lucille. On the edge of the canvas was the large headstone for Colonel Wallace Carson. Right beside it was a smaller one engraved LADY ANN CARSON CHAMBERLIN.

The sight of Royce's name on her grandmother's headstone infuriated Ann. Even in the graveyard, Royce Chamberlin had attached himself to their family. He had used Lady Ann for her money and position, and when she died, he had made sure his name was engraved for posterity along with hers in the cemetery.

"If Grandma'd only said no to the son of a bitch, things would be so different now," Ann thought. "Royce'd be in his cage down at the bank, and we'd all be up here enjoying the view."

A few minutes later, Royce and the girls arrived, surrounded by an entourage of sycophants, including Brubaker and his wife and Van Burin and his family. Besides them were at least twenty others Ann did not recognize. They took their places in the area across from Ann.

The first to notice Ann's presence was Carol. Her already-swollen lip curled into a sneer as she leaned over to her father to alert him. When the others around him heard her, the whispers and glances began. Van Burin's face was a pouty scowl.

"What's wrong with old Van Burin?" Judy whispered to Ellen.

"He looks like he's holding his breath."

Ann saw Royce watching her. His expression was blank and cold, which meant he was furious. He had commanded her presence in his section, and she was sitting where she wanted. There was nothing he could do now.

Anyone who doubted there was bad blood between Ann's family and the Chamberlins would receive a clear affirmation of it now. The two hundred people who attended were split into two distinct groups. On one side was the Chamberlin entourage, which now included some of the merchants from up and down Market Street. The three people who seemed out of place were Olga, who had to come as a Chamberlin employee, and Judge Farnell Post and his wife. Post was the town magistrate. He appeared uncomfortable sitting with this crowd. The people on Ann's side included Doc Powell, Mr. Dobbs from the station, Cecil the barber, and Sheriff Tom Dierkes. With Dierkes and his family was Clem, a new deputy. It was the first time everyone seemed to choose sides.

Ann's gaze moved to the two caskets and the area covered by the canvas. Jack and Lucille would be buried there after the service. She began to feel the quiet impact of the scene. She was alone now. She had held so much inside for so long. "I'll cry about this sometime," she thought. "But I won't cry today."

Reverend Bidwell arrived, wearing his usual beatific smile. This always bothered Ann. "Papa was right about him. He doesn't live in the same world as the rest of us," Ann thought. "His mind's fluttering on a cloud while the rest of him walks around in Winfield."

Royce motioned for the reverend. They conferred quietly. Bidwell glanced disapprovingly at Ann. Suddenly, he flashed his broad, cheerful expression and started over to her.

"My condolences," he whispered. "Your parents were fine people and a spiritual inspiration to us all."

"Thank you," Ann said.

"Will...uh...you be all right sitting here?"

"I'm fine," Ann said.

"Yes, but your family is over there. I'm curious if you might want to sit with them."

"I said I'm fine."

"She's fine with us," Judy said.

"Are you sure? They've suffered a loss, too. Have you stopped to consider their feelings?"

"They seem to be handling it quite well. Did Royce send you over here?"

"Bless you, no," Bidwell said, maintaining the cheerful façade. "I'm only saying that in these troubled times, one should put aside personal resentments and reach out in a spirit of charity and forgiveness."

"I'm happy right here," Ann said.

"Yes, but those are your feelings. This is not a time for selfishness. You must spiritually put aside those petty and vindictive thoughts. It is a time for healing and coming together. Do you understand?"

"I do."

"Don't you want to show your support and gratitude to Royce for all he has done for you?"

"I don't think that matters."

His face began to redden. "And I say it does."

Ann smiled. "Well then, we'll agree to disagree."

The smile became rigid. "In the Lord's name, I am asking you to go sit over there."

"Reverend," Ann said calmly, "this is my parents' funeral, and I'll sit where I damn well please."

"You tell 'em, Ann!"

This loud and clear cry came from Ann's side—a man's voice. Ann turned to see who it was; however, among the faces behind her, she couldn't identify the source. One thing was certain: it was a cry of encouragement. The words had a resounding effect. She had more friends among the citizenry than she had realized.

"She's fine with us, Reverend," Judy's father said.

"So it's settled then," Bidwell said, still smiling, but visibly upset. "Bless you, Ann."

Bidwell took his place in front of the two groups.

"Let us pray," he began. "Oh, gracious Lord, we are gathered here to celebrate two lives—the lives of Jack Hardy and Lucille Carson Hardy, our friends and your devoted servants. We ask you to bless them and remember the good they have left behind with us, your humble servants and their devoted friends."

The words summed up her parents very well. But Ann knew Bidwell was just getting started.

"We celebrated Lucille's birth as the daughter of our own Colonel Wallace Carson, the founder of our town. We celebrated her marriage to your servant Jack and the birth of their daughter, Ann Hardy."

Ann's attention returned to the two caskets. "My parents are dead, and this is their funeral. This is it—the real thing. Many people dread the coming of this moment in their lives. The death of a parent. Now I'm experiencing it. It's right here."

Bidwell continued. "Oh Lord, we acknowledge all the blessings you have given to us in this wonderful world. You have given us your love and a simple list of commandments to follow. You have given us your Son whose sacrifice is our guiding light. We praise you for the blessings you have bestowed upon us each and every day."

As Bidwell droned on, Ann relished the view of Winfield from the hill in Riverside Cemetery. The land would never change. She found comfort in that.

"We praise the institution of family, which you have given us to enrich our lives, and we must praise Royce Chamberlin for his unselfish devotion to family."

"Come again?" Ann thought.

"We ask you to bless him. His generosity. His magnanimous act of stepping in to continue the Carson family traditions and giving up a successful banking career to provide for those in need. We praise Royce and his daughters, Carol and Cassandra, for helping Jack and Lucille in their moments of doubt and struggle."

The gleam in Bidwell's eyes suggested to Ann that the minister's words were not an attempt to curry favor with Royce. This was the glow of a recent convert. Bidwell actually believed it.

"I remember two days ago...Royce and his daughters were leaving the hospital. Jack was gone and word had come that Lucille would soon be joining him. As they were departing, I heard Carol utter a few words that touched my heart. She turned simply to her father and asked, 'What are we going to do about Ann?' Here she was. One family member deceased. Another soon to leave us. And Carol was not thinking of herself or her immediate family. She was thinking of the one human being who was going to suffer. She was thinking of Ann. The care and empathy contained in such a simple phrase. 'What are we going to do about Ann?' Bless Carol for her goodness, Lord. Hold her dearly to your divine heart. Bless her for those simple words: 'What are we going to do about Ann?'"

By now everyone on Royce's side was looking at Ann. She wished that Bidwell had not mentioned her in connection with Carol.

"Having shared that memory, I want to echo the sentiment of everyone here. We're going through some difficult times in Winfield. Every one of us in one way or another."

Deeply moved, he looked down at Royce. "Royce, I want to thank you for all your efforts on our behalf and on behalf of the town and for encouraging us to join your Pheasant Valley project. You're always there for us. God bless you, Royce, for standing up for us in our time of need."

Polite murmurs came from both sides of the assembly. The reverend's using her parents' funeral for a mawkish tribute to the man responsible for much of the town's misfortune irritated Ann but did not surprise her.

Bidwell lifted his gaze and raised his arms heavenward. "We thank you, Lord. In Winfield you have given us a world where the human values we cherish are rewarded by your goodness and mercy. We say good-bye to Jack and Lucille as they are reunited with their loved ones in your heavenly resting place. We thank you, Lord. In Jesus's name..."

"Amen," the group responded in unison. The service was over.

Ann remained in place while a handful of mourners passed by to offer their respects. What surprised her was the larger number of people who remained clustered around Royce and the girls.

"Don't mind them," Judy said. "They're just afraid of Royce."

"Do you know who yelled?" Ann asked.

"I don't know. But I sure liked hearing it."

Ann stepped over to the caskets. She reached out to touch one of them. "Mama...Papa," she said quietly. "I'm saying good-bye to you now. I love you. And I'll see you again—after I've cleaned up the mess down here."

By now Olga had broken away from the Chamberlin entourage. She rushed up to Ann and gave her a big hug.

"I hated sitting over there, Miss Ann. But Mr. Royce said I had to or I'd be fired. He asked every one of those people to sit with him."

"It's all right, Olga. The point is, we're here."

"I wish Reverend Bidwell had talked more about your parents."

"Between you and me, I think the good reverend has a problem."

Then she saw someone crouched behind a sapling about fifty feet away whom she thought she would never see again: lawyer Collinsen.

The image was absurd. He was clutching the trunk and attempting to hide behind it. Since the tree trunk had the width of a large broomstick, he was in plain view of everyone. On first glance one might have thought he was trying to uproot it.

"Excuse me," Ann said, starting for him.

Collinsen appeared terror-stricken. He released the tree and began to back away.

"Did you come to pay your respects?" Ann asked.

"Yes, I did."

"You're a little late. Where were you when we needed you?"

"I...I was there. I came now. But you know...I tried...I did try."

"I thought you came to return our deposit," Ann said.

"What deposit?"

"The five hundred dollars we gave you. You took our money, and you didn't do a damn thing."

Collinsen was wild-eyed. He stumbled away from Ann. "Please don't talk to me that way."

"Why?"

"I have a wife and family."

"You also have our money..."

"I don't have it now," he stammered.

"Then why in hell did you show up?"

With a look of panic, the extraordinary human being from Council Bluffs scurried off to his car.

"Our ex-lawyer," Ann said to Olga.

Ann saw the buckboard from the manor house. Cyrus, the hired hand, was standing by with Ann's suitcase.

"Looks like they want me out of town real fast," Ann said. "Olga, I'll be going back to school now. I don't know when I'll be back."

"I'll write you, Miss Ann."

"I'll write, too. I need to know what's going on here."

Cyrus placed her bag in the back. "Sorry about this, Miss Ann," he said. "Seems I'm always driving you to the station."

Ann gave Olga a hug and got into the buckboard to begin the journey into town. She didn't like leaving Winfield. She wanted to remember it as vividly as possible. On the other hand, Ben would be waiting at the other end. Was it only three days ago that he had given her the roses? With all that had happened since then, it seemed like weeks. Inside, she felt her life was pulling her in two directions. Her past and present were still in Winfield. But her future? She could only imagine the possibilities.

There would be a short wait. The five o'clock train and its change in Minneapolis would get her back to Coon Falls in early evening. She had accomplished a lot in spite of the circumstances. She had been to the funeral, had a meeting at the lawyer's office, and visited the Northeast Quarter. None of these had produced any conclusions, but they were steps.

Even as Ann heard a car approaching, she knew whose it was. Royce turned off Market Street and was heading straight for the station.

"What'll we do about Ann?" she thought.

While the girls waited, Royce stepped out of the car and walked toward her.

Although dressed formally, the girls looked out of place in their attire. It was as if they were trying to project a poise and sophistication that was forever out of reach.

Chamberlin stopped in front of Ann. "Well, here we are again. You have only yourself to blame for this. You sat with the townspeople, and you struck my daughter."

"From my perspective she had it coming," Ann answered.

"Make her apologize! Make her pay!" Carol bawled from Royce's car.

"In due time, Carol," Royce said.

"No! Now! If you love me, you'll do it now!"

Chamberlin appeared more regretful than angry. With all the hatred between them, it seemed peculiar. "When I've decided your future, we'll speak again," he said to Ann.

He paused. He seemed about to make some sort of personal declaration. "This thing we have. You're pushing it about as far as it can go. You know that."

"Good-bye, Royce," Ann said.

Ann watched Royce return to his car and drive away. She sat down on a bench to wait for the train.

46

AN HOUR OUT OF MINNEAPOLIS, ANN'S eyes were on the carriage window, watching the passing scenery. If there was shade, she would look for a reflection of the inside of the car against the glass.

"If anyone's going to do anything, it's going to be me," she thought.

The train began to slow down before its arrival at the next stop. Ann realized she would have seen a silo with a large drawing of a farmer and a plow on the side if there were enough light because she knew the route by heart now.

"Royce is breaking the law. Sometimes he's using the law to do it. And I've been trying to acquaint myself with the law to see what legalities he's bending or breaking. Nobody else is doing this. They're either bought off or afraid."

The train was passing a string of freight cars on a siding. They were all the same color and shape in the late afternoon shade.

"If I were a lawyer, I could take them on myself. I could have stood up to them a long time ago. Perhaps I could have found out what happened to Zachary or maybe even prevented it. I could have stood up to that bunch—for my family and for my neighbors—and saved everyone a load of heartache."

The procession of freight cars began to slow down.

She thought about Arabella Mansfield. "She was a lawyer. She'd have stood up to them. She'd have taken them to court."

Ann smiled and felt the first glow of enthusiasm she'd had in a long time. "I'm going to become a lawyer. That's what I'll do. Yes. That's my plan. I'm going to become a lawyer. I'm going to do it so this will never happen to me or anyone else again."

She was running her decision through her mind over and over again, when slowly a glum and hollow feeling inside began to seep all around it until her effervescence had vanished.

"How the hell am I going to become an attorney?" she thought. "I'm too young. I don't have any money for tuition. And I need all that time to study. A law degree isn't the same as pinning on a badge. And with the finances in Winfield, Royce and everyone would know my plan the first time I applied for admission."

The train creaked and pulled to stop.

"I can't quit and get a job. Most sixteen-year-old girls who try that end up in a whorehouse. No, I'm going to have to wait."

Two businessmen boarded the car ahead of Ann's, and the train slowly rolled out of the station.

"I've got a plan. Something I didn't have before," Ann thought. "Just because I can't do it now, it doesn't mean I can't do it later. Sheriff Dierkes said, 'Hang on and don't fall off.' That's what I've done so far. I'll do it awhile longer."

As she rode in the taxi from Minneapolis to Coon Falls, it was dark outside. It seemed like she had been away a month. She looked forward to seeing Ben and wondered how they would be able to contact each other. She had left so abruptly. She remembered his kiss.

When the taxi turned into the driveway, the school seemed to have retreated into its surroundings. The trees and the buildings were all the same color—it was as if they had blended into a vast etching of lines against a gray backdrop.

Nadia Fairchild was at the desk in her office. Her eyes were shut—as if she were in deep meditation. The remnants of Ann's bouquet were in the same vase on the bookshelf. The phonograph player was on the desk in front of her, along with three cylinders. The player was making a clicking sound that became slower and slower until it finally stopped. Fairchild opened her eyes.

At the sound of the arriving taxi, Fairchild stepped over to the window. She watched Ann as she paid the driver and started for the entrance downstairs.

Ann didn't look up to see if she was being observed. She was tired and wanted to get some rest. She had taken a few steps when she stopped. There was a distinct and strong odor of burnt wood. She glanced at the forest around the school. The air was clear with no sign of smoke, but the scent hung over everything. It couldn't have been a neighboring fireplace since there were no neighbors around. But there had definitely been a fire.

Ann looked across the river toward the speakeasy. It was dark and quiet in the familiar spot near the bridge. No lights. No music. Not a sound. She remembered Ben had told her that Gus was planning to close down. It certainly looked deserted now.

She finished the walk to the front door and knocked. No one answered. Inside, Fairchild had come out of her office. She was standing in the shadows, watching Ann.

Ann knocked again. Fairchild continued to study her, observing Ann go through the inconvenience of being left in the dark—her knock and her reactions when no one came. This went on for a few minutes.

Ann waited and listened to hear if there was any movement inside, but there was nothing. She was raising her hand to knock one more time when Fairchild yanked open the door.

"And so Miss Hardy is back with us," Fairchild said.

She locked the door behind Ann. They were crossing the lobby. "I am told your conduct in Winfield left something to be desired."

Ann was tired. She didn't want to get into a debate on maidenly conduct.

"I am told that you struck Carol."

"Word gets around," Ann said.

"Carol is a very special human being. You should be ashamed of yourself."

Fairchild had moved back into the shadows and was now only a large silhouette in the darkest area in the lobby.

"Is violence part of your nature, Miss Hardy?"

"Can't we talk tomorrow? It's late. I haven't had much sleep."

"Is violence part of your nature?" repeated the voice from the shadows.

"No, ma'am. Violence is not part of my nature," Ann said with a sigh.

"I sensed it the day I met you at our first interview. I sensed it."

"I remember," Ann said.

"I am telling you that if you try any of that around here, I will send you to a doctor—a doctor of mental health issues who is an acquaintance of the school. He will give you an enema to purge you of your anger and violent tendencies. Do you understand?"

"An enema?"

"You heard me."

"Yes, ma'am. But I've behaved myself, haven't I?"

"That's not the point. You know what awaits you."

From the hallway to the students' quarters issued the familiar sound of shoes scuffling along the floor.

"Sounds like Miss Bruner," Ann said.

"What could she be doing up at this hour?" Fairchild grumbled.

"Miss Fairchild, was there a fire here?" Ann asked. "Outside it smells like burnt wood."

"It shouldn't concern you," Fairchild said.

The scuffling grew louder.

"Was there?"

"Yes, if you must know."

"Was it here at the school?"

"I thought you were in a hurry to retire, Miss Hardy."

"I was just wondering."

"It was on the other side of the river, Miss Hardy." Miss Bruner spoke from the entrance to the hallway, clad in a wrinkled floor-length bathrobe and holding a lantern. "A building across the river. The other night it caught fire."

It was the speakeasy after all. Ann immediately thought of Ben. "Was anybody hurt?"

"I don't think so," Bruner said. "It spread to the woods behind it. Took the firemen all night to put it out.

"And do you have your answer now?" Fairchild asked Ann.

"Yes, ma'am," Ann said, still thinking of Ben.

Fairchild returned to Bruner. "You're up awfully late."

"I couldn't sleep. I'm sorry if I disturbed you, Nadia."

"Escort Miss Hardy to her room."

"I'll make it down all right," Ann said, picking up her suitcase.

"Miss Hardy..."

Ann stopped. There was always a final word from Fairchild.

"You've hoodwinked a lot of people around here. Tomorrow after breakfast you clean the showers."

"Yes, ma'am."

Ann and Bruner began the trek down to her room. She knew Bruner would abandon her along the way. That was all right with Ann. She knew her way back in the dark.

47

Only five students remained at Clearwater for the summer break. Every day Miss Fairchild gave each girl a work assignment in a different part of the school. One girl would clean the library; another would polish the doorknobs. Ann didn't mind the work or the solitude. It gave her long periods of time to think of her family.

"I love them and I miss all of them," she would say to herself. "I won't deny how I feel, but I can't let feelings get in my way. Someday I'll cry about it, but not today."

She was also worried about Ben. What had happened across the river? She considered sneaking out at night and venturing across the river to search for answers. But what would she find when she got there? Charred earth and more questions. She would have to wait.

As usual, on Tuesday afternoons, the girls were given two hours of free time in Coon Falls. Ann slipped ahead of the small group and immediately went to the Igloo. Shabby and nearly vacant, it offered her the comfort of familiar surroundings.

Ann sat at her usual table by the window with a chocolate sundae.

"The last day I saw Ben, there wasn't a chance to say good-bye or make a plan or anything. We were here. He'd just given me the roses. Saypin showed up and everything fell apart. I wonder if he's all right. I wonder if he knows how I feel."

Then one day she received a letter. She did not recognize the penmanship on the front, but it was definitely addressed to her. On the back was the name Chamberlin—also in the same writing. It wasn't from Royce or anyone in Winfield. It had been mailed from Cincinnati, and Royce had no business dealings in Cincinnati.

Ann felt a warm glow inside. It could only have come from one person.

Quickly, she tore it open and found a short note. Her eyes went right to the signature at the bottom: Ben.

The message was brief. "Have missed you. Sorry for your loss. Very tough time. Wish I could be there with you. See you at Igloo next Tuesday?"

Ann wanted to cry out with joy. She started to laugh at the way Ben had navigated it through the Clearwater office and right into her hands. With the name Chamberlin on the envelope, nobody dared open it. It wasn't really a love note, but that didn't matter.

⤴

On the following Tuesday afternoon, the girls were preparing to leave for their two hours in Coon Falls. Ann was taking care to select a proper set of clothes. Nothing splashy to stand out from the others, but still special enough for the occasion.

She went straight to the Igloo where Ben was waiting on the small wooden bench outside.

Ann rushed over to him, and before he could get to his feet, she threw her arms around him and kissed him. The passion of the kiss surprised both of them. Ben had not expected it, and, a few seconds before, Ann would never have thought she would greet him this way.

"I've missed you," Ben said, caressing her cheek.

Ann felt wondrous inside. Everything about Ben—his smile, his voice, his appearance—was exactly as she remembered. She wondered how he could seem like a figure from a dream when they were apart and so real when they were together. Everything seemed right. He was the one happy spot in her life.

"I've missed you, too," she said.

"Yes."

"A lot, Ben."

"Me, too."

They stared into each other's eyes for a long time. Nothing needed to be said. Finally, Ann remembered there were unanswered questions and untold news.

"What happened, Ben? We keep hearing about this fire over by the speakeasy. You're OK, aren't you?"

"I'm fine."

"I was worried. What was it?"

"Let's go inside," Ben said.

They went into the Igloo and took seats at their usual table by the window.

"It was late the night of the fifth," Ben began. "Henchawz and his bunch showed up on a drunken bender. Sometime earlier that evening, they'd hit on the idea of driving over and getting their revenge on Gus and me for what happened."

"Oh, brother."

"By the time they showed up, the only one there was Jerry, the watchman. Of course, this didn't set well, so they shot Jerry and set fire to the building. Anyway, Jerry was able to make his way down to Coon Falls and alert the firehouse. He left Henchawz and his crowd up there, laughing at what they had done."

"Jerry's all right?"

"He's a tough one. He's fine. It's Henchawz who's in for it. You see, the Tango Man forgot that the speakeasy is owned by the Gandolfo brothers, so it's gang property. And even though the Gandolfos planned to close it down, they didn't appreciate somebody shooting an employee and putting a match to their building."

"I would imagine not."

"So they've put out a contract on Henchawz and his yes-man. Somewhere out there, the Tango King of Goose Back, Ontario, is on the run for his life."

"I thought something had happened to you," Ann said.

"No. We're all OK—Gus, Lee, Clark. Everyone. We're closed and off the hillside."

Ann was amazed how her own troubles seemed so far away. Ben's presence seemed to place them in a more manageable perspective.

"Now, what about you, Ann? You're the one with the important news."

Ann related all her experiences in Winfield. She finished with her arrival back in Coon Falls.

"I'm sorry, Ann. You've gone through one hell of a lot," Ben said. "Right now, you'll have to depend on what Sheriff Dierkes finds. Can you trust him?"

"He's a good man, Ben."

"Then you'll have to wait."

"I am going to write Fred Brubaker for a copy of the will."

"The will is a good start. Right now, you're not in much of a position to do anything. But there'll come a day when they let their guard down. People with too much confidence and success have a way of letting it go to their heads. They get careless and start making mistakes. Maybe over time this waiting period will work to your advantage."

They sat at the window without speaking. As always, their sundaes were slowly melting away in the sunlight.

"There's another thing. I have to go back to school," Ben said.

"What?"

"I have to get my degree."

"So where does that leave us?"

"Still together," Ben said. "We'll keep in touch by mail. On vacations or semester breaks, I'll come up to see you. We'll figure out a way."

The words were encouraging, but Ann felt sad.

"I'm not leaving you, Ann. I'll give you my address and my telephone number at the dorm. I'll send all my mail with Chamberlin on the envelope. We'll make this work."

Ann was beginning to feel lost and insecure. In spite of his assurances, Ben seemed to be drifting away from her right at the table.

"When do you go?" Ann said finally.

"After Labor Day."

"I'm going to miss you, Ben."

"I'm going to miss you, too. I love you, Ann."

"I love you, too."

He leaned forward and kissed her. "You make a fellow want to follow you. You know that?"

"It's a long road," Ann said.

They sat at the table looking at each other. She felt a warmth inside she had not felt for anyone.

"Let's take a walk," Ben said.

They spent the next half hour strolling along the main street of Coon Falls. There was so little traffic, they might have walked down the center. They walked without saying much, occasionally stopping for a kiss.

When Ann returned to Clearwater, she immediately went to her room and began writing her letter to Fred Brubaker.

48

ANN SENT THE LETTER. WHEN SHE did not receive an answer or a copy of the will, she wrote another request. After a ten-day wait and no answer, she wrote another. This went on for the next eight months.

Finally, on one of the free afternoons in Coon Falls, she went to the post office. Using her school allowance, she placed a call to Fred Brubaker in Winfield.

The call was taken by Kazak, the new teller, who explained that Brubaker, Royce, and Van Burin were all attending an important meeting at the courthouse. But he promised to relay her request to Brubaker. It was only a three- or four-sentence conversation, but Ann believed him. Something in his tone of voice convinced her. It was mocking—not of Ann, but of Van Burin and the others around him.

Ann had never made a direct call before. She was wondering what kind of response it would elicit from Royce and Brubaker. She soon found out.

It was two thirty on a typical sunny May afternoon. Ann was in study hall. The girls had been assigned an essay called "The Power of Feminine Compromise." Ann was working on the final paragraph, detailing how a maiden must choose. Miss Saypin had been the proctor, but she was asleep in her chair at the front of the room. With her head back and her mouth wide open, she was dead to the world. The girls were obediently writing their essays as if nothing were amiss.

The loud bang of a door slamming and the sound of heavy steps across the lobby signaled that Nadia Fairchild on the move.

"Miss Hardy!" she bellowed. "Come here, Miss Hardy!"

Ann didn't try to awaken Miss Saypin for permission to leave. She got up from her chair and went out the door. She saw Fairchild waiting at the edge of the hallway.

"Come here, Miss Hardy!"

"Yes, ma'am?" Ann said when she arrived in front of Fairchild.

They moved out into the lobby.

"You know why I called you," Fairchild said.

"I have an idea."

"Mr. Royce is very displeased with your behavior. He said you called the lawyer's office and demanded a copy of your mother's will."

"They promised me a copy, and they haven't delivered. I thought a call would get results."

"That's neither here nor there. Telling the operator in the Coon Falls post office it was an emergency when it was not is deception, Miss Hardy."

"I wanted the call to go through."

"Deception, Miss Hardy."

"I suppose it was."

Fairchild stopped. She was focused on a ragged clump of weeds out in the driveway.

"I'll have to speak to the gardener about that unsightly clump of weeds. It looks like the shrub clippings from his last visit, wouldn't you say?"

"They are the shrub clippings, ma'am."

By now Ann understood the purpose of their conversation. Even though Fairchild was speaking, Royce had instigated their dialogue.

"Why is the school involved in this?" Ann asked. "It's a family matter."

"The school is the extension of the family, Miss Hardy."

"But I didn't do anything wrong."

"You made the call from Coon Falls, did you not?"

"Yes."

"Not from the school office."

"No, not from the school office."

"Because you knew we wouldn't allow it."

"I figured you wouldn't."

"And had I questioned you, you would have sworn on the heart of our Holy Mother...our Mother of Tears...that you had *never* gone near the post office."

"Probably so."

"Double deception. That makes it a school matter."

"But that didn't happen. What I did and what I might have done are two different things."

"As of today, your allowance is reduced to a dollar a week. All your vacation privileges are suspended. You are here for the duration of the summer."

By now Ann was not surprised at the announcement. She had grown cynical enough to expect the worst.

"We both know this is Royce's doing," Ann said.

"No, this is my doing, Miss Hardy. You may go," Fairchild declared.

Ann started back down the hall.

"Miss Hardy, aren't you going to say anything more?" Fairchild called after her. "React in some way? It would prove I am right about you."

"May I go back to class?" Ann asked.

"Go. Go."

"I'll make the best of this," Ann thought. "I learned long ago to adapt to whatever they throw at me."

As she tiptoed in, Saypin let out a deep snore and stirred in her seat.

"Sure, I'm angry. But I've got to keep a clear head. I learned a couple of things. One, I think I'm right about the will. And two, if I step out of line, if I make one phone call to Winfield, everybody goes through the roof."

Ann resumed writing. "A maiden must choose whether to drift through life, asleep at the switch, or to be alert and allow herself to know herself."

"Their position is clear now," she thought. "But I wonder what they'll do when I graduate."

～

Six weeks later it was the Fourth of July, and Ann was seventeen.

Like the previous summer, only a handful of girls remained for the holiday recess. In Coon Falls there were the usual holiday festivities. The remaining students were allowed to go into town for the afternoon. Ben had planned to come to Coon Falls to celebrate Ann's birthday, but two days before, he had been detained in Chicago with appendicitis, so he and Ann had agreed to meet in Coon Falls on the last Tuesday of the month.

Knowing there would be no gifts, Ann had saved whatever mail she had received over the past week. She would open them in place of presents and then go to the Igloo for a root beer float. There were six envelopes in all.

The first two were cards from Judy and Ellen.

The third was from Royce Chamberlin. Inside was a short note, dated May 10, 1925—around the time Ann had called Brubaker's office—which had been held back for almost two months. She read: "Since you are unable to return for summer recess, I am sure Nadia Fairchild will find plenty of activities to occupy your attention on your birthday. Royce."

Ann crumpled up the letter and tossed it into the wastebasket.

The next envelope was marked "The Right Reverend C. Bidwell, Winfield, Iowa."

"I wonder what you want," Ann said. Inside was another short note: "Dear Miss Hardy: Owing to your recent absences and your lack of financial support to our ministry, it is with deep regret that we strike your name from the church registry. This has nothing to do with your ill-feeling toward Royce and his family. I hope someday you will open your eyes and acknowledge the blessings he has brought. So much has changed in Winfield since he came among us. In Jesus's name, Reverend C. Bidwell."

"Excommunicated on my birthday. Bless you, too," Ann said as she crumpled up the note.

The next one was from Olga. "Dear Miss Ann: Happy Birthday. We're so sorry you won't be coming home. It's not fair, and we're all thinking of you. It's hard to believe you're seventeen. Time flies so much these days. Hope you have a good time celebrating. Hope to meet your young man someday. Old Van Burin is in a mess with that Chaynie Auction House. Starting to get complaints. People aren't getting their money. Van Burin is all in a tizzy. Royce has turned meaner if that is possible. Always up to something. Makes plans and gets angry if anybody disagrees with him. Will sneak this out with the morning mail. Love, Olga."

"I love you, too, Olga," Ann said.

She was looking at the final letter. It came from Chicago with the name Chamberlin on the envelope. She had heard of Ben's emergency in a telegram that arrived a few days earlier. She tore it open. "Dearest Ann: Happy Birthday again. I miss you a great deal. I'll be out of the hospital by the time you receive this. Damned inconvenience. Since it's the appendix, it won't happen again. We still have the summer. Can't wait to see you in three weeks. Love, Ben."

As always, Ben's words lessened the gloomy impact of bad news

"There's so much I want to give him," she thought. "But I can't until the fight is over. I sure hope he'll understand."

Ann reread Ben's note one more time and popped it in the drawer with the cards from Olga and her friends.

"Considering my gains against my losses, it wasn't a bad birthday after all."

49

FALL TERM BEGAN. ANN HAD NOT been home for a year.

The first week in November she received an envelope from Fred Brubaker's office. There were students gathered around her in the lobby opening their mail, so Ann took the envelope over to the window to examine it privately. She was excited because she thought it just might be a copy of the will. But since it came from Brubaker, she prepared herself for any sucker punch it might contain.

She opened the envelope. It was indeed a will, but as she ran her eyes over the contents, she noticed the name Lady Ann Carson in large print. Her heart sank. It was her grandmother's will.

"Bastards," she said to herself. "I should have seen this one coming."

It was the same copy she had held in Brubaker's office years ago. The bequests were the same—half to Ann and her parents and half to the Chamberlins.

On Sunday two weeks later, Ann met Ben at the Igloo. Ben saw Ann's concern immediately.

"What is it?"

"Some news. I finally got the will, but it was the wrong one."

"Your grandmother's will?"

"Yes. They knew which one I wanted."

"They're staying true to form."

"There was a change in Mama's will—I'm sure of it. And it's something they don't want me to see."

"Interesting that they sent the old one anyway," Ben said.

"They're just taunting me—reminding me who's boss."

"It does tell you one thing, and you can take it as a backhanded compliment: They're taking you seriously, Ann."

"I wish I'd picked up the paper Mama tore in half back in the hospital. It was all right there in front of me. Right there on the floor."

Ben touched her arm. "How could you have thought of that back then? Your mind was on a dozen other things. You were in no state of mind for strategy."

"I tell myself that. I've got to find a way to get back to Winfield."

"That'll be difficult. They've got you boxed in here until graduation. That's the middle of next year."

"I'll have to bide my time and wait for an opportunity. Like you say, when a person lets success go to his head, he can get sloppy and overconfident."

"Still true," Ben said.

"I've been hoping that they'll invite me back to be present at some function that honors the family. And while they're congratulating each other, I might slip away long enough to find some answers. I might have a chance."

"Hang on, Ann. It'll happen."

"Yes. Hang on and don't fall off."

Ann waited. Her junior year passed quickly.

⌒

In the fall of 1926, Ann was a senior. She had not seen Winfield for two years.

On a Sunday afternoon in late October, Ann and Ben were sitting beside the riverbank in Coon Falls. Ben had graduated and begun his office job in Chicago. He was still able to visit Ann on Sundays.

Ann had received a letter from Fred Brubaker. "Listen to this," she said to Ben. "'For your information, we are having an auction of some of your mother's possessions and heirlooms at Carson Manor on Friday, November fifth. You might be interested in bidding on some of them—particularly your mother's wedding dress. Lucille once said she hoped you would have it someday. Royce and his family are extending you the invitation.'"

"It's what you've been waiting for."

"Why would they wait that long to auction Mama's things? It's been two years."

"Who knows? You can't worry about that. What matters is what you're going to do."

Ann closed the letter. "I'm going to Winfield on the fifth. It shouldn't be hard to slip over to the courthouse. I know they have a copy of Grandma's will. By now, Mama's will should be there, too."

"How do you plan to do it?"

"My grades are up, and I'm a senior. If I contact Brubaker and say I want to come down for the day to bid on the dress, I'm sure he'll provide a cover letter for the school."

"In one day?"

"It has to be. The shorter the time, the more I can do. If I stayed overnight, I'd have to be out at Carson Manor. This way I'm pretty much on my own."

Ben took her hand. "Then I'm coming with you."

"Oh, Ben." Ann kissed him on the cheek.

"It's time I met this bunch."

"They're quite a group."

"I want to see Winfield. I want to know it. I have a feeling we're going to be taking them on somewhere down the line."

"We?"

"You don't think I'd let you go it alone."

Ann smiled. She had never expected this.

"I want to help, Ann." He gave her a long and tender kiss.

As Ann looked into his eyes, she imagined all of life's possibilities lying ahead of her—for her and for the two of them. The image was beautiful and inviting. But then the reality of Winfield would seep in from the side and color the entire picture. Soon it would become the picture. Ann knew it would always be that way until she made her move.

"Ben, I want to give you more of myself than I can right now."

"I know," Ben said.

Ann looked away from him. "God, I don't want to finish this all bitter and burned out. I've seen what hate does in my own family. I'm not going to be that way."

Very gently, Ben took her face in his hands. "You're just fine. Maybe inside it doesn't feel like that, but on the outside, I see you standing in the middle of a storm. I see goodness. I see strength—tremendous strength. I see someone I want to be with. As for the rest of it, you're worth waiting for."

He kissed her again. Ann felt tears in the corners of her eyes.

"The best way to our future is to win this thing," Ben said. "I'll check the train schedules. We've got a trip to plan."

50

Using the letter from Fred Brubaker that invoked the name of Royce Chamberlin, Ann had no trouble getting permission to go to Winfield. On the morning of the fifth, she left early from school and met Ben in Minneapolis at the downtown station.

By 11:00 a.m. they were stepping off the train in Winfield. There was no one waiting on the platform, and the station seemed closed. Nearby was a new building—a businessman's hotel called the Journeyman.

"I want to show you Market Street," Ann said.

They cut through an alley and walked up Market Street. For a weekday, the town seemed half-awake. Many of the businesses were closed. Some displayed signs that read, "Closed for Auction." Along the way Ann and Ben passed a horse and wagon or the occasional pedestrian. Ann didn't recognize them.

"Funny. Why would they close up so many businesses for an auction of Mama's things? She didn't have that much."

"Maybe it's a county auction."

"Can't be. The last county auction was during the war. Grandpa and Grandma held it to raise money for the troops. If they're having a county auction now, this is serious."

"Hard times, Ann."

Ann looked at the businesses on either side of them. Many of the shops seemed older. Or darker inside. Some of the display windows needed a washing.

"I'm amazed. The whole street looks haggard."

It was not just the auction, but the economy that was affecting Winfield. The cities were not feeling it yet, but for the rural areas and towns like Winfield, the approaching depression had already begun. When they passed the bank and law office at the end of the street, Ann saw that both businesses were closed.

Across the street a For Sale sign had been placed in the front window of Minnie's Ice Cream Parlor.

"Look at that," Ann said. "Minnie's is out of business. I had my first Eskimo Pie in there with Judy and Ellen. Right there in the window. Now it's gone."

"Too bad."

"It's all changed, Ben."

Pomphrey Park was deserted as well. Ann saw the milk truck putt-putting along on the other side, passing the courthouse. The clock tower on the roof began a slow tolling for eleven o'clock.

Ann and Ben went up the steps into the courthouse. The lobby had a creased and worn burgundy rug that had been there for as long as Ann could remember. To the right was a set of double doors with the words COURT OF WINFIELD over them. It was closed and locked. On the left was an open doorway into another room marked RECORDS.

Before they could enter, an argument erupted ahead of them between Jago Hudsen and Betsy Allen, one of the clerks. Betsy was behind the counter that contained the shelves of local records. Jago was lounging against it on the other side. With every exchange, his anger was twisting his posture into a crouch.

"I don't think I can help you, Mr. Hudsen," Betsy was saying.

"Don't give me that," Jago shot back. "You help everybody else. So you find that bill. They're accusin' my papa of stealin' their wagon wheels and puttin' them up all around our property. Papa's a gentleman farmer. He don't do that."

"Jago," Ann whispered to Ben.

Betsy was exasperated. "There is no record of such a bill, Mr. Hudsen. That's why I can't help you."

Jago had made up his mind. "You're not lookin' hard enough."

"I have looked three times for you. And I am going to explain it to once more. Your father says Olaf Dingle lent him the wagon wheels. There's no record of a purchase or a loan."

"You think I'm stupid?"

"I am trying to explain something to you. Whether it was a loan or a theft . . ."

"My papa didn't steal nuthin' . . ."

"Or an accusation of theft, there is no bill. A bill means a purchase. A bill means the item was paid for. Unless there is a purchase record of some kind, I can't help you."

"You got it all figured out, don't you? You and that old man, Dierkes."

"Sheriff Dierkes has nothing to do with this."

Jago turned away from her, only to find the perfect target on whom to take out his rage and disappointment.

"Well, look what come to town," he said to Ann. "Anybody know you're here?"

"They will soon enough."

Betsy looked drained from the encounter with Jago. She was ready to assist Ann, but Jago had not left.

"I can't help you, Mr. Hudsen," she said.

With a grunt, Jago moved to the end of the counter but positioned himself to eavesdrop. Every now and then, he would peer up at the visitors.

"Ann, it's good to see you again," Betsy said with a smile.

"Good to see you, too."

"What may I do for you?"

"I'd like to see a copy of my mother's will," Ann said.

"Isn't there a copy at Fred Brubaker's office?"

"I'm sure there is," Ann replied. "But he's busy right now with the auction. Don't you have a copy here?"

"We should," Betsy said. "We had that fire fifteen months ago. A lot of records were destroyed. But that shouldn't involve your mother."

"I hope not."

"No. If it were over two years, we could ask Lucy to have a look upstairs. But it's not. I think it's down here."

Betsy went over to one of four file cabinets along the wall and began fingering through the folders.

"A year later and we're still getting our files in order from that fire."

Jago remained in place. His rage and frustration were at a boil. "So who's your friend?" he drawled.

"This is Ben Harmon," Ann said.

"You some kind of special friend or somethin'?"

"He is to me," Ann answered. "Now if you'll excuse us."

"Can't he speak for hisself?" Jago snapped. "Don't look like he comes from around here."

"I don't," Ben said.

"So where you come from, friend?"

"Chicago."

Ann glanced over to Ben. He seemed unperturbed. People like Jago and Henchawz always seemed to want to call him out, and Ben always took it in his stride.

"You lookin' down on me?" Jago said.

"Excuse me?"

"I said you lookin' down on me?"

"I don't know you," Ben said. "Now we're busy here."

"Yeah, you're lookin' down on me. You're all soft and polite with that proper gentleman's answer. You're lookin' down on me right now, aren't you, Mr. Harmonsens?"

"Harmon."

Betsy looked up from the drawer. "Why don't you leave them alone, Mr. Hudsen? I said we can't help you."

"You're helpin' *them*, ain't you?" Jago snarled. In an instant, he was back to Ben.

"You nervous, Mr. Harmonsens?"

"No."

Jago snickered. "Sure you are. You're standing there like Mama's Sunday school."

"Think whatever you want," Ben said. "We're busy, OK?"

"I don't think I like you, Mr. Harmonsens."

Neither Ben nor Ann wanted any trouble—not at this point. They had not reckoned on the inconvenience of running into Jago Hudsen. The tension was dispelled by the arrival of another person they had hoped they wouldn't see.

Fred Brubaker appeared in the doorway of the records room. He was whistling, preoccupied in thought, but when he saw Ann at the counter, he stopped.

"Ann, what are you doing here?"

"I thought I'd stop off for a moment."

"You're supposed to be at the auction. You shouldn't be here."

"The auction hasn't started, has it?" Ann countered.

"You didn't tell me you were coming over here."

"It was last minute."

Ben watched the exchange. Ann was going toe-to-toe with an adversary, and she wasn't giving an inch. He was proud of her.

"They came to see some papers, Mr. Brubaker," Jago announced. "That's why they're here."

"And what papers would those be?" Brubaker asked Ann.

"I came to see my mother's will."

"You could have come to me. I could have shown it you."

"I've been asking you for two years," Ann said evenly.

This was something he had not expected. His mind raced quickly to deflect the conversation. "I don't believe I know you," he said to Ben.

"That's Mr. Harmonsens," Jago said with a smirk.

"I'm Ben Harmon."

"Look at him," Jago chuckled. "All polite and proper, just like Mama's Sunday school."

"Don't you have some place to go?" Brubaker said to Jago with some irritation.

"You tellin' me to leave?" Jago said.

"Yes, I'm telling you to leave," Brubaker said.

"Yeah, yeah, I'm leavin'," Jago said with a laugh. "We'll talk again. Right, Mr. Harmonsens?"

Everyone waited as Jago sauntered out of the room.

"Ben Harmon," Brubaker resumed. "I've heard that name mentioned in family conversations. What do you do, Mr. Harmon?"

"I'm an insurance broker."

"I heard you played piano in nightclubs."

"When I need the cash."

"You shouldn't work because you need cash, young man," Brubaker chided. "Work should be dynamic, with job satisfaction and pride in craft the true rewards."

"I'll keep that in mind," Ben replied. "Ann was asking you a question."

Brubaker was beginning to rile. "What question was that?"

"My mother's will," Ann said.

"I didn't know you wanted to see it that badly." He looked over to Betsy. "Is it there?"

"No, Mr. Brubaker. I can't find it."

"Let me know if you do." He returned to Ann. "I can tell you what was in it. Everything is left to your step-grandfather who will act as your trustee until you are twenty-one."

Ann had imagined the possibility of this announcement. But it was still a jolt to hear it from Brubaker.

"She said she was leaving everything to me."

"It looks like she changed her mind, Ann."

"I was with her when she died."

Brubaker adopted his sober, reasonable tone. "She was in tremendous pain and more than a little confused. She must have changed her mind before she saw you and then forgot to mention it after you arrived. Isn't that so, young man?"

"I don't know. I wasn't there," Ben said.

Ann was proud of Ben. In Winfield less than an hour and already he was standing up to both Jago and Brubaker.

Behind the counter, Betsy moved a step from the file cabinet with a folder in her hand. She was about to speak but then changed her mind. She placed the folder on top of the cabinet.

"You got anything going here, Ann? Anything I should know about?" Brubaker asked innocently.

"No."

Brubaker realized there was no further purpose in conversing. Ann had grown increasingly stubborn. The office etiquette he had used with Lady Ann, Lucille, and Jack would not work with her.

"Yes. Well, I dropped in to check on the Clipperton probate papers. Old Man Clipperton died, you know."

"No, I didn't," Ann said.

Betsy moved to another drawer and began to leaf through the files at the front.

"Couldn't keep up with his bank payments. Couldn't afford to hire a crew. Lost the farm."

"Not in yet, Mr. Brubaker," Betsy said from the drawer.

"Coming to the auction?" Brubaker asked Ann.

"I think not," Ann answered.

"You told me you were."

"I changed my mind."

"You lied to me," Brubaker said, affecting hurt. "You lied. You said you were coming down to bid at the auction." There was an uneasy silence. "How long will you be staying?"

"For the day," Ann said.

"Well, let me know if you need anything," he said as he strode out of the room.

"He'll be running to tell Royce," Ann said.

Ann and Ben turned back to the counter. Betsy was nearby, holding the folder she had previously placed on top of the file.

"Is that it?" Ann asked. Betsy handed it to her. "Thank you, Betsy."

"Not everybody likes Mr. Brubaker's taste in ties," Betsy said

Ann took the paperwork out of the folder. It was on standard, off-white paper. She began to read.

"'I bequeath the total of my holdings both real estate and financial to Royce Chamberlin and his daughters Cassandra and Carol.'"

"Plain as day," Ben said.

"No mention of holding it till I'm twenty-one. This is an outright gift."

Ann was staring at the print in front of her. Every word. Every letter. "I can't believe this, Ben."

"May I see it?" Ben said.

On closer look, one thing became apparent. "Look at the print," Ben said. "The print here and the print for the bequest."

The print of the typewriter was different. The typing in the bequest had some distinct characteristics not found in the other parts of the document. The small *h*'s were missing part of the top, and the small *e*'s had an ink spot in the upper area, which made them stand out. The print was darker in this section of the will, and the area behind it looked smudged.

"It's not the same as the other parts," Ann said.

"Not the same at all," Ben said. "It looks like a different typewriter. They changed her will."

"They sure did. This must be what he hasn't wanted me to see. They couldn't force Mama to change it, so after she died, they did it themselves."

"It's so obvious. They left the evidence right out so everybody could see it."

"Around here, who's going to fight them?"

Ann's eyes were riveted on the document. A forged will. Finally, there was some tangible evidence.

"Think we should take it with us?" she asked.

"No," Ben said. "Better let them think we haven't seen it."

They returned to the counter.

"Is everything in order?" Betsy asked.

"Could you please put this back in a safe place where it will never get lost?" Ann said.

"Sure, I'll find a spot here. You can see it whenever you come to town. You won't have to upset Mr. Brubaker."

"Thank you very much."

"Is this your young man?"

"Yes, this is Ben," Ann said.

"You've got a good girl there, Ben. Don't forget that."

"I won't. And thank you for helping us."

"Some of us remember how it was when the colonel was alive. I'll keep this will safe for you."

"Thank you again. We owe you," Ann said. "We'd better get back to the station, Ben."

As they emerged from the courthouse, they were surprised to see who was waiting outside.

"Hello, girlie," said a familiar voice.

Parked across the street was the beat-up car belonging to the Hudsens. Chamberlin, Brubaker, Kurt, and Jago were positioned along the side of the car, their eyes on the courthouse door. Behind them, almost as an echo, the hounds were sitting in a row.

"Word gets around," Ben said.

"I took the liberty of informing Royce," Brubaker said solemnly.

"Wasn't hard. Mr. Royce has been at the bank all morning," Jago added.

"What were you doing in the courthouse?" Chamberlin demanded. "Was that why you came to town?"

"She was showing me around," Ben said.

"Why were you there, Ann? Was it the will?"

Ann struggled to keep from screaming at them that she knew what they had done.

"They didn't have a copy," she said calmly.

"They didn't?" This reaction alone would have confirmed that the court-house did have a copy, even if Ann had not seen it.

"They couldn't find it even though they looked all over. The copy of the will might have been lost in the fire."

"That's what Betsy told us, Royce," Brubaker added.

Chamberlin was more composed. "Fred tells me you were never coming to the auction at all."

"Change of plans," Ann said.

Royce was studying Ben. Evaluating him. He looked like he came from a privileged background. Easy to manipulate. Find his weaknesses. Can he be bought? Does he drink? Can I control him like Jack?

Jago was also sizing up this newcomer. Jago had been trying to court Cassie Chamberlin for years. And this city slicker shows up in town with the colonel's granddaughter. Ben didn't deserve all this good fortune. The whole thing angered Jago. One way or another, he'd have to take Ben down.

"I don't believe we've met," Chamberlin said to Ben, extending his hand. "I'm Royce Chamberlin."

"Ben Harmon," Ben said. He thought Chamberlin's grip was firm, but his touch was cold and lifeless. It was like greeting a statue.

"So you're the young man who plays the piano for a living."

"No, I'm an insurance broker," Ben said.

"What firm?"

"MacMurray and Guild. In Chicago."

"I'm not familiar with them."

"He's familiar with them," Ann thought. "He's trying to get to Ben."

"Tell me, what are your intentions?" Chamberlin asked.

"My intentions?"

"Toward Ann. I'd like to know."

"When we decide, we'll tell you," Ben answered.

Ann stifled a laugh. He was standing up to Royce in a firm and polite manner. She had not seen anyone do that for years.

"I'm still curious about you. Ann never mentioned you in her letters to me. But she told her mother quite a lot about you, isn't that strange?"

"I'm sure Ann has her priorities."

Royce was already viewing Ben as a potential opponent. He certainly wasn't Jack Hardy. He seemed neither impressed nor intimidated by Chamberlin or his position in the town.

"I'm going to have you checked out, young man," Brubaker said.

"He's gonna check you out, Mr. Harmonsens," Jago offered, hoping to stir up something.

"That's enough, boy," Kurt cautioned.

"You tell us you're going into insurance," Chamberlin said. "Could you tell us why?"

"I like the business," Ben answered.

From the start, Ben knew he was being examined and interrogated. It gave him a chance to experience firsthand what Ann and her family had been living with for years. Chamberlin seemed to have no feelings at all.

"Insurance is risky," Chamberlin said. "Business is risky. And in today's economic climate, a wrong decision can lead to ruin. It requires a cool sense of judgment and a good set of nerves. Are you sure you want to take the risk?"

"I'm sure."

"You seem like an enterprising young man." Now Chamberlin's eyes were on Ann. Young Ann was eighteen years old and romantically involved. Royce knew that would happen one day. If Ben was going to be part of the picture, the only course of action was to remove him as a possible opponent. It had worked with Jack.

"I'd like to invite you and Ann to stay the night with us out at the manor house. We can talk more about business. Maybe I can find a place for a young man like you."

Jago grabbed his father's arm. "What's he invitin' him for? Why him and not me?"

"Put a sock in it, boy."

"I'm thinking of starting an insurance office in Council Bluffs," Chamberlin continued. "Maybe this evening we could discuss it over a glass of bourbon. Are you a drinking man, Mr. Harmon?"

"On occasion."

"Good. We have a lot to discuss."

"I think that's up to Ann," Ben said.

"And the answer is no," Ann said.

"Some other time then," Ben said affably.

"I am extending my hospitality."

"I see that, Mr. Chamberlin. But we're going back to Minneapolis."

"Is that final?"

"We're going back," Ann said.

Chamberlin turned away from the conversation. Beneath the icy exterior, his temper was rising.

"Young Ann is going back," Chamberlin said bitterly. "She's gone her own way as long as I've known her."

Suddenly, the emotion he held inside roared to the surface. "Go on then! Get out! Be on the twelve thirty! Kurt, you be damn sure they're on that train! I want them out of here!"

Ann and Ben returned to the station. From a distance, Kurt and Jago lounged beside their car, watching Ann and Ben until the train arrived.

51

"THAT WILL WAS A FORGERY, BEN. You saw it."

Ann and Ben had been riding on the train for half an hour. They were crossing a series of fields where the farmers were finishing the yearly harvest. The yellow of the fields was dotted here and there with wagons surrounded by pockets of people.

"I want to go after them," Ann said angrily. "Everyone—Royce, his daughters, Brubaker, the Hudsens. The whole lot. I want to kick every one of them out."

"It'll happen," Ben assured her.

"But when? Today probably cancelled my chances of any more visits to Winfield."

The train was beginning to slow down.

"Listen," Ben said. "This trip was not a loss. We got what we came for. And for the moment, they don't know we found anything."

Ben's calm was reassuring. With her emotions near the surface, he always gave Ann a chance to reconsider. She saw he was right.

"I don't blame you," he said. "Look what we do have. I think we can count on Betsy. You've got a friend there."

"Unless someone gets to her."

"That's the chance we take."

Ann watched the platform of a tiny depot approaching and coming to a stop in front of their window. It was Woodman, a town no bigger than Coon Falls.

"Funny. I never knew Betsy that well," Ann said. "We were kids in Sunday school. She came from the other side of the county."

"You may have more people on your side than you realize."

"Helping me would be an act of courage. My papa'd been looking for a lawyer for so long. Everyone he talked to was afraid to take us on. And right now, when I get ahold of anything resembling a law book, which is not often in Coon Falls, I try to read up on what they're doing in Winfield...what laws they're breaking. But where am I now? I'm a senior in a godawful finishing school. All I can do is what I've been doing for the past six years. Sit back and watch."

"Then we'll find somebody ourselves," Ben said.

"You're damn right we will."

"It's going to take some time. We can't just pick a lawyer out of the classified ads."

"What are they going to do in the meantime? They must suspect something now."

"Probably nothing. It's worked for them so far. In the meantime, I've started looking in Chicago."

"You have?"

"MacMurray and Guild is a big company. They insure several law firms. We'll find somebody. It may take some time. We'll go slow and easy till we find the right man."

The train was moving out of Woodman. Every now and then the sun was blotted out by passing trees along the tracks.

Even though the circumstances were enraging, they did not seem as dire with Ben beside her. They were in love. And they were facing an obstacle together. They had become a team. But for Ann there was something else. She had never voiced the possibility of her becoming a lawyer. Pursuing the law would change the future completely. It was always with her. She would have to bring it up sometime.

"I am a load of trouble," she said. "Here I am—so wrapped up in my anger, I haven't given us much of a chance. I'm the one on a lifetime quest and you're along for the ride. I don't want that. But that's how it is. I'm sorry."

Ben took her hand. He looked into her eyes. "I wouldn't be with you if I didn't want to be here."

"Then what are we going to do?"

"I've been doing some thinking. We've known each other for two years. You're part of my life. Your fight is my fight, and I love you. So when you graduate, let's get married."

"Excuse me?" Ann was ecstatic. The proposal seemed to pop out of thin air. Unlike the bad news, which she had learned to handle, this one hit her head-on. Still, she did not think she had heard him correctly.

"I'll earn enough at the office. I can still play piano at night. That'll support two people. Then there's our search for the right man. Office people. Night people. Both kinds know lawyers. But getting back to the question—I've never met a girl like you in my life. And I don't want to let you get away. We're good together. This isn't the most romantic way I thought I would propose…"

"Yes, Ben. I'll marry you."

They were both overjoyed. Each saw that the other was sincere, and each saw that the other wanted the same thing.

They watched the passing scenery for several minutes. It was midafternoon. It was the happiest moment in Ann's life. But something was still left unsaid. The easy way would be to get married first and bring it up down the line when it was safe. But this wasn't Ann. She hoped Ben would understand. She didn't want him to be hurt.

"What is it, Ann?"

"I've been doing some thinking, too."

"About us? Second thoughts?"

"Nothing about us. Well, not exactly. There's something I want to do after we're married. I want to become a lawyer."

Ben was completely surprised by the announcement.

"Really?"

"I'm serious, Ben."

He was listening closely, waiting to hear more.

"When did you decide to do this?"

"It's been a long time. You've heard me talk all the time about what I'd do if I could fight this."

"I have."

"This is what I want to do."

"OK." Ben saw her determination. The more determined she was, the quieter she became. But he was still uncertain. "You realize it's a lot of work and preparation. College first and then law study."

"I do."

"There aren't many women lawyers."

"I know that, too. I spent six years watching what Royce and his cronies have done to our family and our neighbors. I don't want anybody in Winfield to have to go through that again. No one was there to stand up for them."

"I see," Ben said.

"Don't be upset, Ben." It came out somewhere between reassurance and a prayer.

Ben didn't speak for a long time. He was staring out the window into the night. Ann could see that he wasn't upset. It was more like he was working something out. She was glad she had brought it up.

Finally, he smiled. "Let's do it," he said.

"So it's not a problem?"

"No, it's not a problem. I've known you long enough. You're not the kind of woman who'd stay home sorting thimbles and baking pies. If you want to do this, I'll help."

Ann leaned over and hugged him, relieved and joyful. "I'm so glad," she said.

"It won't be easy. But we'll do it."

"We do have a full platter, don't we?" Ann said with a laugh.

52

When Ann and Ben arrived in Minneapolis, it was difficult for them to part and go their separate ways. So much had happened in Winfield, and so much had been planned for the future. They sat together on a bench, holding hands and talking for another hour.

After a final hug, Ben was on a train for Chicago and Ann started for the taxi stand. Along the way, she noticed a tiny closet-like structure beside the station waiting room. The words RECORD YOUR VOICE were painted on a sign at the top.

She stopped and pondered a moment. The booth was a primitive operation: put in a few coins and hope for the best. The sounds of the station would be almost as loud as her voice, but she didn't care. "This is too good to pass up," she thought.

When Ann finished, she went on to the taxi stand. And as she rode back to school, she was still bubbling with excitement. Ben, marriage, the forged will, becoming a lawyer. If she tried to concentrate on one subject, another promptly pushed it aside. She wouldn't get much sleep that night, but she didn't care.

She went directly to Fairchild's office. The door was open. Fairchild was hunched at her desk, looking like a peeved Buddha.

"Deception. Deception once again, Miss Hardy," Fairchild grumbled.

"I'm letting you know I'm back," Ann said.

"Another fruitless trip, was it not? Why did you deceive Mr. Royce? Mr. Royce has tolerated more from you than any grandfather should have to endure."

"It's a long story, ma'am."

Miss Fairchild cocked her head. "You told us you were going to bid on your mother's wedding dress."

"I did."

"You never went to the auction."

"No, ma'am."

"Did you ever really want the dress, Miss Hardy?"

"I thought so at the time."

"If you didn't want it, then why did you go to Winfield?"

"Maybe I just wanted to see home," Ann said. "I haven't been there for two years."

"Mr. Royce said you were trying to see your mother's will."

"Did he?"

"And were you able to see it?"

"No, ma'am."

"Is that all?" Fairchild demanded.

"You tell me."

Fairchild waved her hand in front of her. "All right. Get out of here! Go to your room!"

Ann left the office. "Good. They still don't know. They're fishing," she thought. "My next step is to get through this year."

⤳

At Clearwater there was no graduation ceremony, no commencement speaker, and no caps or gowns. Graduation was spread out over a two-day period. It consisted of individual trips to Fairchild's office by each graduating student. Once there, the girl would be given a certificate of completion and a letter describing her growth during her stay at Clearwater. Years ago Fairchild had decided this method was less costly than the trappings of a formal ceremony.

This year the seniors were informed that their last days would be June 14 and 15. Ann would have to wait. Royce Chamberlin had instructed Fairchild to keep Ann at Clearwater until the end of the summer. This was fine with Ann. She and Ben had selected August 23 for their wedding ceremony.

Ann remained on the school grounds for the next two months. Fairchild restricted her activities. There were no visits to Coon Falls. When she was not performing menial tasks, Ann went for walks in the woods nearby. She thought of Ben, their approaching wedding, and their discussions about the future.

Often, she would stand along the riverbank, feeling the soft breeze from the water. Her gaze would always go to the bridge and the hill on the other side. A billboard advertising Campbell's Pork and Beans occupied the space where the speakeasy once stood.

Ben was able to visit her twice, but since Ann was confined to school property, his visits had to be planned in advance. They would sit along the shore watching the passing whitecaps.

Finally, Royce Chamberlin sent word about when Ann could come home. It came through a short note from Brubaker. "You are being allowed to return to Winfield on August 18th. You shall move into the spare room over Bunsenmen's Garage. You will begin employment in the stockroom of Hotstetter's Dress Shop."

Ann contacted Ben. She knew that arrangements would be made for her to take the train from Minneapolis to Winfield. However, instead of returning to Iowa, she would meet Ben at the station in Minneapolis, and together, they would go to Chicago.

On the morning of the eighteenth, Ann rose early. Having already packed, she took a last walk around the Clearwater grounds. She wondered why. She had never liked the school, and she couldn't wait to be with Ben.

"I will not feel any nostalgia for this place," she thought. "Yet I'm out here having a last look."

She took a final glance at the massive building. "In its own rotten way, Clearwater's become part of my life. I can't throw that aside. At the same time, I won't carry it around like a piece of baggage. I'm glad to be out of here."

Ann took her breakfast in the kitchen with some of the staff. Her taxi would be coming at ten. Twenty minutes earlier, she had left her room and had taken her suitcase to the lobby. She plopped her bag along the wall and sat down on a sofa. The place seemed deserted. There were no voices and only the sound of the gentle wind outside. Bruner appeared in the hallway.

"Where were you?" she whispered to Ann. "You weren't leaving early...?"

"No."

"I thought you were running away."

"It's graduation, Miss Bruner. We're all running away," Ann said.

"Please. Don't joke about these things." Bruner cautioned. "Commencement is a serious part of your life."

"Is Miss Fairchild in?"

"Oh yes. In her office."

Ann smiled at Miss Bruner. "You take care now."

Bruner appeared confused at the warmth in Ann's voice.

"At a couple of dark moments, you were there for me. I won't forget that," Ann said.

"Thank you, Miss Hardy."

Ann started for Fairchild's office. When she reached the door, Fairchild was waiting at her desk.

"Come in, Miss Hardy."

The headmistress seemed livelier than usual. Perhaps she was looking forward to this moment as much as Ann.

"And so now is the time," Fairchild said.

"Yes, ma'am."

"I've looked forward to this for many years," Fairchild said. "I would have loved to expel you, but Mr. Royce wouldn't let me."

"We both made our sacrifices," Ann said.

"I am going to read your letter," Fairchild's pudgy hands held up the carefully printed and sealed envelope. With one thumb, she tore it open, ripping the envelope in two.

"'Ann Hardy attended my school for six years. While she was here, she maintained satisfactory attendance and improved her posture. It may be possible that she could achieve adequate success within her level of rustic idiom, but of course, at this time, it remains to be seen.'"

"In other words, I went to Clearwater and learned to walk better."

"I always have the last word, Miss Hardy." Fairchild leaned back in her chair to monitor Ann's reactions. "So what do you plan to do now?"

"Simple. Return home, walk upright, and work in a dress shop."

"You don't mean that, Miss Hardy. I know you. Your flippant attitude. Your snide ripostes."

"It's been quite an education, Miss Fairchild," Ann said as she took the letter from the desk.

"Tell me," Fairchild said. "Was that you who came to my office earlier this morning?"

"Yes, ma'am."

"I wasn't here. Nothing was stolen or damaged."

"No, ma'am."

"Why then?"

"Maybe I couldn't wait to leave."

"Still trying to rile me, aren't you, Miss Hardy?"

"No, ma'am."

"Then why do I have the feeling you're laughing at me?"

Ann stifled a grin. "Me? Laugh at you? Oh no. Never."

"Let me tell you what's going to happen to you, Miss Hardy. I saw the seeds of personal destruction in you from the very first. I will tell you with relish. You'll go to work in that dress shop, but soon you will be lured away by unmaidenly temptations. You'll meet a traveling salesman, and with him and John Barleycorn, you'll sink to the pits of degradation. You will become a tramp, a slut…"

Ann turned to leave.

"Wait a minute. I'm not finished talking to you," Fairchild bellowed.

"But I'm finished listening," Ann said. "My taxi's here."

Ann tossed the letter back onto Fairchild's desk. "You better keep this. If it's the best you could come up with, I'd say I graduated cum laude."

Ann was out of the office and down to the lobby, where she took her bag to wait outside. The taxi was already coming up the driveway.

Ann looked up at Fairchild's window. Sure enough, the headmistress who valued the last word had taken a final position of authority to oversee this troublesome student's departure.

This should have been a moment of victory for Nadia Fairchild. It still might be with the proper element. Fairchild stepped over to her recording machine and cranked it up. She was alone. There was no one to hear and misunderstand. This was her moment. Ann was out of her school forever. Fairchild placed a cylinder in the machine. The cylinder was turning. She was back at the window, relishing the moment.

Ann placed her bag in the trunk of the car. Fairchild watched and waited to see the taxi carry this upstart out the gate for the last time. Then Fairchild heard it—the sound of a girl laughing. It was Ann, laughing at her.

Before climbing into the taxi, Ann glanced up again. Fairchild's face was at the window. Ann's mocking laughter cut through into the deep parts of her that no one else knew. Ann waved a final good-bye, stepped inside, and closed the door. Fairchild smashed her fist through the glass pane. Just as quickly she tore her hand back. It was bloody and cut, but she felt no pain—only the shame and humiliation that now engulfed the whole office.

Fairchild yanked the cylinder out of the machine and threw it on the floor. She stared down at the pieces, blood dripping from the gash in her hand. In her head she still heard Ann's laughter. She would hear it for the rest of her life.

Outside the car was moving away. Fairchild lurched back to the broken window for one more look. The taxi carrying Ann Hardy had vanished.

53

By the time Ann and Ben arrived in Chicago, Ann had begun to experience something she had not expected: second thoughts. "Am I doing the right thing? Am I rushing into this?" she asked herself. "Are there so many things on my plate right now that adding one more is making me fidgety?"

For the next hour she never took her eyes off Ben and tallied all his qualities. He was good. He was loyal. In addition, she hadn't stopped thinking of Ben since the first time she saw him. And now she loved him more than anything. So why the doubts?

"I won't ignore the doubts, but I won't give in. Everything about this tells me it's right."

Shortly after they arrived, Ann sent a telegram to Van Burin. "Since it's Van Burin, I'll stick to his level," she thought. The telegram read, "I am visiting some friends in Chicago for a few days. Fondly, Ann Hardy."

Ann stayed with Ben's parents for the next five days. She found herself accepted into the family right away. Their only reservation was Ann's age. But as the days passed, they were won over by her strength and honesty, as well as her sense of humor.

"You marry someone, you marry their family," Lucille had always said. George Harmon, Ben's father, was a pharmacist, quiet and reserved. His eyes became eager whenever he heard of someone else's successful exploits, which suggested that this soft-spoken man would like to partake in a similar venture if he ever had the chance. Much of his happiness came vicariously through the successes of his son.

Julia, Ben's mother, was a devout woman. Also quiet and reserved, she was given to praying at odd moments when confronted with a four-letter word, an off-color joke, or a raffish situation. Although only fifty years of age, her hair had become prematurely white. Ben had told Ann his father had wanted to be a fund-raiser or spieler for a political candidate, but after meeting and marrying Julia, he had retired into his mild and unassuming shell without any regrets.

"Nothing here is cut-and-dried," Ann thought. "They seem to be nice people. But it looks like they've paralyzed themselves into a quiet, pleasant existence. I can see why Ben left home."

In spite of this, these days were the first genuine family life she had encountered in many years. It was a relief to be removed from the anxiety and tension that had filled her life since Lady Ann had married Royce Chamberlin.

On August 21 Ann sent another telegram to Van Burin: "I shall be marrying Ben Harmon and residing in Chicago. I send this to bring you up to date on my whereabouts. Fondly, Ann Hardy."

On the afternoon of August 23 the wedding and reception were held in a meeting hall that Ben had rented—along with some help from Lee, Clark, and his father. Outside it was raining, but nobody seemed to mind.

The interior of the room appeared worn: a pale pastel green with the occasional scratch and smudge here and there. Most of the time it had been used for union meetings or club gatherings. Today it was a wedding.

Ann and Ben arrived first. Ben was wearing a suit, Ann a white wedding dress. They were strolling about the large room, making sure everything was in order. Two groups of folding chairs faced a podium at the front. On one side was a long table that held a cluster of glasses and some bottled nonalcoholic beverages. At the other end was a white cake and a stack of plates and silverware. An old upright piano that needed tuning and a wooden box with a large umbrella in it stood along the opposite wall.

Ann was pacing back and forth, checking the same things over and over. She was both happy and nervous. The doubts were still in the back of her mind, but she chalked them up to preceremony jitters. Every now and then her eyes focused on a small stack of mail on the top of the piano.

"I think we're set, Ben."

"We're fine." Ben gently stopped her as she was passing him. "It'll be a fine ceremony."

Ann looked to the piano. "I've got that mail. I keep wondering if I should open it."

"Let's wait," Ben said.

"I still keep wondering."

"That's exactly why we should wait. Consider who sent it and where it's from."

Ann smiled. "You're right. We'll wait."

George and Julia came in. "We're early," George said. "We wanted to see if you needed any help."

"I think we have it," Ben said.

"I do wish you two could have had a wedding in the church," Julia said.

"I think the good Lord understands, Mother," Ben said.

"But a church wedding is more appropriate. A proper beginning for a Christian marriage."

"So the kids want it here. Looks good to me," George said. "Hell, it'll be fine."

"George," Julia said with a scolding look.

"Yeah, yeah, watch the cussing."

Julia crossed over to the front row of chairs and sat down. She took out a white handkerchief, and, holding it in her hand, she lowered her head against the cloth and silently prayed.

Ben leaned over to Ann. "She's praying for Dad's soul."

"Put in a good word for me," George said gently.

Julia nodded as she prayed.

Ben smiled. "You're going to catch hell for that one," Ben said to his father.

"I'm entitled to a little wisecrack now and then," George answered. "A man's got to kick up sometime."

Ann noticed the difference between Ben and his father. George was sedentary; Ben was not. George seemed to have surrendered his place in the world; Ben had left home in more ways than one.

"Are any of the people from Winfield going to come?" Julia asked.

"I doubt it," Ann said.

"Well, we're here for you."

Lee and Clark arrived. Ben went to greet his friends. The newcomers immediately plopped their umbrellas in the box and went over to the old piano. Ben sat down at the keyboard and touched a few notes for Lee. George was left alone for a moment, but he surveyed the room and its occupants with great satisfaction. He was proud of his son.

Three older couples arrived, friends of Julia—the Billings, the Ryans, and the Browns. Since Julia was occupied, George went over to greet them himself.

Ann's eyes were back searching the room, checking to see if everything was on schedule. She wondered if she was really looking for some mishap that would ruin the occasion. Everything was fine. Once again, she was looking at the letters on the piano. Did they contain anything that would upset the festivities? What was in them?

Soon there were at least thirty people there, almost the full number on the guest list. The guests were present. The food was in place. But one important person was missing.

"Where's Reverend Peet?" Ann asked.

"He's coming. He said he'd be on time," Ben said.

"Oh good. You're being married by the clergy," Julia said.

"I told you we were, Mother. We're fine," Ben said.

"Then where is he? Where's the pastor?"

"He's coming, Mother. I spoke to him last night."

"Oh? At church?"

"No. At the Ruby Spoon where I was playing piano."

"Oh sacred Lord," Julia gasped.

With handkerchief out, she was on her way to join George.

"My dad could have been a diplomat," Ben said. "Mother? Well…"

"She's all right," Ann said.

"You can say it," Ben laughed. "Mother is Mother. She won't be in our way."

"I wish Peet would get here," Ann said.

"He'll be here," Ben said. "Remember, he's the only clergyman who would marry us."

"And you met him in a gin mill," Ann said with a grin.

"But he's a teetotaler."

Reverend Peet entered, shaking the rain from his topcoat and closing his umbrella. Ben went up the aisle to greet him.

Peet was short and round. From a distance he looked like a ball of dough in a raincoat, a man who spent his entire life rolling into a headwind.

"I'm sorry, Ben. My taxi hit a milk cart, and there was an altercation between the drivers. Punches were thrown. Milk was spilled. It was a catastrophe."

"I'm glad you're here," Ben said.

"We're set," Lee told Ben from the piano.

Ben and Ann took their places at the podium with Reverend Peet

Lee began to play the wedding march. Ann knew she would have a lot to accomplish before she could fully dedicate herself to the promises inherent in a marriage. As she stood there beside Ben, however, she knew she had made the right decision.

Reverend Peet gazed out over the assembled faces in the room.

"Dearly beloved, we are gathered here to celebrate the marriage of two loving people, Ann Hardy and Ben Harmon. I have gotten to know them over the past two weeks, and I must say I think they will make an ideal couple. However, I have to pause a moment. When I first met them, I said, 'Are you sure you want to go through with this, particularly you, Miss Hardy? If you marry this man, you will be known as Ann Hardy Harmon. That will either sound like an avid sports enthusiast or a double dip in the road.' Ann and Ben said it did not matter to them. And that is as it should be. It is the journey we celebrate."

Ann and Ben were laughing. While it wasn't the essence of wit, it was funny coming from this individual.

"Ben, do you take this woman, Ann Hardy, to be your lawful wedded wife? To have and to hold, to cherish and honor, as long as you both shall live?"

"I do," Ben said.

"And do you, Ann, take this man, Ben Harmon, as your lawful wedded husband, to have and to hold, to cherish and honor, as long as you both shall live?"

"I do," Ann answered.

"Do we have the ring?"

Ben reached in his coat pocket for a tiny box. He took out a small ring that he put on Ann's finger.

"Then by the power invested in me by the holy church and the state of Illinois, I now pronounce you man and wife. You may kiss the bride."

Ben leaned forward and kissed Ann. They could hear sniffles here and there around the room. Julia was daubing her eyes with the handkerchief.

"Ladies and gentlemen, Mr. and Mrs. Ben Harmon."

Suddenly, the room was filled with claps and cheers. Ann and Ben looked at each other happily and then gazed out at the assembled guests. The ceremony had been quick and unorthodox, but it was the beginning for them.

Everyone got up from the seats and drifted over to the side table. Ann cut the cake and put the slices on plates that Ben handed to the guests. There were murmurs all-around of "Congratulations! Great ceremony." Somehow, the unconventionality did not detract from the joy of the moment.

"Everything's going well," Ann thought. "I keep thinking something's going to come along and mess it up."

There was still the mail on the piano. She remembered Ben's words. This mail might only bring disappointment. Still, it came from home.

"You want to open them," he said.

"Let's get it over with."

Ann scooped up the three envelopes.

"Are these well-wishes from home?" Julia asked.

"Well, they're from home," Ann said.

"See? They didn't forget you."

"It's a little more complicated than that, Mother," Ben said.

"Nonsense. The good Lord is looking after her."

Ann opened the first letter. "Patrick Van Burin...my legal guardian until fifteen minutes ago."

Ann began to read. "'You have disappointed us beyond belief. We must deplore your choice of a bootlegger for a husband. Your grandfather must be turning in his grave. With deep regret, Patrick Van Burin and family.'"

"Oh dear," Julia murmured. "Oh dear."

"My boy's no bootlegger," George said.

Ben was shaking his head. "I don't understand it. I'm an insurance broker."

Ann was smiling, almost ready to laugh. True, the words were meant to hurt, but they came from Van Burin after all.

She opened the second letter.

"It's from Olga." She began to read. "'All my love to my little girl. I wish I could be there to give you a hug. I look forward to meeting Mr. Ben one day. It sounds like you found an excellent young man. You deserve the joy and happiness that somehow your mama and her mama never found. They would be so proud of you today. I work at the county farm now. Mr. Royce said I was not performing my duties in a manner promoting harmony in the house.'"

Ann looked up from the page, startled at how quickly hostility and rage had overtaken her. She loved Olga. She didn't deserve this. "They fired her. The son of a bitch fired her."

"Oh Lord," Julia whispered.

Ann returned to the letter. "'It does not matter to me, Miss Ann. I didn't like working for them anyway. Carson Manor wasn't the same with everybody gone. Judge Post's wife is still sick. It is too bad. She is a fine lady. Old Van Burin just can't keep from stepping in it.'"

"Van Burin wrote the first letter," George said.

"Yes," Ben said.

Ann resumed. "'Old Man Posner had a loan at the bank like a lot of people right now. He wanted to sell that Audubon painting he had over his mantelpiece to pay off some of the loan. Van Burin said his friends at Chaynie Auction House could sell it for Posner for two thousand dollars, so Posner gave the painting to Van Burin. He waited for his money. Nothing happened. No auction. No sale. Nothing. Finally, Posner looked into it. Van Burin said he sold the painting in an earlier auction. Then Van Burin gave Posner fifty dollars, apologized for the misunderstanding, and foreclosed on the property.'"

"What kind of people are these?" Julia asked.

Ann returned to Olga's letter. "'I'm fine out at the farm. They can certainly use someone who knows what she is doing. Remember I love you always. Olga.'"

"That certainly restores one's faith in humanity," Julia said. "See? The Lord is watching out for you."

Ann opened the third letter. She was still feeling irritated and angry.

"Fred Brubaker," Ann said. She began to read. "'Of course, this marriage will change your legal status. I must bring to your attention that there is an outstanding balance of $6,758, which is still unpaid. Please remember that payment is

due the first of every month. Be sure that this amount is paid before your statement incurs late fees. I send you the best on your wedding day. Sincerely, Fred.'"

Ann looked to Ben. What she feared had happened. Winfield had wormed
its way into her wedding as an uninvited guest. Brubaker's words were as indeco-
rous and insulting as Van Burin's. She crumpled up the paper and held it.

"They just had to stick it in and twist it," she said.

"What kind of people are these?" Julia asked again. "A bill on your wedding
day?"

"It's not the bill. It's the thought behind the bill," Ann said.

George was concerned. "Do you kids need help?"

"No. Thanks, Dad. We'll be all right," Ben answered.

"It's almost sixty-eight hundred dollars."

"He'll just take it out of my account in town," Ann said.

George was still puzzled. "Then what was this letter about?"

"Fred's telling me that times have changed," Ann said. "He and Van Burin
are probably doing their best to strip my name off everything in the bank. I'm
married now, so they can do it."

"You poor dear," Julia said.

Ann stepped away from everyone and moved among the empty chairs. She
wanted to be alone to compose herself. Ben caught up with her.

"You were right, Ben. I should never have looked. It's like they waited for the
right moment—the one time they could hurt me."

Ben gently took her arm. "If this is the best they could come up with..."

"What?"

"A bill and an insult? That's not much."

Ann was looking into his eyes. She loved it when he held an obstacle up to
the light and then cut it down to size—a bill and an insult. He was right.

"One day we're going to take care of those two. And I'm going to be right
beside you," Ben said. "But today they're not worth our time."

None of the guests had left. Many were gathered along the wall enjoying
their cake, and others stood in clusters around the room. They were all happy—
even with the rain pouring outside.

"Look at them. All having a good time," Ben said. "They're our friends.
They count. Anybody else is bystander."

Ben leaned over and kissed her. When he stepped back, Ann was surprised
how excited it made her feel. All the anger had evaporated.

"Why, Mr. Harmon," she said with a smile.

"Let's mingle a bit," Ben said. "Let them know we appreciate their coming.
Then we'll leave."

Ben took her arm and gestured to the largest group, still gathered beside the long table. Already the cake was gone, but the beverages were still plentiful.

"Shall we mingle, Mrs. Harmon?"

"Yes, let us mingle," Ann said, feeling happy once again.

54

ANN AND BEN SETTLED INTO THEIR apartment. It was a cozy one-bedroom place on the fifth floor on Wooster Street. The street was lined with small mom-and-pop businesses—a hardware store here, a vegetable man across the street, a meat vendor, a laundry, and a pharmacist at the end of the block. Unlike the businesses in agricultural areas, there was no sign of economic hardship.

Ben continued to work at the insurance company. Ann got a job as a waitress. Together their salaries enabled them to afford their apartment. This put them a notch above many other couples where the husband worked and the wife did not.

Every now and then Ben would play a night booking. These were usually at a country club or a Knights of Columbus celebration. But they were in Chicago in the 1920s, which more frequently brought them engagements in speakeasies. And this in turn drew them into closer contact with the gangster elements in Chicago.

It was good money, but Ann cautioned Ben not to be too reckless in the choice of jobs he accepted. This was Al Capone's town, not Coon Falls.

In her spare time, Ann went to the public library and read law books. She knew it would be some time before she could pursue her goal of becoming a lawyer, but that didn't matter.

A year passed. It was September 10, 1928. Ann was twenty years old. She had made quite a journey from the manor house to the one bedroom on Wooster Street. She was happy here. She had found a place of contentment, and she had found Ben Harmon. But she knew she would never find true fulfillment in her life until she had kept the promise to her grandfather.

On this September evening, Ann and Ben decided to have dinner at a neighborhood place. Sollie's was the kind of establishment a person might walk past if he were a visitor to Chicago. It was nondescript on the outside—the *O* and the second *L* on the sign needed a paint job—but inside it was warm and welcoming. Each table had a straw basket with matching salt and pepper shakers. Draped here and there along the walls were crossed Italian and American flags. Between them were paintings of Italian seascapes and coastlines. The air was always alive with the odor of baking garlic bread. Ann and Ben had discovered Sollie's the first week in the apartment. Since then, it had become their special place.

That night, they arrived at five thirty. There were two other couples occupying tables for two, and except for some boisterous talk and laughter from the kitchen, it was a quiet night. Ann and Ben snuggled into their favorite booth along the back wall.

"First your news," Ben said.

"No, yours."

"All right, I'll cut to the head of the line." Ben took a tiny box with a red ribbon from his pocket. It was obvious that Ben had selected and tied the ribbon because it was too big for the box.

"What's this?" Ann said. "What have you gone and done?"

She opened it and took out a tiny necklace, gold with a little heart at the bottom.

"It's beautiful, Ben. Oh, thank you!" She leaned over and kissed him.

"I know you like hearts," he said.

Ann remembered they were a couple trying to make ends meet. "You shouldn't have done this," she said. "Did you spend our food money to pay for this?"

"I got a raise. Five dollars," he said. "Also a small promotion."

Ben watched while Ann put the necklace around her neck and fastened it.

"You look terrific," Ben said. "Of course, you always look terrific."

"Oh, Ben."

Octavia, the owner's daughter, came and took their orders. As usual, they split a large plate of spaghetti Bolognese.

"Now what's your news?" Ben asked.

"I got a promotion, too. I'm the greeter at Lakeside Tea Room. No more waitressing, although I'll step in when one of the girls is sick. Now I greet people at the door and escort them to their table."

"Excellent. You've got a way with people. You'll do fine."

"Three dollars more."

"This is great," Ben said. "We're getting there."

Ann noticed that Ben was still smiling. He had what she called his Cheshire cat expression—like he was relishing something good and ready to share it.

"What's the other news?" she asked.

"Well, I'm getting to that. I think I've found our lawyer."

Ann was not sure she heard him correctly. They had been waiting so long for this.

"What? Who is it?"

"His name is Thaddeus Hopkins. Remember last Tuesday when I came in really late?"

"I was wondering about that," Ann said.

"There's a little story behind it."

"OK."

"It was cloudy that night, and we thought it was going to rain."

"What happened, Ben?"

"We had a gig at a place called Cicero's Flute. I know I shouldn't have, but the money was good."

"I told you it was a borderline place."

"More than borderline. There was a raid."

"Oh, Ben!"

Ann was more annoyed than anxious. She could see that Ben was OK since he was sitting in front of her.

"It was all right. I was on my break. Lee and Clark had stepped outside for a smoke. They hightailed it when they saw the cops arrive."

"What about you?"

"I happened to be downstairs in the men's room at the time. Anyway, when I walked in, there were these two thugs working over another guy. A young guy in a blue suit. He looked out of place in that neighborhood. These two guys were laughing and holding him head down over the toilet."

"Didn't you call for help?"

"Ann, I had to go something terrible. I asked them if they could take their business somewhere else."

"Yes, yes…"

"Well, one of the thugs took a swing at me, and I found myself in the middle of it. Blue Suit immediately took on the other one. Just then, we heard this loud bang and crash upstairs. It sounded like the cops had come busting through the front door with a snowplow. There was all this yelling and running around up above us. The thugs took off. Blue Suit grabbed my arm and said, 'Help me get out of here.' There was a window just above our heads that opened into the alley. I grabbed the trash can and smashed it through the glass. Then I helped him onto the sink, and he climbed up and out into the alley. I heard the cops coming down the stairs, so I climbed out after him."

"You ran from the police?"

"I had to get out of there. I followed Blue Suit to the end of the alley. When we reached the street, he went one way, and I went the other."

"You're a fugitive, Ben."

"Not really. I just left in a hurry. You should have seen the front of the place. This truck the cops used was half in and half out. It was like a battlefield."

Ann was relieved that Ben had escaped from this predicament, but she knew it wouldn't prevent him from getting into another one.

"Before we go any further, I'm going to say one thing: I don't want you playing in any more speakeasies—not like that one. I don't want you to end up in jail or floating in the river."

"I'll be careful."

"What about this Hopkins?"

"On Friday this was delivered to me at the office."

Ben handed Ann a business card that read, "Thaddeus Hopkins, Attorney at Law, 557 Fedder Street, Chicago." On the back was a printed message: "Thank you for helping my associate. T. Hopkins."

Ann was intrigued. It was brief, professional, and to the point. And it came out of nowhere.

"How did he find you?"

"Blue Suit must have told him the piano player got him out of a tight spot. Then Hopkins made some calls. It's amazing. I took this to Bill Sanders, assistant manager. He's heard of Hopkins. Said he's a retired lawyer who spent years with Southern Pacific. Now he works out of a little office off Wabash. Bill thinks he might be able to help us."

"What kind of cases does he handle?"

"Bill and I did some checking. Hopkins was down in Oklahoma last year representing some Indians who were being evicted from their reservation because somebody found it was sitting on a fortune in oil. Year before that he was in Louisville. Some investors were taking on a bank that had swindled them out of their life savings."

"That sounds more like it."

"He keeps a very low profile. He doesn't seem to be tied down to any one type of case or client. I guess when you're retired, you can pick and choose what you want."

"What's his success rate?"

"Bill says he's never lost a case. He was honored five times by the Illinois Bar Association."

Ann felt a surge of enthusiasm. She had been preparing for this fight for nearly ten years. Royce and the others had been dishing it out for a long time. Finally, here was a chance to shove it back.

"I want to go see him," Ann said.

"I think we should, too."

"He may be our man. Maybe this is it."

"I'll call him tomorrow," Ben said.

55

THREE DAYS LATER, ANN AND BEN were walking along Fedder Street, a narrow thoroughfare pinched between a row of tall buildings that put everything below in a permanent shade. It was hard to believe they were only a few blocks from the bustle and movement of Wabash Avenue.

They arrived in front of a small tailor shop. The address over the door was 555. The next business, a laundry, had 559 over its entrance. Between the two was a single unmarked door with clouded and wired glass across the top.

Ben pointed. "This has to be it."

Inside were stairs that led to the second floor. At the top was an office door with the words T. HOPKINS, ATTORNEY. Ben knocked.

"Come in," answered a woman's voice from inside.

A young woman in her twenties was sitting at the reception desk. She wore spectacles and had her hair pulled into a bun. Her appearance suggested an actress in a character role rather than a real person.

"Good afternoon," she said. "Mr. and Mrs. Harmon?"

"Yes," Ben said.

"Mr. Hopkins is expecting you."

The young woman got up from her seat. Before she could reach the office, the door opened. A medium-sized man with sparse gray hair stood in the entrance. To Ann he looked like a relaxed southern politician or an easygoing traveling salesman. He appeared to be someone who was completely comfortable within his own skin. Behind his smile was a calm that gave the impression that he did not ruffle easily.

"Mr. and Mrs. Harmon, I'm Thaddeus Hopkins," he said. "Come in."

Ann and Ben followed him into his office, which was well furnished, but small and cramped. It was the opposite of Fred Brubaker's mahogany extravagance.

Ann and Ben took their seats while Hopkins sat down at his desk.

"First, I want to thank you again for helping my associate."

"Glad I could be there," Ben said.

"I'd be careful where you take jobs from now on," Hopkins said. "In some neighborhoods where we've done business, the police and the gangsters live by the same code of conduct. The only way you can tell them apart is the badge."

"I'll be careful," Ben said.

"Good," Hopkins replied. "Do you mind if Vesper sits in?"

"Not at all," Ann said.

The young woman sat down in a chair along the wall.

"How may I help you?" Hopkins said.

Ann had waited a long time for this moment. She began a torrent of words, trying to be brief and clear and wanting to leave nothing out.

"We need to challenge the validity of my mother's will," she said. "You see, I made a promise to my grandpa before he died, and then I was with my mother when she died. She said she was leaving all her part to me, which would uphold my promise to my grandpa. Then all of a sudden, we discovered a copy of her will, and we saw her bequest had been changed. It was typed over."

"Let's start at the beginning, way back when it all began," Hopkins said. "In fact, start a little before that. Paint the whole picture."

Ann started again. She noticed that Vesper was taking notes.

"It all begins on my tenth birthday, July fourth, 1918, in Winfield, Iowa. I'm Colonel Wallace Carson's granddaughter."

For the next two hours, Ann related the entire story.

"So we went to the courthouse," she said in conclusion. "Finally we saw a copy of the will. Her bequest to me had been changed."

"They couldn't force her to change it while she was alive, so they made the changes after she passed away," Hopkins said.

"With a different typewriter," Ann said. She reached in her purse and took out two folded letters that she handed to Hopkins. Both were correspondence from Royce Chamberlin.

"It looks very much like the print on the will," Ann said.

Hopkins examined both letters. "The characters are distinct enough," he said. "The small *h*'s are cut across the top. There's a tiny ink spot in the small *e*'s. The capital *O*s have a smudge across the top."

"Exactly," Ann said.

Hopkins handed them to Vesper, who studied them carefully.

"And with the help of Brubaker and the banker, Van Burin, Royce Chamberlin set himself up as trustee of the estate, and he's done what he's pleased for the past ten years."

"Yes."

"Now he has everything pretty much sewn up in Winfield. And nobody has challenged him?"

"Not that I know of," Ann said.

"That might work in your favor. He's left evidence all over the place. He's gotten away with things for so long that he hasn't bothered to hide it."

"I think he had Zachary killed," Ann said.

"We need evidence to prove that. Is there any evidence?"

"No. Sheriff Dierkes looked into it twice. All I have is suspicion."

"That's a problem."

Ann knew that Hopkins was right. Royce had had a lot of time to falsify or destroy evidence.

"Let me ask you a question," Hopkins said. "Think carefully before you answer. Do you want revenge, or do you want your land back?"

Ann paused for a moment. The more she thought about the question, the more she felt the weight behind it. On one side, she felt anger seething right beneath the surface. On the other, she was guided by a calmer and more rational response.

"I know what I want to answer," she said. "But I also know what I'm going to answer. I want the land back."

"Can you help us?" Ben asked.

"I have another question. A courtroom is not a place where good triumphs over evil, although that can be a side benefit. A courtroom is a battlefield. To win, you have to learn the ways of your opponent. To beat him, you adapt to his code, learn his tactics, and use those same tactics to defeat him. If that happens, it can be very rough. Some people are going to be hurt. Victory is sweet, but there is always a price. Can you accept that?"

"Yes," Ann said. "We'll do what we have to do."

Hopkins seemed satisfied.

"This won't be easy. We have to focus on what we can do and put aside what we can't. Unanswered questions like Zachary's death, your parents' accident, even Nadia Fairchild and her peculiar recordings of children—we have to let them go and concentrate on the job at hand. We're going up against a man who has had the financial and legal backing of the entire county for a decade. No doubt there's evidence embedded in nooks and crannies all over Winfield and Franklin County. It's our task to dig it out."

"How do we do that?" Ben said.

"That's your next decision. It's going to require more people than myself to work on it. I have a small group of...well, I call them researchers. You met one of them, Ben. They will be out gathering every scrap of information they can find. Chamberlin's bunch will block every effort we make to secure evidence from their records. So we will have to go after copies at the state capital and county seat."

Ann nodded.

"This brings us to the question of money—expenses. I'll take your case, but the opening fee is a thousand dollars."

Ann was stunned. "A thousand?"

"You're hiring a team of five."

Ben took out his wallet and placed several bills on Hopkins's desk. "This should cover it."

Ann had almost gotten over the first shock, and now here was another.

"We can eat at home for a few months," Ben said. He turned back to Hopkins. "Where would the trial take place?"

"In Winfield. We take the case right into their courthouse."

"In town?" Ann asked.

"A strategy of mine. Of course, they're going to play dirty. But the court of public opinion is a powerful ally. They're going to have to show their true selves in front of their friends and neighbors."

"They've done that already."

"But not in a courtroom."

"What if everyone's crooked?" Ben asked.

"I don't believe that," Hopkins said. "It's my belief there's a fundamental decency in the human heart. There are good people in Winfield. Right now they're in hiding."

"After ten years it's hard to remember that," Ann said.

"The first thing we need is to get a copy of that will. Is your friend Betsy still at the records office?"

"Yes," Ann said.

"Vesper, call a meeting tonight. Get the gang together. Once we have the will, we'll need a sample of the print from the typewriter in Chamberlin's office."

"Will do," Vesper said.

"Mrs. Harmon, I'll need a map of Winfield and everything you can tell me about the layout of Chamberlin's office—doors, windows, what's outside. Everything you can remember."

"All right," Ann said.

"Good," Hopkins said. "Once we've assembled the preliminary material, we'll meet again."

56

WHEN THEY WERE BACK IN THE street, Ann's mind had already started running through the events of the meeting. She was excited—probably more than she realized. She needed to get her bearings and think over the questions asked, the words in the conversation, and her recitation of events. Had she left out anything? This was the first step to fulfilling her promise.

"What do you think?" Ben said.

"It looks good. I'd like to say more, but right now I can't put too much hope in anything." She stopped herself. "No. I think we've got a capable man here."

"And I made some phone calls from the office. He's low-key but very good. He seems to believe we've got something. I think he's the right man."

"But, Ben...a thousand dollars?"

"I might have questioned it, but remember—I met one of his researchers. Whoever that kid was, he was tough as nails."

"You were there to help him," Ann said.

"But he was brave enough to go it alone," Ben mused. "And if they're all like him..."

Ann's mind was still on the finances. "Where did you get a thousand dollars?"

Ben smiled. "I've been saving it."

"How? From where?"

"From that job everyone wants me to give up."

"The piano?"

"I've been saving here and there ever since we got engaged."

Ann was not sure what to say. The night job held its share of risks, but here it was, coming to the rescue.

"I knew you'd be taking on Chamberlin someday, so I started a war chest."

"Why didn't you tell me?"

"I should have. But you'd have been wanting to spend it on carrots or new curtains or something, so I kept quiet."

Ann caressed his cheek. "You didn't have to."

"I'm in this, too, you know." Ben took her hand as they started across a street.

Tears were beginning to well up in her eyes. It was moments like this that Ann was not prepared to handle. "No, no," she said to herself. "I'll cry sometime. But not today. Not today."

They started back to the apartment. Ann didn't talk much. She was letting it all sink in for another time.

⟋

Around ten thirty, Ann woke up. She was wide awake. She knew it was from excitement—not the heart-stopping excitement of a harrowing event but rather a quiet invigoration. There was no sound except the clock ticking on the night table. She pondered all the events that had led up to the afternoon meeting. In her mind she saw herself poised in a doorway. All she could do was wait. She tried to go back to sleep, but she could not. So she lay quietly beside Ben, listening to the clock.

⟋

At that moment, on the other side of town, the little coffee pot was steaming on a burner in the corner of Thaddeus Hopkins's waiting room. Papers and folders were strewn around the floor and coffee table. Hopkins and Vesper had pulled two chairs from his office out into the waiting area. They were seated and conferring with three others who occupied the waiting room chairs.

The newcomers were two men and a woman—all in their midtwenties. The first was Joel. With his husky build and thatched sandy hair, he could pass for an amiable farm boy. The man next to him was Sherman. Studious, bespectacled, and dressed in a blue suit, he could pass for the shy and serious boy next door, a budding scientist, or a clergyman. The young woman was Deirdre, who was a brunette and, like Vesper, had an appearance that could be altered one way or another to accommodate a variety of professions. She was attractive, but she had a worn and weary look that could gain her entry to many lower levels of society where the others in the room might have stood out as visitors.

They were surrounded by plates with half-eaten portions of pasta.

Hopkins slid his empty cup to one end of the coffee table. "All right," he said, pointing to the cup. "We have Ann Harmon over here...all alone. She made a promise to her grandpa and wants her land back." He pointed to the other cups around the table. "Over here we have Chamberlin, Brubaker, Van

Burin, the Hudsens, and Lord knows who else. It's a David-and-Goliath situation. We're going to even the odds."

There was a general nod of agreement.

"First up, Royce Chamberlin's typewriter—as soon as Ann gets us a layout of the bank."

Vesper raised her hand. "I'll take it."

"Have a plan?"

"He seems partial to helpless women. I'll use that."

"Be careful," Hopkins said. "You're there to get the sample and get out quick. Have Harry Todd drive."

"Will do," she replied.

"Next item: financial dealings of Carson Manor—utility bills, seed bills, maintenance bills. We want to know who pays what. And let's get anything we can on how that bank is tied in with Pheasant Valley Power and Electric. We'll subpoena the records, but we're better tracking down the copies at the county seat or the state capital."

"I'll go," Sherman said. "I'm the bookworm."

"You'll be helping the fellow who bailed you out at the Flute."

"Good. I owe him."

"Next item," Hopkins said. "Questionable business procedures. Families who have been evicted by the bank. My guess is everyone who got an eviction notice was visited first by father and son Hudsen. They're Chamberlin's hired muscle. I want to know their working relationship with Chamberlin, Van Burin, and that bank."

"I'll do it," Joel said. "I look like everyone's lost cousin from Keokuk."

Everybody chuckled. They were a long-established team.

"And finally," Hopkins said. "From the funny business to the Funny Business—Royce Chamberlin himself. Personal and private practices. Chamberlin and his girls."

"Close," Joel said.

"Abnormally close," Sherman added.

"Royce and daughter Cassandra...these trips of theirs to Kansas City. Somebody turn over a few rocks. Hotels and hospitals. See what's crawling underneath."

"I'll take it," Deirdre said. "I'm the only one left."

"You're the only one of us who can do it," Joel said.

"One day you're coming with me, Joel," Deirdre said with a laugh.

"Lots of ground to cover. We've done it before," Hopkins said.

Again, there were nods around the room.

"Bring me everything you can find. We're going to point and punch this one. Bait and switch. We'll file suit for the forged will. The typewriter. They'll focus all their attention on defending that area. Then we hit them from the side with all the data we've dug up on them."

"It'll be a righteous avalanche," Sherman said.

"So what are we looking at?" Hopkins said.

"The odds are against us, and the situation is grim. It's right up our alley," Deirdre said.

"Then let's get to work."

57

~~~

Patrick Van Burin had grown nervous and edgy over the years. He was becoming more concerned about the freshness of his ever-shrinking daily flower order from Sidford's. He was also troubled by Kazak, the teller, who didn't seem to be banking material.

Around 11:00 a.m., Van Burin was puttering around the waiting area of the bank. Kazak, a slender blond youth who seemed to regard the world with cynical eyes, was watching him with amused disbelief. Van Burin was scrupulously examining the latest floral arrangement. As far as Kazak was concerned, a bank president shouldn't be throwing a hissy fit over a bouquet.

"Kazak, are you sure these are fresh?"

"Yeah, yeah. I mean, yes, sir."

"They don't look fresh to me. The stems are wilted, and there's a touch of dry spoil on the petals."

"They were fresh at the florist, sir." Kazak sighed.

"I run a reputable business here. If I seem fussy and unreasonable, it's because appearances are important."

"I know that, Mr. Van Burin. Sheez."

"What?"

Kazak took a crumpled sheet of paper from his hip pocket. "Here's the receipt, if you don't believe me."

Van Burin read it carefully. "It says they're fresh. According to the florist, they're fresh. What's the matter with Trudie Dinkwell? She should pay better attention to her inventory."

"From over here they look fresh, you know."

Van Burin's voice rose a decibel. "But they're not. Don't you see? Flowers make us human. They bring out the best in us. They're our welcome mat. Our smile. You can never tell who's going to walk in here. Don't you see? Don't you understand at all what I'm trying to teach you?"

"Yeah. Sure."

"I don't think you do. It's not peaches and plums in here, Kazak."

Vesper entered the lobby. Although dressed simply and conservatively, her appearance suggested a person of privilege who was downplaying her circumstances.

"You have to be more observant," Van Burin prattled. Realizing that Kazak's attention was on something else, he turned to see.

"May I help you?" Van Burin said to Vesper with an eager smile.

"I think you can. I certainly hope so," Vesper replied demurely. "Is Mr. Royce Chamberlin here?"

"No," Van Burin said. "But he's expected at any moment."

Vesper moved cautiously into the bank, her eyes casing every corner. "I really want to meet Mr. Chamberlin. I've come a long way, and so much has happened. My papa, God rest his soul, once met an associate of his in Lawrence, Kansas, and this man told us if we were ever in the market for farmland, then Mr. Chamberlin is the man to see."

"He is," Van Burin said, adjusting his tie. "I'm Patrick Van Burin, president of the bank. Perhaps I may be of service."

"Perhaps you can," Vesper said. "My papa always said that when you need something at the bank, you speak to the banker in charge."

Kazak marveled at how quickly his fussy boss had been reduced to a schoolboy. Van Burin wasn't sure what to make of the visitor, but he wanted to put up a good appearance. Then he caught sight of Kazak's expression.

"Kazak, haven't you got something to do?"

Kazak sauntered back to the teller's cage. Neither he nor anyone outside the bank noticed the roadster parked along the Pomphrey Park side of the building. Nor did anyone notice the man standing beside the open hood, pretending to be looking at the engine.

Vesper was already focused on Chamberlin's office. She had wandered over to see the interior—where the desk was, where the window was, if the desk was as Ann described it, and above all, the location of the typewriter.

"Why did you want to see Mr. Chamberlin?" Van Burin asked.

"I'm Susan Seggersen. Our family used to own land just over the line in Belland County."

Van Burin brightened. "Sven Seggersen?"

"My great-uncle. It was a long time ago, back when Colonel Carson was alive."

"My wife is from Belland County," Van Burin said. "Some of her family still live there."

"Oh?" Vesper answered, smiling but wary.

Van Burin thought he heard a snicker from the teller's window. When he looked to see, Kazak was sorting some bills.

Vesper became serious. "I want to buy a farm. You might say I'm doing it for my papa."

"Is he a farmer?"

"He was. He died two years ago."

"I'm sorry."

Vesper edged a step backward toward Chamberlin's office. She wanted to go inside, but she could see that for the moment she had been waylaid by local hospitality.

"It was his dream to move to Franklin County and raise corn. He never got the chance."

"Farming's a demanding life. But I suppose you know that."

"Is that Mr. Chamberlin's office?" Vesper asked abruptly. "Do you mind if we wait inside?"

"Mr. Chamberlin doesn't like people in his office without his permission," Van Burin answered. "We could wait in my office. That's the one over here."

Vesper shot a glance at the tiny room next to Royce's.

"No. No, thank you," she said.

"It's perfectly comfortable."

"I'm sure it is, but I get uneasy in cramped quarters. I hope you understand."

The exchange had been brief, but Van Burin felt hollow. It was so long ago that he had possession of the large office and Royce was the teller. Things seemed smoother then. There was less anxiety and more bouquets—better bouquets. Then the colonel died.

Chamberlin entered. By now he had grown to regard anything out of the ordinary with a cold glare of suspicion.

"What's this?" he said.

"Oh, good morning, Royce," Van Burin said.

"Royce?" Vesper said expectantly. "Mr. Royce Chamberlin?"

"It might be," Chamberlin replied, studying her. Who was she? Van Burin seemed charmed by her. Kazak did not. At the same time, she seemed vulnerable and helpless.

"I've come a long way to meet you," Vesper said.

"A long way, Royce," Van Burin echoed. "Royce, this is Susan Seggersen. Her family's from Belland County."

"Never heard of them," Royce said.

"They haven't been there for a while. I knew some of them some time ago . . ."

"Never heard of them."

"We're from Minnesota now," Vesper said.

"She's looking to buy some property, Royce."

"Do you know anything about farming?" Chamberlin asked Vesper.

"Dairy farming...until two years ago. When my papa died."

Vesper felt Chamberlin's eyes all over her. He was not as susceptible to her charms and vulnerability as Van Burin, but then again, he hadn't turned away.

"She wants to carry out her father's wishes," Van Burin offered.

"And what are those?"

"She wants to buy a farm here in Winfield."

"Let her tell it," Chamberlin said.

"He wanted to raise corn all his life," Vesper said. "But we followed my grandpa to Minnesota. I have an inheritance now, so I can do this for him."

Chamberlin was pensive. "For your papa?"

"I just wondered if you could help me."

"Perhaps we can," Van Burin began. Chamberlin shot him an irritated glance.

"I'll take care of the young lady," Chamberlin said. "Do you want to talk in my office?"

"Yes."

With a grin, Kazak watched her enter Chamberlin's office. Chamberlin paused a few seconds and then drew Van Burin over to the teller's window.

"Check her out," Chamberlin ordered quietly.

"Why?" Van Burin asked in surprise.

"Just a hunch. Go next door. Have Fred call the Belland County Courthouse. Check the Seggersen family."

"Sven Seggersen," Van Burin said to Kazak, already delegating the task.

"Who they are. Grandniece named Susan. I want to know who she is."

"You want me to go now?" Kazak asked.

"You heard the man," Van Burin said sternly. "Remember, it's Sven Seggersen. Not Sig Sorensen. Not Sven Stephensen. Sven Seggersen. Understand?"

"Yeah, yeah." Kazak stepped out of the cage and crossed the lobby.

Inside the office, Vesper's eyes were taking note of everything. The typewriter was on the corner of the desk. A small stack of paper was at the other side. The window was closed. Before she made her move, it would have to be open.

On the wall was a map of the Carson estate. Fourteen of the twenty properties had a tiny slip of paper pinned to that particular piece of land. On each of these slips was a name, the name of a stock, and a number of shares written on it. Many of them had Pheasant Valley scribbled beneath the stock. All of the properties had the name Chamberlin written on them in ink, including the Northeast Quarter.

"When I was coming into town, I passed some of these properties you own. Then I heard that some of them were for sale."

"Who told you that?" Chamberlin asked.

"I'm sorry. Is that something I'm not supposed to know? I was told by that young man whose father has a pack of hounds and all those farm implements in his yard."

"Jago Hudsen," Chamberlin muttered.

"I can understand if some of your properties are not for sale. But is there something else available?"

"There might be," Chamberlin said. His tone was more probing. "But first, tell me about this promise to your papa."

Next door, Kazak was explaining Royce's order to Fred Brubaker.

"He wants you to call Belland County Courthouse. He wants you to check out the Sig Svensen Family."

"I don't know them."

"Just a verification. Who they are. If they're legitimate. And especially if they have a grandniece named Susan."

"Sig Svensen?" Brubaker asked.

"Yeah. That's it. One of those Swedish names."

"Royce is getting kind of particular in his old age," Brubaker said with a smile.

"You want me to wait?"

"Yes. We should get an answer right away." He reached for the telephone. "Morning, Willa," he said. "Fred Brubaker. Get me Finchville, the records room at the courthouse."

Back in his office, Chamberlin had moved over to the map. Vesper saw the opportunity. She slid two blank papers nearer the typewriter. Unknown to both of them, Van Burin was lingering near the doorway outside, listening.

"So you talked with Nichols in Lawrence, and he referred you to me."

"Mr. Nichols said if we were ever looking to purchase farmland, then you were the man to see."

Chamberlin turned to face her. "You were very close to your papa."

"Mr. Chamberlin, what I need is direction. I know how it is for a woman in a man's world. That's why I came to see you."

Seemingly satisfied with her response, Chamberlin began to peruse the map. "I hadn't planned to sell any more farms. The economy's changing. Investments seem to be one way to ride it out. Then, of course, there's the land."

"Yes." Vesper glanced back to the closed window. She wondered if it opened easily. Would it be stuck? She had to find out.

Royce was pointing at one of the properties with the name Cooley pinned to it. "Maybe one of these . . . possible foreclosures. How long are you in town?"

"I can stay a few days."

"Stay at the Journeyman. It's our new hotel."

"Thank you."

Chamberlin kept his finger on the Cooley property. "I could sell you this one. It's close by, and the soil is prime for corn. I could drive you out there tomorrow."

"That would be very kind."

"I'll get a more detailed map of the property," he said, starting for the door. Van Burin scurried away and into the lobby.

"Do you mind if I open the window?" she asked.

"Go ahead."

Vesper went to the window. It stuck, but with a little effort, it slid open. She could hear the purr of the roadster's engine.

By now Chamberlin was out in the lobby. Vesper heard him pause to give some orders. In a flash she was beside the desk, slipping some paper into the typewriter.

"Where's the kid?" he asked Van Burin.

"Still next door."

"I need paperwork for section thirteen."

"I'll get it," Van Burin offered.

"I'll go," Chamberlin declared. "Fred must have found something."

Vesper rapidly began typing keys, making sure she included the *h*, the *e*, and the *O*. It made a loud clacking sound.

"What's that?" Van Burin said.

Vesper pulled the paper out of the typewriter just as Van Burin appeared in the doorway.

"Hey! What are you doing there?"

Vesper rushed to the open window, clutching the paper. As she reached the sill, Van Burin grabbed her.

"I've got her! I've got her!' he cried desperately.

Vesper pushed him. He fell down beside the desk. She turned back to climb out as Van Burin was scrambling to his feet.

"Oh no you don't!" he shouted.

Vesper spun back into the room and kicked the desk drawer shut on Van Burin's hand. He let out a scream and collapsed backward onto the floor. Vesper was out the window and gone. A split second later, the roadster roared away.

Chamberlin rushed into the office. The screaming continued. "Ah! Ah! My hand!"

Ignoring the cries, Chamberlin stepped over to the open window and looked out. The sound of the speeding car had disappeared.

"Ah! Ah! Ah!"

Chamberlin was still staring at the park and courthouse, but his mind was somewhere else, his thoughts cool and collected.

Footsteps sounded in the lobby, and Brubaker and Kazak appeared in the doorway.

"What's going on in here?" Brubaker asked. "A car goes speeding away, and there's all this caterwauling in here."

Kazak was observing Van Burin with a condescending smirk. He reached out to help the fallen banker to his feet.

"Get away from me! Get away!" Van Burin shrieked.

"What are you doing on the floor, Patrick?"

"Ah! Ah! Ah!"

"You want me to call Dierkes?" Brubaker asked Chamberlin.

"No. By the time Dierkes gets here, they'll be in the next county."

"Then what the hell was that all about?'

A rare smile spread across Royce Chamberlin's face. He felt young again— eager, alive, full of enthusiasm.

"I think our Little Ann just declared war," he said.

Part Three

THE TRIAL

58

ON JANUARY 10, 1929, ANN AND Ben were seated in Hopkins's office. It was a Chicago winter evening, and the radiator along the wall was clanking and hissing. Hopkins was examining the copy of Lucille's will along with the typing samples from Royce Chamberlin's office.

"The typewriter is definitely the same," Hopkins said.

"Then we know the will was changed in his office," Ann said.

"We know it was changed there, but we have no proof of when or by whom," Hopkins replied.

"I know what Mama told me before she died."

"In the eyes of the court, it's your word against Chamberlin's. As I told you, this isn't going to be easy. The way we can approach it is to say the will was invalid and all your mother's possessions should go to you. Their argument will probably be that Lucille made the changes before you arrived at the hospital, and the pain from her injuries prevented her from remembering to tell you."

"That's not true," Ben said.

"Of course not. And I'm sure half the people in Winfield know it, too. As for the other part of the estate, your grandmother's share, I'm afraid that's lost."

"So we're back to the strategy," Ann said.

"Most likely, when they receive our notice, they'll start arming themselves with typewriter experts, character witnesses, doctor's reports, and so on. And while they're doing that, we come in from the side."

"Court of public opinion."

"Chamberlin. His whole life. His dealings in Winfield. Every scrap we can get on him. A man like that is not used to being questioned or challenged. He'll be standing before his fellow citizens."

"Everybody in Winfield knows what kind of man he is."

"Truth has a way of cutting a bully down to size. It boils down to how long he can take it."

"It's a good plan," Ann said. "Now I see why we have a team of researchers."

Hopkins picked up another paper on the desk. He began to read. "Here's what we have. 'Plaintiff—Ann Harmon. Defendants—Royce Chamberlin, Cassandra Chamberlin, Carol Chamberlin, Kurt Hudsen, Jago Hudsen, and Patrick Van Burin.' I'm purposely leaving Fred Brubaker off the list. I'm hoping he'll take the job defending them. If he does, we'll keep dropping evidence of his involvement with the others. It won't make their case look so good."

"He's been with them from the start," Ann said.

"Our side of the lawsuit claims that Royce Chamberlin forged your mother's will and that Kurt Hudsen is not related to you and, therefore, is living illegally on the Carson estate. Specifically, he and his son are living there without paying rent to the proper owner, Ann Harmon. In addition, Hudsen is damaging the land and is, therefore, allowing a perfectly good agricultural property to go to ruin. Consequently, he should be evicted and the property restored to its rightful owner, Ann Harmon."

Ann could picture how Royce and the others might react. Even though the initial charge was a ruse, she could see them rushing to respond to it. No one had challenged them before. She wondered if they would overreact or respond in a calculating manner, like a move in a game of chess. Whichever way it went, this was the beginning.

⁓

On January 25 Royce Chamberlin called a meeting in his office at the bank. The notice of the lawsuit had arrived a few days earlier, and although he had spoken privately with Brubaker, this was his first formal strategy session.

It was late morning. Dull gray clouds hovered over Winfield. The surface of Pomphrey Park was splotched here and there with areas where the snow had partially melted and then turned to black ice.

Seated in front of Royce were Brubaker and an uneasy Judge Farnell Post. As usual, Patrick Van Burin was late.

"While we're waiting," Chamberlin muttered. "Where is he, anyway?"

"Doc Powell," Brubaker said. "He said it wouldn't be long."

"He should know that when I call a meeting…"

Brubaker seemed full of confidence. He was eager to explain his strategy for the upcoming confrontation, and the irritation of waiting a few minutes didn't bother him.

"Gentlemen, I really shouldn't be here," Post said.

"I asked you in an advisory capacity only," Chamberlin said. "What we decide will affect the entire community."

"Our friends and neighbors, Your Honor," Brubaker added.

"I understand," Post said.

"How's Rose?" he said to the judge, changing the subject.

"Coming along," Post answered. "That's about all we can say."

"Unfortunate... But this Ann Hardy case shouldn't take too long. A day or two at the most. You'll be out of the courtroom and able to arrange your hours any way you want. Spend more time with Rose."

Post turned away to look out the window. His expression said much about his wife's condition, but Chamberlin and Brubaker never noticed.

Van Burin burst into the lobby, taking off his coat and scarf. "Sorry I'm late. I was at Doc Powell's. My hand, you know." He went to the remaining vacant chair.

"You've all read the transcript," Chamberlin said.

"We'll respond to it, Royce. No problem," Brubaker said confidently.

"Maybe not for you," Van Burin said plaintively. "That woman hurt my hand. She came in here, pushed me around, and kicked my hand."

"We know about the hand," Chamberlin growled.

"Nothing's broken, Patrick," Brubaker said. "It'll heal. Doc Powell tells you that every time you go see him."

"Who was that woman? Does anybody know who she was? People just can't come into the bank and...and...and do what she did."

Brubaker nodded sagely. "It was a terrible thing, Patrick. A tragic thing."

"It hurts, Fred."

Noting that Chamberlin's scowl had intensified, Brubaker returned to business.

"Royce, the estate is covered in a satisfactory manner. We'll let them come and have their day in court. Once it's settled, we'll have no more trouble with Ann Hardy."

"No trouble?" Chamberlin mused.

"They come, we respond, and we're done with it. Right, Your Honor?"

"As long as it follows courtroom procedure," Post said.

"That goes without saying. But you think we should file our response and get it over quickly?"

"I think that is for the best. Yes."

Chamberlin had been brooding during the entire exchange. "I am on a different page," he said.

"Why, Royce?" Brubaker asked. "We suspected a lawsuit. It's a simple thing to handle."

"A simple thing that merits the proper response."

"That's what I've been proposing," Brubaker said.

"It's not enough," Chamberlin said.

Brubaker was momentarily caught off guard, but continued, "Royce, listen. We can *win* this. All we need are the experts on typewriter print, doctor's opinion, and two or three nurses to testify to Lucille's mental state."

"Get them."

"Tracy Stabb's already approached me," Van Burin eagerly interjected. "Anything we want her to testify to—anything—she'll be glad to say it."

"We *see* where they're launching their attack." Brubaker said. "We meet them with experts and knowledgeable testimony, and at the end of the day, we'll be home for supper."

"We're going to countersue," Chamberlin said firmly.

Brubaker was stunned. He recognized the stony glare in Chamberlin's eyes.

"Why? We don't have to."

The hard features seemed to soften. "I've waited a long, long time for that little girl to come calling."

"Then let her call and let her go. We've got more important matters to consider here."

"This *is* important," Chamberlin announced. "I've created a position of authority and respect in this town. I've built a community everyone who lives here can be proud of. When someone challenges this community, they challenge my life's work—my legacy. And for that, they must be answered with strength and authority to the fullest extent."

Brubaker groped for the right words. In his mind a person should never make a reckless move unless absolutely necessary. "I don't think this is a wise move," he said.

Chamberlin slid a piece of paper across the desk. "I have a list of forty names. Add them to our countersuit."

Brubaker stared at the paper. The names were upside down and rapidly scribbled. But they spread down the sheet all the way to the bottom, where the last four were bunched together. The volume was astounding.

"Forty names?"

"I *can* countersue, can't I?" Chamberlin said to the judge.

"If that's what you choose."

"We don't need to," Brubaker said.

"Sometimes numerical strength gives the impression of moral predominance," Post said.

"It can and it will," Chamberlin declared. "We countersue to preserve the Carson estate."

"But the question is, should you do it? Fred has a point."

"Forty to one can create undue sympathy for Ann Harmon," Brubaker said.

"I built something from the estate," Chamberlin said. "What has she done?"

"It's still forty to one," Brubaker implored. "Judge Post, can't you see what I'm talking about?"

"I do indeed. You gentlemen have something to consider here."

"We've considered," Chamberlin said. "We're going to countersue."

Judge Post stood up. "Gentlemen, it's time for me to leave. Now that you've decided a course of action, we shouldn't see each other, even socially, until after a verdict is reached."

"Of course. I understand. Thank you, Your Honor," Brubaker said.

"Thank you for coming," Chamberlin said as Judge Post left.

Brubaker was reading the names on the list. The first entry made him recoil.

"Warren Hyatt? He spends all day drunk at his father's farm. You don't want him. If you call him to testify, you'll get a lecture on social reform."

"Replace him, but leave the others." Chamberlin began to recite some of the names himself. "Sam Hyatt, Edith Hyatt, Charles Hartom, Thome Mainwaring, Dick Ryan Story, Olaf Ziering,..."

"Some of these people hardly know her," Brubaker said.

"They'll sign," Chamberlin said.

"And what about Buddy Brenner and Bob Ishie? You lent them money after Lady Ann sacked them for theft."

"They were paid for services rendered."

"I just wish you'd reconsider; I think this is a terrible mistake."

"Where's your nerve, Fred?" Chamberlin cried.

"I'm not talking nerve. I'm talking common sense."

Brubaker saw that Chamberlin was unwavering, yet he made one more effort. "We don't know anything about this Thaddeus Hopkins except that he worked for the railroad."

"We can handle any outside attorneys," Chamberlin said.

He was smiling contentedly, relishing the coming fight. "Ann and I have a day of reckoning long overdue. Let her come with her big-city attorney. You do it, Fred. That's what you're paid for."

"Very well," Brubaker said with some resignation.

"Ann Hardy...coming back to Winfield. Well, let her come. Let her come."

59

THE INTRODUCTION OF FORTY NAMES TO the countersuit created a delay in the scheduling of the trial. Hopkins immediately sent the researchers to Winfield to investigate the forty and determine their actual involvement in the suit against Ann. Except for Vesper, who remained in Chicago, they arrived in various disguises—usually as someone passing through, seeking work, or traveling to visit a cousin in the next county.

Hopkins suspected that Chamberlin had rounded up the names in haste, recruiting them much in the manner of a press-gang gathering conscripts for the navy along the London docks. He figured most of the forty agreed to be on the list just to stay on Royce's good side. If this were true, their degree of involvement might benefit Ann.

The trial date was set for July 23, 1929. It was evident that the entire town would turn out to watch. Winfield had had trials in its time, but this one was special. The granddaughter of Colonel Wallace Carson was taking on the man who had married into the family and then cast her out. No matter what one thought of Ann or Chamberlin, this was the culmination of a blood feud. It was as close to a range war as Winfield, Iowa, would ever get.

Hopkins, Sherman, and Joel visited Winfield a few weeks earlier for the jury selection. Hopkins wanted a jury trial. He was not so much concerned with specific jury members as he was with cramming as many people into the room as possible when he went to work on Royce Chamberlin.

On the afternoon of July 21, Ann and Ben arrived on the 2:40 p.m. train from Omaha. Hopkins and some of his team were already there. Everyone would be staying at the Journeyman Hotel a block off the center of Market Street.

They were met by Olga as well as Ann's friends, Judy and Ellen. For an instant it seemed to Ann like a scene from childhood—a flashback to a time before all the trouble started. She wanted to relish the moment in her mind, but it was gone. The truth was right in front of her. Everyone was older. Everyone's lives had taken separate paths.

The five started for the Journeyman. Ann did not talk. She was listening to all the gossip from Olga and her friends. Both girls had married out of high school. Ellen married Bud Swenson and lived on the Swenson farm out near the county line. Judy had married Ricky Spell, whose father ran the dry goods store. Ricky was being groomed to take over the place, so Judy found herself working in linens all day.

Ann had not taken much notice of the Journeyman, the successful business-man's hotel, whose primary attraction was its proximity to the depot. It faced the backs of the buildings along Market Street, but the left half of the porch did offer a glimpse of the corner of the courthouse and one side of Pomphrey Park.

Something was different. There was a lemonade stand at the corner of the park in front of the courthouse. Next to it three men were putting up slats to create another booth. A sign reading COTTON CANDY was tilted at an angle on the curb nearby.

"Look at that," Ann said. "What are they celebrating?"

"It's the trial, Miss Ann," Olga said.

"There's a couple more on the other side of the park," Ellen said.

"Some of the merchants think it's a big deal for the town," Judy echoed.

"It's a damn Roman circus," Ann said.

She was about to start up the steps onto the porch when she saw the bulky shape of the Hudsen's car. It was parked along a row of trash cans at the back of one of the Market Street buildings. Doss Claypool, wearing his baggage handler uniform, and the Hudsens were slouched against the fender and running board, observing their arrival. The hounds were lined in the backseat, with their eyes haughtily fixed on Ann and her group. As usual, Goliath, the terrier, had managed to get a view, but was pushed out of sight when one of the larger dogs shifted his weight.

"I see them," Ben said.

"Royce must have sent them."

"Ignore them. They're reprobates," Judy whispered.

Doss started nudging Jago, as if to egg him on. Kurt's eyes were on the visitors, but he seemed preoccupied.

"Would you look at that," Doss drawled loudly. "It's Miss Ann...home from the big city."

Ann started up the steps.

"Don't you see Old Dawz over here?"

Ann stopped. "Hello, Doss."

"Leave us alone, Doss," Olga said. "We don't want any trouble."

"I don't want any trouble either," Doss continued. "What happened? Big city life too much for you? Come home to claim the old homestead? Maybe we start callin' you Lady Ann."

"Tell Royce we're here, Doss," Ann said, not even looking at him.

Jago cleared his throat and spat on the ground. "Oh, Mr. Harmonsens! Remember me, Mr. Harmonsens?"

"Let's go in," Ann said.

"I'm talkin' to you, Mr. Harmonsens."

"I remember you," Ben answered.

Jago snickered. "Don't be nervous now, Mr. Harmonsens. You don't have to be afraid of me."

"What do you want, Jago?"

"One thing and I'm gonna say it. You're here to make trouble for Mr. Royce and Miss Cassie. You ain't gonna do that, Mr. Harmonsens."

"We're here for the trial," Ben said. "Anything more is your doing."

Jago's face reddened with anger. Ben always seemed to put him in his place without any effort. Kurt reached out and took his son's arm. "Let 'em go," he said.

"Why?"

"'Cause I said so."

"I wanna bust that Mr. Harmonsens."

Ann and Ben and the others crossed the porch and entered the hotel.

"This ain't the time," Kurt said.

"We were just havin' fun," Doss said.

"What's wrong with you, Papa?" Jago asked.

"You listen to me. Both of you," Kurt said, keeping the focus on his son. "I been thinkin'. And you better start thinkin' too."

"About what?"

"About if we get called on the witness stand. If that happens, we better have a damn good idea what we're gonna say."

60

ANN WANTED BEN TO SEE THE manor house and the Northeast Quarter. He had joined her in her struggle, but he had never seen what she was fighting for.

The morning of the twenty-second, Olga was in town with the buckboard from the county farm. She had been sent to pick up three crates due to arrive on the 8:30 a.m. freight train. However, Mr. Dobbs informed her that the cargo had been mistakenly put on the noon train. That gave her over two hours of free time, which she did not mind at all.

She went immediately to the Journeyman to meet Ann and Ben.

They were soon riding into the countryside. It was the beginning of a warm summer day in Winfield. The crops were almost ready for harvest.

"Mr. Ben," Olga said, "I'm so glad to finally meet you. Sorry it has to be under these circumstances."

"I'm glad to meet you, too," Ben said.

"I've been with this family all their lives. My heart is with the colonel's family...with Miss Ann. She's so young, and she was all alone till you came along. All those people gangin' up on her. If they had their way, they'd have stripped everything, and she'd be selling apples on the roadside."

"That's not going to happen," Ben said.

Ann noticed that Ben's eyes were fixed more and more on the landscape—the fields, the passing farms. Other than the trip to Winfield with Ann, the only place in Iowa he had ever visited was Omaha. This was his first time in the countryside, and he was taking in everything.

"What do you think?" she asked.

"It's immense. It's beautiful."

"It's Iowa," Ann said.

"It's home, Mr. Ben."

They had reached two dirt roads intersecting in the middle of a sweep of cornstalks. The harvest colors of the plants stretched to the hilltops and horizons in the distance.

They heard a crackling among the cornstalks to the right of them and the sound of a large animal running. All at once a deer with antlers darted out of one field, crossed the road, and plunged into the field on the other side. There was more crackling and then silence.

"Deer," Olga said. "They stick to the wooded areas mostly, but when the corn's high, they come down."

After a few minutes, they rounded a curve. Ahead, against the blue sky, was a cluster of buildings surrounded by two barns, a bunkhouse, and two corrals. One structure dominated the scene—a large, white stone house with a pointed shingle roof.

"There it is," Ann said. "Carson Manor."

It had been years since she had seen home. The memory was vivid. It was still the same, but in her mind, it had taken on a certain grandeur.

"Amazing," Ben said. "It's like a chunk of Old England come to life in the cornfields."

"It's what Grandpa wanted," Ann said. "My grandma's people were from England. Grandpa had the house brought over so she wouldn't feel homesick."

When they reached the driveway, Olga stopped the buckboard. The hum of the wires was audible between the gatehouse and the main house.

Olga was scowling. "Mr. Royce is keeping it up pretty well. He's got this thing about appearances."

"You grew up there," Ben said to Ann.

"I did," Ann said. "I had the run of the place."

The front door of the main house opened. Carol Chamberlin strode out to see who was parked in the road. Over the years she had grown plump. She had a clenched, agonized expression, as if every minute in her life was imposing on her time. She cupped her hands around her eyes to get a better view.

"It's Carol," Ann said.

"Miserable girl. Just miserable," Olga muttered.

"She's let herself go," Ann said.

"We better move, Miss Ann. We don't want trouble, and we have to get back."

Olga flicked the reins. Soon they were bumping and rolling along once again.

Every now and then, they would pass a farmhouse and barn with a white sign in the front yard as well as two or three on the fence that lined the road.

"Foreclosures?" Ben asked.

"Fusspot Van Burin and his bank," Olga declared. "He says he's everybody's friend. There ought to be a law to protect people from bankers like him...him and that Fred Brubaker. Take the property. Resell it with a loan. Put all the money in that power and electric company, making themselves rich. It's like they're feeding a beast that's always hungry. It never stops, Miss Ann."

"And Royce calls the shots every inch of the way," Ann said.

In a few minutes, the Hudsen property came into view. It had degenerated into a conglomeration of weeds, wagon parts, and trampled soil—with a farmhouse in the center that now resembled a line shack.

"I don't want to stop. You'll get a glimpse as we go by," Olga said to Ben.

They were jostling past the property. The large car and the hounds were not in the front yard.

"It's worse than I remember," Ann said.

"It's a sore sight. That's for sure."

Ann took a final glance back. "It would be a challenge to turn that place back into a working farm."

Ben noticed that everyone had become serious and contemplative, as people would be before entering a church.

A minute more and Olga pulled the reins to stop.

"Here we are. The Northeast Quarter," Ann said.

Ben's eyes had found the special plot of land on their own. Up ahead the soil became deeper than any of the other sections they had passed. The cornstalks were taller and greener. The place did not trumpet its excellence. It drew a person in.

"It's been a long time," Ann said.

"You see, Mr. Ben?"

Ben had never taken his eyes off the vegetation before him. The quarter was already working its wonders.

"Incredible. It looks more like a garden," he said.

"Some say it was irrigated by the Fountain of Youth," Olga said.

Ben focused on a single cornstalk. He started with the soil and followed it all the way to the top, ten feet above them. Everything was perfection—from the deep green that rose from the ground to the bright yellow at the top. It looked like a special life form that might flourish undisturbed for centuries in a rain forest.

"So it all began here," he said.

Ann was proud of Ben. Most city folk would dismiss the quarter as a better than average cornfield. Ben did not. On his first visit, he had seen and understood what Ann and her family had known for years. It was only when a person stopped to give some time to the quarter that it began to give him something in return.

"Every plant looks perfect," Ben said.

"They are," Ann said

"And you harvest them?"

"With reverence."

"And it grows back the same way?"

"Every year the same way, Mr. Ben," Olga said. "Tall…strong…finest corn in the state."

Ann was glad they came. After all her experiences since her last visit to the quarter, she had felt discouraged—as if her promise to her grandfather had become a chore rather than a willing act. She remembered the colonel's final words to her and felt herself being filled with a sense of purpose. Before long, a feeling of strength and renewal had taken over her.

"Miss Ann uses the word 'majestic' when she describes it," Olga said.

"It is a wonder," Ben said.

"Now you see what we're fighting for," Ann said.

61

The First Day of the Trial

The morning of the twenty-third, Ann, Ben, and Hopkins walked from the Journeyman to the courthouse. The day was already hot, and the sky was cloudless. The square in front of the courthouse was lined with cars and a few carriages. The cicadas were beginning to warm up in the trees around the square. On each side of the square, there was a makeshift lemonade stand. The cotton candy stand was fully assembled. There was even a man attempting to sell balloons, though he was not having much luck. Lemonade was a temporary antidote for a hot day. A balloon was just something to hold until one got tired of it. People had begun to arrive at 7:30 a.m.—just to get a seat inside. Dierkes had taken on two temporary deputies—on loan from Sheriff Tibbs in Exira—for traffic and crowd control around the courthouse.

Van Burin stepped out of the bank. Ann had not seen him for a while. He pretended to ignore them as he placed a sign that read CLOSED FOR THE TRIAL on the door of the bank. He glanced over at the law office. Brubaker was standing in the doorway, watching the passersby.

Brubaker had attempted to put down Hopkins as a has-been in his meetings with Royce, but seeing him in person was another matter. Even during the jury selection, he couldn't get a handle on the man. Brubaker watched him intently. Hopkins, on the other hand, nodded to Brubaker once, just enough to acknowledge his existence.

Brubaker continued to watch them as they crossed Pomphrey Park on their way to the courthouse. He heard the sound of an approaching carriage. It was Chamberlin and the girls. They had deliberately entered Winfield on Market Street, so they could make a grand entrance by passing all the shops and businesses on their way to the courthouse. They could have taken the car, but a carriage gave them a distinctly regal air.

"See you in court, gentlemen," Chamberlin said as they rolled past.

Royce and the carriage made the trip around the park to the courthouse. As they passed the faces of the arriving and curious, they were greeted with a scattering of calls: "Good luck, Royce. We're with you, Royce. You'll win this one, Royce."

The clock over the courthouse tolled a single note, signaling it was 9:45 a.m. Cassie looked up to see the clock face. She had passed the clock and courthouse many times, but this was the first time her father had ever come to court to fight for something. The sound from the clock seemed more ominous than a mere signal of the time of day.

By now Ann, Ben, and Hopkins were at the door of the courthouse. There was a wall of spectators on either side. Ann glanced at the faces. As she expected, over half of them were people she didn't know.

"Oh, Lady Ann . . . Are you solvent?"

Ann saw the leering face of Doss Claypool in the crowd. She ignored the slur, and they entered the courtroom. As she and the others moved along the side of the populated room, she caught a glimpse of another familiar face. Warren Hyatt was standing sullenly at the back. He had arrived too late to find a seat. Ann was amazed how much he had changed. Spite and alcohol had made him spindly and sallow. His features had hardened, and his eyes seemed sunken into their sockets.

They reached the front. There were two tables facing the judge's bench. Behind them were sixteen rows of seats, which were already packed with early arrivals. The jury box was on the left side of the room, which faced the park. Two fans turned slowly overhead. As they took their seats, the rustling and vocal hum in the room went up.

Less than a minute later, Chamberlin and his daughters entered to take their places at the other table. As they made their way through the room, there was the same chorus of encouragement from the crowd: "We're with you, Royce. Don't worry, Royce. They're city; we're Winfield." From his position alongside the jury box, Dierkes watched Royce and the girls as they sat down. He had nodded to Ann and Ben when they entered, but he offered no such acknowledgment to the Chamberlins.

His attention was diverted by a discussion in the back of the room. Kurt and Jago had just arrived, and they wanted a whole row to move over, so they could squeeze themselves in along the aisle. Jago looked immediately for Mr. Royce and the girls.

Chamberlin maintained an air of flinty dignity. Carol was as cold and forbidding as always. No one had greeted her individually, and she rationalized this lack of solicitude as respect for her social position. Cassie, on the other hand, remained aloof from everyone. She was dressed as if she were the belle of a Winfield social function.

Immediately, Jago was out of his seat. Kurt looked up in alarm. This was not the time to make a scene. When one is in a courtroom, one should keep a low profile.

Jago was beside Royce's table, attempting to smile, but in front of so many people, he felt clumsy and awkward.

"Uh, morning, Miss Cassie. It's me, Jago."

Cassie sat rigidly upright, pretending she had not heard him.

"I just want to say that we're gonna get through this."

"Answer the boy," Chamberlin said.

Cassie continued to look straight ahead. "What did he say, Papa?"

"Why you look away from me, Miss Cassie? I was just sayin' that we ain't got anything to worry about."

"My papa will take care it," Cassie replied stiffly.

By now Kurt had reached the table, attempting a hearty demeanor. He was concerned about his son making a fool of himself in front of the whole town.

"Why don't you sit down, Jago?" Carol blared loudly.

Jago felt the disapproval, but he had to make sure they understood. "It ain't right what they're doin' to you, Miss Cassie. I gotta tell you that. I gotta say it."

"Come on, boy," Kurt said.

Jago caught sight of the Harmons at the next table. In his mind, Ben was the cause of all the troubles. It was obvious, yet no one else saw it. Already there were whispers from the sea of faces watching him. They all knew Jago.

"Good morning, Mr. Harmonsens," Jago said mockingly.

"Good morning," Ben answered,

"Break that up," Chamberlin whispered to Kurt.

Kurt was beside his son now. "Sit down," he said urgently.

"If you think you're gettin' away with somethin', Mr. Harmonsens..."

Dierkes had left his position along the wall. He crossed over to Kurt and Jago.

"Not in the courtroom, Jago," Dierkes said.

"Why not? *He's* in the courtroom! You lookin' out for him, Dierkes?"

"Because I'm telling you," Dierkes was saying.

"You on his side? That's it! You're on his side!"

"You sit down, or I'll lock you up," Dierkes said firmly.

Kurt reached out for his son's arm. "Better listen, boy. It's the law talking."

Jago shrugged and grinned. "All right, Papa, all right. I know when I'm bein' told."

Jago and Kurt started back up the aisle.

"Thank you, Sheriff," Ann said.

"It's all right, Miss Ann. Everybody's a little jumpy."

There was a rise in murmurs as the Hudsens took their seats.

Ann turned around in her seat to look at the assembly behind her. Brubaker and Van Burin were arriving. Behind them was a mural of faces, men and women of every age.

"It's like the whole town has come out," Ann said. "I never expected this. Like it's the first time something like this has happened in Winfield."

"It probably is," Hopkins said.

Ann had been telling herself she could use the trial as a learning experience for her ambition to be a lawyer. But she knew she would be too emotionally involved in the proceedings to ever view it objectively.

In the front of the room, the wood-paneled door to the judge's chambers opened. Judge Post entered, clad in his robes.

"All rise!" Dierkes boomed. "Hear ye! Hear ye! The court of Winfield, Franklin County, Iowa, is now in session! Judge Farnell Post presiding."

Post sat down in his place at the front of the room.

"Be seated," Post said and then waited until the rustling had subsided. "Good morning," he began. "This is a case involving inheritance. On one side we have the granddaughter of our town's founder, Colonel Wallace Carson. On the other, we have one of Winfield's most prominent citizens. The courtroom is the highest place in the land for resolution of the moral and legal dilemmas in our daily lives. This is a civil proceeding. Witnesses will be called. Differing points of view will be expressed. But remember, this is the temple of the law. We shall adhere to the proper code of conduct at all times."

Post gazed out over the room. Here and there people had produced fans, which were fluttering at various speeds.

"I can see the plaintiffs and the defendants are both present with their counsel. I suggest we begin with Mr. Hopkins."

Hopkins rose from his seat at the table and addressed the court.

"Good morning," Hopkins began. "Ladies and gentlemen, my client is suing for the return of the property she feels is rightfully hers. She claims the defendant tampered with her mother's will so that he and his daughters might seize her inheritance. This is clear enough. We shall produce a copy of the will that shows a distinct difference in the typewriter print in the areas relating to the bequests to my client."

Ann saw Brubaker exchange a knowing glance with Chamberlin. They were behaving exactly the way Hopkins had hoped.

"All this is clear enough," Hopkins continued. "My client has sued a total of six defendants. However, the other side, in turn, has rounded up thirty-four other names to respond in their countersuit."

"Maybe a lot of them feel the land isn't hers," Brubaker said with a poker face.

"That is what we're here to determine," Hopkins replied.

"My clients are quite clear in their position, Your Honor," Brubaker said.

"Are they all present?" Hopkins asked.

"Now, we won't have any cross talk here," Post admonished.

"I don't mind it, Your Honor," Hopkins said. "It helps me get to know the town and the other side as well. I was asking if all the plaintiffs in the countersuit are present."

"Are they, Mr. Brubaker?" Post inquired.

"All but Stillsen, Bergesen, and Pike."

There was a smattering of cries from the assembly. "We're here, Your Honor! Pike's here! Hey! Olaffsen's here!"

"Order! Order!" Post barked.

"Do any of them know they are involved in a countersuit?" Hopkins inquired.

"I'm sure they do, Mr. Hopkins," Post commented.

"Perhaps. But I'm not sure if all of them know why," Hopkins replied. He took a folded sheet of paper off the table, opened it, and read aloud. "Todd Stillsen...'I am signing this lawsuit paper because Mr. Royce told me to.'"

"I guess he knows which side to be on," Brubaker said with a smirk.

There was laughter from the courtroom. Post did not command them to stop, at least not immediately. Ann knew that this was to be expected. The local boy received a pass on the enforcement of courtroom behavior.

"It seems to me that when Royce Chamberlin says, 'Jump,' everyone jumps," Hopkins stated. "They jump without even thinking. It would be interesting if the next time he says, 'Jump,' someone asks, 'Why?' I may subpoena Mr. Stillsen."

"Can't do that," Brubaker said. "Stillsen's in Exira buying feed."

"For Royce Chamberlin no doubt."

"Of course."

"I still may subpoena Mr. Stillsen. Can you make note of that?"

"What?" Brubaker said.

"Court stenographer, what did I say?"

Ellie, the court stenographer, held up her notes and read, "I still may subpoena Mr. Stillsen. Can you make note of that?"

"So it's in the record," Hopkins said.

Hopkins looked around the room, taking in the jury as well as the entire assembly. "Forty to one. That's what we're looking at. During the process of the trial, I'd like you to think of something very carefully. Ask yourselves, 'Why?' If this case is so easy, then why forty to one? I'm not sure myself. As we move through the course of the trial, maybe we can find out together. Thank you."

"Is that all?" Post said.

"It's all for now, Your Honor," Hopkins replied.

Brubaker and Chamberlin were observing the proceedings with smug expressions. Ann had to smile, too. Hopkins had baited the trap, and they were walking right in.

Post cleared his throat. "If that's all he has to say, then, Mr. Brubaker, you may proceed."

Brubaker stood up and, in a grand manner, moved around the courtroom.

"Good morning, everyone," he said. "This is really a local matter. You all know me. You all know Royce Chamberlin. We're neighbors. We all go to church on Sunday. We go to the same Labor Day picnic."

He paused to let the words sink in.

"And you certainly are acquainted with the plaintiff, Mrs. Ann Harmon. As His Honor said, this is a case involving inheritance, but it is also a case about the failure of one generation to appreciate the benign and subtle generosity of another. This young woman is suing her step-grandfather. And for what reason? It is because the step-grandfather had the…well, how should I phrase it? Because the step-grandfather had the occasion to fall in love with the widow of a great man."

Again he paused. There were a number of approving nods around the room.

"For the next ten years, this man tried his best. No, he *did* his best to provide for the great man's family as well as his own. And here"—his voice rose in an accusatory tone—"*here* is the result. The fruit of his labors. Spoiled. Ungrateful. And after having been given all the advantages of her class and station, she shows her ingratitude by flaunting tradition and eloping to Chicago with a dealer in bootleg whiskey."

"Yeah!" It was a shout from the back of the room. Everyone turned to see Warren Hyatt—glowering, defiant, bloodshot, and petulant as ever.

"Who was that?" Post demanded. When he saw it was Hyatt, he shook his head, but maintained a stern tone. "I'm going to warn you. Any further outbursts and I will clear the courtroom."

Hyatt's face was crimson, either from the alcohol he'd consumed while on the way to the trial or embarrassment from the judge's rebuke. Before their eyes he seemed to retreat back inside himself.

"Continue, Mr. Brubaker," Post said.

"Thank you, Your Honor. As I was…"

"Excuse me, Your Honor," Hopkins said. "We want to get the correct occupation entered into the court record. Mr. Harmon is senior underwriter for MacMurray and Guild Insurance in Chicago."

"Point taken. May I continue?"

"Is it entered into the court record?" Hopkins inquired.

"Mr. Harmon is senior underwriter for MacMurray and Guild Insurance in Chicago," Ellie read.

"I'm a stickler for the facts," Hopkins said.

Post seemed to regard these events with a raised eyebrow. "Mr. Hopkins, we all know you're a big-shot lawyer from Chicago. You may think this is a roomful of rubes and country boys, but we're not. You and I both went to law school. We both worshipped at the same altar of American legal jurisprudence. But *I'm* the judge here, and you're the attorney."

"Your Honor," Brubaker interjected, "since he elected to interrupt me, may the counselors approach the bench?"

"Of course," Post replied.

Brubaker and Hopkins crossed to Judge Post.

"Frankly, Your Honor," Brubaker said, "I think this is waste of the court's time. We can try the case and go through it all. But we have witnesses and experts who will confirm the inaccuracy of my learned colleague's accusations as well as the time the changes were made in Lucille Hardy's will."

"Mr. Brubaker is asking if you wish to drop the case," Post said to Hopkins.

"No, I just got here," Hopkins answered. "I want to stick around and see how you do things."

"Well, go ahead, gentlemen," Post said. "Mr. Brubaker will conclude his opening statements."

"Thank you, Your Honor," Brubaker said. "I will not lower myself to say that the interruption from my learned colleague was an effort to disrupt the flow of my communication with you. In a court of law, we are above that—even if we come from Chicago."

His eyes brushed the faces in room, making contact with friends and neighbors.

"This case is tragic to my heart. Tragic on one side because it is unnecessary. And tragic because it involves a friend of mine, a friend to all of us—Royce Chamberlin. We all know him. An honorable man. A pillar of the community."

Murmurs of agreement about the room.

"We all know the story, but I will condense it for you. Royce began here as a bank teller. He served everyone with unyielding zeal and a desire to be of service to his fellow citizens. He rose in stature in the community, but he never forgot his humble origins. He is a contributor to 4-H clubs, to the Red Cross, to the

Iowa Corn Huskies. He is a member of our city council. And he is the father of Cassandra and Carol, two lovely daughters, who have come here to sit in support of their father. Thanks to him, we are a better town. We are better people."

He took a few steps toward Ann's table.

"And over here, we have Ann Harmon. Her only claim is through blood-line. But businesses and towns are founded and maintained by more than bloodline. What about her? Assuming she had control of the properties in question, could she handle the responsibility? Is she prepared? Is she even ca-pable? We will show she is not. She is antagonistic, impulsive, and emotionally volatile. In the current economic climate, these qualities make her a danger and a casualty in business dealings. She is not ready. Bloodline is not enough."

There was a commotion in the back of the room as people moved out of the way to make room for something or someone. Two wheelbarrows, pushed by Joel and Sherman, were making their way along the wall to Hopkins's table.

Ann had to smile. Hopkins had told her the team had dug up a fair amount of evidence. But the sight of it stacked neatly in two wheelbarrows was surpris-ing. She hadn't realized how much they had found.

Post's eyebrows went up again. "What's this? Who are you people?"

"My apologies, Your Honor," Hopkins said pleasantly. "I have to take re-sponsibility for this."

"You certainly better if this is your doing. What is it?"

"Evidence, Your Honor. Notes and files," Hopkins replied. "My learned colleague across the aisle was unable to provide me with copies of these due to irregularities such as burglaries, courthouse fires, and the like, so we had to send for them at the state capital."

"Isn't that irregular, Mr. Hopkins?"

"It seems so to me, Your Honor. Most of these are already in Mr. Brubaker and Mr. Chamberlin's possession. It's all a matter of catching up." He cast a knowing gaze toward the Chamberlin table. "We're all caught up now."

"I certainly hope so," Post declared.

"You were saying, Mr. Brubaker?" Hopkins said.

"I don't think we need to continue," Brubaker said. "Royce Chamberlin is our friend and neighbor. My learned colleague may have a pair of wheel-barrows, but truth, character, and human values are on our side. We will be watching how you conduct yourself, Mr. Hopkins."

When Brubaker returned to his place at the defendants' table, Chamberlin drew him over. "What's he up to?" Royce asked.

"I don't know and I don't care," Brubaker answered. "We're going to show Ann's big shot lawyer how we do things."

Post regarded the assembly for a few seconds. "Mr. Hopkins, you may call your first witness."

"I'd like to call Patrick Van Burin to the stand."

Van Burin crossed to the witness stand. Dierkes was waiting there with a Bible.

"Raise your right hand," Dierkes said. "Do you solemnly swear to tell the truth, the whole truth, and nothing but the truth, so help you God?"

"I do."

"Be seated."

Hopkins approached the witness stand. Ann was watching intently. Van Burin was trying to put his humble public-servant façade on display, but he had foreclosed on enough property in the past few years that he had become a poster begging to be hit with a spitwad.

"Mr. Van Burin, are you the president of the Iowa Trust Bank here in Winfield?"

"I am, and I am proud to hold the position."

"Tell us a little about your working relationships with Colonel Carson and Royce Chamberlin."

"Objection," Brubaker declared.

"On what grounds?" Hopkins inquired. "I'm just asking how things are run here."

"I have to go with Mr. Hopkins," Post said. "Overruled."

"Both men...the pinnacle of human endeavor...human achievement," Van Burin rhapsodized. "Both...men of quality, insight, integrity."

"Honesty?"

"Yes. Honesty."

"And Royce Chamberlin?"

"A hard working man, a credit to the community, the epitome of the American dream. If Colonel Carson was the man who lit the torch for our town, Royce is the keeper of the flame."

"Continue," Hopkins said.

"Why, I remember years ago, when Royce applied for the job of teller at the bank, I said to him, 'Royce, you have an honest face. I think we can work together.'"

"And did you?"

"Yes. Emphatically. Yes."

"Would you say that he has been a patient and caring family member to Mrs. Harmon?"

"Patient and loving...But I must add that Mrs. Harmon was a trial to everyone's patience."

"How?"

"Too much affluence and not enough upbringing. We sent her to the best schools possible; gave her the best that money can buy." Then as an afterthought, something he couldn't resist. "And she wouldn't even buy an honorarium for her grandmother's memorial service."

A ripple of murmurs and whispers.

Royce was watching Hopkins suspiciously. "Why isn't he challenging any of this?" he asked in a whisper.

"No matter, Royce," Brubaker replied. "Let him make our case for us."

"But in spite of this apparent ingratitude," Hopkins continued. "You have been patiently managing the affairs of the Carson estate ever since the colonel's passing."

"With patience and care...as if it were my very own."

"And *that* is exactly why you're up here," Hopkins stated.

Van Burin paled, realizing that he had been lulled into some kind of trap. He glanced over to Chamberlin and Brubaker for help. They were watching to see how he handled himself.

"Mr. Van Burin, you *are* president of the bank," Hopkins said.

"That's what I said."

"Yet you don't occupy the president's office."

"I'm the president. Anywhere I work is the president's office."

"You don't occupy the big office with the word *President* on the door, do you?"

"I object," Brubaker said.

"I am merely trying to establish a working picture of the bank, Your Honor."

"Overruled."

"Who does occupy that office?"

"Why is that so important?" Van Burin sputtered. "All right, it's occupied by Royce Chamberlin."

"He doesn't work for the bank. How did this happen?"

Van Burin suddenly turned to Judge Post. "Do I have to answer, Your Honor?"

"I'm not condemning him," Hopkins said. "I just want to know the working relationships within the bank. What's he doing in your office?"

"Answer the question, Patrick," Judge Post said.

"I decided to give the office to Royce Chamberlin because he...he controls the majority of the funds in the bank."

"So you took a smaller office and gave the larger one to Royce."

"Just for convenience. That's all."

"Did you volunteer or did Royce Chamberlin ask you to move?"

"I object, Your Honor."

"Sustained."

"Did anybody ask you to move?"

"I object, Your Honor."

"Sustained."

"Then you made this magnanimous decision on your own."

"Yes. Yes, I did."

"We'll accept you at your word," Hopkins said. "Now, Mr. Van Burin, you are in charge of all the accounts on the Carson estate. You also supervise the payroll and cash flow of all the properties."

Ann watched Chamberlin conferring with Brubaker. She knew the whole room was observing the same psychological phenomenon. Van Burin had become very fragile without a stronger force to protect him.

"You pay the bills. You balance the books. And you oversee the investments of the estate."

"I do."

"Then you're more of a bookkeeper."

"I am the *president*," Van Burin fumed.

"I object, Your Honor."

"Sustained. Watch your tone, Mr. Hopkins."

Hopkins turned to the courtroom and addressed Joel and Sherman, who had taken a position at the back of the room. They were standing beside what appeared to be a five-foot-by-five-foot framed poster and an easel.

"Set up the display, please," Hopkins said. "Let's put it up where everyone can see it."

Joel and Sherman came down to the front. Sherman opened the easel and they both placed the poster on it. Written on the large placard were five rectangles on the left side, an oval in the center, and a solitary rectangle on the right. Each rectangle had the number of a bank account printed in the center.

"These are the accounts for the Carson estate," Hopkins began. "We have five accounts on the left side lined up like a squad on guard duty. From top to bottom, we have 8890-56-2232, 8890-56-2234, 8890-56-1278, 8890-56-1258, and 8890-56-1259. Then all the way over here, we have this little one all by itself, 8890-56-0709. Do you recognize them?"

"Of course I do," Van Burin said.

"Could you tell the court who they belong to?"

"2232, 2234, 1278, 1258, and 1259 belong to Royce Chamberlin."

"Could you be more specific?"

"2232 belongs to Royce Chamberlin. 1258 and 1259 belong to Carol and Cassandra, Mr. Chamberlin's two daughters. 2234 is what we call the Operating Account for the estate. 1259 is what we call the Farm Account. Out of that account are paid the bills specifically pertaining to profits and expenses from the year's harvest."

"So it is a mixture of personal and business accounts."

"Yes."

"Where are you leading with this, sir?" Post inquired from his perch.

"I'm acquainting the court with bank operations, Your Honor," Hopkins said.

Ann was watching Van Burin. She knew he was the right man to call first. A true crook would have lied his way out or put on a convincing show. Patrick Van Burin's tragedy was that beneath the surface, he had a streak of honesty.

"So theoretically," Hopkins continued, "if a bill came in to the estate, it would be paid out of the accounts of one of the individuals or from one of the two operating accounts."

"That is correct. It's neatly organized."

Hopkins pointed to the little rectangle on the right. "What about 0709 over here? This little fellow all by himself?"

"Ann Harmon," Van Burin sniffed.

Hopkins stepped up to the board. He pointed at the oval in the center. On second glance, one could notice that the oval was a piece of paper that covered something.

"Mr. Van Burin," Hopkins said. "We haven't mentioned this other account. The one right here in the middle of things."

"An account? I...I...I don't see an account."

Hopkins pulled the paper off. It had been concealing another rectangle with the number 8890-57-5555 in the center.

"Do you recognize it now?"

"Yes... It's more a...technical thing than an account."

"8890-57-5555. What is it?"

Chamberlin leaned over to Brubaker. "What is this?"

"Patrick will be fine," Brubaker said.

"Mr. Van Burin?" Hopkins queried.

"It's a holding account."

"For?"

"For transfer of funds."

"Do something," Chamberlin whispered to Brubaker.

"What funds go into this account?" Hopkins said.

"It's hard to say...money goes in, and money goes out."

"I object, Your Honor. This has no bearing on Ann Harmon's suit," Brubaker declared.

"On what grounds?" Hopkins countered. "There are no funds missing. We're not accusing anyone. I just want to know how it was used."

"This has no bearing on the case," Brubaker repeated.

"Your Honor, it does."

"Mr. Hopkins may continue," Post said. "As long as he does not continue too long."

"It seems to be another operating account," Hopkins said to Van Burin.

"It's like a fiduciary middleman," Van Burin said. "That's all it is. It's temporary. We put funds there while we decide which account will pay for them. Then we transfer the money to the appropriate account, and the bill is paid from that one."

"Temporary?"

"It's a holding account. That's all it is. A holding account."

"It's more than that, Mr. Van Burin."

Rustles and murmurs arose from the courtroom.

Hopkins reached into one of the wheelbarrows and pulled out a stack of papers that numbered about twenty pages.

"Exhibit A," he said. Sherman and Joel reached into the wheelbarrow and took out matching stacks of twenty pages. They began distributing them to Brubaker, Chamberlin, and Post, as well as to the jury. Hopkins held his out to Van Burin.

"What we have here is a financial statement," Hopkins said. "Carson Manor for two months—September and October of 1925."

Chamberlin's face was white.

"I object, Your Honor," Brubaker said. "This has no relevancy to Mr. Van Burin's role as Ann Harmon's financial and legal guardian."

"I have to disagree, Your Honor," Hopkins said. "I am simply trying to establish for the court that my client *does* appreciate all that is being done in her behalf."

"Where did you obtain this?" Post demanded, holding up his copy.

"I'd like to know that myself," Van Burin stated cagily.

Hopkins stared down at him. "When your bank was unable to provide me with paperwork, I subpoenaed them from state bank records in Des Moines. I got the rest from county tax records."

Hopkins returned to Van Burin. The banker seemed to be shrinking.

"Now, Mr. Van Burin, will you explain to the court the financial activity for the month of October."

"I don't...I don't have my glasses," Van Burin whispered.

Hopkins stifled a smile. "Do you know where they are?"

"I object, Your Honor," Brubaker declared. "There's no point in continuing if the witness can't see."

"Where are they, Patrick?" Dierkes asked.

"Over at the bank. I...uh..."

"Clem, could you go fetch them?"

"No need, Your Honor," said a voice from the back of the room.

There was movement among the spectators. Kazak was out of his seat and sauntering cockily toward the bench. With an insolent smirk, he held up a pair of glasses.

"These are his glasses right here," Kazak said. "He forgot them at the bank."

"You're an observant young man," Post said.

Kazak handed them to Van Burin. "I saw you put them on your desk as you were leaving. I thought you might need them."

"Thank you, Kazak," Van Burin said forlornly. "You didn't have to..."

"My pleasure...sir." Kazak returned to his place in the back.

Van Burin looked nervously around the room. The faces, the fluttering fans, and the eyes on him all made him desperately wish to be somewhere else.

He put on his glasses and saw that Hopkins was patiently watching him.

"Can you see now?"

"Yes."

"Then we may proceed," Hopkins said. "Ladies and gentlemen, look at October 1925. What essentially occurred this month, and most other months, is this. Funds come to my client or her mother Lucille Hardy. They are placed in the middle account 5555. Funds come to Chamberlin and his daughters. They go right into 2232, 1258, or 1278. Now a bill comes for the Chamberlins. It is paid out of 5555 or even 0709. In other words, the bills are paid out the holding account or my client's personal account."

Hopkins shot a glance over to Brubaker. "In short, my client is paying for most of *your* client's expenses."

Post glanced up from his copy. "It does seem to be that way."

"I have no knowledge of this," Brubaker announced. "It must have been a one-time occasion when funds were low."

"It happens every month," Hopkins countered. "We can dip into the wheelbarrow for another."

He turned to address the court. "Trace the harvest money," he said. "It comes in October tenth. It is deposited into 2232, Chamberlin's personal account. Then comes a bill for fence repair. Funds are moved out of 5555 and deposited into 0709."

Ann observed this with a mixture of anger and glee: anger that this had happened and glee that Chamberlin's chicanery was finally being exposed. No wonder Van Burin avoided sending her copies of the bank statements.

"I have to object, Your Honor," Brubaker said, adopting his sober mien. "This was obtained without our knowledge."

"I'm not condemning anybody," Hopkins said matter-of-factly. "No funds were stolen. I'm not accusing anyone. Just acquainting myself with the workings of the bank."

"Overruled," Post said. "The witness is president of the bank. He had to be aware of something."

Hopkins pointed to the top of the paper. "Will you read the name on the account?"

"Ann Harmon," Van Burin said tentatively.

"Can you describe for us the ebb and flow of funds for this particular month?"

"I object, Your Honor," Brubaker said. "This information is being obtained under duress."

"I caution you, Mr. Hopkins," Post said.

"I understand, Your Honor," Hopkins replied. "As I said, I'm not making accusations. The funds are all accounted for. I'm interested in the way the funds were moved around."

Van Burin appeared to be crouching in his seat.

"What account paid for the bills that month?" Hopkins asked.

"It looks like the holding account, 5555."

"And what account funded the holding account?"

"I'd have to look carefully."

"Take your time," Hopkins said gently. "You did it every month."

Van Burin jerked his eyes up from the paper, a desperate look on his face. "Why are you talking to me this way?" he wailed. "You're just trying to trip me up here!"

"Just gathering information."

"All right. It's just a method for cash flow that we devised."

"We?"

"At the bank. The way we do things at the bank."

"And the account number?"

"It's 0709."

"Ann Harmon's account."

Louder murmurs and whispers came from the spectators. Ann knew this cross-examination was starting to have an effect. Hopkins stepped over to the table and picked up a letter. He handed it to Van Burin.

"This is a bill from Mr. Brubaker for services rendered. Which account paid for those services?"

"Mr. Brubaker is the attorney for the estate," Van Burin protested. "Aren't we going to focus on Lucille Hardy's will? That's what you're suing about."

"We'll get to the will later. Right now, I want to talk about this. Whose account paid for Mr. Brubaker's services?"

"I object, Your Honor," Brubaker said. "How my bills are paid has no bearing on the plaintiff's complaint. And I further caution my learned colleague that his tactics and innuendos have no place in the legal community. Mr. Hopkins, the town is watching you."

"Sustained."

"How this bill was paid has a large bearing on this case," Hopkins replied. "And if the town is watching us, maybe that's a good thing." He held out the paper to Van Burin. "Was Ann Harmon billed for any of these services?"

"I object, Your Honor."

"Sustained."

"Was Ann Harmon billed for any of the preparation work for this trial?"

"I object, Your Honor."

"Sustained."

"Was the bill sent to Ann Harmon's account?"

"I object, Your Honor."

"Sustained."

Hopkins paused. "We have a bill here. Where did it go, Mr. Van Burin?"

"I...I don't recall...A lot of bills are paid by the bank."

"Such as this one here. The bill *was* paid, wasn't it?"

"I object, Your Honor."

"I can see why my learned colleague is objecting, Your Honor. He doesn't want the town to know who's paying his legal fees."

"All right," Van Burin said. "Ann Harmon."

"Excuse me?" Hopkins queried.

"Ann Harmon...Ann Harmon paid for this. The funds went from 0709 to 5555 and then in a check to Mr. Brubaker."

"Then, theoretically, she could be paying for the cost of the entire trial."

"Once again, I must object," Brubaker declared.

"She's paying to sue herself and to countersue as well."

"No, no." Van Burin moaned. "It's not that..."

There were more whispers all around, and then someone shouted from the back of the room, "Goddamn banker!"

"Don't say that. Don't say that," Van Burin cried.

Chamberlin spun around in his chair. With a murderous glare, he was staring down the rows behind him.

"Who said that?" he snarled. "Which one of you?...If I find out who it was..."

Post banged his gavel. "Order. Order."

"Settle down!" Dierkes shouted. "Quiet!"

The murmurs quieted down until the only sound was the noise of a passing car. Chamberlin slowly sat down.

Post turned his focus on the one person he could conveniently blame. "Mr. Hopkins, I warn you. If you turn this courtroom into a shambles, I shall fine you."

"It won't happen again, Your Honor," Hopkins said. He turned back to the squirming banker.

"In conclusion, might we not say that Ann Harmon is not only paying for the cost of this trial, but also financially supporting the defendants?"

"I object, Your Honor," Brubaker said. "Support cannot be assigned until ownership is proven. I move that remark be stricken from the record."

"Objection sustained," Post replied. "The jury is instructed to strike that remark."

"Your Honor, I move that all of Patrick Van Burin's testimony be stricken from the record. In fact, I move that all of the plaintiff's evidence be stricken. The defense has not had time to view it and prepare an adequate response or rebuttal."

"That's not exactly true, Your Honor," Hopkins countered. "The defense is quite familiar with all the evidence. He's been sitting on it for years. We're the ones who've had to play catch-up."

"The man has a point," Post said. "Mr. Brubaker, you have had the evidence far longer than your learned colleague. It is certainly not new to you. Overruled."

Chamberlin leaned toward Brubaker another time "You better find a way to stop him."

"Don't worry, Royce," Brubaker answered. "We're covered. Every move he makes, we've got him with an objection."

"It's what he squeezes in between that I don't like."

Hopkins stood beside Van Burin with another paper in his hand. The banker was leaning as far away from Hopkins as he could.

"Mr. Van Burin, I have here a receipt for a hundred bushels of corn. Where did those funds go?"

"I don't know what you mean."

"You have your glasses. The funds from this sale did not go into any of the accounts on our diagram."

"I can assure the court that they did."

"The funds for that transaction went into an account we have not seen before: 8890-45-3939."

Van Burin blanched.

"Look at the paper, Mr. Van Burin."

"Objection."

"Sustained."

"On what grounds, Your Honor?" Hopkins asked.

"For badgering the witness."

"All right." His eyes returned to the quivering Van Burin. "I won't badger the witness."

Hopkins paused. "This is *your* account, isn't it?"

"Objection."

"Sustained."

"Whose account is it?"

"Objection."

"Sustained."

Hopkins decided that Post was one of the most erratic judges he had ever seen. One minute he seemed open-minded to both sides, the next he was plainly biased to the defense. But Hopkins was not about to give up. He waited. Then he turned to the courtroom and held up the paper.

"We have here an account where the proceeds from a sale seem to have been deposited erroneously. I say erroneously because no one in the room seems to want to claim it. It's a simple piece of paper with an account number and a name on it."

He replaced it in front of Van Burin. "Can you at least read the name of the bank?"

"Objection."

"On what grounds this time?" Hopkins asked.

Brubaker seemed incredulous. "On what grounds?"

"You're the one who's objecting all the time. What is it now? A few minutes ago, someone out there yelled, 'Goddamn banker.' For Mr. Van Burin's peace of mind, I hope we can settle this before it happens again. Don't you want the court to know that it is Patrick Van Burin's personal account?"

"I warn you, sir," Post declared. "I shall hold you in contempt of court."

"Mr. Van Burin?"

"Yes. Yes, it's my account," Van Burin said. "It's my account."

Murmuring resumed around the room. Banks were not held in high esteem right now. No matter what one thought of Ann or Royce, Hopkins had found a figure of derision on which everyone could agree.

"And how did it end up in your account?"

"Objection."

"I'll answer. I'll answer," Van Burin cried. "Anything. Anything to stop this."

"Patrick, you don't have to," Brubaker cautioned.

"I'm tired of this. I'm so tired of this," Van Burin moaned. "I did the best I could. It wasn't supposed to be..." His voice trailed off. Realizing that everyone's eyes were on him, he attempted to recapture his professional dignity.

"It was my payment for managing the funds for the estate. Royce arranged it so we all could share in the harvest."

"It doesn't look like you shared any of that harvest."

"I don't care what it looks like. It's the way it was."

"Mr. Van Burin, you've accumulated a sizable fortune in the stock market, haven't you?"

"Objection."

"Sustained."

"And all this good fortune occurred after Royce Chamberlin moved you out of your office at the bank."

"Objection."

"Sustained."

"And all of your money has been invested in Pheasant Valley Power and Electric."

"What if it was?" Van Burin moaned. "I've been fortunate. That shouldn't be held against me."

"Objection, Your Honor," Brubaker said. "I move the witness be excused..."

"No," Van Burin said. "I know what I'm saying. I just wish this grilling was over. I'm not made for this..."

"Patrick..."

"I'm going to answer. I'm not ashamed of my good fortune. I'm not a goddamn banker any more than you're a goddamn lawyer, Fred..."

"Of course you're not..."

"I'm a hard working businessman. I have nothing to hide. I'm a citizen here like everyone else. Like everyone in this room."

"Yes," Hopkins said. "A fellow citizen. Hardworking. And in addition, you were Ann Harmon's appointed guardian, were you not?"

"I was."

He leaned close to Van Burin, looking him directly in the eye. "What's the matter with you?"

"What?"

"Your witness," Hopkins said to Brubaker.

"Mr. Brubaker, you wish to cross-examine?" Post inquired.

"Yes, Your Honor," Brubaker said. He was moving across to the witness chair. Van Burin seemed both dazed and relieved.

"Mr. Van Burin, a lot of activities have been implied here over the past several minutes."

"Yes."

"If it were in your power, as a banker, to repair any errors or damages made by the bank, would you do it?"

"Of course I would."

"And in your professional capacity as a banker, have you always been willing to make reparations for any errors or misunderstandings if the occasion ever arose?"

"I have. I always have. My intentions have always been honorable."

"Thank you," Brubaker said.

"The witness may step down," Post said.

Van Burin left the witness stand. When he found his seat in the courtroom, he crouched, looking at the floor, trying to avoid any eye contact with those around him.

"Good intentions," Ann thought, "They don't erase a damn thing."

Post banged his gavel.

"Court's adjourned till two p.m. this afternoon."

62

Fortunately for everyone, the temperature was no hotter in the afternoon than in the morning. All of the windows were open. In addition to the overhead fans, Sheriff Dierkes had brought in four smaller fans from other rooms in the courthouse and positioned them in various places around the room, hoping their air current would do some good. The easel and the poster had been removed, but their earlier presence had made an impression.

"Everybody is present," Judge Post announced. "We may now continue, but before we go further, would both counsels approach the bench?"

Hopkins and Brubaker appeared in the area below Judge Post.

"I've been doing some deliberating in chambers," Post began. "And I've decided to make a change in the proceedings for the trial. I felt that with our last witness, the defense was not allowed to present his side adequately. Consequently, since there is a countersuit, we will go with that imputation and allow the defense to lead off in the cross-examinations."

"That would be fair, Your Honor," Brubaker said.

"I feel that in doing this, both sides will have a chance to present their cases in an open forum. Any objections?"

Brubaker was smiling. "I have none. It takes the pressure off my learned colleague here. We accept graciously."

Hopkins smiled back at them. The ruling was an advantage for the home team. They were trying to hide it with an overlay of folksiness.

"I don't hear anything from you," Post said to Hopkins.

"It doesn't matter to me, Your Honor." Hopkins answered. "Just so I have a crack at them afterward."

Ann began to wonder if she were not seeing a glimpse of the future, a point where human evolution was separating into two paths, a high road and a lower one. She wondered if the lawyers in the remainder of this century would be like

Thaddeus Hopkins: the way a lawyer ought to be—someone who could not be deterred, who would fight tenaciously for his client no matter what the odds or where the location, who could not be bribed or bought off, and who would carry the fight all the way to the end. Or would future lawyers be like Fred Brubaker? An ethically muddled individual who would sell out his client if he received a higher offer. Would men be like Ben or Tom Dierkes or her grandpa? Or would the prototype of the twentieth-century man devolve into something like Warren Hyatt, a spineless individual whose response to pressure or a coming conflict was not a battle cry but a whine? Was she watching the end of an era and the beginning of something worse?

Hopkins returned to his place beside her and Ben.

"Next witness," Post said.

"What happened?" Ben asked.

"They didn't like the way we handled Van Burin."

"I'd like to call James Noble to the stand," Brubaker announced.

A thin, middle-aged man with a flowing moustache crossed to the witness stand. He was clad in a blue suit, which gave the impression that he was an authority of some kind.

"Raise your right hand," Dierkes said.

"He's their typewriter man," Hopkins said.

"State your name, please," Brubaker said.

"James Noble."

"Mr. Noble, you are an authority on mechanical dactylographics, are you not?"

"Yes," Noble said. "I have some knowledge of the workings of typewriter inscription."

"In other words, you can tell the difference between the letters or marks of various typewriters—even when, to the layman, the print looks the same."

"Yes."

"Could you elaborate?"

"It's a little like footprints. In some ways... in the basic ways, they are the same. The letters of the alphabet are the same. But, on closer examination, each typed letter is different. Each machine is different. It's the minute details that show us the difference."

Brubaker handed Noble four sheets of paper.

"We have presented you here with some samples of various typewriter fonts, including the copy that Ann Harmon claims was used to change her mother's will."

"I have seen them. Yes."

"Could you tell us about them?"

"I can. They are all typed on the same machine."

"Could you swear to it?"

"Most definitely. Mr. Chamberlin's typewriter has what we call in the industry a 'sticky finger.' This means that no typing differences are consistent. If you type a correspondence one time and then type a copy of the same correspondence, the flaws in the first will not be identical to the flaws in the second."

"What causes that?"

"Faulty labor at the factory is usually the cause."

"Could you tell us about Lucille Hardy's will?"

"Yes," Noble answered. "It could be argued that the will *was* changed. But who can say when? Mr. Chamberlin says that Lucille Hardy came to him a year ago and made the changes."

"But…?"

"Objection," Hopkins said from the table. "Leading the witness."

"Overruled," Post declared.

"There are not enough distinctions between these samples to determine when Mr. Chamberlin's typewriter made the changes."

"And how long did it take you to arrive at this conclusion?"

"A week. Two weeks. There is a typewriter out at Carson Manor—one used by the Carson family. It's quite similar to the one used in Royce Chamberlin's office. Sticky fingers. Both of them."

"Then you could swear that it is impossible to ascertain if the typewriter in Royce Chamberlin's office was used to change the will at all?"

"I could. And I could also swear that it is impossible to ascertain whether the will had been changed in the first place."

"Thank you, Mr. Noble. Your witness."

Ann watched Brubaker return to his seat with a smug expression.

"Mr. Noble," Hopkins said, "you have told us that the sticky finger phenomenon makes it impossible to ascertain anything about any typewriter print?"

"Only certain machines that are afflicted by the phenomenon," Noble stated.

"How do you know which ones are afflicted and which ones are not?"

"Through constant study. Vigilance. And humble expertise."

"What is humble expertise?"

Noble smiled. "Knowing that you're good at something…and not having to brag about it."

"It still amounts to guesswork, doesn't it?"

"Guesswork through experience," Noble retorted.

"Here is a copy of the will Lucille Hardy signed a year before her death. It was signed and notarized in Mr. Brubaker's office on October first, and you can see the beneficiary."

"It says, 'To my daughter Ann.'"

"Objection, Your Honor," Brubaker said. "What Lucille intended a year before her death has no bearing on her final decision."

"Sustained."

"Here is the updated will. The one that my client says was changed. It is also signed and notarized. What is the date on that?"

"It says July fifth."

"From July fourth onward, Lucille Hardy was bedridden here at the hospital with severe injuries. She was unable to sign anything."

"I object, Your Honor."

"Sustained."

"In addition, there was no available typewriter at the hospital. It had been sent to Omaha on July first for repairs, and it didn't get back until the seventh."

"I object, Your Honor. This is hearsay."

"We have the shipping order signed by William Dobbs at the station."

Sherman stepped over to Hopkins with a piece of paper. Hopkins passed it to Brubaker, who glanced at it and placed it on his table.

"That's all," Hopkins said. "Thank you, Mr. Noble."

Post banged his gavel. "Court's adjourned till ten o'clock tomorrow morning."

63

The Fifth Day of the Trial

The next three days of the trial were spent hearing the testimony of many of the individuals who had signed the countersuit against Ann. As predicted, the majority did not appear to have had much contact with either Ann or any of her family.

The courtroom remained packed on these days as well, more from the interest in seeing friends or neighbors on the stand than hearing what they had to say. For Hopkins, it was to introduce a pattern in the testimony—the similarity of the responses each witness gave when asked why he or she signed the countersuit. Somewhere during the cross-examination, almost every person recited a variation of the following words. "The colonel was a man of vision. A vision for the harvest and a vision for the land. The colonel had that vision. Royce Chamberlin has it, too." By early afternoon of the fourth day, they had finished.

Over the weekend, Ann and Ben stayed near the Journeyman and took an occasional walk around town. On Saturday night, they had a dinner and strategy session with Hopkins, Joel, and Sherman. Deirdre was in Kansas City, interviewing a character witness they might use against Royce Chamberlin.

During these meetings and during the trial, Ann managed to learn something from the way Hopkins was conducting the case, especially the way he prepared, his methods of cross-examination, and how he handled objections from opposing counsel. It confirmed what she already knew—there was far more to being a lawyer than learning what was in law books.

By early afternoon of Monday, July 29, everyone was back in place in the courtroom.

"Call the next witness," Post announced.

"I'd like to call Tarvin Balch," Brubaker said.

Balch, a scruffy-faced individual, crossed to the stand. Ann thought he seemed grim and tight, as if he wanted to spit out his testimony as quickly as possible and leave as fast as he could.

Brubaker began. "Mr. Balch, you work for Iowa Power and Electric, do you not?"

"I do."

"And for the record, that has nothing to do with Pheasant Valley to the north."

"No."

"And in what capacity are you employed?"

"I'm the local representative for Franklin County. Sometimes I'm a field worker."

Ben leaned over to Ann. "You know him?"

"I'm not sure."

As Ann listened, she thought she could place Balch from sometime in the past. She couldn't remember when or where. One thing was certain: he avoided looking anywhere near Ann's table. In fact, he was doing his best not to focus on any of the assembly in front of him.

Ann began to feel sorry for him. He was a Chamberlin witness, but his heart wasn't in it.

"And you've been out to the manor house several times over the years for work, have you not?"

"Yeah." The reply was emotionless and noncommittal.

"Could you tell us the nature of the work?" Brubaker asked.

"Whatever needs to be done."

"Surely you can elaborate for us."

"I do whatever work needs to be done," Balch said curtly.

"I was right. He doesn't want to be up there," Ann thought.

"Four years ago you witnessed an event out at Carson Manor. Could you share it with the court?"

"Yeah. Yeah, I was at the manor."

"Do you remember the day?" Brubaker prodded.

"It was July fifth, five years ago. July fifth, 1924."

"What did you see, Mr. Balch?"

"Mister, I'm not comfortable talkin' about this," Balch said.

"And we're not comfortable bringing it up," Brubaker answered. "But it has to be said. What did you see?"

Balch stared at the floor.

"Start at the beginning."

Balch was about to speak, but stopped.

"You were summoned by subpoena, Mr. Balch," Brubaker said. "You're here to tell us what you saw."

By now Ann suspected what this was about. July 5 was the morning her mother died. Ann had stayed away from Carson Manor until after dinner. In the early evening, she had the altercation with Carol in the gatehouse.

Balch took a breath. "It was four thirty in the afternoon. I was at the gatehouse. The wiring near the window needed to be replaced because it gets frayed all the time. There are only two windows in the gatehouse."

"And what did you see?"

"I saw Ann Harmon strike Carol Chamberlin."

There were gasps from behind Ann.

"Could you tell us more?" Brubaker invited.

"She was trying to comfort Miss Ann in her grief," Balch said in a monotone. "Her mother'd just died, you know. She'd just lost her mother. Carol was trying to comfort her."

Ann could have sworn she heard a derisive chuckle from somewhere behind her. Carol wasn't the type to offer comfort to anyone.

"You're saying Ann Harmon struck her?"

"Yeah."

"And then what happened?" Brubaker continued.

"I don't remember."

"You did earlier."

Another breath. The whole testimony seemed to stick in his throat. "OK, she walked over and kicked Carol."

"I see," Brubaker said solemnly. "Did you try to help Carol?"

At this point, Balch's eyes found Ann's. He was both scared and ashamed. Whatever compassion Ann may have felt was evaporating. He was up there lying, and no amount of hesitation on his part could change that. Still, he was being squeezed in front of the whole town.

"I was too surprised," Balch said.

"What else happened?" Brubaker asked

Ben leaned over to Ann. "They're pulling it out like a tooth."

"Look, Mister," Balch said. "I told you what I saw."

"You're not finished," Brubaker said.

"Miss Ann told Carol that she was going to do it again if she didn't watch out."

Ann glanced over at Carol. The Chamberlin girl was sitting upright in her seat. With her chin up and a triumphant smile, her appearance suggested an outraged penguin. Obviously, the whole testimony had been fabricated from what Carol had told them. Carol must have been planning this a long time.

"And you saw and heard all this very clearly?" Brubaker asked.

"Yeah, I did."

"Your witness," Brubaker said.

Hopkins crossed to the witness chair. "An interesting story," he began. "You say this took place at four thirty p.m.?"

"Yeah."

"The fact is, at four thirty p. m. on that day, Mrs. Harmon was about to have dinner with Judy Spell and her family. They will testify to that. Mrs. Harmon didn't arrive at Carson Manor until seven thirty."

"Your Honor, I object," Brubaker said.

"Overruled."

"And Mrs. Harmon can testify that Carol struck her several times on occasion over the past ten years."

"I didn't know that," Balch said. "I could have got the time wrong."

Hopkins assumed a gentler tone. "We know you're under oath here. And if what you said is true, then you have nothing to worry about."

"I said what I said," Balch said.

"You don't look too comfortable about it. You were subpoenaed. You didn't come voluntarily."

"That's right."

"Were you promised something for coming in and giving testimony?"

"Objection," Brubaker said.

"Sustained," Post said.

"Were you threatened with something if you didn't come?"

"Objection."

"Sustained. Mr. Hopkins, we'll have none of that."

"Sorry, Your Honor," Hopkins said.

Ann was watching Balch's face. Hopkins's questions had touched a nerve.

Hopkins returned to Balch. "A few questions about your job. You're in a position to know about the electrical output of many of the houses in Winfield as well as the billing procedures for each residence in town."

Ann was puzzled. When Hopkins touched on the subject of billing, Balch tensed up again. He was afraid, but now he seemed mournful, even regretful.

"Your Honor, may we ask where this is going?" Brubaker inquired.

"Make your point, Mr. Hopkins," Post said.

"In some cases, you supervise the setting up of electric service at individual houses in Winfield."

"I do, or I did."

"I want to talk for a minute about the manor house and the gatehouse." Hopkins held up two papers. "I have here the electric bills for Royce Chamberlin and Ann Harmon, or for the court records, the manor house and the gatehouse."

"They're billed to two different places," Balch said.

"We'll get to that," Hopkins answered.

Brubaker leaned toward Chamberlin. "What is this, Royce?"

"They're grabbing at straws," Chamberlin answered.

"I'm asking you to have a look at them," Hopkins said, handing the sheets to Balch. "According to these bills, the manor house is charged twenty dollars a month—the bill that is paid by Mr. Chamberlin's account. And then we have the gatehouse, which is charged two hundred dollars a month—the bill that is paid by Ann Harmon's account. This happened during the years when Ann Harmon was away at school."

Balch looked up from the bill with a startled expression. "You mean nobody was living there? All that time?"

"I object, Your Honor," Brubaker declared.

"Bear with us, Your Honor," Hopkins countered. "I am trying to ascertain if my client owes any money to the Carson estate."

Even though Hopkins's tone had been polite, Post recognized the statement's underlying sarcasm. He was about to say "sustained," but he stopped.

"Go ahead then," Post stated.

Hopkins turned back to his witness. "Either this is a clerical error, or it's something else."

"It's no clerical error," Balch said.

"And it's been going on for the past five years."

"I didn't think it would go that long," Balch said sadly.

Hopkins paused. "Would you care to tell us how this all got started?"

"Objection."

"Overruled."

Balch was clutching the arms of the chair. He was ready to speak, but once again, the words weren't there.

"Do the names Bidwell and Bartman mean anything to you?"

Balch seemed to let out a sigh of relief. "Yeah," he said. "I know 'em."

"Tell us what happened on October fifth, 1924."

Balch gathered some energy and sat up. "There were three of us: me, Bidwell, and Bartman."

"For the record, this is not Reverend Clarence Bidwell, the clergyman."

"No. It's the brother, Kenton Bidwell, the posthole digger."

"And you three were out at the Carson estate on that day. On October fifth, did you not rewire the Carson estate, so the manor house electricity would pass through the gatehouse? That way the gatehouse would pay for most of the electricity out there."

"I object, Your Honor," Brubaker said. "You didn't tell me about this," he whispered to Royce.

"Sustained."

Hopkins pressed forward. "And did you not do this on Royce Chamberlin's orders? You, Bidwell, and Bartman?"

Brubaker was aghast. "Why did you do this? What were you thinking?" he said to Royce.

"Who have both signed affidavits to that effect—"

"I object, Your Honor," Brubaker declared.

"Of course you'll object," Hopkins said to Brubaker. "It makes your client look like the cheapskate of all time."

"Order," Post stated loudly. "I will not have cross talk between counsels."

"Did you not do this on Royce Chamberlin's orders?" Hopkins repeated.

"We did. But we didn't know what it was till we got there," Balch answered. "That day we went out there to do a job."

"Objection!" Brubaker cried. "This has no bearing on the case. This was enacted almost five years ago. We were different people. It has no bearing on who we are now."

"The bill hasn't changed," Hopkins stated.

"Please, Your Honor. I gotta finish this," Balch implored. "They got me up here, and I gotta say it. It's been hanging on me for years."

"Continue," Post said.

"We got out there. We saw what we were being asked to do."

More chuckles from the room.

"I know it may seem funny to you, but it's not," Balch said. "Not when you think about it. We saw what it was. Forcing the electricity of a mansion through a one-room shack. We didn't want to do the job. The whole thing was wrong. I said to Mr. Chamberlin over there, 'Why are we doing this?' And he said, 'Why do you care? You value your jobs, don't you?'"

"Objection. I object, Your Honor."

"So we did it. He said it would ease expenses for him and the girls. I don't know why. They're rolling in money out there."

"Mr. Balch, confine yourself to answering the questions," Post cautioned.

Balch shifted in his seat to face Ann. "It's always been bothering me, Miss Ann. I'm a workman. I pride myself on what I do. But not this time. You were always good to my youngest, Susie, when you were in school together. I haven't forgotten that. But this has been bothering me. In fact, I'm ashamed, Miss Ann."

Balch was staring up at Post from the witness chair. "Your Honor, Miss Ann doesn't deserve this."

"Your Honor," Brubaker cried, "I move we strike this part of the testimony…"

"Yeah, yeah, go ahead and strike it," Balch fired back. "I'm not proud of what we did. I wish we could undo it. Those crackling wires are a damn fire hazard."

"I move that this man's entire testimony…"

Suddenly, Balch's eyes were on Chamberlin. "And about Miss Ann hitting Carol, I could be wrong, you hear me, Mr. Royce? I could be wrong!"

The hum began to rise all around the courtroom.

"Hey, Royce! How do you keep warm out there?" someone shouted.

"Who pays your bills now, Royce?"

"Cheep! Cheep!"

There was a roar of laughter.

Chamberlin leaped to his feet, glaring at the rows of faces.

"Who said that?" he shouted. "Stand up so I can see you! Stand up back there!"

Post was banging his gavel. "Order! Order!"

"Quiet!" Dierkes shouted. "Everybody settle down!"

The hum quickly died out. Chamberlin took his seat.

"Any further question, Mr. Hopkins?" Post inquired.

"No, Your Honor," Hopkins answered.

"You may step down, Mr. Balch," Post said.

Balch left the witness stand and made his way for the exit. As he approached Ann and Ben, he looked down at her. The shame and embarrassment were there, but now he seemed relieved. Ann was still angry. She wanted to let him pass without comment, but she couldn't.

Ann reached out and touched his arm. "Thank you," she said.

64

THAT EVENING BEN, ANN, AND HOPKINS were having dinner at the Bluebird Café on Market Street. Their waitress, Celeste, a slim, blond woman, arrived at their table with three servings of fried chicken and baked potatoes.

"Many folks here don't realize it, but Ann's fight is a community fight," Celeste said. "Royce Chamberlin's had his hands in everything for too long. Everyone just sat back and took it. Ann here drew the line."

"How's your father doing?" Ann asked.

"He's doing fine—at least he is now. He got a job in Des Moines at a big lumberyard. It was touch and go after Royce got our land, but we're OK."

"I'm glad to hear it."

"Everybody out there seems to have gone crazy on the stock market," Celeste said. "At least with this job, he's gotten something solid. He can look at a board he's cut and say, 'That's going to build a house, not a dream somewhere.'"

The bell over the front door tinkled. A middle-aged couple arrived for dinner.

"We're keeping our fingers crossed for you," Celeste said, going over to greet them.

"Amazing," Ann said after she had left. "I never knew Celeste very well. Some people I never expected have turned out to be friends. Her, Betsy at the courthouse, Tarvin Balch."

"A trial can show you who your friends are," Hopkins said.

"I should remember that more often. It's easy to get cynical when you only count your enemies."

For the next few minutes they enjoyed their meal.

"What do you think of Judge Post?" Ben asked Hopkins.

"A major irritation," Ann said.

"He's on the fence," Hopkins said. "He favors the home team, but he can't refute what he's hearing."

"His wife's sick," Ann said. "That has to be weighing on him."

Hopkins took a sip of coffee. "Possibly. He's not an evenhanded jurist. In fact, some days he's downright erratic. If this were the big city and he had a family emergency, he could probably recuse himself. Unfortunately, we're stuck with him."

"We sure are," Ann said.

"You know, I was almost appointed a judge, but I turned it down," Hopkins said.

"Why? You'd make a good judge," Ben said.

"I can do better as a lawyer. Out here, I'm a free agent. There's something about the judiciary that challenges a person's character. Every judge starts out as a lawyer. Then he's appointed to the bench. Some of them become good judges. But others? All that power can change a person. It can go to his head. He forgets what made him want to become a lawyer in the first place."

"You've just described Fred Brubaker," Ann said.

"Let me ask you something. You said you want to become a lawyer."

"I do."

"Why?"

"It started with my family situation, and it just grew," Ann said. "For ten years I've been asking myself, 'How can I fight Royce? My family's not doing anything.' There was no one around. No one to lift a hand. Then I began to think, 'If it boiled down to me, what could I do?' Somewhere along the line, it changed from 'What could I do?' to 'What would I do?' to 'I'm going to do it.' And it hasn't changed."

"Solid reason," Hopkins said pensively.

"Ann gets her inspiration from Arabella Mansfield," Ben said.

"Mansfield's a pioneer. Just remember: she passed the bar, but she never took on a case," Hopkins said.

"She could have," Ann said.

Hopkins saw Ann's determination. "How do you plan to start?"

"School. Definitely school," Ann said. "I know that some people study for the bar and pass it without going to law school, like getting a mail order diploma. I don't want that. I want school."

"We've been looking into Portia School of Law," Ben said.

"Boston. A good school. But it's women only," Hopkins said.

"We've talked about that," Ann said.

"As soon as we're done here, I suppose we'll live in Boston for a while," Ben added.

"These are tough times. What about your work, Ben?" Hopkins asked.

"A friend from college has a job with Boston Mutual. He said he could take me on if we decided to make the move. Plus, there's always the piano."

"You've both done some thinking," Hopkins said.

"She really wants this," Ben said.

"Well, when you're ready to make your application, contact me. Maybe I can put in a word for you."

"Thank you. Thanks very much," Ann said, touched by the offer. It was another unexpected kindness.

"If you're going to come in, please close the door."

Celeste was speaking to Doss Claypool, who had entered halfway and stopped in the doorway to watch Ann's table.

The Woodchuck ambled over.

"Excuse me, Miss Ann, Mr. Harmon…Mr. Royce and Fred Brubaker are over at the bank. They'd like a word with you and your attorney."

"Did they say why they want to see us?" Hopkins inquired.

"Well now, I didn't ask."

"If they want to see us, why don't they come here?" Ann said.

"You know them better than that." Claypool leered. "Around here they do the askin'."

The three continued to eat their dinners.

"Now, you folks do what you want. Finish your food for all I care," Doss declared. "I'm just sayin' they're waitin' at the bank."

"Tell them we'll be over," Hopkins said.

"And when'll that be?"

"When we've finished our dinner," Ann said.

"All right, all right," Claypool mumbled. "I'll go to the bank. Tell 'em Old Dawz ran the message."

Claypool was across the room and out the door.

"What do you figure that's about?" Ann asked.

"They're going to offer us a deal," Hopkins said.

"A sign we're winning?" Ben said.

"Let's just say we're having an effect on them."

Twenty minutes later, Ann, Ben, and Hopkins were on their way up Market Street to the bank. It was early evening. The sun had set, but the town was still visible. To Ann, the street seemed shorter now. When she'd made the trip by wagon with Lucille or Lady Ann, it always seemed like a journey from one end to the other, passing the various businesses one by one. Now it was a simple three blocks.

She was reflecting on this when she heard the sound of an automobile engine. Up ahead, along Pomphrey Park, the Hudsen's car swayed and lurched across in front of them and disappeared in the dusk. Ann could not see who was driving or who was riding in the car. She hoped the Hudsens were on the way out of town.

The bank's front shades had been pulled. When they entered, there was only a lamp lit in the big office. The lobby was dark.

Claypool was crouched, silent and watchful, on the hardwood floor. Ann could barely make him out. It was as if he had run his errand and then been told to go sit in the corner.

Royce was seated in his plush armchair with Brubaker and Van Burin in folding chairs on either side of him. They were in a row like three grim gargoyles. In front of the desk were three chairs for the plaintiffs.

"Thank you for coming. I think we can get right to business," Brubaker began.

Ann listened, waiting for the hook.

"Ann, you and your attorney have put up a terrific fight," he announced grandly. "A magnificent argument for your case. I applaud you."

"What do you want, Fred?" Ann said.

"Oh, I'm back to Fred now. Well, we're certainly keeping it in the family."

"Not my family," Van Burin murmured. His cheeks were flushed. He looked like he had either been weeping or holding his breath.

Brubaker continued. "The point is, I think you're beginning to realize you'll never win this. A valiant effort, but you're lost. Why don't you give it up?"

"No," Ann said.

"Come again?"

"My wife said no," Ben said.

"But why? It's such a waste of time and money."

"No, it's not," Ann shot back. "According to the testimony, I'm paying for all of it."

"All the more reason now..."

"So I'll decide whether it's a waste...of time or money."

"Fred, they're not *receptive*," Chamberlin snapped.

Brubaker smiled. "All right, we're prepared to offer you a tidy sum to drop the case."

There it was—the hook.

"How much?" she asked.

"Thirty thousand dollars. We pay you thirty thousand dollars, and you drop the lawsuit. I think you should take it."

"No," Ann said.

Chamberlin's eyes were flickering in the lamplight. "I'd listen if I were you."

"You can go to hell, all of you," she said.

Brubaker feigned an expression of tolerant impatience. "You know, I've been thinking of Jack recently. He was more reasonable... more pliable. In fact, your father pretty much let anybody do anything to him, wouldn't you say?"

His words stung Ann, and she dug her fingernails into her hand.

"Come again?"

"I'm just saying that you're not like your father."

"You're damn right I'm not," Ann said angrily. "Now here are *my* terms. We continue with the trial."

"Until?" Brubaker asked.

"Until you relinquish what's mine and you walk."

"Give up what I own?" Chamberlin declared.

"Give up what you took." Ann glanced over to Brubaker with the same mocking expression. "I'm quite clear in my demands. Right, Fred?"

"And the demands are," Hopkins repeated, "give up the property you have left. It belongs to my client."

"No!" Chamberlin snarled. "No, I'll never do that. You can't come in here and rearrange the plans of a lifetime. The empire belongs to me. You try to take it, and I'll fight. This is our fight, Ann, and it always has been."

"They're not receptive," Ann said to Hopkins.

"You have our answer, gentlemen," Hopkins said to Brubaker. "See you in court."

They were standing up when Van Burin spoke out. His words came out in a sputter.

"Just a minute. Just a minute there."

"Patrick, no," Brubaker cautioned.

"I want to know about that blond woman. I know she works for you. She came in here... into this bank... into this room. She struck me, and she hurt my hand. See my hand?"

"It looks OK to me," Ann said innocently.

"I'm not giving up on this. She was Danish... and deranged. A deranged Dane. I know she works for you. She does work for you, doesn't she?"

"We can't help you," Ann answered.

"Good night, gentlemen," Hopkins said.

Ann, Ben, and Hopkins were out of the cave and on the street. Behind them, they heard Chamberlin shouting. Soon they were walking beside Pomphrey Park.

"Well, what do you think?" Ann asked Hopkins.

"We stay the course."

"I'm proud of you, Ann," Ben said.

"This is the first time I've ever seen Royce come close to being scared," Ann said.

"We're shaming him in front of the town. He doesn't like it," Hopkins said. "And it's going to get rougher. We stand our ground. They stand theirs. They play dirty. We respond. It continues until one side has had enough."

"Well then, we stay the course," Ann said.

"You two going to turn in?" Hopkins said.

"I'd like to take a little walk with Ben," Ann said.

"OK," Hopkins said. "Be careful. Remember what I said about it getting rougher."

"Will do," Ann said.

"See you at breakfast tomorrow," Hopkins said.

"Thank you again," Ann said.

"Good night," Hopkins said, starting back to the Journeyman.

Ann and Ben strolled hand in hand across the park. It seemed deserted until a horse and carriage appeared on the way to the station.

"I still love this town, in spite of everything," Ann said.

"It's peaceful," Ben agreed.

"It never changes. It's almost the same as the pictures Grandpa had of the place when Mama was a baby."

Two streetlights switched on. Here and there some crickets had begun their nighttime chirping.

"Let's take another walk down Market," Ann said.

They reached the edge of the park, started down the center of the street, and passed the bank. It was totally dark. Everyone had cleared out rapidly after the meeting. The only sounds were some voices down the street in the Bluebird Café.

They walked past the dress shop and hardware store and found themselves facing Kurt and Jago and Doss Claypool. The car was along the side of a building in the shadows. Claypool was fingering a broomstick that protruded from a barrel on the side of the hardware window.

"Hello, girlie," Kurt said affably.

"Good evening again, Lady Ann," the Woodchuck drawled. "You left the bank in such a hurry. Mr. Royce wanted you to think over his offer."

"Don't go runnin' off now, Mr. Harmonsens," Jago said.

"Watch it, Ben," Ann whispered.

"We didn't mean to scare you. Just talk," Kurt said.

"If you wanted to talk, why didn't you give us a call?" Ben said.

A slow, dull grin appeared on Kurt's face. "Well now, I don't have much use

for the telephone. We don't even have one out at the farm. If a man's got a problem, I like to work out our differences face-to-face."

"That means man-to-man, Mr. Harmonsens," Jago said loudly.

"So we talk," Ben said.

Ann saw that Ben was remaining quiet and polite. Claypool, on the other
hand, was watching eagerly, hoping the situation would escalate. And Jago was
going to be trouble.

"I don't think Jago likes you, *Mr.* Harmon," Doss drawled.

"I'll be brief," Kurt said. "It's true that Mr. Royce sent us. But me and my
boy, we got a good life here. We'd be happy if this trial stopped."

"That's not going to happen," Ann said.

"Now, that's just what I thought you'd say. We thought maybe you'd be reasonable."

"No, things stay as they are," Ben said.

"You ain't gonna reason with them," Claypool said. "They're big city. Use
words to talk their way out of tough spots all the time."

"That means they're yellow," Jago said. "You yellow, Mr. Harmonsens?"

"Sure he is. Plain yellow." Claypool sneered. "Run from a good fight. Say
things like brains over violence. Courtesy over force. Don't hit me; let's talk it
over."

"Mr. Harmonsens is yellow," Jago repeated.

"Words aren't gonna do it, Kurt," Claypool urged. "You can see that."

Ann saw where this was headed. There was no way to escape now. She looked
up and down the street for anyone who might help.

"We did ask politely," Kurt said. "You don't leave us much choice."

"Talk's over, Lady Ann," Claypool said.

"Bust him," Kurt said.

Jago went right for Ben.

"Get him!" Claypool cried.

Jago swung, but Ben blocked him. With one punch, Ben sent Jago reeling
backward.

Jago had recovered, but before Ben could move, Kurt hit him from behind.
Ben staggered forward. Kurt moved toward him, along with Claypool, who finally had found safety in numbers.

Ann was searching wildly about for something to use—anything to help
Ben. Spotting the broomstick, she raced forward and pulled it out of the barrel. On the bottom was a clump twisted bristles. Kurt laughed when he saw
her holding it. He thought she looked foolish. He was still laughing when she
rammed the bristles into his face. With a roar of pain, Kurt clutched his eyes.

Ann turned on Claypool and advanced on him, jabbing with the bristles.

By now Ben was on his feet. Jago struck him once, knocking him against the wall. His face bloodied, he moved for Ben. More angry than calculating, he simply wanted to inflict damage. Ben was fighting off every effort.

Footsteps sounded from the alley. It was Sheriff Dierkes and Clem, the deputy.

"All right! Hold it!" Dierkes yelled.

Doss saw Jago attacking Ben. Hoping the fight would continue, he tore the broomstick out of Ann's grasp, and, holding it crosswise, he moved to block Dierkes and Clem.

"Now, Sheriff, you don't want to get into this."

"Out of the way, Claypool."

Ignoring the warning, Doss strode toward them, his arm out to stop their approach. "Hey! Come on, Sheriff! Let 'em fight!"

As Dierkes emerged from the shadows, Ann caught a glimpse of his right hand. One second it was moving for his gun, and the next the gun was out of the holster. Dierkes brought the barrel down on Claypool's head. The Woodchuck collapsed onto the pavement.

Jago made a last rush at Ben, who punched him three more times, knocking him flat.

"OK?" Dierkes asked Ann.

"Yes, thank you, Sheriff."

"Thanks, Sheriff," Ben said.

Kurt was over beside his son, who was sprawled on the ground.

"How'd you find us?" Kurt asked Clem.

"When you drive around in that big car and don't park, you sort of announce yourselves," Clem said.

"Kurt…You, Jago, and Claypool are under arrest," Dierkes announced. "You're spending the night in jail."

Kurt tensed up. "You're the law," he said under his breath.

Jago had already regained consciousness and was humiliated, bloodied, and enraged. "You ain't lockin' us up, Dierkes. It was Mr. Harmonsens."

"Sure it was. Three to one?" Clem said.

"You two help Claypool," Dierkes said to Kurt.

"I don't see you puttin' *them* in jail!" Jago shouted.

"Shut up, boy. That's the law talkin'," Kurt growled.

"I don't care whose law it is!"

"I do. Now shut up!"

Jago and Kurt each had an arm around Claypool. The Woodchuck was regaining consciousness.

"Let's go," Clem said.

Clem was shepherding the three up the street to Pomphrey Park and the courthouse.

"Thank you again, Sheriff," Ann said.

"You going back to the Journeyman?"

"Yes. Thank you again," Ben said.

They watched as Dierkes and the others arrived at the edge of the park and disappeared into the night.

65

The Sixth Day of the Trial

The following morning as she waited for the session to start, Ann wondered where the case stood. It was difficult to say who was ahead, but Hopkins was winning many of the verbal skirmishes. She saw Olga in the spectators' section. She had managed to come in from the county farm to sit on Ann's side of the room. At the other table, Royce was grim and glowering. Carol and Cassie retained their expressions of haughty indifference. For them, the trial was just an inconvenience.

Dierkes and Clem appeared at the back with the Hudsens. Jago was surly. Kurt, on the other hand, was serious and watchful.

Jago's mood quickly soured. Nobody was paying any attention to him. Cassie Chamberlin would not return his greeting. And now his father was being called to the witness stand.

"I'd like to call Kurt Hudsen," Hopkins said.

Kurt lumbered up to the witness chair. Dierkes swore him in.

"Mr. Hudsen," Hopkins began, "you're a resident of Winfield, are you not?"

"That's right."

"And what is your profession?" There were some chuckles from the spectators.

"I'll have it quiet in here," Post said.

"What do you *do*, Mr. Hudsen?"

"I'm a farmer," Kurt replied with his easygoing smile. "Some of the good people around here have other ideas."

"And why is that?"

"Objection."

"Sustained."

Hopkins paused. "You say you're a relative of my client."

"That's right. I'm her Uncle Kurt."

"But you're not really related to Ann Harmon."

"No, we're not really related."

"Then why do you say you are?"

Kurt sat back expansively in the chair. "Well, where I come from, East Oklahoma, everybody's somebody else's uncle or cousin. Just bein' neighborly."

The big man cast a confident look over to Jago.

"Now, you and your son live on Section Two of the Carson estate."

"That's right."

"For how long?"

"About eight years."

From his seat, Royce was listening with suspicion. He knew Hopkins would make some kind of surprise move. He remembered what had happened with Van Burin.

"Do you pay rent?" Hopkins asked Kurt.

"I object. Payment of rent is a private matter," Brubaker said.

"Your Honor," Hopkins countered, "I am trying to establish the financial connections between my client, Mr. Hudsen here, and Mr. Chamberlin."

"I don't see the problem, Mr. Brubaker," Post said.

"Do you pay rent?" Hopkins repeated.

"I pay rent," he said finally.

"How much?"

"I don't think it's anybody's business."

"But if you're getting a good deal, I'm sure the court would want to know."

Ann realized a talent she would have to develop later was how to withdraw emotionally from the conflict in a cross-examination. She saw its practicality. She had a temper, and she would vent it on any one of her enemies. If they were asking for it, she spoke up. Right now, Kurt was asking for it. Sitting up there, he was both folksy and smug. Her first inclination would be to ridicule him with some remarks before starting the questions, but Hopkins never did that. Instead, he focused his entire effort on extracting what he wanted to hear and nothing more. Personal feelings were held in check.

"Yeah, I can see they would," Kurt drawled. He shot a quick glance to the Chamberlin table. They were not offering any lifesaving objections.

"OK. Ten dollars a month," he said.

"What was that?"

"I said ten dollars a month."

There was another wave of snickers and chuckles. Kurt tried to spot the source of the merriment, but all he could see in front of him was a wall of serious expressions punctuated with the fluttering of fans. Whoever was mocking him was out of view.

Hopkins continued. "Ten dollars a month. That's one hundred twenty dollars a year. What do you do out there?"

"I told you, Mister."

"Could you tell us again?"

"I'm a...I'm a farmer."

A wave of laughter rippled across the courtroom. This time Kurt saw the smiles, the smirks, and the mocking expressions.

Ann turned around to see. Many of these people, she didn't know. They may not have been on her side, but they certainly weren't on Kurt's.

"Somebody laughin' at us?" Kurt asked jovially. "Why don't you let me in on the joke?"

"Order," Post said.

"All right, settle down," Dierkes echoed.

"Whoever you are laughin' out there," Kurt continued, "you wouldn't be laughin' so hard if you let me see you. That way it's me and you, face-to-face. You'd be all by your lonesome."

"That may have been so in the past, Mr. Hudsen," Hopkins said. "But right now it's you and them, face-to-face, right here."

Kurt shifted his weight in the seat, his homespun air barely concealing a threat. "You enjoyin' yourself?" he asked Hopkins.

"Excuse me?"

"Are you havin' *fun?*"

"It's my job," Hopkins replied. "On your farm, what do you raise out there?"

"Cattle. Some corn."

"That's interesting. I've been by your place twice. I didn't notice any livestock. Only your dogs."

"What about my dogs?" Kurt asked.

"Objection, Your Honor. Badgering the witness."

"You want to say something about my hounds?"

"That's enough, Mr. Hudsen," Post said.

"What about the bottles, Kurt?" called a voice from the spectator section, followed by another chorus of chuckles.

"Who said that?" Kurt roared. "Sounds like Caleb Brown to me!"

Jago sprang out of his seat "You shut up, Caleb Brown! You shut up!"

"Order! Order!" Post said loudly. "I know these proceedings can be stressful, but unless there is some kind of decorum, I will clear the courtroom for the duration of the trial."

"Jago, sit down," Dierkes said.

"It's always me, ain't it, Dierkes?"

"Sit down."

Jago took his seat.

"You do seem to have a collection of wagon parts, empty bottles, and boxes out there as well," Hopkins said.

"What can I tell you? Times are hard," Kurt said.

"And you don't have a telephone."

"I got no use for telephones."

"You don't like telephones."

"Nah. Telephone's the easy way out. You want to say somethin', you come see me."

"Then how do you explain the fact that Ann Harmon has been paying your phone bill?"

"Is that a fact now?" Kurt asked.

"In Mrs. Harmon's checking account, there is a monthly transfer of funds to Royce Chamberlin's account. A deposit of twenty dollars a month for the Hudsen telephone bill."

"I told you I don't have a telephone."

"It's been going on for six years."

"Objection," Brubaker said.

"Overruled," Post replied.

"Do you pay taxes on this property?" Hopkins inquired.

"No. I rent."

"What about your other taxes?"

"What about what other taxes?" Kurt retorted.

"Do you pay any taxes at all?"

"Objection."

"Overruled. The court would like to hear the answer."

"You don't pay any taxes, do you? Mr. Chamberlin pays them for you."

"Objection."

"They're paid by Mr. Chamberlin out of Ann Harmon's account. Same as your telephone bill."

By now the flow of whispers and murmurs was heard all over the room.

"Good deal there, Kurt!" cried someone in the back.

"Order," Post said again. "Mr. Hopkins, once again, you are treading very dangerously."

Ann wondered about Judge Post. It seemed like he still wanted to be on Royce's side, in spite of every new piece of incriminating evidence. "But at least the people are hearing it," she thought.

"What you do out there must keep you awfully busy," Hopkins said, crossing over to his table. He scooped up an envelope and returned to the witness chair. "Mr. Hudsen, I have here a letter from the State Board of Agriculture. It says you're about to be cited for letting the land go to seed."

Hopkins handed the letter to him. Kurt squinted.

"Hell, it's addressed to Royce Chamberlin," Kurt said.

"Objection," Brubaker said. "I'd like to know where my learned friend got a copy of that."

"Mr. Hopkins?" Post directed.

"From the State Board of Agriculture. They claim this is their third letter to you."

Brubaker was on his feet again. "I object, Your Honor. I request this part be stricken from the record. How Mr. Hudsen manages his property has no bearing on this case."

"It does if my client is paying his taxes," Hopkins replied.

By now Brubaker was in the center of the room, the words streaming out. "But you have to understand. Running an empire requires a lot of dedication and diversification of attention. The responsibility of each property forcibly demands every degree of concentration he possesses, and he gives it. By God, he gives it. But Mr. Chamberlin is only human. If he has a flaw, it's that his attentions are focused on so many things at once, he neglected to take care of one farm. *One* farm. And he has been notified. He'll get to the bottom of this. And he'll take care of it. I move we strike this portion of the testimony."

"Mr. Hopkins, make your point, or I'll have to sustain," Post said.

"Mr. Hudsen, my question is this," Hopkins said. "With all this privileged treatment you seem to be getting from Mr. Chamberlin, is there anything you do for him in return?"

"Royce Chamberlin's a good man," Kurt said.

"And he's a man of vision. Loves the land. And so responsible he pays another man's telephone bill. We've heard it before."

"I am losing my patience, Mr. Hopkins," Post cautioned

"I apologize, Your Honor," Hopkins said. "I hope to establish a link between this man's duties for Royce Chamberlin and an event that occurred at the Nelson farm eight years ago."

Post seemed to flinch. It wasn't a big movement, but it was enough to show Hopkins that something in those words had touched him. Ann knew that Hopkins had hit another bull's-eye.

"What are you talking about?" Post said.

"You're familiar with the event, Your Honor," Hopkins said.

"Of course. The accident. That's what the Nelsons told us," Post said.

Hopkins was facing the courtroom. "For the record, may we say that the Nelsons are third cousins to Rose Post, the wife of Your Honor here?"

"That's true. But why are we bringing it up?" Post said.

Brubaker leaned close to Chamberlin. "What's he talking about, Royce?"

"Never mind. Try to get Kurt out of there."

Post was still mystified. "They're distant cousins, but they're family. We haven't seen them as much as we'd liked since they moved. What does it have to do with Kurt Hudsen?"

"That's what we'd like to examine," Hopkins said.

"I object, Your Honor," Brubaker said. "That was eight years ago. We were all different people."

"I'll decide that," Post said.

Brubaker was on the move again. "We all know what happened. A tragic thing. A simple accident. Peter Nelson broke his arm. It became infected and had to be amputated. They couldn't make their harvest. They lost the farm."

"Is that what you were told, Your Honor?" Hopkins asked.

"They never talked much about it."

Hopkins scooped a letter from the table. "I'd like to introduce this as testimony."

"Your Honor, we know nothing of this," Brubaker interjected.

"May both counsels approach the bench while His Honor examines it?" Hopkins asked.

"Granted," Post said.

Both Brubaker and Hopkins headed to the bench.

Ben glanced over at Ann. She was getting the satisfaction of seeing another enemy held up before the town. "I shouldn't be liking this so much, but I do," she whispered to him. "It's like yanking up a floorboard and seeing the roaches scatter."

Post began to read the letter. "We should consider the possibility of a conflict of interest," Brubaker said.

"If it is, I'll take the necessary action," Post said.

"But Your Honor..."

"When I've finished, Mr. Brubaker."

"Is that Charlie Nelson's handwriting?" Hopkins asked Post.

"It is."

"May we introduce it as evidence?"

"Yes." Post handed the letter to Brubaker. Within seconds, Brubaker began to react.

"Your Honor. This is hearsay. Third party to say the least..."

"Is that an objection?"

"Yes."

"We'll wait. Mr. Hopkins was still addressing the court."

"May I have the document?" Hopkins said. Brubaker handed him the paper.

"This should refresh your memory, Mr. Hudsen," Hopkins said.

Hopkins began to read. "'It wasn't an accident like we first said. We were afraid. We owed money to Royce's bank. Kurt and Jago showed up that morning claiming we owed them money. Then they pretended they were helping us get ready for the harvest. Threw my son Peter under the wagon. Crippled his arm. Couldn't finish the harvest. We couldn't pay the bank. Lost the farm. They had to cut off Peter's arm. Didn't tell anybody because we feared what Royce Chamberlin might do to us. We're not afraid now."

Assorted whispers rustled around the room.

"Finally," Ann thought. "Finally, someone has come out and said it. Right out in the open. And it's the judge's family. I just hope Post gets off the fence."

"Once again, I object, Your Honor," Brubaker said. "This was dictated from emotion. It is not sworn testimony."

"Overruled," Post said. "I want to hear the witness."

"But Your Honor, there are two sides to every story."

"And we're going to hear one of them, Mr. Brubaker," Post declared. "Do I make myself clear?"

Hopkins moved closer to the chair. "Mr. Hudsen, Royce Chamberlin sent you out to Charlie Nelson's farm to collect a debt, did he not?"

"It was eight years ago. How the hell would I know?" Kurt growled.

"Your objective was to get possession of the farm for Chamberlin and the bank. You went there on the pretext of collecting a gambling debt."

"It was a long time ago…"

"So you asked Peter Nelson to pay. And when he and Charlie told you that they couldn't, you and your son proceeded to cripple Peter by rolling a wagon wheel over his arm."

"Objection."

"Overruled." Post leaned forward to get a full view of Kurt in the witness chair. "One way or another, we're going to have an answer."

"Don't tell him, Papa!" Jago shouted.

"Quiet!" Dierkes said.

"We are waiting, Mr. Hudsen," Post said.

Kurt squirmed. "I don't remember. It was a financial matter…a gambling debt between them and my son. I teach my boy that a man always lives up to his obligations. But as I say, I don't remember back that far."

"The Nelson family does. I have a signed affidavit," Hopkins said.

"All right. It was a financial matter."

"They didn't pay you then."

"No. They didn't pay me then. They couldn't. Too bad it worked out the way it did."

"For the record, you admit you were there."

Kurt sighed. "Yeah, I was there. It was an accident. Nobody meant to do anything. It got outta hand."

"So, having heard this, can we say that you are Mr. Chamberlin's bill collector?"

Kurt scowled. "No. Nobody can say that."

"If he wants somebody reasoned with or even removed, he sends you."

"I object," Brubaker cried. "Nobody said anything about removing people."

"That's right. That's a damn lie," Kurt bellowed in agreement.

"The Nelson family has already signed a complaint against you."

Brubaker was up from his table. "Your Honor, this development is as stunning to us as it is to you. I move this entire testimony be stricken, and further I request that we declare this a mistrial. A mistrial through no fault of your own."

Ann admitted that Brubaker was a wily legal opponent. He had lost his ethical values a long time ago, but he had sharpened his talent for spinning any argument out of the flimsiest of pretexts.

"You've done your best, Your Honor. A magnificent job. But hidden revelations create a conflict of interest. And in light of legal objectivity, I request we call it a day."

"That's what I thought you'd say," Post said tersely. "And I can fully understand your reasoning."

Hopkins, too, was up. "Your Honor, I agree that this was an unusual revelation, but it shows the degree of corruption that has found its way into Winfield and Franklin County. Most of the witnesses we have seen have either been perpetrators or victims. And I warrant many of the spectators in this room have been affected as well."

The courtroom was hushed.

Hopkins continued. "Have there been other incidents like the one at the Nelson farm? I would warrant that there have. Looking around, I would say it's time for Winfield to stand up for itself."

"That is a discussion for another time, Mr. Hopkins," Post said. "Do you have any further questions?"

"I do," Hopkins answered. He was facing Kurt in the witness chair. "Mr. Hudsen, before you came here, you used to work in Kansas City."

"I worked a lot of places."

"One of them was the Rose/Fentress warehouse. You worked as a watchman at the same warehouse where Royce Chamberlin was partners with Daniel Rose."

"It could have been."

Ann saw Chamberlin motion Brubaker closer to him to whisper some instructions. This was an area Chamberlin did not want discussed.

"That was where Delmond Rose had his accident. He came out to Carson Manor to accuse Royce Chamberlin of having an affair with his mother."

Kurt shrugged. "I don't know anything about that."

"Objection."

"Overruled."

"Four weeks later, Delmond Rose fell to his death in the warehouse. And a month after that, you showed up here to take over Section Two."

"It's the economy. I had to move."

"Possibly."

"You're not sayin' I had anything to do with that kid fallin'..."

"No. I'm just following the links in the chain," Hopkins replied.

"What's Rose Senior say about it?" Kurt asked.

"He's afraid. He lost both his wife and his son. He says he'll talk, but only under subpoena."

Kurt sat back, flashing a big, contented grin. His movement said more about his knowledge of the events at the warehouse than any cross-examination.

"Your Honor, this is all innuendo. I object," Brubaker said. "What happened in Kansas City has no bearing on this case."

"We're not making any accusations concerning Kansas City, although I have my own opinion on that," Hopkins replied. "At the conclusion of this trial, I move that there be an investigation of this man's whereabouts during the time of his employment for Royce Chamberlin."

"You're making some far-flung suppositions, Mr. Hopkins," Post said.

"We're just trying to establish where certain people were at certain times. However, in light of what we've discussed, it might be a good idea to widen the scope to include Mr. Hudsen's activities directly before he came to Winfield."

"I'll take it under advisement," Post said. "Mr. Hudsen, you have a choice. You remain in Franklin County under your own recognizance, or you be remanded to the custody of Sheriff Dierkes."

"What?" Kurt said, almost accusatorily.

"This is the decision of the court."

"But I haven't done anything."

"Then you have nothing to worry about."

Kurt looked over to Royce's table. He was on his own.

"We're waiting, Mr. Hudsen," Post said.

"I'll stay in the county," Kurt mumbled.

"No! You ain't gonna do that to Papa!" Jago yelled from his seat.

"I can do it to you as well," Post stated. "Do you want to spend the rest of the trial in jail for contempt?"

"No," Jago answered.

Brubaker crossed over to Judge Post. "Your Honor, please. Permission for both counsels to approach the bench."

"Granted."

Hopkins joined Brubaker in front of Judge Post.

Brubaker's tone was urgent. "Your Honor, we didn't know anything about what happened at Nelson's farm. We knew that money was owed, but my client is very upset to hear about it. We have to chalk it up as a well-intended misunderstanding. Mr. Hudsen was acting in our best interests."

"Mr. Brubaker, this court believes a man is responsible for his actions."

"It's *me* he wants," Chamberlin cried. He was up from his table to join the others at the bench.

Ann tried to listen as closely as she could.

"What's your price?" Chamberlin said to Hopkins.

"You relinquish all claim to the remaining property and you walk."

"Never."

Hopkins studied him carefully. "I seriously think you should reconsider. This morning we discussed your employees. This afternoon will be closer to home."

"In what way?"

"Your family. You should think of your family. I'm going to be asking some questions."

"My family?"

"I'm hoping you'll use this opportunity to reconsider your position."

Chamberlin was amazed. "You're threatening me? You're coming in here and threatening me and my family?"

"I'm prepared to take this as far as we have to. You have the power to end it."

"You go straight to hell."

Brubaker felt a chill. He didn't know much about Royce Chamberlin's personal life because Royce's severe demeanor always made him afraid to ask.

"I ask you again to reconsider," Hopkins said to Chamberlin.

Brubaker's concern was growing now. Royce always had a stubborn streak, but lately, it was becoming self-destructive.

"Use my family as a weapon to intimidate me? If he wants to attack me with those tactics, he'll have to do it right here…in front of everybody."

"My client has answered you," Brubaker said.

"But he didn't hear me," Hopkins said.

He was looking up at Judge Post. "Your Honor, I'm asking permission for a change of venue for the next part of the trial. Perhaps your chambers."

"Why?" Post said.

"The nature of the testimony. Certain bills. I said it would cover his family, but I'm also thinking of their welfare."

"What's he talking about, Royce?" Brubaker said.

"It's a bluff."

Post was pensive. "Well, if you think it's better. But I'd like to know more. How long do you think it would take?"

"Thirty minutes at the most."

Brubaker felt pinned. He had to try to something. Royce wasn't thinking clearly, and he wouldn't back down. "We don't know what they're going to talk about, Royce."

"It doesn't matter. This is my town. Our town and our community. We've put our blood and sweat into it, and we're not caving in. Not for any slander or innuendo. It's a bluff. We'll have it right out here."

He turned away from the bench to face Ann. In a loud voice he said, "We'll take it right to the end, won't we?"

The rage and anger on his face would have been frightening if Ann did not perceive the underlying dread. In the past, when Royce was angry, he took on a stone-like appearance. This was the opposite. His emotions were out in the open, and the façade was beginning to crack.

"Your Honor, might we have a recess?" Brubaker asked.

"I think that would be best for everyone," Post said. "Court's adjourned until two o'clock this afternoon."

66

Every noon Judge Post would go to the hospital to sit with his wife Rose. Today when he arrived, he found her asleep. She had been ailing for a long time. Breathing softly, she seemed to have grown smaller over the past two weeks.

The judge was glad to be away from this case. The testimony made him uncomfortable. He wasn't guilty of anything, but why did he have a faint feeling of culpability every time a witness was sworn in? If conditions were as bad as the cross-examinations revealed, then why hadn't he, as a representative of the law, tried to do something about it? He knew he could always use his concern for his wife's health as an excuse. But what about the violence at the Nelson farm? He told himself he didn't know about it. In truth, he didn't. But he kept wondering if he really suspected all along and never wanted to think about it.

He looked up to see Chamberlin and Brubaker in the doorway. Royce appeared angry and shaken. Brubaker was wearing his concerned expression.

"Excuse us for intruding, Your Honor," Brubaker said.

"What is it?" Post asked. "You shouldn't be here."

"How's she doing?" Brubaker answered as they entered the room.

"Sleeps more and more."

"She needs her rest," Brubaker said.

Post wavered between being touched and agitated. He appreciated the show of interest, but their presence was a violation of court procedure.

"It's her blood, and she's not going to get any better. Now what are you doing here?"

"We'd like a moment," Chamberlin said. The tone was cold and emotionless, a stark contrast to Brubaker's calculated empathy.

"Is opposing counsel with you?" Post asked. "You know the rules. I'm not supposed to confer with you unless opposing counsel is present."

"Why don't we step outside?" Brubaker said.

The three stood in front of the massive oil painting of Royce and his daughters. The large figures on the wall seemed to loom over them like a cloud.

"What is it, gentlemen? You know this is highly irregular."

Chamberlin and Brubaker picked up on his anxiety right away. While Chamberlin observed, Brubaker adopted a mediating tone.

"Your Honor, we know the protocol and procedure of a trial. But something has come to our attention. Ann Harmon has been conferring with some financial advisors in Chicago."

"So? What's wrong with that?"

"It seems that if she wins her lawsuit, she plans to take over the bank and call in all the loans."

"Ann Harmon? I find that hard to believe. Where did you hear this?"

"Claypool at the station. Two of Hopkins's team were having a little conference outside the baggage room."

"That's why opposing counsel is not present," Chamberlin said.

"Now, I take this very seriously," Brubaker continued. "A lot of the bank's funds come from the Carson estate. Her position is she lost her land. She wants it back, and if there are people living on it, that's their problem."

"I can't picture Ann Harmon doing that to anyone," Post said. "She's Wallace Carson's granddaughter. Of course, I didn't have much time for him or any of her family."

"You've heard the testimony so far. It's spiteful, thoughtless, and vindictive."

"Yes, yes. But Claypool is one step up from a rat catcher. I wouldn't trust anything he says."

"We're talking about Ann," Chamberlin said. "I know her character. I know her better than anyone."

Post wasn't sure whether to believe them or not. It sounded true. On the other hand, Royce and Brubaker had a tendency to conceal their real intentions within a request for something else.

"Assuming what you say is true, she won't be doing any of this until after the trial," Post said. "She has to win the case first."

"That's small consolation to the town," Brubaker answered.

"Show him the letter," Chamberlin said.

Brubaker handed a wrinkled sheet of paper to Post.

Post read: "'Please help us. Save our farms. Please don't let her take us down that road. If we lose our farm, we lose everything.'"

"Quite clear," Brubaker said.

"Who wrote this?" Post asked. "It's not addressed to anybody. It's not signed by anyone."

"A cry for help."

"Who wrote it?"

"One of the forty individuals."

"Who, Fred?"

"We'd rather not say unless we have to."

"*Who* wrote it?" Post demanded. "I need a name."

"Ellis Burr."

"Burr? He's as dependable as a weather vane. No better than Claypool."

By now Post was irritated by the ambiguity of the whole presentation. It might be true, but he was beginning to doubt it. And right now he was too wrapped up in his worries to give it a thorough consideration.

"Burr brought it to me, Your Honor," Brubaker said.

"How did he find out? And who was he writing to?" Post asked.

"He didn't say. He's afraid. He doesn't want to lose his land," Brubaker said. "You couple this with what Claypool overheard, and you have a disturbing picture."

Post knew there had been bad blood for years between Ann and the Chamberlins. Still, Brubaker's claim might be possible. Post wanted to be a good judge. He had always prided himself on being honest and fair, but he suspected that Brubaker and Royce were after something else. His mind went back to the morning's events. What had they requested? A mistrial. It was time to get it out of them.

"I'm going to have to talk to Mrs. Harmon and opposing counsel," he said.

"They'll deny it," Brubaker said. "You think they're going to admit something like that? Of course, they'll deny it."

"So what are you suggesting?"

"I'm going to repeat my suggestion for declaring a mistrial."

"I thought that was it," Post said.

"But now it's an emergency," Brubaker exclaimed. "This goes beyond the scope of two parties in a lawsuit."

Chamberlin had once again adopted his stone-like demeanor. "What you need to do is take a step back from this—for the good of the town."

"Think of your neighbors," Brubaker agreed. "Think of your family. Think of Rose in there."

Post was feeling the pressure. This was what they wanted all along. Chamberlin's blunt approach and Brubaker's empathetic tone were closing in from both sides.

"You're asking me to throw the trial. You want me to declare a mistrial and declare all the evidence inadmissible."

"You said yourself there's a possible conflict of interest," Brubaker said.

"It hasn't influenced my handling of this case," Post said.

Chamberlin was annoyed. He never liked to pause for ethical considerations. He shot a glance at Brubaker, who resumed.

"I realize we're in a gray area. We're thinking of the town. It's the only way we can stop her."

"No, I'm not going to do this on the basis of an unsigned scrap of paper. For all I know he could be writing a note to Van Burin."

"Right now the only people who know about this are we three and Claypool. We're the only ones who can take action. It's for the good of the town."

"It's also good for your case," Post said.

"We're asking you to help us," Brubaker said.

"No. A trial follows rules. The answer is no."

Brubaker assumed a pensive expression. "All right, but we can declare a mistrial from our side. It would be a little messier and drawn out a little longer, but we can do it."

"It's a legal option," Post said. "But we're going to finish this trial first."

"Why?"

"Because we have to do it. We've let a lot of things happen over the past few years, things that never should have happened. We've let them go by, and they haven't made us better as people. It's time we put a stop to this."

For once, Brubaker was truly mystified. "I don't understand."

"I can't explain it any other way."

"What if we walked out of the courtroom? What if we withdrew ourselves until the new trial?"

"Then this trial will go on without you."

By now Chamberlin was furious. Brubaker's methods should have worked, but they had not.

"Now we'll look at this economically," he declared. "The bank holds notes on twenty-five farms in Franklin County."

"And most of these families pay their interest every month," Post said.

"A few have difficulty."

"These are difficult times," Brubaker added.

"And out of the twenty-five, two of them belong to you," Chamberlin said. "Two farms."

"And I keep up on my payments," Post said.

"We know you do," Brubaker said. "In fact, sometimes the bank has given you an extra month now and then when money's tight."

"And I appreciate that."

"You've managed the bills—the room and all the care the hospital provides."

"I have."

"What if that were taken away?" Chamberlin said, more as a statement than a question.

Post was jolted by the directness of his words. "What are you saying, Royce?"

"He's asking you to step back from your personal circumstance and think of your neighbors," Brubaker said, maintaining his sympathetic tone. "We're asking you to do this for the sake of the town."

"Everything I've done has been for the sake of the town," Chamberlin said. "Without me, we wouldn't have this hospital. Without me, Rose wouldn't have the care she's getting here. I've given. I'm asking you to do the same."

"It's only fair, Your Honor," Brubaker said.

Post's temper was rising. They were dangling Rose in front of him as a reason to accept a bribe. He also knew that he couldn't afford to care for her without the loan. The loan was paying for everything.

"In your case," Chamberlin said, "whoever holds your loans at the end of the day is in the position of foreclosing . . . or forgiving them."

"Forgiving them?"

"Both mortgages. A remaining balance of thirty thousand dollars. You help us, and I'm prepared to forgive both loans."

Post was stunned. He had never taken a bribe in his life. All the same, he wanted to hear the offer again.

"Repeat that," he said.

"Help us and you're free and clear."

"It's a generous offer," Brubaker said.

"It's a bribe. That's what it is." Post felt a swirl of emotions—tears mixing with the anger as well as the relief that would come if he were free of financial difficulty. He wanted desperately to accept it. It would solve everything. But it would also betray everything he had stood for in his legal career.

"No, no. It's not a bribe," Brubaker said.

"What would you call it, Fred?"

"An offer. A beneficial offer."

"Thirty thousand dollars free and clear," Chamberlin said.

"We're thinking of Rose," Brubaker said solemnly.

"No, you're thinking of yourselves," Post said. "What if I refuse?"

"Then it's out of our hands."

"What'll you do then? Foreclose if I can't pay?"

Post felt suffocated. He could use the money, and he was afraid of what might happen if he refused. He hated himself for even considering the offer. But more and more he was insulted that Brubaker and Chamberlin had thought he would be such a pushover.

"What are you afraid of?" he asked. The question seemed to pop out of him.

"Wrong question," Chamberlin said.

"There's something you're afraid of—something you don't want brought up, isn't there?"

"Who says there's anything?"

"It's going to come up. Hopkins has all but raised a red flag. And if that's the case, then what you're doing isn't about protecting the town at all. It's about you. What have they got on you?"

"Gentlemen, we're all getting off in the deep end," Brubaker said. "Let's not raise our voices. Rose is asleep in there."

"You leave my wife out of this," Post said.

"Are you with us or not?" Chamberlin demanded.

Post took a few steps. Slowly, he turned and whispered, "No...no, I'm not. I've taken about as much as I can. An evil shows up, and you look the other way. It starts to grow, and you tell yourself it won't hurt the town. A few people are hurt, but more prosper; you even tell yourself that maybe it's good for the town. You try not think about it. But finally it shows up on your doorstep, bigger than life and staring you in the face, so you can't ignore it anymore."

His eyes were on Royce as his voice began to rise. "You come to me with this offer. You come right into my family...right up to my wife's deathbed. How dare you? How dare you?"

Everyone was silent. The sudden display of anger was unexpected.

"I sure hope you know what you're doing," Chamberlin said slowly.

"This is my family, sir. My *family*."

Without a word, Chamberlin stormed across the lobby to the front door. Post appeared exhausted. Brubaker knew the judge's decision would cost him dearly if Royce called in the loan. But in spite of it, Post was a fellow jurist, and Brubaker could sympathize with a fellow jurist. Brubaker felt he should say something before walking away.

"You know, it might not turn out so badly. Rose isn't going to be with us much longer. We all know that. Afterward, you won't have to worry about all those payments."

Post's eyes flashed. His teeth were clenched, as if he were ready to scream.

Brubaker hadn't expected that reaction. "I'm just saying that if you see it that way, it's not so bad."

Realizing his words had only aggravated the situation, Brubaker quickly crossed the lobby to join Royce.

Judge Post remained under the oil painting. He felt very small and all alone.

He would have to deal with this back in the courtroom, but thankfully he had an hour before the afternoon session began. Right now he wanted to be with his wife. He returned to her room and sat down in the chair beside her bed.

67

AFTER HE LEFT THE HOSPITAL, ROYCE Chamberlin locked himself in his office at the bank. Outside, some people were strolling in the park, while others were gathered in clusters having picnic lunches. Chamberlin was inside looking out at the world—just the way he had at the teller's window long ago. The room whose view of the park and courthouse had helped fuel his ambitions had now become a refuge from the outside world.

Carol and Cassie tried to communicate with their father, but he did not open the door. Alone and brooding, he spent the rest of the time running his eyes over the map of the Carson empire. Everywhere he could, he had changed the name on the properties from Carson to Chamberlin—even those whose ownership Ann was contesting. It was reassuring to look at the map. The exchange with Judge Post had backfired. He didn't know that Brubaker's subsequent efforts to attenuate the situation had made things even worse.

Ann and Ben had a makeshift lunch in the park with Olga. Ann's thoughts were on what would transpire that afternoon. She was thinking back to something Hopkins had asked her: would winning her case be worth the price of victory? Her answer never wavered. "You can't half-keep a promise," she said.

At 2:00 p.m. Judge Post banged his gavel. Ann thought that Post looked different. He was deliberate and focused, almost as if running on new reserves of energy. She wondered what had happened to him during lunch. If his wife had died, he wouldn't be there. What had happened?

"Mrs. Harmon, the court has a question," Post said.

This surprised Ann. For most of the trial the judge had behaved as if she weren't even in the room. She stood up to face the bench.

"Something has been on my mind," Post said. "There's no right or wrong answer here. And in no way is it a prediction of any legal outcome. If the court ruled in your favor and the properties were returned to you, what would you do with the ones that have loans from the bank?"

Ann was not sure how to respond. She had been on the receiving end of many trick questions during the past few years. Was this another? She tried to imagine the implications this question might conceal and then formulate an answer to the hidden part of the question, but she could not. Her best recourse was to answer honestly.

"You mean what would happen to the people living on them?" she asked.

"Yes."

"Well, I sure wouldn't kick them off, Your Honor. We've had enough of that around here."

"Thank you," Post said. "Mr. Hopkins, we may now begin."

"I'd like to call Royce Chamberlin to the stand," Hopkins said.

Chamberlin rose from his seat. The ferocious opponent from her childhood was now on the defensive, although trying his best not to show it.

"Your turn in the hot seat!" a voice called from the wall of faces.

Chamberlin stopped. "Mighty vocal when you're in a crowd, Caleb," he purred. "Step out and show yourself."

"I'll have order in the court," Post said.

As Ann watched Chamberlin being sworn in, she knew that she wasn't alone. In her mind, the colonel, Lady Ann, Lucille, Jack, and even Zachary had all gathered alongside her to witness what was about to occur. "This is it," she thought. "Vindication."

Hopkins began. "Mr. Chamberlin, we just heard the testimony of Kurt Hudsen. We've heard that you allowed him to live on one of your properties for ten dollars a month while you retained him as your personal bill collector."

"Objection."

"Overruled."

"We've also heard how my client is paying your utility bills, the taxes for all the remaining properties, as well as your attorney's fees."

Chamberlin caught sight of Patrick Van Burin arriving late. The banker was furtive, as if the shame of his own cross-examination was following him around like an embarrassing smell. Van Burin was trying to find a seat, but each time he approached one of the few available places, the person beside it would move over slightly to prevent him from sitting down.

"I want to talk about the will for a minute," Hopkins said. "Of course, we are challenging Lucille Hardy's will. And we have shown the difference in type on the final copy of the will. It makes a curious bequest. In effect, Lucille Hardy rescinds her daughter's claims and instead bequests everything to your daughters, Cassandra and Carol."

"It was her choice."

"Yet they were already profiting from inheritance of the remaining parts of the estate."

"Lucille was quite clear in her bequest," Brubaker announced from his table.

"That's what happened," Chamberlin said in a matter-of-fact tone. "Lucille came into the office shortly before the accident."

"She did?"

"That's what I said."

"No, earlier you said you weren't aware of it," Hopkins countered. "Earlier you told us you weren't aware that anything had been changed until Mrs. Harmon filed suit against you. Now you say that Lucille came in and made the changes. Which was it?"

"A change is a change."

"You said you were there. That means you were present."

"Objection, Your Honor. We've covered this before," Brubaker said.

"Overruled."

"Were you or were you not present when the will was changed? Why did you tell us you were unaware of a change and then tell us Lucille came to the office and made the changes?"

Chamberlin waited. He saw Van Burin along the back wall. He remembered the banker's time on the stand. He knew Hopkins was hoping to wear him down.

"Of course, I had to be aware," Chamberlin said. "The bequest was going to my daughters. It was a generous offer on Lucille's part, and we were appreciative. A man, if he's any kind of man, should look after his family. Lucille came to the office and said she wanted to make some changes. I told her to make them on the original, and we would draw up a formal copy of the new will at a later date."

"And did you draw up a formal copy?"

"Of course not. Lucille died."

"And, of course, you were aware of the importance of this change in bequests."

"I considered it a tremendous compliment to my girls."

"I'm sure you did," Hopkins said. "Usually when a change is made in these circumstances, such as writing over an earlier bequest, the person making the changes is required to sign and date or at least initial and date the area beside the new bequest."

"So?"

"It isn't there, Mr. Chamberlin."

"Come again?"

"It isn't there. Did you remind Lucille to initial and date it?"

"I must have."

"It's still not there. As a result, this last-minute inclusion is dubious without her initial or signature. Without it, it might seem like someone made the changes at the last minute and hoped nobody would notice."

"Now we've got him," Ann thought. "I've been waiting for this ever since we saw the will in the records room."

"The changes were valid," Chamberlin declared.

"I'm sure they were to the person who made them. Without an initial and date, they are only changes."

"I say they were valid and legal, Mr. Hopkins. You'll never prove otherwise."

"Perhaps not." Hopkins cast an eye to the jury. "But if you were so convinced of the success of your claim, why did you round up forty people to file a countersuit?"

"I thought what I did was fair."

"Forty to one?

"It's the way I do things."

"This brings us to another observation. As we have mentioned, my client has been paying most of your living expenses. And you, during all this time, have taken all the profits from the estate and made investments elsewhere, particularly Pheasant Valley Power. The one exception is a portion of your medical bills, specifically the medical bills of your daughters Carol and Cassandra."

For the first time in his life, Chamberlin felt vulnerable. Up until now his family's privacy had been protected. Maybe this was where Hopkins had been going all along. It still could be a bluff. He glanced over at his daughters. Cassie appeared worried. Carol was hunched over and clenched up—as if preparing for a fight.

"What about these bills? Why are they so important?" Chamberlin asked.

"You've paid for these yourself."

"What's wrong with that? A man should look after his family."

Brubaker stood up. "Your Honor, my client has been under a great deal of stress. I request a recess."

"A strange request, Mr. Brubaker," Post answered. "Especially since we just got here. Request denied."

"About the bills," Hopkins said.

Chamberlin shifted posture and expression, transforming from the accused witness to sensitive man of the people.

"I'll answer about the bills," he said warmly. "But before I do, I want to say something. Up here on the stand…we're expected to be truthful. It brings us close to who we are as people."

"He's afraid," Ann thought. "He's sidestepping. Maybe I'm the only one here who sees through it. If he talks long enough, maybe everyone'll see what I see."

Chamberlin slowly stood up to address the courtroom as if they were all fervent supporters.

"A man, even in the most trying of circumstances, should always strive to be better than himself. He should rise above his instincts. And if confronted with rumor or slander, as I seem to be at this moment, then he should answer with truth and with humility. To answer you truthfully, I want to talk about us. You and me. Our sense of community. A courtroom is not always the easiest place to do this, but we *are* community. We are worth addressing."

Ann had heard Chamberlin's fake sincere tone for as long as she had known him. He used it when he was courting Lady Ann. It always worked when the listener did not know Chamberlin or his methods. Obviously, he hoped it would work again.

"I came here some time ago. I worked at the bank for many years. Serving the community. In getting to know Winfield, I grew to love this town and the people in it. The town. The sense of purpose. The unity. It was the American spirit. The freedom to choose how to live your life and be of service to your fellow human beings. Winfield, Iowa...I like the sound of that...I love what it stands for."

Had Chamberlin not been so wrapped up in his delivery, he would have noticed that he was addressing a wall of irritated faces. Here everyone knew him.

"I love it, and I will fight to preserve it. I will fight for me and for anyone in this room," Chamberlin declared. "This is why, when someone comes to Winfield and seeks to destroy our way of life, I will challenge his right to do so. This is our town. These are our families. I will fight for that."

He slowly turned to address Hopkins in a sternly accusatory manner. "How we live our lives is a private matter. You leave my family alone, Mr. Hopkins."

Hopkins was politely waiting. He offered no objections. From the expressions of the spectators, he knew Chamberlin was making his case for him.

"I've had my say. What about the rest of you?" Chamberlin said to the assemblage.

Silence.

"What about it? We're all in this together."

Again no response.

"If you've finished, the opposing counsel was asking you about a bill," Post said. "You were saying, Mr. Hopkins."

"I don't deny a man the right to express his opinions," Hopkins said. "If you go back over the court records, at no point have I condemned any of Mr. Chamberlin's actions. I have simply held them up to the light of day. You say a man should look after his family. Let's examine this for a minute."

Ann knew where this was headed: Chamberlin's peculiar relationship with his girls. Ann remembered the night long ago when she had looked out the gatehouse window to see Chamberlin and Cassie walking in the moonlight while Carol remained behind, shivering in the doorway. Royce and Cassie behaved as if they were lovers taking a stroll in the park.

"Before we do, let me say that it is you we are questioning, not Carol or Cassandra. In no way are they to be judged or condemned."

Cassie seemed to pale at the sound of his words.

Brubaker was worried. Chamberlin seemed determined to remain on the stand while Hopkins maneuvered him into some incriminating testimony. There had to be a way to get Royce out of there.

"I'd like to go over five bills," Hopkins said.

"I paid all of them. I don't owe the doctors anything."

"I don't question that they were paid. I want to examine what they paid for."

"Objection," Brubaker said. "If my client doesn't owe any money..."

"Overruled."

"Why? If they were paid, why do we need to dig anything up?" Chamberlin said. "If it was owed money, that's a different matter. It has nothing to do with this lawsuit."

"That's what we want to find out. These were the only bills you paid from your personal checking account."

Hopkins went to his table and returned with a handful of papers. "The first one is for Carol's ear infection. The bill was from Dr. C. B. Wright in Chicago. He treated Carol for an infection six years ago."

"Yes, yes, Dr. Wright. A reputable man. Surely you're not attempting to drag his name into this."

"I'm looking for some clarification," Hopkins said. "And these other bills certainly need clarification. They concern your other daughter, Cassandra."

A quiet, mewing noise came from where Carol and Cassie were seated. Cassie was trembling. Carol reached over and, without looking at her sister, clamped her hand over Cassie's arm, like a nurse restraining a patient.

Ann saw the impact the questioning was having on the Chamberlins. Each was reacting in a different way. Cassie becoming more frightened, Carol more controlling, while their father appeared to be ignoring them altogether.

"They're starting to crack," Ann thought. "It's about time."

"This one here is from Doc Powell. I'm sure you recognize it."

Chamberlin glanced at the paper. It was familiar. He was mystified at how much evidence Hopkins had been able to dig up. There was nothing incriminating yet, but there were three more to come.

"I move that this interrogation take another course," Brubaker said. "Your

Honor, bills my client paid have no bearing on this case. Mrs. Harmon is suing for bills she alleges she paid."

"The court is still curious why Mr. Chamberlin paid these bills himself," Post answered.

"Then please, yesterday opposing counsel suggested a change of venue. Admittedly, I was skeptical. Let me join him in renewing that request."

"Request denied for both counsels."

"But Your Honor…"

"Continue, Mr. Hopkins," Post stated.

"You recognize the bill," Hopkins said.

"It's none of the court's business. It's private business," Chamberlin said.

Ann wondered why Chamberlin was just sitting there and allowing this to happen to him. Did he feel he was invincible?

"What's the bill for?" Hopkins asked.

"Read it yourself."

"Can you tell the court?"

"A tonsillectomy."

Hopkins handed him a third paper. "What about this one?"

Murmurs came from the Chamberlin table. Cassie was squirming and Carol holding fast.

Judge Post also noticed the commotion. "Mr. Chamberlin, I'm beginning to suspect the direction we are about to take. I am asking if you might consider your options."

"What options?" Chamberlin retorted. "I built an empire here, and Hopkins is going to unspeakable lengths to tear it down. I am sure that if he returned to law school to bone up on courtroom tactics, he might discover that he has provided my side with enough to sue for disbarment."

Post's tone became severe. "Mr. Chamberlin, a little earlier today we had a talk about family. I'll remember that talk for the rest of my life. If you want to sit up there and show everyone how much you can take, you might first think of your family. Look where you are."

"I know damn well where I am," Chamberlin said.

"Continue, Mr. Hopkins."

"The bill is for an appendectomy performed by Dr. Powell on April ninth, 1921," Hopkins said.

"That's correct," Chamberlin answered. "The last time I looked, there was no law against having your tonsils or appendix out."

"Are you acquainted with the name Armand Szerbicki?" Hopkins said.

"Never heard of him."

In the back of the room, Deirdre and Sherman entered, accompanied by two deputies and a rumpled, unshaven man in an ill-fitting suit. Wearing handcuffs, Szerbicki was middle-aged and squinty—as if he had spent years in the dark, peering out at the day through a slit in the wall. He was getting accustomed to the light in the room when he caught sight of Royce in the witness chair. Once fixed on Chamberlin, he never stopped looking at him.

Cassie buried her face in her hands, as if hiding her view of the new arrival would make him go away.

Chamberlin was returning the gaze of the man in the ill-fitting suit. They looked like one enemy sizing up another.

"Your Honor, may we approach the bench?" Brubaker said.

Both Hopkins and Brubaker were in front of Judge Post.

"Your Honor, in a sense of fairness, I request we have a recess. Mr. Hopkins hasn't prepared us. He hasn't provided us with one bit of information about these bills or this witness."

"I provided you with copies of all the bills," Hopkins countered. "They were sent to your office yesterday afternoon by registered mail."

"I never received them."

"You certainly did, and we have the receipts." Hopkins went over to his table and came back with two pieces of paper.

"May I see them?" Post asked.

Brubaker passed them to Judge Post.

"Looks like you did, Mr. Brubaker. All stamped and signed," Post said. "We were talking about bills."

"I'm going to ask you again to think of your client's family," Hopkins said.

"Permission to confer with my client," Brubaker said.

"Make it quick."

"Who is he, Royce?" Brubaker whispered.

"Nobody."

"He's not nobody. He looks like death warmed over, he came here under armed guard, and he knows you. Give me something to work with. I can't help unless you give me something."

"You're on the court's time, gentlemen," Post said.

Brubaker was exasperated. "Your Honor, my client didn't know these transactions were going to be brought up at a later date. They're private. There's no reason for us to look at them now."

"Then why did he leave them around for anybody to find?" Hopkins asked. "Half the evidence in this trial was strewn about all over the county. Right out in the open. Was he expecting somebody to find it?"

Brubaker returned to his table. Had Chamberlin grown so big that he thought he was indestructible? The evidence was advancing on him from all directions. He and Royce had crossed ethical boundaries many times. For them it was business. At that moment he realized that their biggest blunder was to try to intimidate the judge.

"Dr. Armand Szerbicki...of Kansas City," Hopkins said.

A cry came from the Chamberlin table. Cassie was on her feet, pulling her arm out of Carol's grasp. She ran sobbing to the back of the room. As she passed Jago Hudsen, he started to go after her, but Kurt yanked him back into his seat.

"I'll see to her, Papa," Carol said, striding along the wall with loud, clumping steps.

Hopkins resumed. "Dr. Armand Szerbicki...I have here a bill from Dr. Szerbicki for the rental of a surgical room..."

"I don't know about that," Chamberlin said.

"For the performance of an appendectomy on Cassandra Chamberlin on October tenth, 1913."

"I don't know what you're talking about. Surely, you're working at the bottom of the cage when you bring in a convict..."

"How do you know he's a convict?"

"He came in under guard. What else could he be?"

Chamberlin was becoming desperate. Ann knew he had tried to stand his ground with denials and threats, but it wasn't working.

"Doc Powell and his staff have signed a sworn statement that he removed Cassandra's appendix in 1921. So what is this first appendectomy?"

"How can I answer? I never saw him before..."

"Doc Powell performed a successful operation in Winfield."

"Powell's a reputable doctor," Chamberlin said. "I don't know what you're trying to prove here by relying on the word of a convict. I don't know that man back there. I tell you I don't..."

Ann listened to the exchange with a ferocious glee. All her rage and resentment were being expiated with each question and answer. This didn't have to do with legal precepts. She saw her father being broken by Royce years ago, Carol's fist driving into her face when she was too young to defend herself, and Royce and Brubaker lurking around the deathbeds of both Lady Ann and Lucille. "Finally," Ann thought, "the son of a bitch is getting what's coming to him."

"1913," Chamberlin said. "That was years ago. Cassandra was sick. We had to do something."

"What did you do?"

Brubaker was feeling helpless. He wanted to try something—a delaying tactic, anything. The questions just kept on coming.

"What was this first operation?" Hopkins asked.

"I don't know why you're stirring this up..."

"What was it, Mr. Chamberlin?"

"I refuse to answer."

Hopkins moved closer to Chamberlin. "Do you recognize the man at the back of the room?"

"Why should I?"

"He certainly recognizes you."

Chamberlin gestured to the handcuffed man. "His testimony is inadmissible. He's no obstetrician. He's a convict now."

"Then you knew him before."

"I never said that."

"Then how did you know he was an obstetrician?"

"I didn't."

"Better tell dem, Mr. Royce," the handcuffed man said. "Time to pay de bill." The words were heavy and loud and seemed to resonate in every corner of the room.

"You shut your mouth!" Chamberlin yelled.

"If you don't tell dem, I vill, Mr. Royce."

"Where did you find him? Where did you dig him up?" Chamberlin shouted.

"Order," Post said from the bench.

"Dr. Szerbicki says he performed two operations on Cassandra. One in 1913 and the other in the summer of 1915."

"He's a liar!"

"If you don't tell dem, I vill," the man said loudly.

"You're a liar!"

"Svear me in. I vill tell dem, Mr. Royce."

"No! It won't end this way! You won't end it this way!"

"Order," Post said to Chamberlin.

"The operation in 1913 was for termination of a pregnancy," Hopkins said. "Cassandra was pregnant, and you took her to Szerbicki..."

"I have a family. I look after my children," Chamberlin sputtered. "A father looks after his children."

"Cassandra was thirteen, Mr. Chamberlin. In the summer of 1915, he performed a second operation that was also described as an appendectomy."

Brubaker rose again. "Your Honor, permission to speak with my client."

"Granted."

He rushed over to Chamberlin. "Royce, can't you see what's happening? It's over. We take our losses and walk."

"I'd listen to counsel," Post said.

"I can see what you're doing. All of you. You want to tear down everything I've built?"

"Do you relinquish?" Hopkins said.

"Never."

"Dr. Szerbicki says the second operation was not an appendectomy either," Hopkins continued. "I have both statements from Dr. Szerbicki right here. The second operation was a hysterectomy. Ordered by you. Paid for by you. The operation was to ensure that Cassandra would never get pregnant again."

"You had no right. No right," Chamberlin railed, his voice becoming weaker.

"He can come up here and repeat what I just said. He'll do it willingly because he believes you turned him over to the authorities a year after the second operation."

"He's a blackmailer!"

Chamberlin caught himself. He felt the energy seeping out of his body. He knew this declaration spelled trouble the moment he said it. It was an admission to everything Hopkins had been describing.

"Was he blackmailing you?"

"No. I mean yes."

"Now Cassie was only fifteen. There are many more questions we can examine, such as the identity of the father."

Chamberlin was paralyzed. Hopkins had backed him into a corner, and every answer he gave served as a cue for another question. He was aware of the people around him, but he felt all alone in a void.

"Do you relinquish?"

"Go to hell."

"What kind of father are you?" Hopkins said. "The girl was only thirteen the first time and when she's fifteen you let her be carved up again. None of this was her fault. She was a child. And just now, she ran out of the courtroom in tears. Aren't you the least bit curious what she's feeling?"

Ann was still savoring every question and evasive answer. Royce deserved every bit of what he was getting. But what about Cassie? Ann wanted to feel something, but memories of all the years of mistreatment had cancelled any possibility of pity. "You can't half-keep a promise," she thought.

"Maybe Dr. Szerbicki can tell us the rest of the story."

Something in these words prodded Chamberlin to look up at his accuser. He knew the questions wouldn't stop until they had destroyed him.

"No. No more," he said.

"Then you relinquish?" Hopkins said.

Ann was riveted. She knew Royce had lost. All she needed now was for him to concede.

"Do you relinquish?"

"All right," Chamberlin said after a long time. "I relinquish."

"And this is your decision now?"

"I relinquish my claim." His tone was tired, almost lifeless.

Post looked down from the bench. "Is this your final decision?'

"It's over," Chamberlin said. "Give it to her."

"For the court record," Post said. "Do you, Royce Chamberlin, relinquish all claims to the property and holdings in question?"

"I do."

"And this includes the eviction of the Hudsens from property that is not their own?"

"Yes. It's over."

"Then the court rules in favor of the plaintiff, Ann Harmon," Post said. He banged his gavel once. "Court's adjourned."

Ann shut her eyes. She pictured Colonel Carson, sitting at the long table as he did so long ago. "Grandpa. We did it. We won," she said in her thoughts. When she opened her eyes, she felt tired rather than joyful. It was a feeling of accomplishment rather than celebration. It wasn't how she imagined it would be, but it was good enough.

She reached over and gave Ben a hug. "Thank you," she said.

"For what?"

"For being you."

In the next instant, they were surrounded. Olga, Judy, Ellen, and their families were all around Ann, congratulating her at the same time.

"Oh, child," Olga was bubbling. "You won. You beat them. Your parents and your grandpa would be so proud."

"Yeah, I kept my promise. We saved the Northeast Quarter," Ann said.

"You should be proud, Ann," Judy said.

"It's been a fight," Ann said. She smiled. "And I'm asking myself, 'What do I do now?'"

The spectators got up from their seats to clear the room. Post quietly retired to his chambers. Jago Hudsen bolted away from his father and elbowed his way to the nearest door.

Brubaker was immediately engaged in damage control. "Maybe it worked out for the best, Royce. You still have the house. Your monetary assets. And, of course, your major interest in Pheasant Valley."

Van Burin joined them, talking as he came. "You did it, Royce. Still on top. The brat didn't get everything."

"Where's Cassandra?" Chamberlin asked.

"She ran outside. Carol's with her," Brubaker said.

"Sitting on a park bench, I bet," Van Burin added. "Putting it all behind her."

"I wonder how she can do that," Chamberlin muttered, as he brushed Van Burin aside. Followed by Brubaker, he made his way through the milling spectators to the exit.

"Papa!"

It was a little girl's voice—almost a scream. Pitched high and shrill, it pierced through the summer air.

"Papa!"

"You hear that?" Olga asked.

"Who is it?" Judy said

"Somebody call Sheriff Dierkes!" another voice from outside shouted. "Cassie's up in the clock tower and won't come down!"

The orderly procession of humanity turned into a rush for the doors, with pushing and shoving as people hurried to get outside. Ann saw Dierkes emerging from Judge Post's chambers. Deputy Clem was coming in from the street.

"It's Cassie Chamberlin. She locked herself up in the tower," he said.

"Come on," Dierkes said.

Ann, Ben, Olga, and the others started into the street along Pomphrey Park. A crowd was gathering below the courthouse clock. The mix of departing cars, carriages, and pedestrians had stopped.

Up above, Cassie had one hand on a side railing. She was an inch away from jumping. Her eyes were wild. She was searching desperately among the faces below for the one person who could make all the pain go away.

The reactions below her were mixed. Some were genuinely concerned, others morbidly curious. Mostly they were just waiting to see what she would do next.

"Don't do it, Cassandra!" one voice called.

"You poor dear, you poor, poor dear," an old woman cried.

"Come down from there," another old lady scolded.

Ann and Ben arrived at the front of the crowd as Dierkes was giving instructions to Clem.

"Try to get up the stairway behind her," Dierkes said.

Ann saw Clem edge his way back through the onlookers and into the courthouse. She didn't like Cassie, but she was up there all alone. In spite of her feelings, Ann began wondering what she could do to help talk her down.

Dierkes stepped forward, cupping his hands. "Cassie! This is Sheriff Dierkes! We don't want anything to happen to you! Come down now!"

"What if I don't want to?" Cassie answered.

"Then that would be a very sad thing. Now, we can talk about this."

"No talk! I want my papa!"

Ann went over to Dierkes. "Sheriff, let me see what I can do."

"You think you can help her?"

"I can try."

"Be careful now," Dierkes said.

Ann took a few steps in front of Dierkes.

"What are you going to tell me, Ann? What are you going to say?" Cassie yelled.

"I think you're making a big mistake," Ann replied.

Cassie emitted a mocking laugh. It was the first time she sounded like Carol.

"Cassie, I know a little about innocence and guilt," Ann said. "I know you were a child when it all started."

Another laugh. "Are you talking about yourself?"

"I'm talking about both of us. You can't blame a child for being innocent. Think back now. Did you ever have a say? You aren't to blame."

"She's right, Cassie," Dierkes said. "It wasn't your fault. None of it was."

"Nobody's blaming you for a thing," Ann said.

Cassie laughed again. "Oh, listen to you. Trying to talk me down. Don't tell me that you're my friend."

"Your friend? You haven't given me much to work with," Ann answered. "But I'll be honest with you. This isn't the way."

"Why did you have to ruin everything?" Cassie screamed. "We were all so happy and loving until you came back!"

"It started long before that. But it doesn't have to end here," Ann said. "We can all start over."

"I hate you, Ann! I hate you!" Cassie yelled.

The voices in the crowd began to editorialize. "Look at her up there."

"Sick girl."

"Doesn't know what she's saying."

"Where's my papa?"

Farther back, along the edge of the crowd, Jago wanted to rush in and help. Nobody was doing a thing for Cassie. He could get her down. Maybe this time he could prove his worth to her. He could show her he was the only one in the world who cared.

"Don't even think it, boy," Kurt growled.

"I'm gonna get her down," Jago said.

"You leave it alone."

"Why, Papa? She's gonna jump."

"It's Chamberlin business."

"Then why isn't he helpin' her?"

"He knows best. You stay out of it."

"You go to hell!" Jago cried.

Jago made a move to leave. Kurt twisted his son's arm behind his back and held it firmly.

"Ow! Ow! What are you doin'?"

"Keepin' you out of this," Kurt said.

"Let me go, Papa! You goddamn old man."

Jago struggled, but the big man held his son fast. The people around them were focused on Cassie.

"You move, I'll break it."

"You're hurtin' me!"

"You haven't got the sense of a hound dog pup," Kurt said. "In case it slipped your mind, we got our own problems. We been kicked off our land. Where we gonna live?"

Jago tried to move again. "You're hurtin' me, Papa!"

"That girl in the tower. That's Royce's problem," he rasped in Jago's ear. "Chamberlins live by their own rules. They make their own mess. We get near it, and we get pulled down with them."

"Papa!" Cassie screamed.

"You let me go!" Jago yelled.

On the other side of the crowd, Chamberlin appeared with Carol at his side and Brubaker and Van Burin trailing behind. Cassie saw them.

"Papa! Why didn't you stop them? Why didn't you look after me?"

Carol gazed up impassively at her sister. "Cassie, come down from there. It's time to go home," she ordered. She might as well have been summoning a child on the playground.

"She doesn't know what she's saying," Van Burin said.

Chamberlin knew perfectly well what she was saying. Their secrets had been made public, and he had pulled into himself for protection. He joined the others in watching. The situation would resolve itself one way or another.

"I was everything to you!" Cassie screamed. "Aren't you going to answer me?"

"Is Clem up there?" Ann asked Dierkes.

"She must have blocked the door," Dierkes said.

By now Cassie had stopped listening to Dierkes and Ann. She looked imploringly to her father for answers, but he had become a silent onlooker.

"Papa, why won't you answer me? Why are you just standing there?"

Brubaker was puzzled by Royce's silence. "She's your daughter, Royce. Say something."

"I can't," Chamberlin said, almost a whisper.

All at once a smile appeared on Cassie's face—a radiant smile like the one she wore when she danced with Royce at the wedding reception. She stepped over to the edge.

"Don't do it, Cassie!" Dierkes yelled.

Behind Cassie there was the sound of wood splintering as someone was trying to force open the door.

"Look, Papa! Look at me! This is for you!"

Cassie pitched forward out of the tower. There was a surge of screams and gasps from the people below. Her body hit the pavement in front of the courthouse. Up above, Clem peered over the edge. Everyone stood in shock. Before them was the body of the girl who had once been Cassandra Chamberlin.

Dierkes knelt down beside Cassie. She was dead. Her eyes were open, and there was blood gathering on the pavement along one side of her head. Doc Powell was moving through the crowd with his bag. Others began to follow him. Royce and Carol were swept along with them.

"Everybody stay back!" Dierkes said to the crowd. "Stay back! Somebody call the hospital!"

Doc Powell was beside Cassie. He took out his stethoscope and listened.

"I'm sorry, Royce. She's gone," he said.

There was no reaction from Royce Chamberlin. He was staring at his daughter's body.

"You know I couldn't help her," he said to Carol. "You know that, don't you?"

Carol's gaze had settled on the blood beside Cassie's head. "Does this mean you'll love me now, Papa?" she asked.

For Ann the scene seemed like a hallucination. Cassie was alive one minute and dead the next. Instead of grieving, her father and sister seemed more concerned about how the event affected them. Everything they did was true to character, but with death in the mix, their behavior seemed even more bizarre.

Jago and Kurt had seen the whole thing. Jago felt his chest tighten, as if his insides were strangling him.

"She's dead, Papa," he said. "We coulda done something."

"Better we stayed out of it."

Kurt released him. "I'm letting you go. You may not understand why I did that. Maybe one day you will."

Jago sprang away from him. "You let her die, Papa. You the same as helped kill her."

Kurt was amazed at his son's pigheadedness. "You're stupid. The girl had no time for you. Don't you see that?"

Jago dove through the crowd toward the spot where Cassie lay. He stopped abruptly when he saw the blood. He wasn't aware of anyone around him, only Cassie's body on the pavement.

"Everybody back!" Dierkes ordered. "Give us some room here!"

Jago was boiling and ready to tear down anything that moved the wrong way.

"Nobody did nuthin' for her," he repeated over and over. "Nobody did nuthin'..."

Kurt caught up to his son. "We're leaving, boy. Right now before we make a fool of ourselves."

Jago turned to the crowd. He didn't care who he was yelling at. They were all to blame.

"You all killed her!" he shouted. "You coulda done somethin'! You just stood around and watched!"

With so many faces around, Jago didn't know where to vent his anger. He needed a face, a target. Then he found it. Standing a short distance away were Ann and Ben.

"You just stood and watched, didn't you, Mr. Harmonsens?" Jago challenged. "A great lady died because of you!"

Ann and Ben saw him immediately. Jago was always angry, but this time he seemed in the grip of a fever.

"I see you, Mr. Hamonsens! I see you hidin' over there!"

Kurt was approaching his son cautiously. He could see now that his efforts to keep Jago out of trouble had only pushed him over the edge.

"A man fesses his actions, Mr. Harmonsens!"

"Come on, boy. We're going home," Kurt said.

Chamberlin observed the outburst from his place beside Cassie's body. He was becoming increasingly agitated at Jago's display.

"What stirred him up?" he said.

"It's the last thing we need," Brubaker said.

"A great lady's dead, Mr. Harmonsens!" Jago shouted over his father's entreaties. "Blood on your hands!"

"I should have gotten rid of him a long time ago," Chamberlin growled.

"We don't need the trouble, Royce," Brubaker said.

Chamberlin's temper was already rising. In his mind, Jago's words had become another finger pointing at him in front of the whole town. "Dierkes! Break that up!" he shouted.

Dierkes was already on his way over to Jago. "Settle down, Jago!" he ordered.

"The law's coming. Now you plug it," Kurt said.

"That's enough," Dierkes said as he walked up to Jago. The two men were almost eye to eye.

"Who says? You tellin' me what to do?"

"It's over because I say so."

"Let me take him home," Kurt said.

"You gone soft, Papa?" Jago yelled. "You takin' their side?"

"He's the law."

"Bought and paid for law. Washed-up old lawman, he stood back and let her jump, didn't you, Dierkes?"

Dierkes remained calm. "Jago, you're going to jail till you settle down."

"Why? For tellin' the truth?"

"No, because you don't listen." Clem had emerged from the clock tower. "Take Jago back to the office," Dierkes told him. "Put him in the empty cell till he cools off."

"You just wouldn't leave it alone, would you?" Kurt said as Clem led Jago away.

Jago and Clem started along the sidewalk in front of the courthouse. Jago flashed a wide and chilling grin at Ann and Ben.

"Calm down," Clem said to him.

Ann and Ben watched. "We're going to hear from him again," Ben said.

Ann knew Ben was right, but compared with the scope of her victory, it was a minor detail. Jago Hudsen was going to jail for now. Still, there was something about that grin.

She had seen Jago when he was angry on numerous occasions. Rage was as natural to him as breathing. Now he seemed to be walking peaceably with the deputy. But when they reached the end of the courthouse, Jago slowed his pace and began to address Clem in a fawning manner.

"He's going to try something," Ann said.

"What?"

"I know him, Ben."

Jago continued his chatter. Clem kept moving him along. When the two reached the last doorway of the courthouse, Jago sprang at the deputy, shoving him inside. Clem reeled into a side wall and was struggling to his feet when Jago tore the gun out of the deputy's holster and fired a shot into him. From the distance, it sounded more like a firecracker.

"He shot Clem!" Ann exclaimed.

Gun in hand, Jago was back on the sidewalk, looking to see if anyone had heard the shot.

When he saw Ann and Ben, he started directly for them.

Jago fired a shot into the air. "Mr. Harmonsens!"

"Come on!" Ben grabbed Ann's hand. They searched frantically for cover. The nearest thing was a row of carriages across the street.

"Blood on your hands, Mr. Harmonsens!"

Once again, the area erupted in confusion.

"Sheriff! He just shot Clem!" came a shout.

"Doc! Clem's in trouble!" Dierkes yelled.

Jago advanced rapidly, waving the pistol. "Mr. Harmonsens!"

Ann and Ben made a dash for a carriage across the street. There was another shot, and Ben let out a yell, grabbing his side. There was a bloody rip along his shirt where the bullet had grazed him. Ann pulled him down behind the cover of a wheel.

"It's all right," Ben said.

"But you're shot."

"Just tore my shirt."

People were scurrying for safety. Some ran across the park, others back into the courthouse.

"I'm gonna kill you, Mr. Harmonsens!"

Ann looked for their next place of cover. She saw Dierkes and Kurt scrambling to stop the rampage—probably the only time both men would be united in the same purpose. To one side were Royce and his entourage. Brubaker and Carol were alarmed. Chamberlin showed no emotion at all. He was staring at Jago as if he were a nuisance. Slowly, he stood up to face him. Grim and determined, he was a stone statue come to life.

Chamberlin was striding forcefully toward Jago. "Jago!" he shouted. "Jago!"

Jago turned to greet him with a smile. Maybe Mr. Royce understood after all.

"We're gonna make 'em pay, Mr. Royce!"

Chamberlin stormed right up to Jago. He lunged for his pistol in Jago's hand. Jago clung to it, more out of surprise than anger. The two grappled for control of the weapon. The struggle went on for several seconds with Chamberlin's hand around the barrel while Jago's grip was on the handle and trigger. Suddenly, the gun went off. Chamberlin screamed and staggered backward, clutching his abdomen.

"Papa!" Carol shrieked. She and Brubaker rushed over to where Chamberlin had fallen.

"I didn't want to shoot Mr. Royce," he said. "Why this have to happen?"

Kurt was beside him, his anger overwhelmed by the grief building up inside. One son in prison and now this.

"You crazy mutt!" he shouted. "What's the matter with you?"

"Why'd Mr. Royce come at me?"

"Give me the gun."

"No, Papa. I ain't gonna do that."

Jago laughed. His father's rage almost matched his. As a reflex, Jago squeezed the trigger. Kurt's hand went to his shoulder, his only reaction to having been shot. If Kurt felt physical pain, he didn't show it. His emotional pain was overwhelming. He was losing Jago before his eyes, and there was nothing he could do to stop it.

Neither of them had noticed the arrival of Sheriff Dierkes. Dierkes's gun was out of its holster and pointed at Jago.

"Put the gun down," Dierkes said. He gazed steadily at Jago, and he spoke slowly and soothingly, spacing his words so each one would sink in. "Put it down before anything else happens."

"Can't do that," Jago answered.

"You don't want to hurt any more people."

Jago smiled mischievously. "Who says?"

"I said you don't want to shoot any more people."

"Listen to him," Kurt said. "He's giving you a chance."

"What kind of chance is that?"

"We don't want it to go any further," Dierkes said. "Put the gun down and step away."

"Listen to him, boy," Kurt entreated. "Do what he says. Please."

Jago laughed. "You never said please before, Papa. You turnin' soft?"

"I'm trying to keep you alive," Kurt said.

"Don't force me, boy," Dierkes said. "We can still walk away."

"And then what? Go to jail?" Jago snickered. "I can take you, washed-up old lawman."

With a cry, Jago raised his pistol to shoot. Dierkes fired a shot that spun Jago around. Jago stared desperately at everything around him, as though he realized this was his last view of the world. He dropped to his knees and fell dead onto the pavement.

From behind the wagon, Ann and Ben saw Dierkes slowly lower his gun. He didn't put it in the holster. He was waiting to see what Kurt would do next. Ann never felt sympathy for either of the Hudsens, but she was touched by what was happening. Kurt was sitting in the street, cradling his son's head in his lap.

"You stupid…you stupid," Kurt stammered. It was as close as he would ever get to tears. "Why'd you do it? Why didn't you listen? One goddamn lawman. You could have walked away."

Dierkes kept his eyes on Kurt. With the death of Jago, the sparks of defiance and aggression were rapidly seeping out of the big man.

Finally, Kurt looked up at the sheriff. His eyes were glazed. "You gave him a choice, Dierkes. I saw it. You gave him a chance."

Kurt got to his knees and picked up Jago's body. He had become a shell of the man he was when his son was alive.

"I'm taking my boy to the hospital. I know I'm supposed to stay in the county," Kurt said. "But I'm taking my boy to the hospital."

Ann watched Kurt carry Jago's body across the park to their car, amazed at how easily he had picked him up. Kurt must have been far stronger than anyone realized. He placed Jago on the dusty contours of the backseat. Soon the car headed away from Pomphrey Park.

By now they could hear the clanging of an ambulance approaching. Two vehicles that resembled white delivery vans came up Market Street. People were coming out from where they had sought cover.

Ann and Ben came out from behind the carriage.

"We're getting you to the hospital," she said.

"It's just a scratch, Ann."

Royce Chamberlin lay on the pavement a short distance ahead of them. With Carol beside him, he was battling for consciousness.

Ann paused to look at him. So many of her emotions were wrapped up in her struggles and final victory. She hated him for all he had done to her and her family. She wouldn't have minded if he died in the next two minutes. They had been locked in a duel that had lasted ten years. And he was right on the pavement in front of her.

"Come on," she said to Ben.

When Chamberlin saw her approaching, he seemed to rally. "Come to finish me off?" he said.

A flood of responses crowded into Ann's mind, hurtful words that could drive a stake into this monster once and for all. Trouble was, the urge to drive in the stake was evaporating.

"I got what I came for," she said.

Ann took Ben's arm to leave.

"Ann..."

She turned for one last look at Royce Chamberlin.

"You'll never forget me," he said, still smiling,

Doc Powell arrived with his bag to examine Royce. He saw the blood spot on Ben's shirt.

"You want to ride in the ambulance?" he said to Ben.

"We'll walk," Ben said.

Two attendants arrived with a stretcher. With Powell supervising, they began to ease Chamberlin onto it. They took him to the first ambulance and returned for Cassie.

Hopkins emerged from the courthouse his arm around Clem. For the entire trial, Hopkins had been neatly dressed and businesslike. Yet here he was, with blood on his suit. The attendants from the other ambulance rushed over to them. They helped the wounded deputy onto their stretcher. Ann and Ben joined them.

"All right?" Hopkins said to Ben.

"He grazed me. What about Clem?"

"I'll live. I've been shot before," Clem said from the stretcher. "Kinda stings, doesn't it?"

"A little," Ben said.

Ann's mind was still a blur. Concern for Ben. Victory in the trial. The explosion afterward. What she would do next. But here was the man who made it all possible.

"Thank you, Mr. Hopkins," Ann said. "We owe you a lot."

"Thanks for everything," Ben said.

"You're welcome," Hopkins said. "Was it worth it?"

"Every bit. But it had a price tag."

The ambulance carrying Royce and Cassie was driving away.

"I'll be back at the hotel," Hopkins said. "We can say good-bye before I take the train."

Hopkins left and was crossing the park on his way to the Journeyman.

"He was asking if we had second thoughts," Ben said.

"I know."

"Do you?"

Ann already knew the answer. "Considering who we were up against and the time we had to wait, I doubt if it could have ended any other way."

Epilogue

THADDEUS HOPKINS HAD ALWAYS SAID THAT, in a trial, the triumph of good over evil was a fringe benefit. The Harmon case was no different. If there were just desserts in the outcome, the quantities were unevenly distributed, to say the least.

Kurt and Jago Hudsen

Instead of going to the hospital as he had promised, Kurt drove back to section two with his son's body. To the few who saw him, Kurt seemed in a trance. He didn't drive recklessly. He wasn't even aware of how long it took to get home.

Kurt stopped just short of section two, and taking a shovel, he buried his son's remains in one of the cornfields. A passerby was to say later that he had spotted Kurt burying something out in section four. Or was it section three? No one to this day knows the exact location of Jago Hudsen's grave. In the decades that followed, rumor had its way and a portion of section five became known as Jago's Acre—but only on Halloween.

What followed was performed almost like ritual. Quietly and calmly, Kurt returned to the house, where he rounded up all his dogs and turned them loose in the yard. Once they were there, he loaded his two shotguns and began to fire over their heads. The dogs scattered in terror and disappeared in the surrounding cornfields.

After the last hound was gone, Kurt went to the barn and returned with two cans of kerosene. He doused the interior and front porch with the liquid. When both cans were empty, he lit a match and set the place on fire.

For the next hour, Kurt stood and watched the flames devour the house. When the house had become sufficiently engulfed in the holocaust, he simply turned and walked out the driveway.

Kurt Hudsen was never seen in Winfield again. Some say he went to Long

Beach, California, and hired himself out as muscle for management in labor disputes, only to be killed in a fracas on the docks in San Pedro.

One member of the Hudsen homestead remained at large: the bull terrier Goliath. When the shotgun blasts started, he scampered across the road and hid among the stalks of the Northeast Quarter. The other hounds were quickly caught, but Goliath roamed the countryside for several months.

Fred Brubaker

Brubaker was one of those ethically challenged individuals who always seemed to avoid retribution and land on their feet.

The day after the trial, Brubaker decided to leave Winfield. All the revelations about scandalous activity out at Carson Manor would not bode well for any future career in Winfield. Over the next few days, he removed and destroyed any incriminating evidence that had not been brought out at the courtroom. A week later, he was on a train heading west, where he finally disembarked in Phoenix, Arizona.

In Phoenix Fred Brubaker set up a legal practice that developed into one of the most profitable law firms in the state. He died in his bed at age eighty-five—beloved by his colleagues and surrounded by his adoring family.

The Depression

For those who remained in Winfield, it was a different story.

The official date was October 29, 1929.

In Winfield there was no thunderclap to announce its arrival. The bank simply did not open one morning. Everyone who had put money in stocks or futures was left penniless. They were pulled into the abyss along with the rest of the country. The only people in Winfield who stood a chance were the ones who had held onto their land.

Royce and Carol Chamberlin

Royce Chamberlin's gunshot wound left him incapacitated. He was unable to walk and had permanent internal damage from which he had not been expected to survive. Somehow, he defied the odds and remained alive.

In his hospital room, he spent his days raging about a countersuit: how Ann had hoodwinked him with her killer attorney and how he would have his revenge. He sent requests to law firms all over the state—none of which were interested in taking his case.

When Pheasant Valley Power and Electric went under, Chamberlin and Carol found themselves without any manner of support. All of Royce's investments failed, and his remaining fortune, having been used to fund other investments, was targeted as unpaid debt or back taxes. Royce and Carol were destitute and without land in one fell swoop.

Royce sold the manor house to the county to pay for his care. But when those funds were gone, he and Carol moved to the one place in Winfield that would take them for free: the county farm.

Ironically, they were given Zachary Carson's old room, where Chamberlin spent his time planning his return to financial stability or spinning revenge plots against Ann. Carol had no interest in anything more than being a facilitator to her father. She shared the room with him and acted as a self-appointed chief nurse.

On June 1, 1930, Royce Chamberlin died in his room in the county farm. The gravity of his injuries was listed as the primary cause, but most likely what killed him was the inability to put any of his schemes into action. He simply wallowed in his own bile until he drowned.

Carol remained in his room at the county farm. Speaking to no one, she rarely went outside. Six months later, Carol Chamberlin followed her father. One morning, Nurse Tracy Stabb found her dead—sitting in the chair with her father's sweater across her lap. The certificate would read death by natural causes. Carol was thirty-one.

Today, the name Royce Chamberlin is not found on any court records from this period. All the maps of Winfield show the name Carson on cartography of the old Carson estate. It is as if the town was trying to forget a dreadful period that had been allowed to engulf their ancestors.

The Manor House

The manor house fell into disrepair during the Depression years. Nobody had bothered to correct the faulty electrical connection between the gatehouse and the main house. In 1933, the wiring finally erupted into a series of sparks and then a fire. The gatehouse burned to the ground, but the volunteer fire department was able to save most of the manor house. Today it stands as the Winfield Iowa Historical Museum.

Patrick Van Burin

Van Burin was one of the casualties of the events surrounding the fall of the Carson empire.

After the trial, he could never understand why he was resented so much. He felt he had done his job as ethically as possible under the circumstances. It was Royce Chamberlin's fault. Nobody understood that their problems were caused by Chamberlin's ambitions and financial overreaching.

On November 1, 1929, several of the citizens made their way to the bank.

They began stoning the windows and yelling that it was high time somebody burned it down. Windows were broken. Manure was thrown at the front door. A facsimile of an outhouse was left outside with the words "Van Burin's Office" scrawled across the side.

Van Burin hid at his home. In the eyes of his family, he had become the shame of Franklin County. Very soon his wife and family left him. Van Burin was crushed. Everything he had advocated and believed in had betrayed him. Now everyone despised him.

On February 10, 1930, Van Burin quietly snuck away from his home. He took some cash from the jar in the kitchen and a bottle of champagne from his cellar. He went to Kansas City, and under an assumed name, he checked into a cheap hotel near the stockyards. After dinner at a nearby café, he returned to his sixth-floor room and drank the bottle until it was empty. Around midnight, he placed the bottle in the wastebasket and straightened up the room so it looked as it did when he arrived. He walked over to the window and opened it. He stood quietly, letting a gentle breeze caress his face. He thought he smelled a perfumed fragrance from somewhere in the night. He tried to identify it, but it was gone. Then he stepped out of the window.

Van Burin's body was found in the alley the next morning. Since he had checked in under a false name, and there was no identification on him, he was considered a vagrant. He was buried in Kansas City's equivalent of potter's field and remained there until his family located his remains.

Nobody sent flowers.

Sheriff Tom Dierkes

Dierkes remained in Winfield as its peace officer. He was elected three more times before he retired in 1940. To this day no one has ever learned where he spent the first part of his life.

Thaddeus Hopkins

Hopkins returned to Chicago to continue his practice with his group. Due to the change in financial circumstances, Ann and Ben paid him for his services by deeding him two of the remaining farms. His office used the crop money to help finance the activities of his research team. He and the Harmons remained in contact for the rest of their lives. After the final debts were paid, Ann and Ben were left with Sections Two and Three and the property across the road, the portion that had started it all: the Northeast Quarter.

Ann and Ben

Ann and Ben remained married for the next seventy years.

Ann became a lawyer and opened her office in Winfield, the first female lawyer in Franklin County. She remained a local lawyer, looking after her neighbors as she had promised. In the thirty-eight years she practiced law, she never lost a case.

Ben opened an insurance office next door. By the time he retired, he had branched out to ten regional offices around the state.

Ben passed away in the summer of 1998—one day before their seventy-first anniversary. Ann lived for eight more years and died in 2006.

Before Ann began her law studies, she and Ben decided to settle on Section Two—the old Hudsen property. It would be a challenge to restore, but it was across the road from the Northeast Quarter. By March of 1930, they had removed the remains of the Hudsen house as well as the junk that had littered the property. By May of that year, construction had begun on their new house.

However, there was one piece of unfinished business.

Little Goliath had made his way all around Franklin County, foraging for food and sleeping wherever he could find an open barn or storeroom. He managed to visit most of the farms in the county—providing there was a warm nook or no watchdog to scare him away.

In late spring of 1930, he headed for home.

When he arrived, he was surprised to see that the dwelling he had once known had vanished. He remembered Ann had never tried to harm him, but most humans were not to be trusted. He promptly hid under the house. Although Ann and Ben tried their best to coax him out, all they received for their efforts was a pair of silent eyes staring back at them from beneath the floorboards. They started leaving him a ration of food and water along the side of the building. Goliath ate the food and drank the water, but he remained out of sight. Ann remembered how he had been mistreated over the years—beaten, kicked, taunted, and even used for target practice. No wonder he sought comfort in the dark.

But then, on July 4, 1930, Goliath the bull terrier decided to come out.

It was Ann's birthday—her first celebration on her own property since the birthday party hosted by Colonel Carson and Lady Ann so many years ago. The celebration of the Fourth of July as a day of thanks was a tradition worth continuing, so Ann invited several of her new friends to reinstate the family tradition.

It was a bright and warm day. The field around the new house was beginning to recover from its lack of attention and use by showing off several rows of new cornstalks. It was not enough for a harvest, but enough to show that health was returning to the land.

Across the road, in the Northeast Quarter, the rows of corn towered over everything around them. The stalks were of the purest green imaginable, a deep, full color that radiated the special quality of the earth beneath it. For Ann, the vitality of the plants in the quarter was a sign of hope. The good times would return.

So far the house was a one-bedroom dwelling with marked-off portions where more rooms would be added. On the front side, there was a porch, and on the porch, in an effort to carry on the tradition, there was another long table—actually five card tables pushed together and covered by a tablecloth. It was big enough for sixteen places—seven on each side and one place at each end. To one side of the long table were two more card tables soon to be covered with food.

There was a piano inside the house. Ben, Lee, and Clark were pounding out their rendition of "Tiger Rag." Olga was seated at the table. Judy and Ellen were inside mixing salad while their husbands were helping set the table. Betsy was standing beside her husband as he carved the steaks. Celeste was opening some pastry from the café.

Little by little, they finished their tasks, brought the food to the side table, and began serving themselves.

Under the floorboards beneath them, Goliath was having a major struggle. He had been able to live comfortably by himself until today. Now he smelled the food, particularly the steaks. He would wriggle out of the dark to the edge, sniffing the feast upstairs. Then someone would laugh or step on the floor loudly, and he would dive back to safety. The trouble was, the aroma of the feast would follow him, too, particularly the steaks.

As Ann was making one of the last trips in from the kitchen, she noticed Olga struggling to get out of her seat.

"I can help, Miss Ann," Olga was saying. "Let me do something."

Ann put down her tray and gave Olga a hug. "You sit down," she said. "You've helped me all these years. Now it's my turn."

When everyone was seated, Ann said the blessing. They were just starting to eat when Ann saw it: a bad memory come back to life. The image brought back everything in the journey Ann had made for the past eleven years. The figure of a man was standing outside in the road looking at the house as if waiting to say something or perhaps gather up the nerve to come in. It was the same man as on that fateful Fourth of July so many years ago: Warren Hyatt.

Fortune and social revolution had not been kind to Hyatt over the intervening years. His family had lost their farm and had been taken in by relatives in Keokuk. With no land and no financial support, Warren Hyatt had become a local hobo. People would see him wandering on the roads, cadging money or offering to do work just long enough to receive a handout. Whatever had fired him up in the past about social change had fermented into a simple case of class envy.

"What's *he* doing here?" Olga said.

Hyatt glared at them from the road. The sight must have bothered him to no end. The mighty Carsons had been brought down by circumstance, and, instead of feeling sorry for themselves, they were rebuilding.

"Uh…hello. Hello there. Hello, I say," he called.

No one answered.

"Don't ignore me. I'm right here, you see."

"Who is that guy?" Lee asked.

"A man who always uses ten words when one will do," Olga scoffed.

"Isn't it beneficial to see the humbling of a great family? You were brought down by circumstances you could not control but which you undoubtedly deserve."

There was no reply from the porch.

"I'm very proud not to have accepted one bit of charity from your family all these years. I stood up against the financial depredations of your grandfather and your parents. And I've watched how benevolent existence and social justice have caught up with you over the years. I can't say as I've shed any tears for you, but that's life, isn't it?"

Warren smiled proudly, relishing every point he had just made.

"And now, would it be too much to prevail upon your humanity? Would it be too much to ask you for some food?"

"You want me to talk to him?" Ben asked.

"I'll take care of it," Ann said.

Ann went to the side table. She took a plate and scooped off a piece of steak and a baked potato.

"You're not giving him any food, are you?" Judy asked.

"I don't give a plugged duck about him," Ann replied. "It's something I've got to do."

"What?"

"I'm closing the books."

Taking the plate, Ann started out the driveway. From beneath the house, the little terrier stuck his nose out to watch.

"Well, look at this," Hyatt sneered. "I would never have expected one ounce of charity from the high and mighty Carsons."

Ann faced him.

"Let me understand this," Ann said. "You're saying we had it coming."

"That's right."

"And then you're asking for food."

"That's right."

Ann held out the plate to him.

"Is this some effort to reach out to me? Or are you just feeling guilty for being born into wealth and privilege?"

Hyatt snatched the plate and began to eat.

"I forgive you, Warren," Ann said, smiling at him.

Hyatt looked up at her in shock.

"What did you say?"

"I forgive you for killing my grandpa," she said, letting each word register.

"Oh no! Oh no!" Hyatt shouted. "You're not going to do that. I will not let you do that!"

Ann knew she had him. There was no way he could respond.

"I will not let you do this to me!"

There was a movement. A white blur appeared along the driveway beside Ann. She looked down and saw Goliath standing beside her.

"You have my forgiveness and my good wishes. And you've got some food," Ann said. "Now get the hell off my land."

"No! No! You can't do that!" Hyatt screamed.

The terrier bared his fangs and began to growl.

"Uh, what's the matter with that dog?"

Goliath lunged forward and began to snap at Warren Hyatt's legs. Hyatt stumbled backward, trying to hold on to his plate.

"Stop him! Call him off!" Hyatt cried.

On the porch, everyone had stopped eating to watch the spectacle. Hyatt reeled out of the driveway, followed by Goliath, who seemed to be enjoying his newfound courage.

"Get that dog away! Get that dog away from me!"

Goliath stopped at the edge of the driveway. He wasn't timid now. He'd just chased an intruder off the property.

Ann looked back at her guests. "I knew this little guy was good for something," she said.

From the road, Hyatt made one final effort to assert himself. "I'm not to blame for the colonel! I'm not to blame for what happened! I'm not!"

"Good-bye, Warren," Ann said.

Something snapped inside of Warren Hyatt.

"All right!" he screamed. "All right! I killed your grandpa! I killed him! I killed your grandpa!"

He hurled his plate of food onto the road.

"I killed him! What are you going to do about it?"

"It's not a moment of triumph, but it'll do," Ann thought. "Who knows? Maybe one day I will forgive him."

"What are you going to do about it?" Hyatt shouted. He stormed his way up the road, sputtering and arguing with the demons that plagued him.

One last time Ann heard the words, "What are you going to do about it?" Then there was only the breeze through the cornstalks. She never saw Warren Hyatt again.

Goliath scurried out into the road, snatched up the steak from the ground, and darted back up the driveway.

"You earned it," Ann said, looking down at him. "Come on. Let's eat."

She took her place at the end of the table.

"Trouble?" Ben asked.

"Not anymore," she replied.

Ann looked at the company. She picked up her glass and began to speak.

"My grandpa used to do this every July fourth," she began. "I guess now it's my turn. It's been a long journey to this moment. Some good things happened, and some not so good, but we overcame them. I could be cynical about it, but I choose not to be because cynicism only holds you down. And if we have the ability to survive, then we also have the ability to rebuild."

She paused a moment to take in the faces at the table. The colonel had done this every time he'd spoken.

"We're building a new house here. Right by the Northeast Quarter. It's smaller than the manor house, but times have changed. When we're finished, we'll have two bedrooms: one for us and one for guests."

Ann was trying to remember how her grandfather handled one of these speeches. She decided to say what she felt.

"As I look around the table, I see new families. New strengths. You were friends at a time when it didn't look like I had any. You became a rock. A foundation. Seeing you here means a great deal. We've just started a depression, and it doesn't look like we're going to see the end of it very soon. It seems like the only people who survive are the ones with the land. Grandpa said, it always comes back to the land. He began with the Northeast Quarter. We'll do the same. I am so thankful for that."

Ann glanced out to the surrounding cornfields—the familiar and reassuring rolling hills of green and yellow under a bright summer sky.

"As I stand here on our nation's birthday, I give thanks for many things. For Ben, my beloved husband, who has stood by me always. For you, my new friends and family. The faces have changed over the past eleven years. I hope what we've started will give us the strength to survive and move forward. New faces. New hopes. We're still a new country. We're down, but not out. For that I give thanks. It's our nation's birthday..."

"And your birthday," Olga said.

"Lucky timing." She raised her glass. The others at the table followed, raising their cups and glasses.

"Happy birthday to our country, and God bless the United States of America."

Everyone at the table drank the toast.

Ann looked down the table at Ben. It was a smile just for him, the one she had been waiting to give him for a long time.

"And now we begin," she said.

Acknowledgments

To Lorraine, who lived with these characters and their shenanigans for six years—from first word to last line—with much love and appreciation.

To Richard Marek, my editor, who spent three years helping me whip the narrative into shape. An excellent teacher and advisor.

To Connie and Jay Stein for all their encouragement.

To Chris Ceraso and the gang in the Works-in-Progress Playwrights Lab at Manhattan Theatre Club Studios—who were there when it all began.

A Note About Winfield
and Franklin County

THE TOWN OF WINFIELD IN *THE Northeast Quarter* is not to be confused with the city of Winfield in Henry County, Iowa. *The Northeast Quarter* is a work of fiction, set almost one hundred years ago. To create a perfect community for the narrative, I selected two favorite names: Winfield, which I love for the name itself, and Franklin for the county because of its traditionally American sound. For native Iowans I may have monkeyed with the road map, but I wanted the image of an idealized American small town—almost a paradise or heaven on earth for the Carson family until all hell breaks loose.

About the Author

S. M. HARRIS BEGAN WRITING FOR the theater professionally in 1991 when he was invited by the Ensemble Studio Theatre in New York to attend a summer conference. The experience led the native Californian to move to New York and become a playwright. Several of his plays have been produced Off Broadway and around the country, among them *Onna Field,* produced by Diverse City Theater Company, and *Colleen Ireland*, about a ninety-year-old retirement home resident and her great-granddaughter. *Colleen Ireland* played in New York, Spokane, and other cities, including Hamilton, Ohio, where it won Best Play at the Fitton Center One-Act Playwriting Contest. A follow-up to *Colleen* was *Spindrift Way*, the first of ten more plays in the series. *The Northeast Quarter* began as a full-length play developed by the Works in Progress Theatre Lab at Manhattan Theatre Club Studios. Harris put playwriting on hold in order to weave the story of generations of Iowan farmers into his new historical novel. He lives in Brooklyn.

CPSIA information can be obtained
at www.ICGtesting.com
Printed in the USA
BVOW09s0555020217
474942BV00002B/7/P